Bernhard Tauchnitz

The Works of Lord Byron Complete in Five Volumes

Bernhard Tauchnitz

The Works of Lord Byron Complete in Five Volumes

ISBN/EAN: 9783742874078

Manufactured in Europe, USA, Canada, Australia, Japa

Cover: Foto ©Raphael Reischuk / pixelio.de

Manufactured and distributed by brebook publishing software
(www.brebook.com)

Bernhard Tauchnitz

The Works of Lord Byron Complete in Five Volumes

COLLECTION

OF

BRITISH AUTHORS

TAUCHNITZ EDITION.

VOL. 10.

THE WORKS OF LORD BYRON

Second Edition.

IN FIVE VOLUMES. — VOL. 3.

LEIPZIG: BERNHARD TAUCHNITZ.

PARIS: C. REINWALD & Cⁱᵉ, 15, RUE DES SAINTS PÈRES.

COLLECTION

OF

BRITISH AUTHORS.

VOL. X.

THE WORKS OF LORD BYRON.

IN FIVE VOLUMES.

VOL. III.

THE WORKS

OF

LORD BYRON

COMPLETE IN FIVE VOLUMES.

Second Edition.

VOL. III.

LEIPZIG

BERNHARD TAUCHNITZ

1866.

CONTENTS

OF VOLUME III.

CONTENTS OF VOLUME III.

THE BRIDE OF ABYDOS,

A TURKISH TALE.

"Had we never loved so kindly,
Had we never loved so blindly,
Never met or never parted,
We had ne'er been broken-hearted."

BURNS.

TO

THE RIGHT HONOURABLE

LORD HOLLAND,

THIS TALE

IS INSCRIBED, WITH

EVERY SENTIMENT OF REGARD

AND RESPECT,

BY HIS GRATEFULLY OBLIGED

AND SINCERE FRIEND,

BYRON.

THE BRIDE OF ABYDOS.

CANTO THE FIRST.

I.

Know ye the land where the cypress and myrtle
　Are emblems of deeds that are done in their clime,
Where the rage of the vulture, the love of the turtle,
　Now melt into sorrow, now madden to crime?
Know ye the land of the cedar and vine,
Where the flowers ever blossom, the beams ever shine;
Where the light wings of Zephyr, oppressed with perfume,
Wax faint o'er the gardens of Gúl* in her bloom;
Where the citron and olive are fairest of fruit,
And the voice of the nightingale never is mute:
Where the tints of the earth, and the hues of the sky,
In colour though varied, in beauty may vie,
And the purple of Ocean is deepest in dye;
Where the virgins are soft as the roses they twine,
And all, save the spirit of man, is divine?
'Tis the clime of the East; 'tis the land of the Sun —
Can he smile on such deeds as his children have done?**
Oh! wild as the accents of lovers' farewell
Are the hearts which they bear, and the tales which they tell.

II.

Begirt with many a gallant slave,
Apparell'd as becomes the brave,.

---

* "Gúl," the rose.
**　　　"Souls made of fire, and children of the Sun,
　　　With whom revenge is virtue."
　　　　　　　　　　　Young's Revenge.

Awaiting each his lord's behest
To guide his steps, or guard his rest,
Old Giaffir sate in his Divan:
  Deep thought was in his aged eye;
And though the face of Mussulman
  Not oft betrays to standers by
The mind within, well skill'd to hide
All but unconquerable pride,
His pensive cheek and pondering brow
Did more than he was wont avow.

III.

"Let the chamber be clear'd." — The train disappear'd —
"Now call me the chief of the Haram guard."
With Giaffir is none but his only son,
  And the Nubian awaiting the sire's award.
"Haroun — when all the crowd that wait
Are pass'd beyond the outer gate,
(Woe to the head whose eye beheld
My child Zuleika's face unveil'd!)
Hence, lead my daughter from her tower;
Her fate is fix'd this very hour:
Yet not to her repeat my thought;
By me alone be duty taught!"
"Pacha! to hear is to obey."
No more must slave to despot say —
Then to the tower had ta'en his way,
But here young Selim silence brake,
  First slowly rendering reverence meet!
And downcast look'd, and gently spake,
  Still standing at the Pacha's feet:
For son of Moslem must expire,
Ere dare to sit before his sire!

"Father! for fear that thou shouldst chide
My sister, or her sable guide,
Know — for the fault, if fault there be,
Was mine, then fall thy frowns on me —

So lovelily the morning shone,
 That — let the old and weary sleep —
I could not; and to view alone
 The fairest scenes of land and deep,
With none to listen and reply
To thoughts with which my heart beat high
Were irksome — for whate'er my mood,
In sooth I love not solitude;
I on Zuleika's slumber broke,
 And, as thou knowest that for me
 Soon turns the Haram's grating key,
Before the guardian slaves awoke
We to the cypress groves had flown,
And made earth, main, and heaven our own!
There linger'd we, beguiled too long
With Mejnoun's tale, or Sadi's song;*
Till I, who heard the deep tambour**
Beat thy Divan's approaching hour,
To thee, and to my duty true,
Warn'd by the sound, to greet thee flew:
But there Zuleika wanders yet —
Nay, Father, rage not — nor forget
That none can pierce that secret bower
But those who watch the women's tower."

IV.

"Son of a slave" — the Pacha said —
 "From unbelieving mother bred,
 Vain were a father's hope to see
 Aught that beseems a man in thee,
Thou, when thine arm should bend the bow,
 And hurl the dart, and curb the steed,
 Thou, Greek in soul if not in creed,

---

 * Mejnoun and Leila, the Romeo and Juliet of the East. Sadi, the moral poet of Persia.
 ** Tambour. Turkish drum, which sounds at sunrise, noon, and twilight.

Must pore where babbling waters flow,
And watch unfolding roses blow.
Would that you orb, whose matin glow
Thy listless eyes so much admire,
Would lend thee something of his fire!
Thou, who would'st see this battlement
By Christian cannon piecemeal rent;
Nay, tamely view old Stambol's wall
Before the dogs of Moscow fall,
Nor strike one stroke for life and death
Against the curs of Nazareth!
Go — let thy less than woman's hand
Assume the distaff — not the brand.
But, Haroun! — to my daughter speed:
And hark — of thine own head take heed —
If thus Zuleika oft takes wing —
Thou see'st yon bow — it hath a string!"

v.

No sound from Selim's lip was heard,
  At least that met old Giaffir's ear,
But every frown and every word
Pierced keener than a Christian's sword.
  "Son of a slave! — reproach'd with fear!
  Those gibes had cost another dear.
Son of a slave! — and *who* my sire?"
  Thus held his thoughts their dark career;
And glances ev'n of more than ire
  Flash forth, then faintly disappear.
Old Giaffir gazed upon his son
  And started; for within his eye
He read how much his wrath had done;
He saw rebellion there begun:
  "Come hither, boy — what, no reply?
I mark thee — and I know thee too;
But there be deeds thou dar'st not do:
But if thy beard had manlier length,
And if thy hand had skill and strength,

I'd joy to see thee break a lance,
Albeit against my own perchance."

As sneeringly these accents fell,
On Selim's eye he fiercely gazed:
   That eye return'd him glance for glance,
And proudly to his sire's was raised,
   Till Giaffir's quail'd and shrunk askance —
And why — he felt, but durst not tell.
"Much I misdoubt this wayward boy
Will one day work me more annoy:
I never loved him from his birth,
And — but his arm is little worth,
And scarcely in the chase could cope
With timid fawn or antelope,
Far less would venture into strife
Where man contends for fame and life —
I would not trust that look or tone:
No — nor the blood so near my own.
That blood — he hath not heard — no more —
I'll watch him closer than before.
He is an Arab* to my sight,
Or Christian crouching in the fight —
But hark! — I hear Zuleika's voice;
   Like Houris' hymn it meets mine ear:
She is the offspring of my choice;
   Oh! more than ev'n her mother dear,
With all to hope, and nought to fear —
My Peri! ever welcome here!
Sweet as the desert fountain's wave
To lips just cool'd in time to save —
   Such to my longing sight art thou;
Nor can they waft to Mecca's shrine
More thanks for life, than I for thine,
   Who blest thy birth, and bless thee now."

* The Turks abhor the Arabs (who return the compliment a hundred fold) even more than they hate the Christians.

VI.

Fair, as the first that fell of womankind,
  When on that dread yet lovely serpent smiling,
Whose image then was stamp'd upon her mind —
  But once beguiled — and ever more beguiling;
Dazzling, as that, oh! too transcendent vision
  To Sorrow's phantom-peopled slumber given,
When heart meets heart again in dreams Elysian,
  And paints the lost on Earth revived in Heaven;
Soft, as the memory of buried love;
Pure, as the prayer which Childhood wafts above;
Was she — the daughter of that rude old Chief,
Who met the maid with tears — but not of grief.

Who hath not proved how feebly words essay
To fix one spark of Beauty's heavenly ray?
Who doth not feel, until his failing sight
Faints into dimness with its own delight,
His changing cheek, his sinking heart confess
The might — the majesty of Loveliness?
Such was Zuleika — such around her shone
The nameless charms unmark'd by her alone;
The light of love, the purity of grace,
The mind, the Music * breathing from her face,

* This expression has met with objections. I will not refer to "Him
who hath not Music in his soul," but merely request the reader to recollect,
for ten seconds, the features of the woman whom he believes to be the most
beautiful; and, if he then does not comprehend fully what is feebly expressed in the above line, I shall be sorry for us both. For an eloquent
passage in the latest work of the first female writer of this, perhaps of
any, age, on the analogy (and the immediate comparison excited by that
analogy) between "painting and music," see vol. iii. cap. 10. DE L'ALLE-
MAGNE. And is not this connection still stronger with the original than
the copy? With the colouring of Nature than of Art? After all, this is
rather to be felt than described; still I think there are some who will
understand it, at least they would have done had they beheld the countenance whose speaking harmony suggested the idea; for this passage is not
drawn from imagination but memory, that mirror which Affliction dashes
to the earth, and looking down upon the fragments, only beholds the reflection multiplied!

The heart whose softness harmonized the whole —
And, oh! that eye was in itself a Soul!

    Her graceful arms in meekness bending
    Across her gently-budding breast;
At one kind word those arms extending
    To clasp the neck of him who blest
    His child caressing and carest ·
    Zuleika came — and Giaffir felt
    His purpose half within him melt:
    Not that against her fancied weal
    His heart though stern could ever feel;
    Affection chain'd her to that heart;
    Ambition tore the links apart.

VII.

"Zuleika! child of gentleness!
    How dear this very day must tell,
When I forget my own distress,
    In losing what I love so well,
    To bid thee with another dwell:
    Another! and a braver man
    Was never seen in battle's van.
We Moslem reck not much of blood;
    But yet the line of Carasman*
Unchanged, unchangeable hath stood
    First of the bold Timariot bands
That won and well can keep their lands.
Enough that he who comes to woo
Is kinsman of the Bey Oglou:
His years need scarce a thought employ;
I would not have thee wed a boy.
And thou shalt have a noble dower:
And his and my united power

* Carasman Oglou, or Kara Osman Oglou, is the principal landholder
in Turkey; he governs Magnesia: those who, by a kind of feudal tenure,
possess land on condition of service, are called Timariots: they serve as
Spahis, according to the extent of territory, and bring a certain number
into the field, generally cavalry.

Will laugh to scorn the death-firman,
Which others tremble but to scan,
And teach the messenger * what fate
The bearer of such boon may wait.
And now thou know'st thy father's will;
    All that thy sex hath need to know:
'Twas mine to teach obedience still —
    The way to love, thy lord may show."

                    VIII.

In silence bow'd the virgin's head;
    And if her eye was fill'd with tears
That stifled feeling dare not shed,
And changed her cheek from pale to red,
    And red to pale, as through her ears
Those winged words like arrows sped,
    What could such be but maiden fears?
So bright the tear in Beauty's eye,
Love half regrets to kiss it dry;
So sweet the blush of Bashfulness,
Even Pity scarce can wish it less!
Whate'er it was the sire forgot;
Or if remember'd, mark'd it not;
Thrice clapp'd his hands, and call'd his steed, **
    Resign'd his gem-adorn'd chibouque, †
And mounting featly for the mead,

---

* When a Pacha is sufficiently strong to resist, the single messenger, who is always the first bearer of the order for his death, is strangled instead, and sometimes five or six, one after the other on the same errand, by command of the refractory patient; if, on the contrary, he is weak or loyal, he bows, kisses the Sultan's respectable signature, and is bowstrung with great complacency. In 1810, several of these presents were exhibited in the niche of the Seraglio gate; among others, the head of the Pacha of Bagdat, a brave young man, cut off by treachery, after a desperate resistance.

** Clapping of the hands calls the servants. The Turks hate a superfluous expenditure of voice, and they have no bells.

† "Chibouque," the Turkish pipe, of which the amber mouth-piece, and sometimes the ball which contains the leaf, is adorned with precious stones, if in possession of the wealthier orders.

With Maugrabee* and Mamaluke,
His way amid his Delis took,**
To witness many an active deed
With sabre keen, or blunt jerreed.
The Kislar only and his Moors
Watch well the Haram's massy doors.

IX.

His head was leant upon his hand,
   His eye look'd o'er the dark blue water
That swiftly glides and gently swells
Between the winding Dardanelles;
But yet he saw nor sea nor strand,
Nor even his Pacha's turban'd band
   Mix in the game of mimic slaughter,
Careering cleave the folded felt †
With sabre stroke right sharply dealt;
Nor mark'd the javelin-darting crowd,
Nor heard their Ollahs †† wild and loud —
   He thought but of old Giaffir's daughter!

X.

No word from Selim's bosom broke;
One sigh Zuleika's thought bespoke:
Still gazed he through the lattice grate,
Pale, mute, and mournfully sedate.
To him Zuleika's eye was turn'd,
But little from his aspect learn'd:

* "Maugrabee," Moorish mercenaries.
** "Delis," bravos who form the forlorn hope of the cavalry, and always begin the action.
   † A twisted fold of felt is used for scimitar practice by the Turks, and few but Mussulman arms can cut through it at a single stroke: sometimes a tough turban is used for the same purpose. The jerreed is a game of blunt javelins, animated and graceful.
   †† "Ollahs," Alla il Allah, the "Leilies," as the Spanish poets call them, the sound is Ollah; a cry of which the Turks, for a silent people, are somewhat profuse, particularly during the jerreed, or in the chase, but mostly in battle. Their animation in the field, and gravity in the chamber, with their pipes and combololos, form an amusing contrast.

Equal her grief, yet not the same;
Her heart confess'd a gentler flame:
But yet that heart alarm'd or weak,
She knew not why, forbade to speak.
Yet speak she must — but when essay?
"How strange he thus should turn away!
Not thus we e'er before have met;
Not thus shall be our parting yet."
Thrice pac'd she slowly through the room,
    And watch'd his eye — it still was fix'd:
    She snatch'd the urn wherein was mix'd
The Persian Atar-gul's* perfume,
And sprinkled all its odours o'er
The pictured roof** and marble floor:
The drops, that through his glittering vest
The playful girl's appeal address'd,
Unheeded o'er his bosom flew,
As if that breast were marble too.
"What, sullen yet? it must not be —
Oh! gentle Selim, this from thee!"
She saw in curious order set
    The fairest flowers of eastern land —
"He lov'd them once; may touch them yet,
    If offer'd by Zuleika's hand."
The childish thought was hardly breathed
Before the Rose was pluck'd and wreathed;
The next fond moment saw her seat
Her fairy form at Selim's feet:
"This rose to calm my brother's cares
A message from the Bulbul† bears;

* "Atar-gul," ottar of roses. The Persian is the finest.
** The ceiling and wainscots, or rather walls, of the Mussulman apartments are generally painted, in great houses, with one eternal and highly
coloured view of Constantinople, wherein the principal feature is a noble
contempt of perspective; below, arms, scimitars, &c. are in general fanci-
fully and not inelegantly disposed.
† It has been much doubted whether the notes of this "Lover of the
rose" are sad or merry; and Mr. Fox's remarks on the subject have pro-

It says to-night he will prolong
For Selim's ear his sweetest song;
And though his note is somewhat sad,
He'll try for once a strain more glad.
With some faint hope his alter'd lay
May sing these gloomy thoughts away.

XI.

"What! not receive my foolish flower?
    Nay then I am indeed unblest:
On me can thus thy forehead lower?
    And know'st thou not who loves thee best?
Oh, Selim dear! oh, more than dearest!
Say, is it me thou hat'st or fearest?
Come, lay thy head upon my breast,
And I will kiss thee into rest,
Since words of mine, and songs must fail,
Ev'n from my fabled nightingale.
I knew our sire at times was stern,
But this from thee had yet to learn:
Too well I know he loves thee not;
But is Zuleika's love forgot?
Ah! deem I right? the Pacha's plan —
This kinsman Bey of Carasman
Perhaps may prove some foe of thine.
If so, I swear by Mecca's shrine,
If shrines that ne'er approach allow
To woman's step admit her vow,
Without thy free consent, command,
The Sultan should not have my hand!
Think'st thou that I could bear to part
With thee, and learn to halve my heart?
Ah! were I sever'd from thy side,
Where were thy friend — and who my guide?

voked some learned controversy as to the opinions of the ancients on the
subject. I dare not venture a conjecture on the point, though a little inclined to the "errare mallem," &c. *if* Mr. Fox *was* mistaken.

Years have not seen, Time shall not see
The hour that tears my soul from thee:
Ev'n Azrael,* from his deadly quiver
   When flies that shaft, and fly it must,
That parts all else, shall doom for ever
   Our hearts to undivided dust!"

XII.

He lived — he breathed — he moved — he felt;
He raised the maid from where she knelt;
His trance was gone — his keen eye shone
With thoughts that long in darkness dwelt;
With thoughts that burn — in rays that melt.
As the stream late conceal'd
   By the fringe of its willows,
When it rushes reveal'd
   In the light of its billows;
As the bolt bursts on high
   From the black cloud that bound it,
Flash'd the soul of that eye
   Through the long lashes round it.
A war-horse at the trumpet's sound.
A lion roused by heedless hound,
A tyrant waked to sudden strife
By graze of ill-directed knife,
Starts not to more convulsive life
Than he, who heard that vow, display'd,
And all, before repress'd, betray'd:
"Now thou art mine, for ever mine,
With life to keep, and scarce with life resign;
Now thou art mine, that sacred oath,
Though sworn by one, hath bound us both.
Yes, fondly, wisely hast thou done;
That vow hath saved more heads than one;
But blench not thou — thy simplest tress
Claims more from me than tenderness;

    * "Azrael," the angel of death.

I would not wrong the slenderest hair
That clusters round thy forehead fair,
For all the treasures buried far
Within the caves of Istakar.*
This morning clouds upon me lower'd,
Reproaches on my head were shower'd,
And Giaffir almost call'd me coward!
Now I have motive to be brave;
The son of his neglected slave,
Nay, start not, 'twas the term he gave,
May show, though little apt to vaunt,
A heart his words nor deeds can daunt.
His son, indeed! — yet, thanks to thee,
Perchance I am, at least shall be;
But let our plighted secret vow
Be only known to us as now.
I know the wretch who dares demand
From Giaffir thy reluctant hand;
More ill-got wealth, a meaner soul
Holds not a Musselim's** control:
Was he not bred in Egripo?†
A viler race let Israel show;
But let that pass — to none be told
Our oath; the rest shall time unfold.
To me and mine leave Osman Bey;
I've partisans for peril's day:
Think not I am what I appear;
I've arms, and friends, and vengeance near."

* The treasures of the Pre-adamite Sultans. See D'Herbelot, article Istakar.
** "Musselim," a governor, the next in rank after a Pacha; a Waywode is the third; and then come the Agas.
† "Egripo," the Negropont. According to the proverb, the Turks of Egripo, the Jews of Salonica, and the Greeks of Athens, are the worst of their respective races.

XIII.

"Think not thou art what thou appearest!
  My Selim, thou art sadly changed:
This morn I saw thee gentlest, dearest;
  But now thou 'rt from thyself estranged.
My love thou surely knew'st before,
It ne'er was less, nor can be more.
To see thee, hear thee, near thee stay,
  And hate the night I know not why,
Save that we meet not but by day;
  With thee to live, with thee to die,
  I dare not to my hope deny: .
Thy cheek, thine eyes, thy lips to kiss,
Like this — and this — no more than this:
For, Alla! sure thy lips are flame;
  What fever in thy veins is flushing?
My own have nearly caught the same,
  At least I feel my cheek too blushing.
To soothe thy sickness, watch thy health,
Partake, but never waste thy wealth,
Or stand with smiles unmurmuring by,
And lighten half thy poverty;
Do all but close thy dying eye,
For that I could not live to try;
To these alone my thoughts aspire:
More can I do? or thou require?
But, Selim, thou must answer why
We need so much of mystery?
The cause I cannot dream nor tell,
But be it, since thou say'st 't is well;
Yet what thou mean'st by 'arms' and 'friends,'
Beyond my weaker sense extends.
I meant that Giaffir should have heard
  The very vow I plighted thee;
His wrath would not revoke my word:
  But surely he would leave me free.
  Can this fond wish seem strange in me,

To be what I have ever been?
What other hath Zuleika seen
From simple childhood's earliest hour?
  What other can she seek to see
Than thee, companion of her bower,
  The partner of her infancy?
These cherish'd thoughts with life begun,
  Say, why must I no more avow?
What change is wrought to make me shun
  The truth; my pride, and thine till now?
To meet the gaze of stranger's eyes
Our law, our creed, our God denies;
Nor shall one wandering thought of mine
At such, our Prophet's will, repine:
No! happier made by that decree,
He left me all in leaving thee.
Deep were my anguish, thus compell'd
To wed with one I ne'er beheld:
This wherefore should I not reveal?
Why wilt thou urge me to conceal?
I know the Pacha's haughty mood
To thee hath never boded good;
And he so often storms at nought,
Allah! forbid that e'er he ought!
And why, I know not, but within
My heart concealment weighs like sin.
If then such secrecy be crime,
  And such it feels while lurking here;
Oh, Selim! tell me yet in time,
  Nor leave me thus to thoughts of fear.
Ah! yonder see the Tchocadar, *
My father leaves the mimic war;
I tremble now to meet his eye —
Say, Selim, canst thou tell me why?"

* "Tchocadar" — one of the attendants who precedes a man of authority.

XIV.

"Zuleika — to thy tower's retreat
  Betake thee — Giaffir I can greet:
And now with him I fain must prate
Of firmans, impost, levies, state.
There's fearful news from Danube's banks,
Our Vizier nobly thins his ranks,
For which the Giaour may give him thanks!
Our Sultan hath a shorter way
Such costly triumph to repay.
But, mark me, when the twilight drum
  Hath warn'd the troops to food and sleep,
Unto thy cell will Selim come:
    Then softly from the Haram creep
    Where we may wander by the deep:
    Our garden-battlements are steep;
Nor these will rash intruder climb
To list our words, or stint our time;
And if he doth, I want not steel
Which some have felt, and more may feel.
Then shalt thou learn of Selim more
Than thou hast heard or thought before:
Trust me, Zuleika — fear not me!
Thou know'st I hold a Haram key."

"Fear thee, my Selim! ne'er till now
Did word like this —"

        "Delay not thou;
I keep the key — and Haroun's guard
Have *some*, and hope of *more* reward.
To-night, Zuleika, thou shalt hear
My tale, my purpose, and my fear;
I am not, love! what I appear."

———

CANTO THE SECOND.

I.

The winds are high on Helle's wave,
  As on that night of stormy water
When Love, who sent, forgot to save
The young, the beautiful, the brave,
  The lonely hope of Sestos' daughter.
Oh! when alone along the sky
Her turret-torch was blazing high,
Though rising gale, and breaking foam,
And shrieking sea-birds warn'd him home;
And clouds aloft and tides below,
With signs and sounds, forbade to go,
He could not see, he would not hear,
Or sound or sign foreboding fear;
His eye but saw that light of love,
The only star it hail'd above;
His ear but rang with Hero's song,
"Ye waves, divide not lovers long!" —
That tale is old, but love anew
May nerve young hearts to prove as true.

II.

The winds are high, and Helle's tide
  Rolls darkly heaving to the main;
And Night's descending shadows hide
  That field with blood bedew'd in vain,
The desert of old Priam's pride;
  The tombs, sole relics of his reign,
All — save immortal dreams that could beguile
The blind old man of Scio's rocky isle!

III.

Oh! yet — for there my steps have been;
   These feet have press'd the sacred shore;
These limbs that buoyant wave hath borne —
Minstrel! with thee to muse, to mourn,
   To trace again those fields of yore,
Believing every hillock green
   Contains no fabled hero's ashes,
And that around the undoubted scene
   Thine own "broad Hellespont"* still dashes,
Be long my lot! and cold were he
Who there could gaze denying thee!

IV.

The night hath closed on Helle's stream,
   Nor yet hath risen on Ida's hill
That moon, which shone on his high theme:
   No warrior chides her peaceful beam,
But conscious shepherds bless it still.
Their flocks are grazing on the mound
   Of him who felt the Dardan's arrow:
That mighty heap of gather'd ground
   Which Ammon's son ran proudly round,**
By nations raised, by monarchs crown'd,

* The wrangling about this epithet, "the broad Hellespont" or the "boundless Hellespont," whether it means one or the other, or what it means at all, has been beyond all possibility of detail. I have even heard it disputed on the spot; and not foreseeing a speedy conclusion to the controversy, amused myself with swimming across it in the mean time; and probably may again, before the point is settled. Indeed, the question as to the truth of "the tale of Troy divine" still continues, much of it resting upon the talismanic word "ἄπειρος:" probably Homer had the same notion of distance that a coquette has of time; and when he talks of boundless, means half a mile; as the latter, by a like figure, when she says *eternal* attachment, simply specifies three weeks.

** Before his Persian invasion, and crowned the altar with laurel, &c. He was afterwards imitated by Caracalla in his race. It is believed that the last also poisoned a friend, named Festus, for the sake of new Patroclan games. I have seen the sheep feeding on the tombs of Æsietes and Antilochus: the first is in the centre of the plain.

Is now a lone and nameless barrow!
Within — thy dwelling-place how narrow!
Without — can only strangers breathe
The name of him that *was* beneath:
Dust long outlasts the storied stone;
But Thou — thy very dust is gone!

v.

Late, late to-night will Dian cheer
The swain, and chase the boatman's fear:
Till then — no beacon on the cliff
May shape the course of struggling skiff;
The scatter'd lights that skirt the bay,
All, one by one, have died away;
The only lamp of this lone hour
Is glimmering in Zuleika's tower.
Yes! there is light in that lone chamber,
    And o'er her silken Ottoman
Are thrown the fragrant beads of amber,
    O'er which her fairy fingers ran;*
Near these, with emerald rays beset,
(How could she thus that gem forget?)
Her mother's sainted amulet,**
Whereon engraved the Koorsee text,
Could smooth this life, and win the next;
And by her comboloio † lies
A Koran of illumined dyes;

* When rubbed, the amber is susceptible of a perfume, which is slight but *not* disagreeable.

** The belief in amulets engraved on gems, or enclosed in gold boxes, containing scraps from the Koran, worn round the neck, wrist, or arm, is still universal in the East. The Koorsee (throne) verse in the second cap. of the Koran describes the attributes of the Most High, and is engraved in this manner, and worn by the pious, as the most esteemed and sublime of all sentences.

† "Comboloio" — a Turkish rosary. The MSS., particularly those of the Persians, are richly adorned and illuminated. The Greek females are kept in utter ignorance; but many of the Turkish girls are highly accomplished, though not actually qualified for a Christian coterie. Perhaps some of our own "*blues*" might not be the worse for *bleaching*.

And many a bright emblazon'd rhyme
By Persian scribes redeem'd from time;
And o'er those scrolls, not oft so mute,
Reclines her now neglected lute;
And round her lamp of fretted gold
Bloom flowers in urns of China's mould;
The richest work of Iran's loom,
And Sheeraz' tribute of perfume;
All that can eye or sense delight
   Are gather'd in that gorgeous room:
   But yet it hath an air of gloom.
She, of this Peri cell the sprite,
What doth she hence, and on so rude a night?

VI.

Wrapt in the darkest sable vest,
   Which none save noblest Moslem wear,
To guard from winds of heaven the breast
   As heaven itself to Selim dear,
With cautious steps the thicket threading,
   And starting oft, as through the glade
   The gust its hollow moanings made,
Till on the smoother pathway treading,
More free her timid bosom beat,
   The maid pursued her silent guide;
And though her terror urged retreat,
   How could she quit her Selim's side?
   How teach her tender lips to chide?

VII.

They reach'd at length a grotto, hewn
   By nature, but enlarged by art,
Where oft her lute she wont to tune,
   And oft her Koran conn'd apart;
And oft in youthful reverie
She dream'd what Paradise might be:
Where woman's parted soul shall go
Her Prophet had disdain'd to show;

But Selim's mansion was secure,
Nor deem'd she, could he long endure
His bower in other worlds of bliss,
Without *her*, most beloved in this!
Oh! who so dear with him could dwell?
What Houri soothe him half so well?

VIII.

Since last she visited the spot
Some change seem'd wrought within the grot:
It might be only that the night
Disguised things seen by better light:
That brazen lamp but dimly threw
A ray of no celestial hue;
But in a nook within the cell
Her eye on stranger objects fell.
There arms were piled, not such as wield
The turban'd Delis in the field;
But brands of foreign blade and hilt,
And one was red — perchance with guilt!
Ah! how without can blood be spilt?
A cup too on the board was set
That did not seem to hold sherbet.
What may this mean? she turn'd to see
Her Selim — "Oh! can this be he?"

IX.

His robe of pride was thrown aside,
  His brow no high-crown'd turban bore,
But in its stead a shawl of red,
  Wreathed lightly round, his temples wore:
That dagger, on whose hilt the gem
Were worthy of a diadem,
No longer glitter'd at his waist,
Where pistols unadorn'd were braced;
And from his belt a sabre swung,
And from his shoulder loosely hung
The cloak of white, the thin capote
That decks the wandering Candiote;

Beneath — his golden plated vest
Clung like a cuirass to his breast;
The greaves below his knee that wound
With silvery scales were sheathed and bound.
But were it not that high command
Spake in his eye, and tone, and hand,
All that a careless eye could see
In him was some young Galiongée.*

X.

"I said I was not what I seem'd;
    And now thou see'st my words were true:
I have a tale thou hast not dream'd,
    If sooth — its truth must others rue.
My story now 't were vain to hide,
I must not see thee Osman's bride:
But had not thine own lips declared
How much of that young heart I shared,
I could not, must not, yet have shown
The darker secret of my own.
In this I speak not now of love;
That, let time, truth, and peril prove:
But first — Oh! never wed another —
Zuleika! I am not thy brother!"

XI.

"Oh! not my brother! — yet unsay —
    God! am I left alone on earth
To mourn — I dare not curse — the day
    That saw my solitary birth?
Oh! thou wilt love me now no more!
    My sinking heart foreboded ill;
But know me all I was before,
    Thy sister — friend — Zuleika still.

---

* "Galiongée" — or Galiongi, a sailor, that is, a Turkish sailor; the
Greeks navigate, the Turks work the guns. Their dress is picturesque;
and I have seen the Capitan Pacha more than once wearing it as a kind of
incog. Their legs, however, are generally naked. The buskins described
in the text as sheathed behind with silver are those of an Arnaut robber,

Thou led'st me here perchance to kill;
  If thou hast cause for vengeance, see!
My breast is offer'd — take thy fill!
    Far better with the dead to be
    Than live thus nothing now to thee:
Perhaps far worse, for now I know
Why Giaffir always seem'd thy foe;
And I, alas! am Giaffir's child,
For whom thou wert contemn'd, reviled.
If not thy sister — would'st thou save
My life, oh! bid me be thy slave!"

XII.

"My slave, Zuleika! — nay, I'm thine:
    But, gentle love, this transport calm,
Thy lot shall yet be link'd with mine;
I swear it by our Prophet's shrine,
    And be that thought thy sorrow's balm.
So may the Koran* verse display'd
Upon its steel direct my blade,
In danger's hour to guard us both,
As I preserve that awful oath!
The name in which thy heart hath prided
    Must change; but, my Zuleika, know,
That tie is widen'd, not divided,
    Although thy Sire's my deadliest foe.

who was my host (he had quitted the profession) at his Pyrgo, near Gas-
touni in the Morea; they were plated in scales one over the other, like the
back of an armadillo.

  * The characters on all Turkish scimitars contain sometimes the name
of the place of their manufacture, but more generally a text from the Koran,
in letters of gold. Amongst those in my possession is one with a blade of
singular construction; it is very broad, and the edge notched into ser-
pentine curves like the ripple of water, or the wavering of flame. I asked
the Arminian who sold it, what possible use such a figure could add: he
said, in Italian, that he did not know; but the Mussulmans had an idea
that those of this form gave a severer wound; and liked it because it was
"piu feroce." I did not much admire the reason, but bought it for its
peculiarity.

My father was to Giaffir all
　That Selim late was deem'd to thee;
That brother wrought a brother's fall,
　But spared, at least, my infancy;
And lull'd me with a vain deceit
That yet a like return may meet.
He rear'd me, not with tender help,
　But like the nephew of a Cain;*
He watch'd me like a lion's whelp,
　That gnaws and yet may break his chain.
　My father's blood in every vein
Is boiling; but for thy dear sake
No present vengeance will I take;
　Though here I must no more remain.
But first, beloved Zuleika! hear
How Giaffir wrought this deed of fear.

XIII.

"How first their strife to rancour grew,
　If love or envy made them foes,
It matters little if I knew;
In fiery spirits, slights, though few
　And thoughtless, will disturb repose.
In war Abdallah's arm was strong,
Remember'd yet in Bosniac song,
And Paswan's** rebel hordes attest
How little love they bore such guest:

* It is to be observed, that every allusion to any thing or personage in the Old Testament, such as the Ark, or Cain, is equally the privilege of Mussulman and Jew: indeed, the former profess to be much better acquainted with the lives, true and fabulous, of the patriarchs, than is warranted by our own sacred writ; and not content with Adam, they have a biography of Pre-Adamites. Solomon is the monarch of all necromancy, and Moses a prophet inferior only to Christ and Mahomet. Zuleika is the Persian name of Potiphar's wife; and her amour with Joseph constitutes one of the finest poems in their language. It is, therefore, no violation of costume to put the names of Cain, or Noah, into the mouth of a Moslem. —

** Paswan Oglou, the rebel of Widin; who, for the last years of his life, set the whole power of the Porte at defiance.

His death is all I need relate,
The stern effect of Giaffir's hate;
And how my birth disclosed to me,
Whate'er beside it makes, hath made me free.

XIV.

"When Paswan, after years of strife,
At last for power, but first for life,
In Widin's walls too proudly sate,
Our Pachas rallied round the state;
Nor last nor least in high command,
Each brother led a separate band;
They gave their horsetails* to the wind,
    And mustering in Sophia's plain
Their tents were pitch'd, their post assign'd;
    To one, alas! assign'd in vain!
What need of words? the deadly bowl,
    By Giaffir's order drugg'd and given,
With venom subtle as his soul,
    Dismiss'd Abdallah's hence to heaven.
Reclined and feverish in the bath,
    He, when the hunter's sport was up,
But little deem'd a brother's wrath
    To quench his thirst had such a cup:
The bowl a bribed attendant bore;
He drank one draught** nor needed more!
If thou my tale, Zuleika, doubt,
Call Haroun — he can tell it out.

XV.

"The deed once done, and Paswan's feud
    In part suppress'd, though ne'er subdued,

* "Horse-tail," the standard of a Pacha.
** Giaffir, Pacha of Argyro Castro, or Scutari, I am not sure which, was actually taken off by the Albanian Ali, in the manner described in the text. Ali Pacha, while I was in the country, married the daughter of his victim, some years after the event had taken place at a bath in Sophia, or Adrianople. The poison was mixed in the cup of coffee, which is presented before the sherbet by the bath-keeper, after dressing.

Abdullah's Pachalick was gain'd: —
Thou know'st not what in our Divan
Can wealth procure for worse than man —
    Abdullah's honours were obtain'd
By him a brother's murder stain'd;
'Tis true, the purchase nearly drain'd
His ill got treasure, soon replaced.
Would'st question whence? Survey the waste,
And ask the squalid peasant how
His gains repay his broiling brow! —
Why me the stern usurper spared,
Why thus with me his palace shared,
I know not. Shame, regret, remorse,
And little fear from infant's force;
Besides, adoption as a son
By him whom Heaven accorded none,
Or some unknown cabal, caprice,
Preserved me thus; — but not in peace:
He cannot curb his haughty mood,
Nor I forgive a father's blood.

XVI.

" Within thy father's house are foes;
    Not all who break his bread are true:
To these should I my birth disclose,
    His days, his very hours were few:
They only want a heart to lead,
A hand to point them to the deed.
But Haroun only knows or knew
    This tale, whose close is almost nigh:
He in Abdallah's palace grew,
    And held that post in his Serai
    Which holds he here — he saw him die:
But what could single slavery do?
Avenge his lord? alas! too late;
Or save his son from such a fate?
He chose the last, and when elate

With foes subdued, or friends betray'd,
Proud Giaffir in high triumph sate,
He led me helpless to his gate,
    And not in vain it seems essay'd
    To save the life for which he pray'd.
The knowledge of my birth secured
    From all and each, but most from me;
Thus Giaffir's safety was ensured.
    Removed he too from Roumelie
To this our Asiatic side,
Far from our seats by Danube's tide,
    With none but Haroun, who retains
Such knowledge — and that Nubian feels
    A tyrant's secrets are but chains,
From which the captive gladly steals,
And this and more to me reveals:
Such still to guilt just Alla sends —
Slaves, tools, accomplices — no friends!

XVII.

"All this, Zuleika, harshly sounds;
    But harsher still my tale must be:
Howe'er my tongue thy softness wounds,
    Yet I must prove all truth to thee.
    I saw thee start this garb to see,
Yet is it one I oft have worn,
    And long must wear: this Galiongée,
To whom thy plighted vow is sworn,
    Is leader of those pirate hordes,
    Whose laws and lives are on their swords;
To hear whose desolating tale
Would make thy waning cheek more pale:
Those arms thou see'st my band have brought.
The hands that wield are not remote;
This cup too for the rugged knaves
    Is fill'd — once quaff'd, they ne'er repine:
Our prophet might forgive the slaves;
    They're only infidels in wine.

XVIII.

"What could I be? Proscribed at home,
  And taunted to a wish to roam;
  And listless left — for Giaffir's fear
  Denied the courser and the spear —
  Though oft — Oh, Mahomet! how oft! —
  In full Divan the despot scoff'd,
  As if *my* weak unwilling hand
  Refused the bridle or the brand:
  He ever went to war alone,
  And pent me here untried — unknown;
  To Haroun's care with women left,
  By hope unblest, of fame bereft,
  While thou — whose softness long endear'd,
  Though it unmann'd me, still had cheer'd —
  To Brusa's walls for safety sent,
  Awaited'st there the field's event.
  Haroun, who saw my spirit pining
    Beneath inaction's sluggish yoke,
  His captive, though with dread, resigning,
    My thraldom for a season broke,
  On promise to return before
  The day when Giaffir's charge was o'er.
  'Tis vain — my tongue can not impart
  My almost drunkenness of heart,
  When first this liberated eye
  Survey'd Earth, Ocean, Sun, and Sky,
  As if my spirit pierced them through,
  And all their inmost wonders knew!
  One word alone can paint to thee
  That more than feeling — I was Free!
  E'en for thy presence ceased to pine;
  The World — nay, Heaven itself was mine!

XIX.

"The shallop of a trusty Moor
  Convey'd me from this idle shore;

I long'd to see the isles that gem
Old Ocean's purple diadem:
I sought by turns, and saw them all;*
   But when and where I join'd the crew,
With whom I'm pledged to rise or fall,
   When all that we design to do
Is done, 't will then be time more meet
To tell thee, when the tale's complete.

XX.

"'Tis true, they are a lawless brood,
   But rough in form, nor mild in mood;
And every creed, and every race,
With them hath found — may find a place:
But open speech, and ready hand,
Obedience to their chief's command,
A soul for every enterprise,
That never sees with Terror's eyes;
Friendship for each, and faith to all,
And vengeance vow'd for those who fall,
Have made them fitting instruments
For more than ev'n my own intents.
And some — and I have studied all
   Distinguish'd from the vulgar rank,
But chiefly to my council call
   The wisdom of the cautious Frank —
And some to higher thoughts aspire,
   The last of Lambro's** patriots there
   Anticipated freedom share;
And oft around the cavern fire

* The Turkish notions of almost all islands are confined to the Archipelago, the sea alluded to.

** Lambro Canzani, a Greek, famous for his efforts, in 1789-90, for the independence of his country. Abandoned by the Russians, he became a pirate, and the Archipelago was the scene of his enterprises. He is said to be still alive at Petersburg. He and Riga are the two most celebrated of the Greek revolutionists.

On visionary schemes debate,
To snatch the Rayahs* from their fate.
So let them ease their hearts with prate
Of equal rights, which man ne'er knew;
I have a love for freedom too.
Ay! let me like the ocean-Patriarch** roam,
Or only know on land the Tartar's home!†
My tent on shore, my galley on the sea,
Are more than cities and Serais to me:
Borne by my steed, or wafted by my sail,
Across the desert, or before the gale,
Bound where thou wilt, my barb! or glide, my prow!
But be the star that guides the wanderer, Thou!
Thou, my Zuleika, share and bless my bark;
The Dove of peace and promise to mine ark!
Or, since that hope denied in worlds of strife,
Be thou the rainbow to the storms of life!
The evening beam that smiles the clouds away,
And tints to-morrow with prophetic ray!††

* "Rayahs," — all who pay the capitation tax, called the "Haratch."
** The first of voyages is one of the few with which the Mussulmans profess much acquaintance.
† The wandering life of the Arabs, Tartars, and Turkomans, will be found well detailed in any book of Eastern travels. That it possesses a charm peculiar to itself, cannot be denied. A young French renegado confessed to Chateaubriand, that he never found himself alone, galloping in the desert, without a sensation approaching to rapture which was indescribable.
†† Originally written thus —

"And tints to-morrow with {an airy / a fancied} ray."

The following note being annexed: — "Mr. Murray, choose which of the two epithets, 'fancied' or 'airy,' may be best; or if neither will do, tell me, and I will dream another." In a subsequent letter, he says: — "Instead of — "And tints to-morrow with a *fancied* ray,

Print — "And tints to-morrow with *prophetic* ray;

Or — "And {gilds / tints} the hope of morning with its ray;

Or — "And gilds to-morrow's hope with heavenly ray.
I wish you would ask Mr. Gifford which of them is best; or, rather, *not worst.*"

Blest — as the Muezzin's strain from Mecca's wall
To pilgrims pure and prostrate at his call;
Soft — as the melody of youthful days,
That steals the trembling tear of speechless praise;
Dear — as his native song to Exile's ears,
Shall sound each tone thy long-loved voice endears.
For thee in those bright isles is built a bower
Blooming as Aden* in its earliest hour.
A thousand swords, with Selim's heart and hand,
Wait — wave — defend — destroy — at thy command!
Girt by my band, Zuleika at my side,
The spoil of nations shall bedeck my bride.
The Haram's languid years of listless ease
Are well resign'd for cares — for joys like these:
Not blind to fate, I see, where'er I rove,
Unnumbered perils, — but one only love!
Yet well my toils shall that fond breast repay,
Though fortune frown, or falser friends betray.
How dear the dream in darkest hours of ill,
Should all be changed, to find thee faithful still
Be but thy soul, like Selim's, firmly shown;
To thee be Selim's tender as thine own;
To soothe each sorrow, share in each delight,
Blend every thought, do all — but disunite!
Once free, 'tis mine our horde again to guide;
Friends to each other, foes to aught beside:
Yet there we follow but the bent assign'd
By fatal Nature to man's warring kind:
Mark! where his carnage and his conquests cease!
He makes a solitude, and calls it — peace!
I like the rest must use my skill or strength,
But ask no land beyond my sabre's length:
Power sways but by division — her resource
The blest alternative of fraud or force!
Ours be the last; in time deceit may come
When cities cage us in a social home:

* "Jannat al Aden," the perpetual abode, the Mussulman paradise.

There ev'n thy soul might err — how oft the heart
Corruption shakes which peril could not part!
And woman, more than man, when death or woe,
Or even Disgrace, would lay her lover low,
Sunk in the lap of Luxury will shame —
Away suspicion! — not Zuleika's name!
But life is hazard at the best; and here
No more remains to win, and much to fear:
Yes, fear! — the doubt, the dread of losing thee,
By Osman's power, and Giaffir's stern decree.
That dread shall vanish with the favouring gale,
Which love to-night hath promised to my sail:
No danger daunts the pair his smile hath blest,
Their steps still roving, but their hearts at rest.
With thee all toils are sweet, each clime hath charms;
Earth — sea alike — our world within our arms!
Ay — let the loud winds whistle o'er the deck,
So that those arms cling closer round my neck:
The deepest murmur of this lip shall be
No sigh for safety, but a prayer for thee!
The war of elements no fears impart
To Love, whose deadliest bane is human Art:
There lie the only rocks our course can check;
Here moments menace — *there* are years of wreck!
But hence ye thoughts that rise in Horror's shape!
This hour bestows, or ever bars escape.
Few words remain of mine my tale to close:
Of thine but *one* to waft us from our foes;
Yea — foes — to me will Giaffir's hate decline?
And is not Osman, who would part us, thine?'

XXI.

" His head and faith from doubt and death
   Return'd in time my guard to save;
   Few heard, none told, that o'er the wave
From isle to isle I roved the while:

And since, though parted from my band,
Too seldom now I leave the land,
No deed they've done, nor deed shall do,
Ere I have heard and doom'd it too:
I form the plan, decree the spoil,
'Tis fit I oftener share the toil.
But now too long I've held thine ear;
Time presses, floats my bark, and here
We leave behind but hate and fear.
To-morrow Osman with his train
Arrives — to-night must break thy chain:
And would'st thou save that haughty Bey,
   Perchance, *his* life who gave thee thine,
With me, this hour away — away!
   But yet, though thou art plighted mine,
Would'st thou recall thy willing vow,
Appall'd by truths imparted now,
Here rest I — not to see thee wed:
But be that peril on *my* head!"

XXII.

Zuleika, mute and motionless,
Stood like that statue of distress,
When, her last hope for ever gone,
The mother harden'd into stone;
All in the maid that eye could see
Was but a younger Niobé.
But ere her lip, or even her eye,
Essay'd to speak, or look reply,
Beneath the garden's wicket porch
Far flash'd on high a blazing torch!
Another — and another — and another —
"Oh! fly — no more — yet now my more than brother!"
Far, wide, through every thicket spread,
The fearful lights are gleaming red;

Nor these alone — for each right hand
Is ready with a sheathless brand.
They part, pursue, return, and wheel
With searching flambeau, shining steel;
And last of all, his sabre waving,
Stern Giaffir in his fury raving:
And now almost they touch the cave —
Oh! must that grot be Selim's grave?

XXIII.

Dauntless he stood — "'Tis come — soon past —
One kiss, Zuleika — 'tis my last:
  But yet my band not far from shore
May hear this signal, see the flash;
Yet now too few — the attempt were rash:
  No matter — yet one effort more."
Forth to the cavern mouth he stept;
  His pistol's echo rang on high,
Zuleika started not, nor wept,
  Despair benumb'd her breast and eye! —
"They hear me not, or if they ply
Their oars, 't is but to see me die;
That sound hath drawn my foes more nigh.
Then forth my father's scimitar,
Thou ne'er hast seen less equal war!
Farewell, Zuleika! — Sweet! retire:
  Yet stay within — here linger safe,
  At thee his rage will only chafe.
Stir not — lest even to thee perchance
Some erring blade or ball should glance.
Fear'st thou for him? — may I expire
If in this strife I seek thy sire!
No — though by him that poison pour'd:
No — though again he call me coward!
But tamely shall I meet their steel?
No — as each crest save *his* may feel!"

3*

XXIV.

One bound he made, and gain'd the sand:
  Already at his feet hath sunk
The foremost of the prying band,
  A gasping head, a quivering trunk:
Another falls — but round him close
A swarming circle of his foes;
From right to left his path he cleft,
  And almost met the meeting wave:
  His boat appears — not five oars' length —
His comrades strain with desperate strength —
  Oh! are they yet in time to save?
  His feet the foremost breakers lave;
His band are plunging in the bay,
Their sabres glitter through the spray;
Wet — wild — unwearied to the strand
They struggle — now they touch the land!
They come — 't is but to add to slaughter —
His heart's best blood is on the water.

XXV.

Escaped from shot, unharm'd by steel,
Or scarcely grazed its force to feel,
Had Selim won, betray'd, beset,
To where the strand and billows met;
There as his last step left the land,
And the last death-blow dealt his hand.—
Ah! wherefore did he turn to look
  For her his eye but sought in vain?
That pause, that fatal gaze he took,
  Hath doom'd his death, or fix'd his chain.
Sad proof, in peril and in pain,
How late will Lover's hope remain!
His back was to the dashing spray;
Behind, but close, his comrades lay,

When, at the instant, hiss'd the ball —
"So may the foes of Giaffir fall!"
Whose voice is heard? whose carbine rang?
Whose bullet through the night-air sang,
Too nearly, deadly aim'd to err?
'Tis thine — Abdallah's Murderer!
The father slowly rued thy hate,
The son hath found a quicker fate:
Fast from his breast the blood is bubbling,
The whiteness of the sea-foam troubling —
If aught his lips essay'd to groan,
The rushing billows choked the tone!

XXVI.

Morn slowly rolls the clouds away;
    Few trophies of the fight are there:
The shouts that shook the midnight-bay
Are silent; but some signs of fray
    That strand of strife may bear,
And fragments of each shiver'd brand;
Steps stamp'd; and dash'd into the sand
The print of many a struggling hand
    May there be mark'd; nor far remote
    A broken torch, an oarless boat;
And tangled on the weeds that heap
The beach where shelving to the deep
    There lies a white capote!
'Tis rent in twain — one dark-red stain
The wave yet ripples o'er in vain:
    But where is he who wore?
Ye! who would o'er his relics weep,
Go, seek them where the surges sweep
Their burthen round Sigæum's steep
    And cast on Lemnos' shore:
The sea-birds shriek above the prey,
O'er which their hungry beaks delay,

As shaken on his restless pillow,
His head heaves with the heaving billow;
That hand, whose motion is not life,
Yet feebly seems to menace strife,
Flung by the tossing tide on high,
 Then levell'd with the wave —
What recks it, though that corse shall lie
 Within a living grave?
The bird that tears that prostrate form
Hath only robb'd the meaner worm;
The only heart, the only eye
Had bled or wept to see him die,
Had seen those scatter'd limbs composed,
 And mourn'd above his turban-stone,*
That heart hath burst — that eye was closed —
 Yea — closed before his own!

XXVII.

By Helle's stream there is a voice of wail!
And woman's eye is wet — man's cheek is pale:
Zuleika! last of Giaffir's race,
 Thy destined lord is come too late:
He sees not — ne'er shall see thy face!
  Can he not hear
The loud Wul-wulleh ** warn his distant ear?
 Thy handmaids weeping at the gate,
 The Koran-chanters of the hymn of fate,
 The silent slaves with folded arms that wait,
Sighs in the hall, and shrieks upon the gale,
  Tell him thy tale!
Thou didst not view thy Selim fall!
 That fearful moment when he left the cave
  Thy heart grew chill:
He was thy hope — thy joy — thy love — thine all —

* A turban is carved in stone above the graves of *men* only.
** The death-song of the Turkish women. The "silent slaves" are the
men, whose notions of decorum forbid complaint in *public*.

And that last thought on him thou could'st not save
    Sufficed to kill;
Burst forth in one wild cry — and all was still.
Peace to thy broken heart, and virgin grave!
Ah! happy! but of life to lose the worst!
That grief — though deep — though fatal — was thy
    first!
Thrice happy! ne'er to feel nor fear the force
Of absence, shame, pride, hate, revenge, remorse!
And, oh! that pang where more than Madness lies!
The worm that will not sleep — and never dies;
Thought of the gloomy day and ghastly night,
That dreads the darkness, and yet loathes the light,
That winds around and tears the quivering heart!
Ah! wherefore not consume it — and depart!
Woe to thee, rash and unrelenting chief!
    Vainly thou heap'st the dust upon thy head,
    Vainly the sackcloth o'er thy limbs dost spread:
    By that same hand Abdallah — Selim bled.
Now let it tear thy beard in idle grief:
Thy pride of heart, thy bride for Osman's bed,
She, whom thy sultan had but seen to wed,
    Thy Daughter's dead!
    Hope of thine age, thy twilight's lonely beam,
    The Star hath set that shone on Helle's stream.
What quench'd its ray? — the blood that thou hast shed!
Hark! to the hurried question of Despair:
"Where is my child?" — an Echo answers — "Where?"*

* "I came to the place of my birth, and cried, 'The friends of my youth, where are they?' and an Echo answered, 'Where are they?'" — *From an Arabic MS* The above quotation (from which the idea in the text is taken) must be already familiar to every reader: it is given in the first annotation, p. 67., of "The Pleasures of Memory;" a poem so well known as to render a reference almost superfluous; but to whose pages all will be delighted to recur.

XXVIII.

Within the place of thousand tombs
    That shine beneath, while dark above
The sad but living cypress glooms,
    And withers not, though branch and leaf
Are stamp'd with an eternal grief,
    Like early unrequited Love,
One spot exists, which ever blooms,
    Ev'n in that deadly grove —
A single rose is shedding there
    Its lonely lustre, meek and pale:
It looks as planted by Despair —
    So white — so faint — the slightest gale
Might whirl the leaves on high;
    And yet, though storms and blight assail,
And hands more rude than wintry sky
    May wring it from the stem — in vain —
    To-morrow sees it bloom again!
The stalk some spirit gently rears,
And waters with celestial tears;
    For well may maids of Helle deem
That this can be no earthly flower,
Which mocks the tempest's withering hour,
And buds unshelter'd by a bower;
Nor droops, though spring refuse her shower,
    Nor woos the summer beam:
To it the livelong night there sings
    A bird unseen — but not remote:
Invisible his airy wings,
But soft as harp that Houri strings
    His long entrancing note!
It were the Bulbul; but his throat,
    Though mournful, pours not such a strain;
For they who listen cannot leave
The spot, but linger there and grieve,
    As if they loved in vain!

And yet so sweet the tears they shed,
'Tis sorrow so unmix'd with dread,
They scarce can bear the morn to break
    That melancholy spell,
And longer yet would weep and wake,
    He sings so wild and well!
But when the day-blush bursts from high
Expires that magic melody.
And some have been who could believe,
(So fondly youthful dreams deceive,
    Yet harsh be they that blame,)
That note so piercing and profound
Will shape and syllable* its sound
    Into Zuleika's name.
'Tis from her cypress summit heard,
That melts in air the liquid word:
'Tis from her lowly virgin earth
That white rose takes its tender birth.
There late was laid a marble stone;
Eve saw it placed — the Morrow gone!
It was no mortal arm that bore
That deep fixed pillar to the shore;
For there, as Helle's legends tell,
Next morn 'twas found where Selim fell;
Lash'd by the tumbling tide, whose wave
Denied his bones a holier grave:

* "And airy tongues that *syllable* men's names." — MILTON.

For a belief that the souls of the dead inhabit the form of birds, we need not travel to the East. Lord Lyttleton's ghost story, the belief of the Duchess of Kendal, that George I. flew into her window in the shape of a raven (see Orford's Reminiscences), and many other instances, bring this superstition nearer home. The most singular was the whim of a Worcester lady, who, believing her daughter to exist in the shape of a singing bird, literally furnished her pew in the cathedral with cages full of the kind; and as she was rich, and a benefactress in beautifying the church, no objection was made to her harmless folly. For this anecdote, see Orford's Letters.

And there by night, reclined, 'tis said,
Is seen a ghastly turban'd head:
   And hence extended by the billow,
   'Tis named the "Pirate-phantom's pillow!"
   Where first it lay that mourning flower
   Hath flourished; flourisheth this hour,
Alone and dewy, coldly pure and pale;
As weeping Beauty's check at Sorrow's tale!

THE ISLAND;

OR,

CHRISTIAN AND HIS COMRADES.

———

THE foundation of the following story will be found partly in Lieutenant Bligh's "Narrative of the Mutiny and Seizure of the Bounty, in the South Seas, in 1789;" and partly in "Mariner's Account of the Tonga Islands."

Genoa, 1823.

———

THE ISLAND.

－－－

CANTO THE FIRST.

I.

The morning watch was come; the vessel lay
Her course, and gently made her liquid way;
The cloven billow flash'd from off her prow
In furrows form'd by that majestic plough;
The waters with their world were all before;
Behind, the South Sea's many an islet shore.
The quiet night, now dappling, 'gan to wane,
Dividing darkness from the dawning main;
The dolphins, not unconscious of the day,
Swam high, as eager of the coming ray;
The stars from broader beams began to creep,
And lift their shining eyelids from the deep;
The sail resumed its lately shadow'd white,
And the wind flutter'd with a freshening flight;
The purpling ocean owns the coming sun,
But ere he break — a deed is to be done.

II.

The gallant chief within his cabin slept,
Secure in those by whom the watch was kept:
His dreams were of Old England's welcome shore,
Of toils rewarded, and of dangers o'er;
His name was added to the glorious roll
Of those who search the storm-surrounded Pole.
The worst was over, and the rest seem'd sure,
And why should not his slumber be secure?

Alas! his deck was trod by unwilling feet,
And wilder hands would hold the vessel's sheet;
Young hearts, which languish'd for some sunny isle,
Where summer years and summer women smile;
Men without country, who, too long estranged,
Had found no native home, or found it changed,
And, half uncivilised, preferr'd the cave
Of some soft savage to the uncertain wave —
The gushing fruits that nature gave untill'd;
The wood without a path but where they will'd;
The field o'er which promiscuous Plenty pour'd
Her horn; the equal land without a lord;
The wish — which ages have not yet subdued
In man — to have no master save his mood;
The earth, whose mine was on its face, unsold,
The glowing sun and produce all its gold;
The freedom which can call each grot a home;
The general garden, where all steps may roam,
Where Nature owns a nation as her child,
Exulting in the enjoyment of the wild;
Their shells, their fruits, the only wealth they know,
Their unexploring navy, the canoe;
Their sport, the dashing breakers and the chase;
Their strangest sight, an European face: —
Such was the country which these strangers yearn'd
To see again; a sight they dearly earn'd.

III.

Awake, bold Bligh! the foe is at the gate!
Awake! awake! — Alas! it is too late!
Fiercely beside thy cot the mutineer
Stands, and proclaims the reign of rage and fear.
Thy limbs are bound, the bayonet at thy breast;
The hands, which trembled at thy voice, arrest;
Dragg'd o'er the deck, no more at thy command
The obedient helm shall veer, the sail expand;
That savage spirit, which would lull by wrath
Its desperate escape from duty's path,

Glares round thee, in the scarce believing eyes
Of those who fear the chief they sacrifice:
For ne'er can man his conscience all assuage,
Unless he drain the wine of passion — rage.

IV.

In vain, not silenced by the eye of death,
Thou call'st the loyal with thy menaced breath: —
They come not; they are few, and, overawed,
Must acquiesce, while sterner hearts applaud.
In vain thou dost demand the cause: a curse
Is all the answer, with the threat of worse.
Full in thine eyes is waved the glittering blade,
Close to thy throat the pointed bayonet laid.
The levell'd muskets circle round thy breast
In hands as steel'd to do the deadly rest.
Thou darest them to their worst, exclaiming — "Fire!"
But they who pitied not could yet admire;
Some lurking remnant of their former awe
Restrain'd them longer than their broken law;
They would not dip their souls at once in blood,
But left thee to the mercies of the flood.

V.

"Hoist out the boat!" was now the leader's cry;
And who dare answer "No!" to Mutiny,
In the first dawning of the drunken hour,
The Saturnalia of unhoped-for power?
The boat is lower'd with all the haste of hate,
With its slight plank between thee and thy fate;
Her only cargo such a scant supply
As promises the death their hands deny;
And just enough of water and of bread
To keep, some days, the dying from the dead:
Some cordage, canvas, sails, and lines, and twine,
But treasures all to hermits of the brine,
Were added after, to the earnest prayer
Of those who saw no hope, save sea and air;

And last, that trembling vassal of the Pole —
The feeling compass — Navigation's soul.

VI.

And now the self-elected chief finds time
To stun the first sensation of his crime,
And raise it in his followers — "Ho! the bowl!"
Lest passion should return to reason's shoal.
"Brandy for heroes!" Burke could once exclaim —
No doubt a liquid path to epic fame;
And such the new-born heroes found it here,
And drain'd the draught with an applauding cheer.
"Huzza! for Otaheite!" was the cry.
How strange such shouts from sons of Mutiny!
The gentle island, and the genial soil,
The friendly hearts, the feasts without a toil,
The courteous manners but from nature caught,
The wealth unhoarded, and the love unbought;
Could these have charms for rudest sea-boys, driven
Before the mast by every wind of heaven?
And now, even now prepared with others' woes
To earn mild virtue's vain desire, repose?
Alas! such is our nature! all but aim
At the same end by pathways not the same;
Our means, our birth, our nation, and our name,
Our fortune, temper, even our outward frame,
Are far more potent o'er our yielding clay
Than aught we know beyond our little day.
Yet still there whispers the small voice within,
Heard through Gain's silence, and o'er Glory's din;
Whatever creed be taught or land be trod,
Man's conscience is the oracle of God.

VII.

The launch is crowded with the faithful few
Who wait their chief, a melancholy crew:
But some remain'd reluctant on the deck
Of that proud vessel — now a moral wreck —

Sublime tobacco! which from east to west
Cheers the tar's labour or the Turkman's rest;
Which on the Moslem's ottoman divides
His hours, and rivals opium and his brides;
Magnificent in Stamboul, but less grand,
Though not less loved, in Wapping or the Strand;
Divine in hookas, glorious in a pipe,
When tipp'd with amber, mellow, rich, and ripe;
Like other charmers, wooing the caress
More dazzlingly when daring in full dress;
Yet thy true lovers more admire by far
Thy naked beauties — Give me a cigar!

XX.

Through the approaching darkness of the wood
A human figure broke the solitude,
Fantastically, it may be, array'd,
A seaman in a savage masquerade;
Such as appears to rise out from the deep
When o'er the line the merry vessels sweep,
And the rough saturnalia of the tar
Flock o'er the deck, in Neptune's borrow'd car;*
And, pleased, the god of ocean sees his name
Revive once more, though but in mimic game
Of his true sons, who riot in the breeze
Undreamt of in his native Cyclades.
Still the old god delights, from out the main,
To snatch some glimpses of his ancient reign.
Our sailor's jacket, though in ragged trim,
His constant pipe, which never yet burn'd dim,
His foremast air, and somewhat rolling gait,
Like his dear vessel, spoke his former state;
But then a sort of kerchief round his head,
Not over-tightly bound, nor nicely spread;
And, 'stead of trousers (ah! too early torn!
For even the mildest woods will have their thorn)

* This rough but jovial ceremony, used in crossing the line, has been
so often and so well described, that it need not be more than alluded to.

A curious sort of somewhat scanty mat
Now served for inexpressibles and hat;
His naked feet and neck, and sunburnt face,
Perchance might suit alike with either race.
His arms were all his own, our Europe's growth,
Which two worlds bless for civilising both;
The musket swung behind his shoulders broad,
And somewhat stoop'd by his marine abode,
But brawny as the boar's; and hung beneath,
His cutlass droop'd, unconscious of a sheath,
Or lost or worn away; his pistols were
Link'd to his belt, a matrimonial pair —
(Let not this metaphor appear a scoff,
Though one miss'd fire, the other would go off);
These, with a bayonet, not so free from rust
As when the arm-chest held its brighter trust,
Completed his accoutrements, as Night
Survey'd him in his garb heteroclite.

XXI.

"What cheer, Ben Bunting?" cried (when in full view
Our new acquaintance) Torquil. "Aught of new?"
"Ey, ey!" quoth Ben, "not new, but news enow;
A strange sail in the offing." — "Sail! and how?
What! could you make her out? It cannot be;
I've seen no rag of canvass on the sea."
"Belike," said Ben, " you might not from the bay,
But from the bluff-head, where I watch'd to-day,
I saw her in the doldrums; for the wind
Was light and baffling." — "When the sun declined
Where lay she? had she anchor'd?" — "No, but still
She bore down on us, till the wind grew still."
"Her flag?" — "I had no glass: but fore and aft,
Egad! she seem'd a wicked-looking craft."
"Arm'd?" — "I expect so; — sent on the look-out:
'Tis time, belike, to put our helm about."
"About? — Whate'er may have us now in chase,
We'll make no running fight, for that were base;

We will die at our quarters, like true men."
"Ey, ey! for that 'tis all the same to Ben."
"Does Christian know this?" — "Ay; he has piped all
       hands
To quarters. They are furbishing the stands
Of arms; and we have got some guns to bear,
And scaled them. You are wanted." — "That's but fair;
And if it were not, mine is not the soul
To leave my comrades helpless on the shoal.
My Neuha! ah! and must my fate pursue
Not me alone, but one so sweet and true?
But whatsoe'er betide, ah, Neuha! now
Unman me not; the hour will not allow
A tear; I am thine whatever intervenes!"
"Right," quoth Ben, "that will do for the marines."*

   * "That will do for the marines, but the sailors won't believe it," is an
old saying; and one of the few fragments of former jealousies which still
survive (in jest only) between these gallant services.

CANTO THE THIRD.

I.

THE fight was o'er; the flashing through the gloom
Which robes the cannon as he wings a tomb,
Had ceased; and sulphury vapours upward driven
Had left the earth, and but polluted heaven:
The rattling roar which rung in every volley
Had left the echoes to their melancholy;
No more they shriek'd their horror, boom for boom;
The strife was done, the vanquish'd had their doom;
The mutineers were crush'd, dispersed, or ta'en,
Or lived to deem the happiest were the slain.
Few, few escaped, and these were hunted o'er
The isle they loved beyond their native shore.
No further home was theirs, it seem'd, on earth,
Once renegades to that which gave them birth;
Track'd like wild beasts, like them they sought the wild,
As to a mother's bosom flies the child;
But vainly wolves and lions seek their den,
And still more vainly men escape from men.

II.

Beneath a rock whose jutting base protrudes
Far over ocean in his fiercest moods,
When scaling his enormous crag the wave
Is hurl'd down headlong, like the foremost brave,
And falls back on the foaming crowd behind,
Which fight beneath the banners of the wind,
But now at rest, a little remnant drew
Together, bleeding, thirsty, faint, and few;
But still their weapons in their hands, and still
With something of the pride of former will,

As men not all unused to meditate,
And strive much more than wonder at their fate.
Their present lot was what they had foreseen,
And dared as what was likely to have been;
Yet still the lingering hope, which deem'd their lot
Not pardon'd, but unsought for or forgot,
Or trusted that, if sought, their distant caves
Might still be miss'd amidst the world of waves,
Had wean'd their thoughts in part from what they saw
And felt, the vengeance of their country's law.
Their sea-green isle, their guilt-won paradise,
No more could shield their virtue or their vice:
Their better feelings, if such were, were thrown
Back on themselves, — their sins remain'd alone.
Proscribed even in their second country, they
Were lost; in vain the world before them lay;
All outlets seem'd secured. Their new allies
Had fought and bled in mutual sacrifice;
But what avail'd the club and spear, and arm
Of Hercules, against the sulphury charm,
The magic of the thunder, which destroy'd
The warrior ere his strength could be employ'd?
Dug, like a spreading pestilence, the grave
No less of human bravery than the brave!*
Their own scant numbers acted all the few
Against the many oft will dare and do;
But though the choice seems native to die free,
Even Greece can boast but one Thermopylæ,
Till _now_, when she has forged her broken chain
Back to a sword, and dies and lives again!

III.

Beside the jutting rock the few appear'd,
Like the last remnant of the red-deer's herd;

* Archidamus, king of Sparta, and son of Agesilaus, when he saw a machine invented for the casting of stones and darts, exclaimed that it was the "grave of valour." The same story has been told of some knights on the first application of gunpowder; but the original anecdote is in Plutarch.

Their eyes were feverish, and their aspect worn,
But still the hunter's blood was on their horn,
A little stream came tumbling from the height,
And straggling into ocean as it might,
Its bounding crystal frolick'd in the ray,
And gush'd from cliff to crag with saltless spray;
Close on the wild, wide ocean, yet as pure
And fresh as innocence, and more secure,
Its silver torrent glitter'd o'er the deep,
As the shy chamois' eye o'erlooks the steep,
While far below the vast and sullen swell
Of ocean's alpine azure rose and fell.
To this young spring they rush'd, — all feelings first
Absorb'd in passion's and in nature's thirst, —
Drank as they do who drink their last, and threw
Their arms aside to revel in its dew;
Cool'd their scorch'd throats, and wash'd the gory stains
From wounds whose only bandage might be chains;
Then, when their drought was quench'd, look'd sadly round,
As wondering how so many still were found
Alive and fetterless: — but silent all,
Each sought his fellow's eyes, as if to call
On him for language which his lips denied,
As though their voices with their cause had died.

IV.

Stern, and aloof a little from the rest,
Stood Christian, with his arms across his chest.
The ruddy, reckless, dauntless hue once spread
Along his cheek was livid now as lead;
His light-brown locks, so graceful in their flow,
Now rose like startled vipers o'er his brow.
Still as a statue, with his lips comprest
To stifle even the breath within his breast,
Fast by the rock, all menacing, but mute,
He stood; and, save a slight beat of his foot,
Which deepen'd now and then the sandy dint
Beneath his heel, his form seem'd turn'd to flint.

Some paces further Torquil lean'd his head
Against a bank, and spoke not, but he bled, —
Not mortally ; — his worst wound was within :
His brow was pale, his blue eyes sunken in,
And blood-drops, sprinkled o'er his yellow hair,
Show'd that his faintness came not from despair
But nature's ebb.   Beside him was another,
Rough as a bear, but willing as a brother, —
Ben Bunting, who essay'd to wash, and wipe,
And bind his wound — then calmly lit his pipe,
A trophy which survived a hundred fights,
A beacon which had cheer'd ten thousand nights.
The fourth and last of this deserted group
Walk'd up and down — at times would stand, then stoop
To pick a pebble up — then let it drop —
Then hurry as in haste — then quickly stop —
Then cast his eyes on his companions — then
Half whistle half a tune, and pause again —
And then his former movements would redouble,
With something between carelessness and trouble.
This is a long description, but applies
To scarce five minutes pass'd before the eyes ;
But yet *what* minutes ! Moments like to these
Rend men's lives into immortalities.

v.

At length Jack Skyscrape, a mercurial man,
Who flutter'd over all things like a fan,
More brave than firm, and more disposed to dare
And die at once than wrestle with despair,
Exclaim'd, "G – d damn !" — those syllables intense, —
Nucleus of England's native eloquence,
As the Turk's "Allah !" or the Roman's more
Pagan "Proh Jupiter !" was wont of yore
To give their first impressions such a vent,
By way of echo to embarrassment.
Jack was embarrass'd, — never hero more,
And as he knew not what to say, he swore :

Nor swore in vain; the long congenial sound
Revived Ben Bunting from his pipe profound;
He drew it from his mouth, and look'd full wise,
But merely added to the oath his *eyes;*
Thus rendering the imperfect phrase complete,
A peroration I need not repeat.

VI.

But Christian, of a higher order, stood
Like an extinct volcano in his mood;
Silent, and sad, and savage, — with the trace
Of passion recking from his clouded face;
Till lifting up again his sombre eye,
It glanced on Torquil, who lean'd faintly by.
"And is it thus?" he cried, "unhappy boy!
And thee, too, *thee* — my madness must destroy!"
He said, and strode to where young Torquil stood,
Yet dabbled with his lately flowing blood;
Seized his hand wistfully, but did not press,
And shrunk as fearful of his own caress;
Enquired into his state; and when he heard
The wound was slighter than he deem'd or fear'd,
A moment's brightness pass'd along his brow,
As much as such a moment would allow.
"Yes," he exclaim'd, "we are taken in the toil,
But not a coward or a common spoil;
Dearly they have bought us — dearly still may buy, —
And I must fall; but have you strength to fly?
'Twould be some comfort still, could you survive;
Our dwindled band is now too few to strive.
Oh! for a sole canoe! though but a shell,
To bear you hence to where a hope may dwell!
For me, my lot is what I sought; to be,
In life or death, the fearless and the free."

VII.

Even as he spoke, around the promontory,
Which nodded o'er the billows high and hoary,

A dark speck dotted ocean : on it flew
Like to the shadow of a roused sea-mew;
Onward it came — and, lo! a second follow'd —
Now seen — now hid — where ocean's vale was hollow'd;
And near, and nearer, till their dusky crew
Presented well-known aspects to the view,
Till on the surf their skimming paddles play,
Buoyant as wings, and flitting through the spray; —
Now perching on the wave's high curl, and now
Dash'd downward in the thundering foam below,
Which flings it broad and boiling sheet on sheet,
And slings its high flakes, shiver'd into sleet:
But floating still through surf and swell, drew nigh
The barks, like small birds through a lowering sky.
Their art seem'd nature — such the skill to sweep
The wave of these born playmates of the deep.

VIII.

And who the first that, springing on the strand,
Leap'd like a nereid from her shell to land,
With dark but brilliant skin, and dewy eye
Shining with love, and hope, and constancy?
Neuha — the fond, the faithful, the adored —
Her heart on Torquil's like a torrent pour'd;
And smiled, and wept, and near, and nearer clasp'd,
As if to be assured 't was *him* she grasp'd;
Shudder'd to see his yet warm wound, and then,
To find it trivial, smiled and wept again.
She was a warrior's daughter, and could bear
Such sights, and feel, and mourn, but not despair.
Her lover lived, — nor foes nor fears could blight
That full-blown moment in its all delight:
Joy trickled in her tears, joy fill'd the sob
That rock'd her heart till almost HEARD to throb;
And paradise was breathing in the sigh
Of nature's child in nature's ecstasy.

IX.

The sterner spirits who beheld that meeting
Were not unmoved; who are, when hearts are greeting?
Even Christian gazed upon the maid and boy
With tearless eye, but yet a gloomy joy
Mix'd with those bitter thoughts the soul arrays
In hopeless visions of our better days,
When all's gone — to the rainbow's latest ray.
"And but for me!" he said, and turn'd away;
Then gazed upon the pair, as in his den
A lion looks upon his cubs again;
And then relapsed into his sullen guise,
As heedless of his further destinies.

X.

But brief their time for good or evil thought;
The billows round the promontory brought
The plash of hostile oars. — Alas! who made
That sound a dread? All around them seem'd array'd
Against them, save the bride of Toobonai:
She, as she caught the first glimpse o'er the bay
Of the arm'd boats, which hurried to complete
The remnant's ruin with their flying feet,
Beckon'd the natives round her to their prows,
Embark'd their guests and launch'd their light canoes;
In one placed Christian and his comrades twain;
But she and Torquil must not part again.
She fix'd him in her own. — Away! away!
They clear the breakers, dart along the bay,
And towards a group of islets, such as bear
The sea-bird's nest and seal's surf-hollow'd lair,
They skim the blue tops of the billows; fast
They flew, and fast their fierce pursuers chased.
They gain upon them — now they lose again, —
Again make way and menace o'er the main;

And now the two canoes in chase divide,
And follow different courses o'er the tide,
To baffle the pursuit. — Away! away!
As life is on each paddle's flight to-day,
And more than life or lives to Neuha: Love
Freights the frail bark and urges to the cove —
And now the refuge and the foe are nigh —
Yet, yet a moment! — Fly, thou light ark, fly!

CANTO THE FOURTH.

I.

White as a white sail on a dusky sea,
When half the horizon's clouded and half free,
Fluttering between the dun wave and the sky,
Is hope's last gleam in man's extremity.
Her anchor parts; but still her snowy sail
Attracts our eye amidst the rudest gale:
Though every wave she climbs divides us more,
The heart still follows from the loneliest shore.

II.

Not distant from the isle of Toobonai,
A black rock rears its bosom o'er the spray,
The haunt of birds, a desert to mankind,
Where the rough seal reposes from the wind,
And sleeps unwieldy in his cavern dun,
Or gambols with huge frolic in the sun:
There shrilly to the passing oar is heard
The startled echo of the ocean bird,
Who rears on its bare breast her callow brood,
The feather'd fishers of the solitude.
A narrow segment of the yellow sand
On one side forms the outline of a strand;
Here the young turtle, crawling from his shell,
Steals to the deep wherein his parents dwell;
Chipp'd by the beam, a nursling of the day,
But hatch'd for ocean by the fostering ray;
The rest was one bleak precipice, as e'er
Gave mariners a shelter and despair;
A spot to make the saved regret the deck
Which late went down, and envy the lost wreck.

Such was the stern asylum Neuha chose
To shield her lover from his following foes;
But all its secret was not told; she knew
In this a treasure hidden from the view.

III.

Ere the canoes divided, near the spot,
The men that mann'd what held her Torquil's lot,
By her command removed, to strengthen more
The skiff which wafted Christian from the shore.
This he would have opposed; but with a smile
She pointed calmly to the craggy isle,
And bade him "speed and prosper." *She* would take
The rest upon herself for Torquil's sake.
They parted with this added aid; afar
The proa darted like a shooting star,
And gain'd on the pursuers, who now steer'd
Right on the rock which she and Torquil near'd.
They pull'd; her arm, though delicate, was free
And firm as ever grappled with the sea,
And yielded scarce to Torquil's manlier strength.
The prow now almost lay within its length
Of the crag's steep, inexorable face,
With nought but soundless waters for its base;
Within a hundred boats' length was the foe,
And now what refuge but their frail canoe?
This Torquil ask'd with half upbraiding eye,
Which said — "Has Neuha brought me here to die?
Is this a place of safety, or a grave,
And yon huge rock the tombstone of the wave?"

IV.

They rested on their paddles, and uprose
Neuha, and pointing to the approaching foes,
Cried, "Torquil, follow me, and fearless follow!"
Then plunged at once into the ocean's hollow.
There was no time to pause — the foes were near —
Chains in his eye, and menace in his ear;

With vigour they pull'd on, and as they came,
Hail'd him to yield, and by his forfeit name.
Headlong he leapt — to him the swimmer's skill
Was native, and now all his hope from ill:
But how, or where? He dived, and rose no more;
The boat's crew look'd amazed o'er sea and shore.
There was no landing on that precipice,
Steep, harsh, and slippery as a berg of ice.
They watch'd awhile to see him float again,
But not a trace rebubbled from the main:
The wave roll'd on, no ripple on its face,
Since their first plunge recall'd a single trace;
The little whirl which eddied, and slight foam,
That whiten'd o'er what seem'd their latest home,
White as a sepulchre above the pair
Who left no marble (mournful as an heir)
The quiet proa wavering o'er the tide
Was all that told of Torquil and his bride;
And but for this alone the whole might seem
The vanish'd phantom of a seaman's dream.
They paused and search'd in vain, then pull'd away;
Even superstition now forbade their stay.
Some said he had not plunged into the wave,
But vanish'd like a corpse-light from a grave;
Others, that something supernatural
Glared in his figure, more than mortal tall;
While all agreed that in his cheek and eye
There was a dead hue of eternity.
Still as their oars receded from the crag,
Round every weed a moment would they lag,
Expectant of some token of their prey;
But no — he had melted from them like the spray.

V.

And where was he, the pilgrim of the deep,
Following the nereid? Had they ceased to weep
For ever? or, received in coral caves,
Wrung life and pity from the softening waves?

Did they with ocean's hidden sovereigns dwell,
And sound with mermen the fantastic shell?
Did Neuha with the mermaids comb her hair
Flowing o'er ocean as it stream'd in air?
Or had they perish'd, and in silence slept
Beneath the gulf wherein they boldly leapt?

VI.

Young Neuha plunged into the deep, and he
Follow'd: her track beneath her native sea
Was as a native's of the element,
So smoothly, bravely, brilliantly she went,
Leaving a streak of light behind her heel,
Which struck and flash'd like an amphibious steel.
Closely, and scarcely less expert to trace
The depths where divers hold the pearl in chase,
Torquil, the nursling of the northern seas,
Pursued her liquid steps with heart and ease.
Deep — deeper for an instant Neuha led
The way — then upward soar'd — and as she spread
Her arms, and flung the foam from off her locks,
Laugh'd, and the sound was answer'd by the rocks.
They had gain'd a central realm of earth again,
But look'd for tree, and field, and sky, in vain.
Around she pointed to a spacious cave,
Whose only portal was the keyless wave,*
(A hollow archway by the sun unseen,
Save through the billows' glassy veil of green,
In some transparent ocean holiday,
When all the finny people are at play,)
Wiped with her hair the brine from Torquil's eyes,
And clapp'd her hands with joy at his surprise;
Led him to where the rock appear'd to jut,
And form a something like a Triton's hut;

* Of this cave (which is no fiction) the original will be found in the ninth chapter of "Mariner's Account of the Tonga Islands." I have taken the poetical liberty to transplant it to Toobonai, the last island where any distinct account is left of Christian and his comrades.

For all was darkness for a space, till day,
Through clefts above let in a sober'd ray;
As in some old cathedral's glimmering aisle
The dusty monuments from light recoil,
Thus sadly in their refuge submarine
The vault drew half her shadow from the scene.

VII.

Forth from her bosom the young savage drew
A pine torch, strongly girded with gnatoo;
A plantain-leaf o'er all, the more to keep
Its latent sparkle from the sapping deep.
This mantle kept it dry; then from a nook
Of the same plantain-leaf a flint she took,
A few shrunk wither'd twigs, and from the blade
Of Torquil's knife struck fire, and thus array'd
The grot with torchlight. Wide it was and high,
And show'd a self-born Gothic canopy;
The arch uprear'd by nature's architect,
The architrave some earthquake might erect;
The buttress from some mountain's bosom hurl'd
When the Poles crash'd, and water was the world;
Or harden'd from some earth-absorbing fire,
While yet the globe reek'd from its funeral pyre;
The fretted pinnacle, the aisle, the nave, *
Were there, all scoop'd by Darkness from her cave.
There, with a little tinge of phantasy,
Fantastic faces mop'd and mow'd on high,
And then a mitre or a shrine would fix
The eye upon its seeming crucifix.
Thus Nature play'd with the stalactites,
And built herself a chapel of the seas.

* This may seem too minute for the general outline (in Mariner's Account) from which it is taken. But few men have travelled without seeing something of the kind — on *land*, that is. Without adverting to Ellora, in Mungo Park's last journal, he mentions having met with a rock or mountain so exactly resembling a Gothic cathedral, that only minute inspection could convince him that it was a work of nature.

No more he said; but urging to the bark
His chief, commits him to his fragile ark;
These the sole accents from his tongue that fell,
But volumes lurk'd below his fierce farewell.

IX.

The arctic sun rose broad above the wave;
The breeze now sank, now whisper'd from his cave;
As on the Æolian harp, his fitful wings
Now swell'd, now flutter'd o'er his ocean strings.
With slow, despairing oar, the abandon'd skiff
Ploughs its drear progress to the scarce-seen cliff,
Which lifts its peak a cloud above the main:
That boat and ship shall never meet again!
But 'tis not mine to tell their tale of grief,
Their constant peril, and their scant relief;
Their days of danger, and their nights of pain;
Their manly courage even when deem'd in vain;
The sapping famine, rendering scarce a son
Known to his mother in the skeleton;
The ills that lessen'd still their little store,
And starv'd even Hunger till he wrung no more;
The varying frowns and favours of the deep,
That now almost ingulfs, then leaves to creep
With crazy oar and shatter'd strength along
The tide that yields reluctant to the strong;
The incessant fever of that arid thirst
Which welcomes, as a well, the clouds that burst
Above their naked bones, and feels delight
In the cold drenching of the stormy night,
And from the outspread canvass gladly wrings
A drop to moisten life's all-gasping springs;
The savage foe escap'd, to seek again
More hospitable shelter from the main;
The ghastly spectres which were doom'd at last
To tell as true a tale of dangers past,
As ever the dark annals of the deep
Disclosed for man to dread or woman weep.

x.

We leave them to their fate, but not unknown
Nor unredress'd.   Revenge may have her own:
Roused discipline aloud proclaims their cause,
And injured navies urge their broken laws.
Pursue we on his track the mutineer,
Whom distant vengeance had not taught to fear.
Wide o'er the wave — away! away! away!
Once more his eyes shall hail the welcome bay;
Once more the happy shores without a law
Receive the outlaws whom they lately saw;
Nature, and Nature's goddess — woman — woos
To lands where, save their conscience, none accuse;
Where all partake the earth without dispute,
And bread itself is gather'd as a fruit; *
Where none contest the fields, the woods, the streams: —
The goldless age, where gold disturbs no dreams,
Inhabits or inhabited the shore,
Till Europe taught them better than before:
Bestow'd her customs, and amended theirs,
But left her vices also to their heirs.
Away with this! behold them as they were.
Do good with Nature, or with Nature err.
"Huzza! for Otaheite!" was the cry,
As stately swept the gallant vessel by.
The breeze springs up; the lately flapping sail
Extends its arch before the growing gale;
In swifter ripples stream aside the seas,
Which her bold bow flings off with dashing ease.
Thus Argo plough'd the Euxine's virgin foam;
But those she wafted still look'd back to home —
These spurn their country with their rebel bark,
And fly her as the raven fled the ark;
And yet they seek to nestle with the dove,
And tame their fiery spirits down to love.

    * The now celebrated bread-fruit, to transplant which Captain Bligh's
expedition was undertaken.

CANTO THE SECOND.

I.

How pleasant were the songs of Toobonai,*
When summer's sun went down the coral bay!
Come, let us to the islet's softest shade,
And hear the warbling birds! the damsels said:
The wood-dove from the forest depth shall coo,
Like voices of the gods from Bolotoo;
We'll cull the flowers that grow above the dead,
For these most bloom where rests the warrior's head;
And we will sit in twilight's face, and see
The sweet moon glancing through the tooa tree,
The lofty accents of whose sighing bough
Shall sadly please us as we lean below;
Or climb the steep, and view the surf in vain
Wrestle with rocky giants o'er the main,
Which spurn in columns back the baffled spray.
How beautiful are these! how happy they,
Who, from the toil and tumult of their lives,
Steal to look down where nought but ocean strives!
Even he too loves at times the blue lagoon,
And smooths his ruffled mane beneath the moon.

II.

Yes — from the sepulchre we'll gather flowers,
Then feast like spirits in their promised bowers,
Then plunge and revel in the rolling surf,
Then lay our limbs along the tender turf,

* The first three sections are taken from an actual song of the Tonga
Islanders, of which a prose translation is given in "Mariner's Account of
the Tonga Islands." Toobonai is *not* however one of them; but was one
of those where Christian and the mutineers took refuge. I have altered
and added, but have retained as much as possible of the original.

4*

And, wet and shining from the sportive toil,
Anoint our bodies with the fragrant oil,
And plait our garlands gather'd from the grave,
And wear the wreaths that sprung from out the brave.
But lo! night comes, the Mooa woos us back,
The sound of mats are heard along our track;
Anon the torchlight dance shall fling its sheen
In flashing mazes o'er the Marly's green;
And we too will be there; we too recall
The memory bright with many a festival,
Ere Fiji blew the shell of war, when foes
For the first time were wafted in canoes.
Alas! for them the flower of mankind bleeds;
Alas! for them our fields are rank with weeds:
Forgotten is the rapture, or unknown,
Of wandering with the moon and love alone.
But be it so: — *they* taught us how to wield
The club, and rain our arrows o'er the field:
Now let them reap the harvest of their art!
But feast to-night! to-morrow we depart.
Strike up the dance! the cava bowl fill high!
Drain every drop! — to-morrow we may die.
In summer garments be our limbs array'd;
Around our waists the tappa's white display'd;
Thick wreaths shall form our coronal, like spring's.
And round our necks shall glance the hooni strings;
So shall their brighter hues contrast the glow
Of the dusk bosoms that beat high below.

III.

But now the dance is o'er — yet stay awhile;
Ah, pause! nor yet put out the social smile.
To-morrow for the Mooa we depart,
But not to-night — to-night is for the heart.
Again bestow the wreaths we gently woo,
Ye young enchantresses of gay Licoo!
How lovely are your forms! how every sense
Bows to your beauties, soften'd, but intense,

Like to the flowers on Mataloco's steep,
Which fling their fragrance far athwart the deep! —
We too will see Licoo; but — oh! my heart! —
What do I say? — to-morrow we depart!

IV.

Thus rose a song — the harmony of times
Before the winds blew Europe o'er these climes.
True, they had vices — such are Nature's growth —
But only the barbarian's — we have both:
The sordor of civilisation, mix'd
With all the savage which man's fall hath fix'd.
Who hath not seen Dissimulation's reign,
The prayers of Abel link'd to deeds of Cain?
Who such would see may from his lattice view
The Old World more degraded than the New, —
Now *new* no more, save where Columbia rears
Twin giants, born by Freedom to her spheres,
Where Chimborazo, over air, earth, wave,
Glares with his Titan eye, and sees no slave.

V.

Such was this ditty of Tradition's days,
Which to the dead a lingering fame conveys
In song, where fame as yet hath left no sign
Beyond the sound whose charm is half divine;
Which leaves no record to the sceptic eye,
But yields young history all to harmony;
A boy Achilles, with the centaur's lyre
In hand, to teach him to surpass his sire.
For one long-cherish'd ballad's simple stave,
Rung from the rock, or mingled with the wave,
Or from the bubbling streamlet's grassy side,
Or gathering mountain echoes as they glide,
Hath greater power o'er each true heart and ear,
Than all the columns Conquest's minions rear;
Invites, when hieroglyphics are a theme
For sages' labours or the student's dream;

Attracts, when History's volumes are a toil, —
The first, the freshest bud of Feeling's soil.
Such was this rude rhyme — rhyme is of the rude —
But such inspir'd the Norseman's solitude,
Who came and conquer'd; such, wherever rise
Lands which no foes destroy or civilise,
Exist: and what can our accomplish'd art
Of verse do more than reach the awaken'd heart?

VI.

And sweetly now those untaught melodies
Broke the luxurious silence of the skies,
The sweet siesta of a summer day,
The tropic afternoon of Toobonai,
When every flower was bloom, and air was balm,
And the first breath began to stir the palm,
The first yet voiceless wind to urge the wave   ·
All gently to refresh the thirsty cave,
Where sat the songstress with the stranger boy,
Who taught her passion's desolating joy,
Too powerful over every heart, but most
O'er those who know not how it may be lost;
O'er those who, burning in the new-born fire,
Like martyrs revel in their funeral pyre,
With such devotion to their ecstasy,
That life knows no such rapture as to die:
And die they do; for earthly life has nought
Match'd with that burst of nature, even in thought
And all our dreams of better life above
But close in one eternal gush of love.

VII.

There sat the gentle savage of the wild,
In growth a woman, though in years a child,
As childhood dates within our colder clime,
Where nought is ripen'd rapidly save crime;
The infant of an infant world, as pure
From nature — lovely, warm, and premature;

Dusky like night, but night with all her stars;
Or cavern sparkling with its native spars;
With eyes that were a language and a spell,
A form like Aphrodite's in her shell,
With all her loves around her on the deep,
Voluptuous as the first approach of sleep;
Yet full of life — for through her tropic cheek
The blush would make its way, and all but speak;
The sun-born blood suffused her neck, and threw
O'er her clear nut-brown skin a lucid hue,
Like coral reddening through the darken'd wave,
Which draws the diver to the crimson cave.
Such was this daughter of the southern seas,
Herself a billow in her energies,
To bear the bark of others' happiness,
Nor feel a sorrow till their joy grew less:
Her wild and warm yet faithful bosom knew
No joy like what it gave; her hopes ne'er drew
Aught from experience, that chill touchstone, whose
Sad proof reduces all things from their hues:
She fear'd no ill, because she knew it not,
Or what she knew was soon — too soon — forgot:
Her smiles and tears had pass'd, as light winds pass
O'er lakes to ruffle, not destroy, their glass,
Whose depths unsearch'd, and fountains from the hill,
Restore their surface, in itself so still,
Until the earthquake tear the naiad's cave,
Root up the spring, and trample on the wave,
And crush the living waters to a mass,
The amphibious desert of the dank morass!
And must their fate be hers? The eternal change
But grasps humanity with quicker range;
And they who fall but fall as worlds will fall,
To rise, if just, a spirit o'er them all.

VIII.

And who is he? the blue-eyed northern child
Of isles more known to man, but scarce less wild;

The fair-hair'd offspring of the Hebrides,
Where roars the Pentland with its whirling seas;
Rock'd in his cradle by the roaring wind,
The tempest-born in body and in mind,
His young eyes opening on the ocean-foam,
Had from that moment deem'd the deep his home,
The giant comrade of his pensive moods,
The sharer of his craggy solitudes,
The only Mentor of his youth, where'er
His bark was borne; the sport of wave and air;
A careless thing, who placed his choice in chance,
Nursed by the legends of his land's romance;
Eager to hope, but not less firm to bear,
Acquainted with all feelings save despair
Placed in the Arab's clime, he would have been
As bold a rover as the sands have seen,
And braved their thirst with as enduring lip
As Ishmael, wafted on his desert-ship;*
Fix'd upon Chili's shore, a proud cacique;
On Hellas' mountains, a rebellious Greek;
Born in a tent, perhaps a Tamerlane;
Bred to a throne, perhaps unfit to reign.
For the same soul that rends its path to sway,
If rear'd to such, can find no further prey
Beyond itself, and must retrace its way **
Plunging for pleasure into pain: the same
Spirit which made a Nero, Rome's worst shame,
A humbler state and discipline of heart,
Had form'd his glorious namesake's counterpart †;
But grant his vices, grant them all his own,
How small their theatre without a throne!

* The "ship of the desert" is the Oriental figure for the camel or dromedary; and they deserve the metaphor well, — the former for his endurance. the latter for his swiftness.

**   "Lucullus, when frugality could charm,
          Had roasted turnips in the Sabine farm." — POPE.

† The consul Nero, who made the unequalled march which deceived Hannibal, and defeated Asdrubal; thereby accomplishing an achievement

IX.

Thou smilest; — these comparisons seem high
To those who scan all things with dazzled eye;
Link'd with the unknown name of one whose doom
Has nought to do with glory or with Rome,
With Chili, Hellas, or with Araby; —
Thou smilest? — Smile; 'tis better thus than sigh;
Yet such he might have been; he was a man,
A soaring spirit, ever in the van,
A patriot hero or despotic chief,
To form a nation's glory or its grief,
Born under auspices which makes us more
Or less than we delight to ponder o'er.
But these are visions; say, what was he here?
A blooming boy, a truant mutineer.
The fair-hair'd Torquil, free as ocean's spray,
The husband of the bride of Toboonai.

X.

By Neuha's side he sate, and watch'd the waters, —
Neuha, the sun-flower of the island daughters,
Highborn, (a birth at which the herald smiles,
Without a scutcheon for these secret isles,)
Of a long race, the valiant and the free,
The naked knights of savage chivalry,
Whose grassy cairns ascend along the shore;
And thine — I've seen — Achilles! do no more.
She, when the thunder-bearing strangers came,
In vast canoes, begirt with bolts of flame,
T'opp'd with tall trees, which, loftier than the palm,
Seem'd rooted in the deep amidst its calm:

almost unrivalled in military annals. The first intelligence of his return, to Hannibal, was the sight of Asdrubal's head thrown into his camp. When Hannibal saw this, he exclaimed with a sigh, that "Rome would now be the mistress of the world." And yet to this victory of Nero's it might be owing that his imperial namesake reigned at all. But the infamy of the one has eclipsed the glory of the other. When the name of "Nero" is heard, who thinks of the consul? — But such are human things.

But when the winds awaken'd, shot forth wings
Broad as the cloud along the horizon flings,
And sway'd the waves, like cities of the sea,
Making the very billows look less free; —
She, with her paddling oar and dancing prow,
Shot through the surf, like reindeer through the snow,
Swift-gliding o'er the breaker's whitening edge,
Light as a nereid in her ocean sledge,
And gazed and wonder'd at the giant bulk,
Which heaved from wave to wave its trampling bulk:
The anchor dropp'd; it lay along the deep,
Like a huge lion in the sun asleep,
While round it swarm'd the proas' flitting chain,
Like summer bees that hum around his mane.

XI.

The white man landed! — need the rest be told?
The New World stretch'd its dusk hand to the Old;
Each was to each a marvel, and the tie
Of wonder warm'd to better sympathy.
Kind was the welcome of the sun-born sires,
And kinder still their daughters' gentler fires.
Their union grew: the children of the storm
Found beauty link'd with many a dusky form;
While these in turn admired the paler glow,
Which seem'd so white in climes that knew no snow.
The chase, the race, the liberty to roam,
The soil where every cottage show'd a home;
The sea-spread net, the lightly-launch'd canoe,
Which stemm'd the studded archipelago,
O'er whose blue bosom rose the starry isles;
The healthy slumber, earn'd by sportive toils;
The palm, the loftiest dryad of the woods,
Within whose bosom infant Bacchus broods,
While eagles scarce build higher than the crest
Which shadows o'er the vineyard in her breast;
The cava feast, the yam, the cocoa's root,
Which bears at once the cup, and milk, and fruit;

The bread-tree, which, without the ploughshare, yields
The unreap'd harvest of unfurrow'd fields,
And bakes its unadulterated loaves
Without a furnace in unpurchased groves,
And flings off famine from its fertile breast,
A priceless market for the gathering guest; —
These, with the luxuries of seas and woods,
The airy joys of social solitudes,
Tamed each rude wanderer to the sympathies
Of those who were more happy, if less wise,
Did more than Europe's discipline had done,
And civilised Civilisation's son!

XII.

Of these, and there was many a willing pair,
· Neuha and Torquil were not the least fair:
Both children of the isles, though distant far;
Both born beneath a sea-presiding star;
Both nourish'd amidst nature's native scenes,
Loved to the last, whatever intervenes
Between us and our childhood's sympathy,
Which still reverts to what first caught the eye.
He who first met the Highlands' swelling blue
Will love each peak that shows a kindred hue,
Hail in each crag a friend's familiar face,
And clasp the mountain in his mind's embrace.
Long have I roam'd through lands which are not mine,
Adored the Alp, and loved the Apennine,
Revered Parnassus, and beheld the steep
Jove's Ida and Olympus crown the deep:
But 'twas not all long ages' lore, nor all
Their nature held me in their thrilling thrall;
The infant rapture still survived the boy,
And Loch-na-gar with Ida look'd o'er Troy, *

* When very young, about eight years of age, after an attack of the
scarlet fever at Aberdeen, I was removed by medical advice into the Highlands. Here I passed occasionally some summers, and *from this period* I
date my love of mountainous countries. I can never forget the effect, a

Mix'd Celtic memories with the Phrygian mount,
And Highland linns with Castalie's clear fount.
Forgive me, Homer's universal shade!
Forgive me, Phœbus! that my fancy stray'd;
The north and nature taught me to adore
Your scenes sublime, from those beloved before.

                          XIII.

The love which maketh all things fond and fair,
The youth which makes one rainbow of the air,
The dangers past, that make even man enjoy
The pause in which he ceases to destroy,
The mutual beauty, which the sternest feel
Strike to their hearts like lightning to the steel,
United the half savage and the whole,
The maid and boy, in one absorbing soul.
No more the thundering memory of the fight
Wrapp'd his wean'd bosom in its dark delight;
No more the irksome restlessness of rest
Disturb'd him like the eagle in her nest,
Whose whetted beak and far-pervading eye
Darts for a victim over all the sky;
His heart was tamed to that voluptuous state,
At once Elysian and effeminate,
Which leaves no laurels o'er the hero's urn; —
These wither when for aught save blood they burn;
Yet when their ashes in their nook are laid,
Doth not the myrtle leave as sweet a shade?
Had Cæsar known but Cleopatra's kiss,
Rome had been free, the world had not been his.
And what have Cæsar's deeds and Cæsar's fame
Done for the earth? We feel them in our shame:

few years afterwards, in England, of the only thing I had long seen, even
in miniature, of a mountain, in the Malvern Hills. After I returned to
Cheltenham, I used to watch them every afternoon, at sunset, with a sensation which I cannot describe. This was boyish enough; but I was then
only thirteen years of age, and it was in the holidays.

The gory sanction of his glory stains
The rust which tyrants cherish on our chains.
Though Glory, Nature, Reason, Freedom, bid
Roused millions do what single Brutus did —
Sweep these mere mock-birds of the despot's song
From the tall bough where they have perch'd so long, —
Still are we hawk'd at by such mousing owls,
And take for falcons those ignoble fowls,
When but a word of freedom would dispel
These bugbears, as their terrors show too well.

XIV.

Rapt in the fond forgetfulness of life,
Neuha, the South Sea girl, was all a wife,
With no distracting world to call her off
From love; with no society to scoff
At the new transient flame; no babbling crowd
Of coxcombry in admiration loud,
Or with adulterous whisper to alloy
Her duty, and her glory, and her joy:
With faith and feelings naked as her form,
She stood as stands a rainbow in a storm,
Changing its hues with bright variety,
But still expanding lovelier o'er the sky,
Howe'er its arch may swell, its colours move,
The cloud-compelling harbinger of love.

XV.

Here, in this grotto of the wave-worn shore,
They pass'd the tropic's red meridian o'er;
Nor long the hours — they never paused o'er time,
Unbroken by the clock's funereal chime,
Which deals the daily pittance of our span,
And points and mocks with iron laugh at man.
What deem'd they of the future or the past?
The present, like a tyrant, held them fast:
Their hour-glass was the sea-sand, and the tide,
Like her smooth billow, saw their moments glide;

Their clock the sun, in his unbounded tow'r;
They reckon'd not, whose day was but an hour;
The nightingale, their only vesper-bell,
Sung sweetly to the rose the day's farewell;*
The broad sun set, but not with lingering sweep,
As in the north he mellows o'er the deep;
But fiery, full, and fierce, as if he left
The world for ever, earth of light bereft,
Plunged with red forehead down along the wave,
As dives a hero headlong to his grave.
Then rose they, looking first along the skies,
And then for light into each other's eyes,
Wondering that summer show'd so brief a sun,
And asking if indeed the day were done.

XVI.

And let not this seem strange: the devotee
Lives not in earth, but in his ecstasy;
Around him days and worlds are heedless driven,
His soul is gone before his dust to heaven.
Is love less potent? No — his path is trod,
Alike uplifted gloriously to God;
Or link'd to all we know of heaven below,
The other better self, whose joy or woe
Is more than ours; the all-absorbing flame
Which, kindled by another, grows the same,
Wrapt in one blaze; the pure, yet funeral pile,
Where gentle hearts, like Bramins, sit and smile.
How often we forget all time, when lone,
Admiring Nature's universal throne,
Her woods, her wilds, her waters, the intense
Reply of *hers* to our intelligence!
Live not the stars and mountains? Are the waves
Without a spirit? Are the dropping caves

---

* The now well-known story of the loves of the nightingale and rose
need not be more than alluded to, being sufficiently familiar to the Western
as to the Eastern reader.

Without a feeling in their silent tears?
No, no; — they woo and clasp us to their spheres,
Dissolve this clog and clod of clay before
Its hour, and merge our soul in the great shore.
Strip off this fond and false identity! —
Who thinks of self, when gazing on the sky?
And who, though gazing lower, ever thought,
In the young moments ere the heart is taught
Time's lesson, of man's baseness or his own?
All nature is his realm, and love his throne.

XVII.

Neuha arose, and Torquil: twilight's hour
Came sad and softly to their rocky bower,
Which, kindling by degrees its dewy spars,
Echoed their dim light to the mustering stars.
Slowly the pair, partaking nature's calm,
Sought out their cottage, built beneath the palm;
Now smiling and now silent, as the scene;
Lovely as Love — the spirit! — when serene.
The Ocean scarce spoke louder with his swell,
Than breathes his mimic murmurer in the shell, *
As, far divided from his parent deep,
The sea-born infant cries, and will not sleep,
Raising his little plaint in vain, to rave
For the broad bosom of his nursing wave:
The woods droop'd darkly, as inclined to rest,
The tropic bird wheel'd rockward to his nest,
And the blue sky spread round them like a lake
Of peace, where Piety her thirst might slake.

* If the reader will apply to his ear the sea-shell on his chimney-piece,
he will be aware of what is alluded to. If the text should appear obscure,
he will find in "Gebir" the same idea better expressed in two lines. The
poem I never read, but have heard the lines quoted by a more recondite
reader — who seems to be of a different opinion from the editor of the
Quarterly Review, who qualified it, in his answer to the Critical Reviewer
of his Juvenal, as trash of the worst and most insane description. It is to
Mr. Landor, the author of "Gebir," so qualified, and of some Latin poems,
which vie with Martial or Catullus in obscenity, that the immaculate Mr.
Southey addresses his declamation against impurity!

VIII.

And Neuha took her Torquil by the hand,
And waved along the vault her kindled brand,
And led him into each recess, and show'd
The secret places of their new abode.
Nor these alone, for all had been prepared
Before, to soothe the lover's lot she shared:
The mat for rest; for dress the fresh gnatoo,
And sandal oil to fence against the dew;
For food the cocoa-nut, the yam, the bread
Borne of the fruit; for board the plantain spread
With its broad leaf, or turtle-shell which bore
A banquet in the flesh it cover'd o'er;
The gourd with water recent from the rill,
The ripe banana from the mellow hill;
A pine-torch pile to keep undying light,
And she herself, as beautiful as night,
To fling her shadowy spirit o'er the scene,
And make their subterranean world serene.
She had foreseen, since first the stranger's sail
Drew to their isle, that force or flight might fail,
And form'd a refuge of the rocky den
For Torquil's safety from his countrymen.
Each dawn had wafted there her light canoe,
Laden with all the golden fruits that grew;
Each eve had seen her gliding through the hour
With all could cheer or deck their sparry bower;
And now she spread her little store with smiles,
The happiest daughter of the loving isles.

IX.

She, as he gazed with grateful wonder, press'd
Her shelter'd love to her impassion'd breast;
And suited to her soft caresses, told
An olden tale of love, — for love is old,
Old as eternity, but not outworn

With each new being born or to be born: *
How a young chief, a thousand moons ago,
Diving for turtle in the depths below,
Had risen, in tracking fast his ocean prey,
Into the cave which round and o'er them lay;
How in some desperate feud of after-time
He shelter'd there a daughter of the clime,
A foe beloved, and offspring of a foe,
Saved by his tribe but for a captive's woe;
How, when the storm of war was still'd, he led
His island clan to where the waters spread
Their deep-green shadow o'er the rocky door,
Then dived — it seem'd as if to rise no more:
His wondering mates, amazed within their bark,
Or deem'd him mad, or prey to the blue shark;
Row'd round in sorrow the sea-girded rock,
Then paused upon their paddles from the shock;
When, fresh and springing from the deep, they saw
A goddess rise — so deem'd they in their awe;
And their companion, glorious by her side,
Proud and exulting in his mermaid bride;
And how, when undeceived, the pair they bore
With sounding conchs and joyous shouts to shore;
How they had gladly lived and calmly died, —
And why not also Torquil and his bride?
Not mine to tell the rapturous caress
Which follow'd wildly in that wild recess
This tale; enough that all within that cave
Was love, though buried strong as in the grave
Where Abelard, through twenty years of death,
When Eloïsa's form was lower'd beneath
Their nuptial vault, his arms outstretch'd, and press'd
The kindling ashes to his kindled breast. **

* The reader will recollect the epigram of the Greek anthology, or its
translation into most of the modern languages: —
          "Whoe'er thou art, thy master see —
              He was, or is, or is to be."
** The tradition is attached to the story of Eloïsa, that when her body

The waves without sang round their couch, their roar
As much unheeded as if life were o'er;
Within, their hearts made all their harmony,
Love's broken murmur and more broken sigh.

x.

And they, the cause and sharers of the shock
Which left them exiles of the hollow rock,
Where were they? O'er the sea for life they plied,
To seek from Heaven the shelter men denied.
Another course had been their choice — but where?
The wave which bore them still their foes would bear,
Who, disappointed of their former chase,
In search of Christian now renew'd their race.
Eager with anger, their strong arms made way,
Like vultures baffled of their previous prey.
They gain'd upon them, all whose safety lay
In some bleak crag or deeply-hidden bay:
No further chance or choice remain'd; and right
For the first further rock which met their sight
They steer'd, to take their latest view of land
And yield as victims, or die sword in hand;
Dismiss'd the natives and their shallop, who
Would still have battled for that scanty crew;
But Christian bade them seek their shore again,
Nor add a sacrifice which were in vain;
For what were simple bow and savage spear
Against the arms which must be wielded here?

xi.

They landed on a wild but narrow scene,
Where few but Nature's footsteps yet had been;
Prepared their arms, and with that gloomy eye,
Stern and sustain'd, of man's extremity,
When hope is gone, nor glory's self remains
To cheer resistance against death or chains, —

was lowered into the grave of Abelard (who had been buried twenty years,)
he opened his arms to receive her.

6 *

They stood, the three, as the three hundred stood
Who dyed Thermopylæ with holy blood.
But, ah! how diffcrent! 'tis the *cause* makes all,
Degrades or hallows courage in its fall.
O'er them no fame, eternal and intense,
Blazed through the clouds of death and beckon'd hence;
No grateful country, smiling through her tears,
Begun the praises of a thousand years;
No nation's eyes would on their tomb be bent,
No heroes envy them their monument;
However boldly their warm blood was spilt,
Their life was shame, their epitaph was guilt.
And this they knew and felt, at least the one,
The leader of the band he had undone;
Who, born perchance for better things, had set
His life upon a cast which linger'd yet:
But now the die was to be thrown, and all
The chances were in favour of his fall:
And such a fall! But still he faced the shock,
Obdurate as a portion of the rock
Whereon he stood, and fix'd his levell'd gun,
Dark as a sullen cloud before the sun.

XII.

The boat drew nigh, well arm'd, and firm the crew
To act whatever duty bade them do;
Careless of danger, as the onward wind
Is of the leaves it strews, nor looks behind.
And yet perhaps they rather wish'd to go
Against a nation's than a native foe,
And felt that this poor victim of self-will,
Briton no more, had once been Britain's still.
They hail'd him to surrender — no reply;
Their arms were poised, and glitter'd in the sky.
They hail'd again — no answer; yet once more
They offer'd quarter louder than before.
The echoes only, from the rock's rebound,
Took their last farewell of the dying sound.

Then flash'd the flint, and blazed the volleying flame,
And the smoke rose between them and their aim,
While the rock rattled with the bullets' knell,
Which peal'd in vain, and flatten'd as they fell;
Then flew the only answer to be given
By those who had lost all hope in earth or heaven.
After the first fierce peal, as they pull'd nigher,
They heard the voice of Christian shout, "Now, fire!"
And ere the word upon the echo died,
Two fell; the rest assail'd the rock's rough side,
And, furious at the madness of their foes,
Disdain'd all further efforts, save to close.
But steep the crag, and all without a path,
Each step opposed a bastion to their wrath,
While, placed midst clefts the least accessible,
Which Christian's eye was train'd to mark full well,
The three maintain'd a strife which must not yield,
In spots where eagles might have chosen to build.
Their every shot told; while the assailant fell,
Dash'd on the shingles like the limpet shell:
But still enough survived, and mounted still,
Scattering their numbers here and there, until
Surrounded and commanded, though not nigh
Enough for seizure, near enough to die,
The desperate trio held aloof their fate
But by a thread, like sharks who have gorged the bait;
Yet to the very last they battled well,
And not a groan inform'd their foes *who* fell.
Christian died last — twice wounded; and once more
Mercy was offer'd when they saw his gore;
Too late for life, but not too late to die,
With, though a hostile hand, to close his eye.
A limb was broken, and he droop'd along
The crag, as doth a falcon reft of young.
The sound revived him, or appear'd to wake
Some passion which a weakly gesture spake:

He beckon'd to the foremost, who drew nigh,
But, as they near'd, he rear'd his weapon high —
His last ball had been aim'd, but from his breast
He tore the topmost button from his vest*,
Down the tube dash'd it, levell'd, fired, and smiled
As his foe fell; then, like a serpent, coil'd
His wounded, weary form, to where the steep
Look'd desperate as himself along the deep;
Cast one glance back, and clench'd his hand, and shook
His last rage 'gainst the earth which he forsook;
Then plunged: the rock below received like glass
His body crush'd into one gory mass,
With scarce a shred to tell of human form,
Or fragment for the sea-bird or the worm;
A fair-hair'd scalp, besmear'd with blood and weeds,
Yet reek'd, the remnant of himself and deeds;
Some splinters of his weapons (to the last,
As long as hand could hold, he held them fast)
Yet glitter'd, but at distance — hurl'd away
To rust beneath the dew and dashing spray.
The rest was nothing — save a life mis-spent,
And soul — but who shall answer where it went?
'Tis ours to bear, not judge the dead; and they
Who doom to hell, themselves are on the way,
Unless these bullies of eternal pains
Are pardon'd their bad hearts for their worse brains.

XIII.

The deed was over! All were gone or ta'en,
The fugitive, the captive, or the slain.
Chain'd on the deck, where once, a gallant crew,
They stood with honour, were the wretched few

* In Thibault's account of Frederic the Second of Prussia, there is a
singular relation of a young Frenchman, who with his mistress appeared
to be of some rank. He enlisted and deserted at Schweidnitz; and after a
desperate resistance was retaken, having killed an officer, who attempted
to seize him after he was wounded, by the discharge of his musket loaded

Survivors of the skirmish on the isle;
But the last rock left no surviving spoil.
Cold lay they where they fell, and weltering,
While o'er them flapp'd the sea-birds' dewy wing,
Now wheeling nearer from the neighbouring surge,
And screaming high their harsh and hungry dirge:
But calm and careless heaved the wave below,
Eternal with unsympathetic flow;
Far o'er its face the dolphins sported on,
And sprung the flying fish against the sun,
Till its dried wing relapsed from its brief height,
To gather moisture for another flight.

XIV.

'Twas morn; and Neuha, who by dawn of day
Swam smoothly forth to catch the rising ray,
And watch if aught approach'd the amphibious lair
Where lay her lover, saw a sail in air:
It flapp'd, it fill'd, and to the growing gale
Bent its broad arch: her breath began to fail
With fluttering fear, her heart beat thick and high,
While yet a doubt sprung where its course might lie.
But no! it came not; fast and far away
The shadow lessen'd as it clear'd the bay.
She gazed, and flung the sea-foam from her eyes,
To watch as for a rainbow in the skies.
On the horizon verged the distant deck,
Diminish'd, dwindled to a very speck —
Then vanish'd.   All was ocean, all was joy!
Down plunged she through the cave to rouse her boy;
Told all she had seen, and all she hoped, and all
That happy love could augur or recall;

with a *button* of his uniform. Some circumstances on his court-martial raised a great interest amongst his judges, who wished to discover his real situation in life, which he offered to disclose, but to the *king* only, to whom he requested permission to write. This was refused, and Frederic was filled with the greatest indignation, from baffled curiosity or some other motive, when he understood that his request had been denied.

Sprung forth again, with Torquil following free
His bounding nereid over the broad sea;
Swam round the rock, to where a shallow cleft
Hid the canoe that Neuha there had left
Drifting along the tide, without an oar,
That eve the strangers chased them from the shore;
But when these vanish'd, she pursued her prow,
Regain'd, and urged to where they found it now:
Nor ever did more love and joy embark,
Than now were wafted in that slender ark.

XV.

Again their own shore rises on the view,
No more polluted with a hostile hue;
No sullen ship lay bristling o'er the foam,
A floating dungeon: — all was hope and home!
A thousand proas darted o'er the bay,
With sounding shells, and heralded their way;
The chiefs came down, around the people pour'd,
And welcomed Torquil as a son restored;
The women throng'd, embracing and embraced
By Neuha, asking where they had been chased,
And how escaped? The tale was told; and then
One acclamation rent the sky again;
And from that hour a new tradition gave
Their sanctuary the name of "Neuha's Cave."
A hundred fires, far flickering from the height,
Blazed o'er the general revel of the night,
The feast in honour of the guest, return'd
To peace and pleasure, perilously earn'd;
A night succeeded by such happy days
As only the yet infant world displays.

HOURS OF IDLENESS.

A
SERIES OF POEMS,
ORIGINAL AND TRANSLATED.

Virginibus purisque canto.
HORACE, lib. 3. ode 1.

Μή;τ' ἄρ με μάλ' αἶνεε μήτε τι νείκει.
HOMER, ILIAD, x. 249.

He whistled as he went, for want of thought.
DRYDEN.

[FIRST PUBLISHED IN 1807.]

TO

THE RIGHT HONOURABLE

FREDERICK, EARL OF CARLISLE,

KNIGHT OF THE GARTER, ETC. ETC.

THE SECOND EDITION OF THESE POEMS

IS INSCRIBED,

BY HIS OBLIGED WARD

AND AFFECTIONATE KINSMAN,

THE AUTHOR.

PREFACE

TO THE FIRST EDITION.

In submitting to the public eye the following collection, I have not only to combat the difficulties that writers of verse generally encounter, but may incur the charge of presumption for obtruding myself on the world, when, without doubt, I might be, at my age, more usefully employed.

These productions are the fruits of the lighter hours of a young man who has lately completed his nineteenth year. As they bear the internal evidence of a boyish mind, this is, perhaps, unnecessary information. Some few were written during the disadvantages of illness and depression of spirits: under the former influence, "CHILDISH RECOLLECTIONS," in particular, were composed. This consideration, though it cannot excite the voice of praise, may at least arrest the arm of censure. A considerable portion of these poems has been privately printed, at the request and for the perusal of my friends. I am sensible that the partial and frequently injudicious admiration of a social circle is not the criterion by which poetical genius is to be estimated, yet, "to do greatly," we must "dare greatly;" and I have hazarded my reputation and feelings in publishing this volume. "I have passed the Rubicon," and must stand or fall by the "cast of the die." In the latter event, I shall submit without a murmur; for, though not without solicitude for the fate of these effusions, my expectations are by no means sanguine. It is probable that I may have dared much and done little; for, in the words of Cowper, "it is one thing to write what may please our friends, who, because they are such, are apt to be a little biassed in our favour, and another to write what may please every body;

because they who have no connection, or even knowledge of the author, will be sure to find fault if they can." To the truth of this, however, I do not wholly subscribe: on the contrary, I feel convinced that these trifles will not be treated with injustice. Their merit, if they possess any, will be liberally allowed: their numerous faults, on the other hand, cannot expect that favour which has been denied to others of maturer years, decided character, and far greater ability.

I have not aimed at exclusive originality, still less have I studied any particular model for imitation: some translations are given, of which many are paraphrastic. In the original pieces there may appear a casual coincidence with authors whose works I have been accustomed to read; but I have not been guilty of intentional plagiarism. To produce any thing entirely new, in an age so fertile in rhyme, would be a Herculean task, as every subject has already been treated to its utmost extent. Poetry, however, is not my primary vocation; to divert the dull moments of indisposition, or the monotony of a vacant hour, urged me "to this sin:" little can be expected from so unpromising a muse. My wreath, scanty as it must be, is all I shall derive from these productions; and I shall never attempt to replace its fading leaves, or pluck a single additional sprig from groves where I am, at best, an intruder. Though accustomed, in my younger days, to rove a careless mountaineer on the Highlands of Scotland, I have not, of late years, had the benefit of such pure air, or so elevated a residence, as might enable me to enter the lists with genuine bards, who have enjoyed both these advantages. But they derive considerable fame, and a few not less profit, from their productions; while I shall expiate my rashness as an interloper, certainly without the latter, and in all probability with a very slight share of the former, I leave to others "virûm volitare per ora." I look to the few who will hear with patience "dulce est desipere in loco." To the former worthies I resign, without repining, the hope of immortality, and content myself with the not very magnificent prospect of ranking amongst "the mob of gentlemen who write;" — my readers must determine whether I dare say "with ease," or the honour of a posthumous page in "The Catalogue of Royal and Noble Authors," — a work to which the Peerage is under infinite obligations, inasmuch as many names of considerable length, sound, and antiquity, are thereby rescued from the obscurity which unluckily overshadows several voluminous productions of their illustrious bearers.

With slight hopes, and some fears, I publish this first and last attempt. To the dictates of young ambition may be ascribed many actions more criminal and equally absurd. To a few of my own age the contents may afford amusement: I trust they will, at least, be found harmless. It is highly improbable, from my situation and pursuits hereafter, that I should ever obtrude myself a second time on the public; nor even, in the very doubtful event of present indulgence, shall I be tempted to commit a future trespass of the same nature. The opinion of Dr. Johnson on the Poems of a noble relation of mine,* "That when a man of rank appeared in the character of an author, he deserved to have his merit handsomely allowed," can have little weight with verbal, and still less with periodical censors; but were it otherwise, I should be loth to avail myself of the privilege, and would rather incur the bitterest censure of anonymous criticism, than triumph in honours granted solely to a title.

* The Earl of Carlisle, whose works have long received the meed of public applause, to which, by their intrinsic worth, they were well entitled.

HOURS OF IDLENESS.

ON THE DEATH OF A YOUNG LADY, COUSIN TO THE AUTHOR, AND VERY DEAR TO HIM.*

HUSH'D are the winds, and still the evening gloom,
  Not e'en a zephyr wanders through the grove,
Whilst I return, to view my Margaret's tomb,
  And scatter flowers on the dust I love.

Within this narrow cell reclines her clay,
  That clay, where once such animation beam'd;
The King of Terrors seized her as his prey,
  Not worth, nor beauty, have her life redeem'd.

Oh! could that King of Terrors pity feel,
  Or Heaven reverse the dread decrees of fate!
Not here the mourner would his grief reveal,
  Not here the muse her virtues would relate.

But wherefore weep? Her matchless spirit soars
  Beyond where splendid shines the orb of day;
And weeping angels lead her to those bowers
  Where endless pleasures virtue's deeds repay.

And shall presumptuous mortals Heaven arraign,
  And, madly, godlike Providence accuse?
Ah! no, far fly from me attempts so vain; —
  I'll ne'er submission to my God refuse.

---

* The author claims the indulgence of the reader more for this piece than, perhaps, any other in the collection; but as it was written at an earlier period than the rest (being composed at the age of fourteen), and his first essay, he preferred submitting it to the indulgence of his friends in its present state, to making either addition or alteration,

Yet is remembrance of those virtues dear,
    Yet fresh the memory of that beauteous face;
Still they call forth my warm affection's tear,
    Still in my heart retain their wonted place.

1802.

TO E——.

Let Folly smile, to view the names
    Of thee and me in friendship twined;
Yet Virtue will have greater claims
    To love, than rank with vice combined.

And though unequal is thy fate,
    Since title deck'd my higher birth!
Yet envy not this gaudy state;
    Thine is the pride of modest worth.

Our souls at least congenial meet,
    Nor can thy lot my rank disgrace;
Our intercourse is not less sweet,
    Since worth of rank supplies the place.

November 1802.

TO D——.

In thee, I fondly hop'd to clasp
    A friend, whom death alone could sever;
Till envy, with malignant grasp,
    Detach'd thee from my breast for ever.

True, she has forc'd thee from my breast,
    Yet, in my heart thou keep'st thy seat;
There, there thine image still must rest,
    Until that heart shall cease to beat.

And, when the grave restores her dead,
    When life again to dust is given,
On thy dear breast I'll lay my head —
    Without thee, where would be my heaven?

February 1803.

EPITAPH ON A FRIEND.

"Ἀστὴρ πρὶν μὲν ἔλαμπες ἐνὶ ζωοῖσιν ἑῷος. —
LAERTIUS.

Oh, Friend! for ever loved, for ever dear!
What fruitless tears have bathed thy honour'd bier!
What sighs re-echo'd to thy parting breath,
Whilst thou wast struggling in the pangs of death!
Could tears retard the tyrant in his course;
Could sighs avert his dart's relentless force;
Could youth and virtue claim a short delay,
Or beauty charm the spectre from his prey;
Thou still hadst lived to bless my aching sight,
Thy comrade's honour and thy friend's delight.
If yet thy gentle spirit hover nigh
The spot where now thy mouldering ashes lie,
Here wilt thou read, recorded on my heart,
A grief too deep to trust the sculptor's art.
No marble marks thy couch of lowly sleep,
But living statues there are seen to weep;
Affliction's semblance bends not o'er thy tomb,
Affliction's self deplores thy youthful doom.
What though thy sire lament his failing line,
A father's sorrows cannot equal mine!
Though none, like thee, his dying hour will cheer,
Yet other offspring soothe his anguish here:
But, who with me shall hold thy former place?
Thine image, what new friendship can efface?
Ah, none! — a father's tears will cease to flow,
Time will assuage an infant brother's woe;
To all, save one, is consolation known,
While solitary friendship sighs alone.

1803.

A FRAGMENT.

When, to their airy hall, my fathers' voice
Shall call my spirit, joyful in their choice;

When, pois'd upon the gale, my form shall ride,
Or, dark in mist, descend the mountain's side;
Oh! may my shade behold no sculptur'd urns
To mark the spot where earth to earth returns!
No lengthen'd scroll, no praise-encumber'd stone;
My epitaph shall be my name alone:
If *that* with honour fail to crown my clay,
Oh! may no other fame my deeds repay!
That, only *that*, shall single out the spot;
By that remember'd, or with that forgot.

                                              1803.

ON LEAVING NEWSTEAD ABBEY.

"Why dost thou build the hall, son of the winged days? Thou
lookest from thy tower to-day: yet a few years, and the blast of
the desert comes, it howls in thy empty court." —

                                              OSSIAN.

THROUGH thy battlements, Newstead, the hollow winds whistle;
   Thou, the hall of my fathers, art gone to decay;
In thy once smiling garden, the hemlock and thistle
   Have chok'd up the rose which late bloom'd in the way.

Of the mail-cover'd Barons, who proudly to battle
   Led their vassals from Europe to Palestine's plain,
The escutcheon and shield, which with every blast rattle,
   Are the only sad vestiges now that remain.

No more doth old Robert, with harp-stringing numbers,
   Raise a flame in the breast for the war-laurell'd wreath;
Near Askalon's towers, John of Horistan* slumbers,
 'Unnerv'd is the hand of his minstrel by death.

Paul and Hubert, too, sleep in the valley of Cressy;
   For the safety of Edward and England they fell:
My fathers! the tears of your country redress ye;
   How you fought, how you died, still her annals can tell.

   * "In the park of Horseley," says Thoroton, "there was a castle, some
of the ruins of which are yet visible, called Horistan Castle, which was the
chief mansion of Ralph de Burun's successors."

On Marston,* with Rupert,** 'gainst traitors contending,
  Four brothers enrich'd with their blood the bleak field;
For the rights of a monarch their country defending,
  Till death their attachment to royalty seal'd.

Shades of heroes, farewell! your descendant departing
  From the seat of his ancestors, bids you adieu!
Abroad, or at home, your remembrance imparting
  New courage, he'll think upon glory and you.

Though a tear dim his eye at this sad separation,
  'Tis nature, not fear, that excites his regret;
Far distant he goes, with the same emulation,
  The fame of his fathers he ne'er can forget.

That fame, and that memory, still will he cherish;
  He vows that he ne'er will disgrace your renown:
Like you will he live, or like you will he perish
  When decay'd, may he mingle his dust with your own!

1803.

LINES WRITTEN IN "LETTERS OF AN ITALIAN NUN AND
AN ENGLISH GENTLEMAN: BY J. J. ROUSSEAU: FOUNDED
ON FACTS."

"Away, away, your flattering arts
  May now betray some simpler hearts;
And you will smile at their believing,
  And they shall weep at your deceiving."

ANSWER TO THE FOREGOING, ADDRESSED TO MISS —.

Dear, simple girl, those flattering arts,
From which thou'dst guard frail female hearts,
Exist but in imagination, —
Mere phantoms of thine own creation;

---

* The battle of Marston Moor, where the adherents of Charles I. were
defeated.
** Son of the Elector Palatine, and nephew to Charles I. He afterwards commanded the fleet in the reign of Charles II.

For he who views that witching grace,
That perfect form, that lovely face,
With eyes admiring, oh! believe me,
He never wishes to deceive thee:
Once in thy polish'd mirror glance,
Thou 'lt there descry that elegance
Which from our sex demands such praises,
But envy in the other raises:
Then he who tells thee of thy beauty,
Believe me, only does his duty:
Ah! fly not from the candid youth;
It is not flattery, — 'tis truth.

                                    July, 1804.

ADRIAN'S ADDRESS TO HIS SOUL WHEN DYING.

[ANIMULA! vagula, blandula,
Hospes, comesque, corporis,
Quæ nunc abibis in loca —
Pallidula, rigida, nudula,
Nec, ut soles, dabis jocos?]

AH! gentle, fleeting, wav'ring sprite,
Friend and associate of this clay!
    To what unknown region borne,
Wilt thou now wing thy distant flight?
No more with wonted humour gay,
    But pallid, cheerless, and forlorn.

TRANSLATION FROM CATULLUS.

AD LESBIAM.

EQUAL to Jove that youth must be —
Greater than Jove he seems to me —
Who, free from Jealousy's alarms,
Securely views thy matchless charms.
That cheek, which ever dimpling glows,
That mouth, from whence such music flows,

To him, alike, are always known,
Reserved for him, and him alone.
Ah! Lesbia! though 'tis death to me,
I cannot choose but look on thee;
But, at the sight, my senses fly;
I needs must gaze, but, gazing, die;
Whilst trembling with a thousand fears,
Parch'd to the throat my tongue adheres,
My pulse beats quick, my breath heaves short,
My limbs deny their slight support,
Cold dews my pallid face o'erspread,
With deadly languor droops my head,
My ears with tingling echoes ring,
And life itself is on the wing;
My eyes refuse the cheering light,
Their orbs are veiled in starless night:
Such pangs my nature sinks beneath,
And feels a temporary death.

TRANSLATION OF THE EPITAPH ON VIRGIL AND TIBULLUS.

BY DOMITIUS MARSUS.

He who sublime in epic numbers roll'd
    And he who struck the softer lyre of love,
By Death's* unequal hand alike controll'd,
    Fit comrades in Elysian regions move!

IMITATION OF TIBULLUS.
"Sulpicia at Cerinthum." — *Lib.* 4.

Cruel Cerinthus! does the fell disease
Which racks my breast your fickle bosom please?
Alas! I wish'd but to o'ercome the pain,
That I might live for love and you again:
But now I scarcely shall bewail my fate:
By death alone I can avoid your hate.

* The hand of Death is said to be unjust or unequal, as Virgil was considerably older than Tibullus at his decease.

7*

TRANSLATION FROM CATULLUS.

[Lugete, Veneres, Cupidinesque, &c.]

Ye Cupids, droop each little head
Nor let your wings with joy be spread,
My Lesbia's favourite bird is dead,
  Whom dearer than her eyes she lov'd:
For he was gentle, and so true,
Obedient to her call he flew,
No fear, no wild alarm he knew,
  But lightly o'er her bosom mov'd:

And softly fluttering here and there,
He never sought to cleave the air,
But chirupp'd oft, and, free from care,
  Tuned to her ear his grateful strain.
Now having passed the gloomy bourne
From whence he never can return,
His death and Lesbia's grief I mourn,
  Who sighs, alas! but sighs in vain.

Oh! curst be thou, devouring grave!
Whose jaws eternal victims crave,
From whom no earthly power can save,
  For thou hast ta'en the bird away:
From thee my Lesbia's eyes o'erflow,
Her swollen cheeks with weeping glow;
Thou art the cause of all her woe,
  Receptacle of life's decay.

IMITATED FROM CATULLUS.

TO ELLEN.

Oh! might I kiss those eyes of fire,
A million scarce would quench desire:
Still would I steep my lips in bliss,
And dwell an age on every kiss:

Nor then my soul should sated be;
Still would I kiss and cling to thee:
Nought should my kiss from thine dissever;
Still would we kiss, and kiss for ever;
E'en though the numbers did exceed
The yellow harvest's countless seed.
To part would be a vain endeavour:
Could I desist? — ah! never — never!

TRANSLATION FROM HORACE.

[Justum et tenacem propositi virum, &c.]

THE man of firm and noble soul
No factious clamours can control,
No threat'ning tyrant's darkling brow
 Can swerve him from his just intent:
Gales the warring waves which plough,
 By Auster on the billows spent,
To curb the Adriatic main,
Would awe his fix'd determin'd mind in vain.

Ay, and the red right arm of Jove,
Hurtling his lightnings from above,
With all his terrors there unfurl'd,
 He would, unmov'd, unaw'd behold.
The flames of an expiring world,
 Again in crashing chaos roll'd,
In vast promiscuous ruin hurl'd,
Might light his glorious funeral pile:
Still dauntless 'midst the wreck of earth he'd smile.

FROM ANACREON.

[Θελω λεγειν Ατρειδας, κ. τ. λ.]

I WISH to tune my quivering lyre
To deeds of fame and notes of fire;
To echo, from its rising swell,
How heroes fought and nations fell,

When Atreus' sons advanced to war,
Or Tyrian Cadmus roved afar;
But still, to martial strains unknown,
My lyre recurs to love alone
Fir'd with the hope of future fame,
I seek some nobler hero's name;
The dying chords are strung anew,
To war, to war, my harp is due:
With glowing strings, the epic strain
To Jove's great son I raise again;
Alcides and his glorious deeds,
Beneath whose arm the Hydra bleeds.
All, all in vain; my wayward lyre
Wakes silver notes of soft desire.
Adieu, ye chiefs renown'd in arms!
Adieu the clang of war's alarms!
To other deeds my soul is strung,
And sweeter notes shall now be sung;
My harp shall all its powers reveal,
To tell the tale my heart must feel;
Love, Love alone, my lyre shall claim,
In songs of bliss and sighs of flame.

FROM ANACREON.

[Μεσονυκτιαις ποθ' ώραις, κ. τ. λ.]

'Twas now the hour when Night had driven
Her car half round yon sable heaven;
Boötes, only, seem'd to roll
His arctic charge around the pole;
While mortals, lost in gentle sleep,
Forgot to smile, or ceased to weep:
At this lone hour, the Paphian boy,
Descending from the realms of joy,
Quick to my gate directs his course,
And knocks with all his little force.
My visions fled, alarm'd I rose, —
"What stranger breaks my blest repose?"

"Alas!" replies the wily child
In faltering accents sweetly mild,
"A hapless infant here I roam,
Far from my dear maternal home.
Oh! shield me from the wintry blast!
The nightly storm is pouring fast.
No prowling robber lingers here.
A wandering baby who can fear?"
I heard his seeming artless tale,
I heard his sighs upon the gale:
My breast was never pity's foe,
But felt for all the baby's woe.
I drew the bar, and by the light
Young Love, the infant, met my sight;
His bow across his shoulders flung,
And thence his fatal quiver hung
(Ah! little did I think the dart
Would rankle soon within my heart).
With care I tend my weary guest,
His little fingers chill my breast;
His glossy curls, his azure wing,
Which droop with nightly showers, I wring.
His shivering limbs the embers warm;
And now reviving from the storm,
Scarce had he felt his wonted glow,
Than swift he seized his slender bow: —
"I fain would know, my gentle host,"
He cried, "if this its strength has lost;
I fear, relax'd with midnight dews,
The strings their former aid refuse."
With poison tipt, his arrow flies,
Deep in my tortured heart it lies;
Then loud the joyous urchin laugh'd: —
"My bow can still impel the shaft:
'Tis firmly fix'd, thy sighs reveal it;
Say, courteous host, canst thou not feel it?"

FROM THE PROMETHEUS VINCTUS OF ÆSCHYLUS.

[Μηδαμ' δ πάντα νέμων, κ. τ. λ.]

GREAT Jove, to whose almighty throne
  Both gods and mortals homage pay,
Ne'er may my soul thy power disown,
  Thy dread behests ne'er disobey.
Oft shall the sacred victim fall
In sea-girt Ocean's mossy hall;
My voice shall raise no impious strain
'Gainst him who rules the sky and azure main.

How different now thy joyless fate,
  Since first Hesione thy bride,
When placed aloft in godlike state,
  The blushing beauty by thy side,
Thou sat'st, while reverend Ocean smiled,
And mirthful strains the hours beguiled,
The Nymphs and Tritons danced around,
Nor yet thy doom was fix'd, nor Jove relentless frown'd.

                              Harrow, Dec. 1. 1804.

TO EMMA.

SINCE now the hour is come at last,
  When you must quit your anxious lover;
Since now our dream of bliss is past,
  One pang, my girl, and all is over.

Alas! that pang will be severe,
  Which bids us part to meet no more;
Which tears me far from one so dear,
  Departing for a distant shore.

Well! we have pass'd some happy hours,
  And joy will mingle with our tears;
When thinking on these ancient towers,
  The shelter of our infant years;

Where from this Gothic casement's height,
    We view'd the lake, the park, the dell,
And still, though tears obstruct our sight,
    We lingering look a last farewell,

O'er fields through which we used to run,
    And spend the hours in childish play;
O'er shades where, when our race was done,
    Reposing on my breast you lay;

Whilst I, admiring, too remiss,
    Forgot to scare the hovering flies,
Yet envied every fly the kiss
    It dared to give your slumbering eyes:

See still the little painted bark,
    In which I row'd you o'er the lake;
See there, high waving o'er the park,
    The elm I clamber'd for your sake.

These times are past — our joys are gone,
    You leave me, leave this happy vale;
These scenes I must retrace alone:
    Without thee what will they avail?

Who can conceive, who has not proved,
    The anguish of a last embrace?
When, torn from all you fondly loved,
    You bid a long adieu to peace.

This is the deepest of our woes,
    For this these tears our cheeks bedew;
This is of love the final close,
    Oh, God! the fondest, last adieu!

TO M. S. G.

Whene'er I view those lips of thine,
  Their hue invites my fervent kiss;
Yet, I forego that bliss divine,
  Alas! it were unhallow'd bliss.

Whene'er I dream of that pure breast,
  How could I dwell upon its snows!
Yet is the daring wish represt,
  For that, — would banish its repose.

A glance from thy soul-searching eye
  Can raise with hope, depress with fear;
Yet I conceal my love, — and why?
  I would not force a painful tear.

I ne'er have told my love, yet thou
  Hast seen my ardent flame too well
And shall I plead my passion now,
  To make thy bosom's heaven a hell?

No! for thou never canst be mine,
  United by the priest's decree:
By any ties but those divine,
  Mine, my beloved, thou ne'er shalt be!

Then let the secret fire consume,
  Let it consume, thou shalt not know:
With joy I court a certain doom,
  Rather than spread its guilty glow.

I will not ease my tortured heart,
  By driving dove-eyed peace from thine;
Rather than such a sting impart,
  Each thought presumptuous I resign.

Yes! yield those lips, for which I'd brave
  More than I here shall dare to tell;
Thy innocence and mine to save, —
  I bid thee now a last farewell.

Yes! yield that breast, to seek despair,
  And hope no more thy soft embrace;
Which to obtain my soul would dare,
  All, all reproach, but thy disgrace.

At least from guilt shalt thou be free,
  No matron shall thy shame reprove;
Though cureless pangs may prey on me,
  No martyr shalt thou be to love.

TO CAROLINE.

Think'st thou I saw thy beauteous eyes,
  Suffused in tears, implore to stay;
And heard unmoved thy plenteous sighs,
  Which said far more than words can say?

Though keen the grief thy tears exprest,
  When love and hope lay both o'erthrown;
Yet still, my girl, this bleeding breast
  Throbb'd with deep sorrow as thine own.

But when our cheeks with anguish glow'd,
  When thy sweet lips were join'd to mine,
The tears that from my eyelids flow'd
  Were lost in those which fell from thine.

Thou could'st not feel my burning cheek,
  Thy gushing tears had quench'd its flame,
And as thy tongue essay'd to speak,
  In signs alone it breath'd my name.

And yet, my girl, we weep in vain,
  In vain our fate in sighs deplore;
Remembrance only can remain, —
  But that will make us weep the more.

Again, thou best beloved, adieu
  Ah! if thou canst, o'ercome regret,
Nor let thy mind past joys review, —
  Our only hope is to forget!

TO CAROLINE.

WHEN I hear you express an affection so warm,
  Ne'er think, my beloved, that I do not believe:
For your lip would the soul of suspicion disarm,
  And your eye beams a ray which can never deceive.

Yet, still, this fond bosom regrets, while adoring,
  That love, like the leaf, must fall into the sear;
That age will come on, when remembrance, deploring,
  Contemplates the scenes of her youth with a tear;

That the time must arrive, when, no longer retaining
  Their auburn, those locks must wave thin to the breeze;
When a few silver hairs of those tresses remaining,
  Prove nature a prey to decay and disease.

'Tis this, my beloved, which spreads gloom o'er my features,
  Though I ne'er shall presume to arraign the decree
Which God has proclaim'd as the fate of his creatures,
  In the death which one day will deprive you of me.

Mistake not, sweet sceptic, the cause of emotion,
  No doubt can the mind of your lover invade;
He worships each look with such faithful devotion,
  A smile can enchant, or a tear can dissuade.

But as death, my beloved, soon or late shall o'ertake us,
  And our breasts, which alive with such sympathy glow,
Will sleep in the grave till the blast shall awake us,
  When calling the dead, in earth's bosom laid low, —

Oh! then let us drain, while we may, draughts of pleasure,
  Which from passion like ours may unceasingly flow;
Let us pass round the cup of love's bliss in full measure,
  And quaff the contents as our nectar below.

                                        1805.

TO CAROLINE.

Oh! when shall the grave hide for ever my sorrow?
  Oh! when shall my soul wing her flight from this clay?
The present is hell, and the coming to-morrow
  But brings, with new torture, the curse of to-day.

From my eye flows no tear, from my lips flow no curses,
  I blast not the fiends who have hurled me from bliss;
For poor is the soul which bewailing rehearses
  Its querulous grief, when in anguish like this.

Was my eye, 'stead of tears, with red fury flakes bright'ning,
  Would my lips breathe a flame which no stream could
    assuage,   [ning,
On our foes should my glance lanch in vengeance its light-
  With transport my tongue give a loose to its rage.

But now tears and curses, alike unavailing,
  Would add to the souls of our tyrants delight;
Could they view us our sad separation bewailing,
  Their merciless hearts would rejoice at the sight.

Yet still, though we bend with a feign'd resignation,
  Life beams not for us with one ray that can cheer;
Love and hope upon earth bring no more consolation,
  In the grave is our hope, for in life is our fear.

Oh! when, my adored, in the tomb will they place me,
  Since, in life, love and friendship for ever are fled?
If again in the mansion of death I embrace thee,
  Perhaps they will leave unmolested the dead.

1805.

STANZAS TO A LADY.

WITH THE POEMS OF CAMOËNS.

This votive pledge of fond esteem,
  Perhaps, dear girl! for me thou'lt prize;
It sings of Love's enchanting dream,
  A theme we never can despise.

Who blames it but the envious fool,
　　The old and disappointed maid;
Or pupil of the prudish school,
　　In single sorrow doom'd to fade?

Then read, dear girl! with feeling read,
　　For thou wilt ne'er be one of those;
To thee in vain I shall not plead
　　In pity for the poet's woes.

He was in sooth a genuine bard;
　　His was no faint, fictitious flame:
Like his, may love be thy reward,
　　But not thy hapless fate the same.

THE FIRST KISS OF LOVE.

'Α Βαρβιτος δε χορδαις
Έρωτα μουνον ἠχει.   ANACREON.

Away with your fictions of flimsy romance;
　　Those tissues of falsehood which folly has wove!
Give me the mild beam of the soul-breathing glance,
　　Or the rapture which dwells on the first kiss of love.

Ye rhymers, whose bosoms with phantasy glow,
　　Whose pastoral passions are made for the grove;
From what blest inspiration your sonnets would flow,
　　Could you ever have tasted the first kiss of love!

If Apollo should e'er his assistance refuse,
　　Or the Nine be disposed from your service to rove,
Invoke them no more, bid adieu to the muse,
　　And try the effect of the first kiss of love.

I hate you, ye cold compositions of art:
　　Though prudes may condemn me, and bigots reprove,
I court the effusions that spring from the heart,
　　Which throbs with delight to the first kiss of love.

Your shepherds, your flocks, those fantastical themes,
    Perhaps may amuse, yet they never can move:
Arcadia displays but a region of dreams;
    What are visions like these to the first kiss of love?

Oh! cease to affirm that man, since his birth,
    From Adam till now, has with wretchedness strove;
Some portion of paradise still is on earth,
    And Eden revives in the first kiss of love.

When age chills the blood, when our pleasures are past —
    For years fleet away with the wings of the dove —
The dearest remembrance will still be the last,
    Our sweetest memorial the first kiss of love.

ON A CHANGE OF MASTERS AT A GREAT PUBLIC SCHOOL.

WHERE are those honours, Ida! once your own,
When Probus fill'd your magisterial throne?
As ancient Rome, fast falling to disgrace,
Hail'd a barbarian in her Cæsar's place,
So you, degenerate, share as hard a fate,
And seat Pomposus where your Probus sate.
Of narrow brain, yet of a narrower soul,
Pomposus* holds you in his harsh control;
Pomposus, by no social virtue sway'd,
With florid jargon, and with vain parade;
With noisy nonsense, and new-fangled rules,
Such as were ne'er before enforced in schools.
Mistaking pedantry for learning's laws,
He governs, sanction'd but by self-applause,
With him the same dire fate attending Rome,
Ill-fated Ida! soon must stamp your doom:
Like her o'erthrown, for ever lost to fame,
No trace of science left you, but the name.

                                      July, 1805.

* At Harrow I was a most unpopular boy, but *led* latterly, and have retained many of my school friendships, and all my dislikes — except to Dr. Butler, whom I treated rebelliously, and have been sorry ever since. — *Diary.*

TO THE DUKE OF DORSET.[*]

Dorset! whose early steps with mine have stray'd,
Exploring every path of Ida's glade;
Whom still affection taught me to defend,
And made me less a tyrant than a friend,
Though the harsh custom of our youthful ban
Bade *thee* obey, and gave *me* to command[**];
Thee, on whose head a few short years will shower
The gift of riches and the pride of power;
E'en now a name illustrious is thine own,
Renown'd in rank, not far beneath the throne.
Yet, Dorset, let not this seduce thy soul
To shun fair science, or evade control,
Though passive tutors[†], fearful to dispraise
The titled child, whose future breath may raise,
View ducal errors with indulgent eyes,
And wink at faults they tremble to chastise.
    When youthful parasites, who bend the knee
To wealth, their golden idol, not to thee, —
And even in simple boyhood's opening dawn
Some slaves are found to flatter and to fawn, —
When these declare, "that pomp alone should wait
On one by birth predestined to be great;

[*] In looking over my papers to select a few additional poems for this second edition, I found the above lines, which I had totally forgotten, composed in the summer of 1805, a short time previous to my departure from Harrow. They were addressed to a young schoolfellow of high rank, who had been my frequent companion in some rambles through the neighbouring country: however, he never saw the lines, and most probably never will. As, on a re-perusal, I found them not worse than some other pieces in the collection, I have now published them, for the first time, after a slight revision.

[**] At every public school the junior boys are completely subservient to the upper forms till they attain a seat in the higher classes. From this state of probation, very properly, no rank is exempt; but after a certain period, they command in turn those who succeed.

[†] Allow me to disclaim any personal allusions, even the most distant: I merely mention generally what is too often the weakness of preceptors.

That books were only meant for drudging fools,
That gallant spirits scorn the common rules;"
Believe them not; — they point the path to shame,
And seek to blast the honours of thy name.
Turn to the few in Ida's early throng,
Whose souls disdain not to condemn the wrong;
Or if, amidst the comrades of thy youth,
None dare to raise the sterner voice of truth,
Ask thine own heart; 'twill bid thee, boy, forbear;
For *well* I know that virtue lingers there.

Yes! I have mark'd thee many a passing day,
But now new scenes invite me far away;
Yes! I have mark'd within that generous mind
A soul, if well matured, to bless mankind.
Ah! though myself, by nature haughty, wild,
Whom Indiscretion hail'd her favourite child;
Though every error stamps me for her own,
And dooms my fall, I fain would fall alone;
Though my proud heart no precept now can tame,
I love the virtues which I cannot claim.

'Tis not enough, with other sons of power,
To gleam the lambent meteor of an hour;
To swell some peerage page in feeble pride,
With long-drawn names that grace no page beside;
Then share with titled crowds the common lot —
In life just gazed at, in the grave forgot;
While nought divides thee from the vulgar dead,
Except the dull cold stone that hides thy head,
The mouldering 'scutcheon, or the herald's roll,
That well-emblazon'd but neglected scroll,
Where lords, unhonour'd, in the tomb may find
One spot, to leave a worthless name behind.
There sleep, unnoticed as the gloomy vaults
That veil their dust, their follies, and their faults,
A race, with old armorial lists o'erspread,
In records destined never to be read.

Fain would I view thee, with prophetic eyes,
Exalted more among the good and wise,
A glorious and a long career pursue,
As first in rank, the first in talent too:
Spurn every vice, each little meanness shun;
Not Fortune's minion, but her noblest son.

 Turn to the annals of a former day;
Bright are the deeds thine earlier sires display.
One, though a courtier, lived a man of worth,
And call'd, proud boast! the British drama forth.*
Another view, not less renown'd for wit;
Alike for courts, and camps, or senates fit;
Bold in the field, and favour'd by the Nine;
In every splendid part ordain'd to shine;
Far, far distinguish'd from the glittering throng,
The pride of princes, and the boast of song.**
Such were thy fathers; thus preserve their name:
Not heir to titles only, but to fame.
The hour draws nigh, a few brief days will close,
To me, this little scene of joys and woes;
Each knell of Time now warns me to resign
Shades where Hope, Peace, and Friendship all were mine:
Hope, that could vary like the rainbow's hue
And gild their pinions as the moments flew;
Peace, that reflection never frown'd away,
By dreams of ill to cloud some future day;
Friendship, whose truth let childhood only tell;
Alas! they love not long, who love so well.
To these adieu! nor let me linger o'er
Scenes hail'd, as exiles hail their native shore,

* "Thomas Sackville, Lord Buckhurst, created Earl of Dorset by
James I., was one of the earliest and brightest ornaments to the poetry of
his country, and the first who produced a regular drama."—*Anderson's Poets.*

** "Charles Sackville, Earl of Dorset, esteemed the most accomplished
man of his day, was alike distinguished in the voluptuous court of Charles II.
and the gloomy one of William III. He behaved with great gallantry in the
sea-fight with the Dutch in 1665; on the day previous to which he composed
his celebrated song, 'To all you Ladies now at Land.' His character has
been drawn in the highest colours by Dryden, Pope, Prior, and Congreve."
— *Anderson's Poets.*

Receding slowly through the dark-blue deep,
Beheld by eyes that mourn, yet cannot weep.
   Dorset, farewell! I will not ask one part
Of sad remembrance in so young a heart;
The coming morrow from thy youthful mind
Will sweep my name, nor leave a trace behind.
And yet, perhaps, in some maturer year,
Since chance has thrown us in the self-same sphere,
Since the same senate, nay, the same debate,
May one day claim our suffrage for the state,
We hence may meet, and pass each other by
With faint regard, or cold and distant eye.
For me, in future, neither friend nor foe,
A stranger to thyself, thy weal or woe,
With thee no more again I hope to trace
The recollection of our early race;
No more, as once, in social hours rejoice,
Or hear, unless in crowds, thy well-known voice:
Still, if the wishes of a heart untaught
To veil those feelings which perchance it ought,
If these, — but let me cease the lengthen'd strain, —
Oh! if these wishes are not breathed in vain,
The guardian seraph who directs thy fate
Will leave thee glorious, as he found thee great.
                                1805.

FRAGMENT.

WRITTEN SHORTLY AFTER THE MARRIAGE OF MISS CHAWORTH.

   Hills of Annesley, bleak and barren,
     Where my thoughtless childhood stray'd,
   How the northern tempests, warring,
     Howl above thy tufted shade!

   Now no more, the hours beguiling,
     Former favourite haunts I see;
   Now no more my Mary smiling
     Makes ye seem a heaven to me.
                          1805.

GRANTA. A MEDLEY.

"'Αργυρέαις λόγχαισι μάχου καὶ πάντα Κρατήσαις."

Oh! could Le Sage's* demon's gift
   Be realized at my desire,
This night my trembling form he'd lift
   To place it on St. Mary's spire.

Then would, unroof'd, old Granta's halls
   Pedantic inmates full display;
Fellows who dream on lawn or stalls,
   The price of venal votes to pay.

Then would I view each rival wight,
   Petty and Palmerston survey;
Who canvass there with all their might,
   Against the next elective day.

Lo! candidates and voters lie
   All lull'd in sleep, a goodly number:
A race renown'd for piety,
   Whose conscience won't disturb their slumber.

Lord H——**, indeed, may not demur;
   Fellows are sage reflecting men:
They know preferment can occur
   But very seldom, — now and then.

They know the Chancellor has got
   Some pretty livings in disposal:
Each hopes that one may be his lot,
   And therefore smiles on his proposal.

Now from the soporific scene
   I'll turn mine eye, as night grows later,
To view, unheeded and unseen,
   The studious sons of Alma Mater.

* The Diable Boiteux of Le Sage, where Asmodeus, the demon, places
Don Cleofas on an elevated situation, and unroofs the houses for inspection.
** Edward-Harvey Hawke, third Lord Hawke.

There, in apartments small and damp
  The candidate for college prizes
Sits poring by the midnight lamp;
  Goes late to bed, yet early rises.

He surely well deserves to gain them,
  With all the honours of his college,
Who, striving hardly to obtain them,
  Thus seeks unprofitable knowledge:

Who sacrifices hours of rest
  To scan precisely metres attic;
Or agitates his anxious breast
  In solving problems mathematic:

Who reads false quantities in Seale *,
  Or puzzles o'er the deep triangle;
Deprived of many a wholesome meal;
  In barbarous Latin ** doom'd to wrangle:

Renouncing every pleasing page
  From authors of historic use;
Preferring to the letter'd sage,
  The square of the hypothenuse. †

Still, harmless are these occupations,
  That hurt none but the hapless student
Compared with other recreations,
  Which bring together the imprudent;

Whose daring revels shock the sight,
  When vice and infamy combine,
When drunkenness and dice invite,
  As every sense is steep'd in wine.

* Seale's publication on Greek Metres displays considerable talent and ingenuity, but, as might be expected in so difficult a work, is not remarkable for accuracy.

** The Latin of the schools is of the *canine species*, and not very intelligible.

† The discovery of Pythagoras, that the square of the hypothenuse is equal to the squares of the other two sides of a right-angled triangle.

Not so the methodistic crew,
   Who plans of reformation lay:
In humble attitude they sue,
   And for the sins of others pray:

Forgetting that their pride of spirit,
   Their exultation in their trial,
Detracts most largely from the merit
   Of all their boasted self-denial.

'Tis morn: — from these I turn my sight.
   What scene is this which meets the eye?
A numerous crowd, array'd in white*,
   Across the green in numbers fly.

Loud rings in air the chapel bell;
   'Tis hush'd: — what sounds are these I hear?
The organ's soft celestial swell
   Rolls deeply on the list'ning ear.

To this is join'd the sacred song,
   The royal minstrel's hallow'd strain;
Though he who hears the music long
   Will never wish to hear again.

Our choir would scarcely be excused,
   Even as a band of raw beginners;
All mercy now must be refused
   To such a set of croaking sinners.

If David, when his toils were ended,
   Had heard these blockheads sing before him,
To us his psalms had ne'er descended, —
   In furious mood he would have tore 'em.

The luckless Israelites, when taken
   By some inhuman tyrant's order,
Were ask'd to sing, by joy forsaken,
   On Babylonian river's border.

* On a saint's day, the students wear surplices in chapel.

Oh! had they sung in notes like these,
   Inspired by stratagem or fear,
They might have set their hearts at ease,
   The devil a soul had stay'd to hear.

But if I scribble longer now,
   The deuce a soul will stay to read:
My pen is blunt, my ink is low;
   'Tis almost time to stop, indeed.

Therefore, farewell, old Granta's spires!
   No more, like Cleofas, I fly;
No more thy theme my muse inspires:
   The reader's tired and so am I.

1806.

ON A DISTANT VIEW OF THE VILLAGE AND SCHOOL
OF HARROW ON THE HILL.

Oh! mihi praeteritos referat si Jupiter annos.   VIRGIL.

Ye scenes of my childhood, whose loved recollection
   Embitters the present, compared with the past;
Where science first dawn'd on the powers of reflection,
   And friendships were form'd, too romantic to last;

Where fancy yet joys to retrace the resemblance
   Of comrades, in friendship and mischief allied;
How welcome to me your ne'er fading remembrance,
   Which rests in the bosom, though hope is denied!

Again I revisit the hills where we sported,
   The streams where we swam, and the fields where we
      fought;
The school where, loud warn'd by the bell, we resorted,
   To pore o'er the precepts by pedagogues taught.

Again I behold where for hours I have ponder'd,
   As reclining, at eve, on yon tombstone I lay;
Or round the steep brow of the churchyard I wander'd,
   To catch the last gleam of the sun's setting ray.

I once more view the room, with spectators surrounded,
   Where, as Zanga, I trod on Alonzo o'erthrown;
While, to swell my young pride, such applauses resounded,
   I fancied that Mossop * himself was outshone:

Or, as Lear, I pour'd forth the deep imprecation,
   By my daughters, of kingdom and reason deprived;
Till, fired by loud plaudits and self-adulation,
   I regarded myself as a Garrick revived.

Ye dreams of my boyhood, how much I regret you!
   Unfaded your memory dwells in my breast;
Though sad and deserted, I ne'er can forget you:
   Your pleasures may still be in fancy possest.

To Ida full oft may remembrance restore me,
   While fate shall the shades of the future unroll!
Since darkness o'ershadows the prospect before me,
   More dear is the beam of the past to my soul.

But if, through the course of the years which await me,
   Some new scene of pleasure should open to view,
I will say, while with rapture the thought shall elate me,
   "Oh! such were the days which my infancy knew."
                             1806.

TO M—.

Oh! did those eyes, instead of fire,
   With bright but mild affection shine,
Though they might kindle less desire,
   Love, more than mortal, would be thine.

For thou art form'd so heavenly fair,
   Howe'er those orbs may wildly beam,
We must admire, but still despair;
   That fatal glance forbids esteem.

  * Mossop, a cotemporary of Garrick, famous for his performance of
Zanga.

When Nature stamp'd thy beauteous birth,
  So much perfection in thee shone,
She fear'd that, too divine for earth,
  The skies might claim thee for their own:

Therefore, to guard her dearest work,
  Lest angels might dispute the prize,
She bade a secret lightning lurk
  Within those once celestial eyes.

These might the boldest sylph appal,
  When gleaming with meridian blaze;
Thy beauty must enrapture all;
  But who can dare thine ardent gaze?

'Tis said that Berenice's hair
  In stars adorns the vault of heaven;
But they would ne'er permit thee there,
  Thou wouldst so far outshine the seven.

For did those eyes as planets roll,
  Thy sister-lights would scarce appear:
E'en suns, which systems now control,
  Would twinkle dimly through their sphere.*

1806.

TO WOMAN.

Woman! experience might have told me
That all must love thee who behold thee:
Surely experience might have taught
Thy firmest promises are nought;
But, placed in all thy charms before me,
All I forget, but to adore thee.
Oh memory! thou choicest blessing
When join'd with hope, when still possessing;

---

*   "Two of the fairest stars in all the heaven,
    Having some business, do intreat her eyes
    To twinkle in their spheres till they return." — SHAKSP.

But how much cursed by every lover
When hope is fled and passion's over.
Woman, that fair and fond deceiver,
How prompt are striplings to believe her!
How throbs the pulse when first we view
The eye that rolls in glossy blue,
Or sparkles black, or mildly throws
A beam from under hazel brows!
How quick we credit every oath,
And hear her plight the willing troth!
Fondly we hope 'twill last for aye,
When, lo! she changes in a day.
This record will for ever stand,
"Woman, thy vows are traced in sand."*

TO M. S. G.

When I dream that you love me, you'll surely forgive;
    Extend not your anger to sleep;
For in visions alone your affection can live, —
    I rise, and it leaves me to weep.

Then, Morpheus! envelope my faculties fast,
    Shed o'er me your languor benign;
Should the dream of to-night but resemble the last,
    What rapture celestial is mine!

They tell us that slumber, the sister of death,
    Mortality's emblem is given;
To fate how I long to resign my frail breath,
    If this be a foretaste of heaven!

Ah! frown not, sweet lady, unbend your soft brow,
    Nor deem me too happy in this;
If I sin in my dream, I atone for it now,
    Thus doom'd but to gaze upon bliss.

* The last line is almost a literal translation from a Spanish proverb.

Though in visions, sweet lady, perhaps you may smile,
  Oh! think not my penance deficient!
When dreams of your presence my slumbers beguile,
  To awake will be torture sufficient.

TO MARY,

ON RECEIVING HER PICTURE.

This faint resemblance of thy charms,
  Though strong as mortal art could give,
My constant heart of fear disarms,
  Revives my hopes, and bids me live.

Here I can trace the locks of gold
  Which round thy snowy forehead wave,
The cheeks which sprung from beauty's mould,
  The lips which made me beauty's slave.

Here I can trace — ah, no! that eye,
  Whose azure floats in liquid fire,
Must all the painter's art defy,
  And bid him from the task retire.

Here I behold its beauteous hue;
  But where's the beam so sweetly straying
Which gave a lustre to its blue,
  Like Luna o'er the ocean playing?

Sweet copy! far more dear to me,
  Lifeless, unfeeling as thou art,
Than all the living forms could be,
  Save her who placed thee next my heart.

She placed it, sad, with needless fear,
  Lest time might shake my wavering soul,
Unconscious that her image there
  Held every sense in fast control.

Through hours, through years, through time, 'twill
    cheer;
  My hope, in gloomy moments, raise;
In life's last conflict 'twill appear,
    And meet my fond expiring gaze.

TO LESBIA.

Lesbia! since far from you I've ranged,
  Our souls with fond affection glow not;
You say 'tis I, not you, have changed,
  I'd tell you why, — but yet I know not.

Your polish'd brow no cares have crost;
  And, Lesbia! we are not much older
Since, trembling, first my heart I lost,
  Or told my love, with hope grown bolder.

Sixteen was then our utmost age,
  Two years have lingering past away, love!
And now new thoughts our minds engage,
  At least I feel disposed to stray, love!

'Tis I that am alone to blame,
  I, that am guilty of love's treason;
Since your sweet breast is still the same,
  Caprice must be my only reason.

I do not, love! suspect your truth,
  With jealous doubt my bosom heaves not;
Warm was the passion of my youth,
  One trace of dark deceit it leaves not.

No, no, my flame was not pretended;
  For, oh! I loved you most sincerely;
And — though our dream at last is ended —
  My bosom still esteems you dearly.

No more we meet in yonder bowers;
  Absence has made me prone to roving;
But older, firmer hearts than ours
  Have found monotony in loving.

Your cheek's soft bloom is unimpair'd,
  New beauties still are daily bright'ning,
Your eye for conquest beams prepared,
  The forge of love's resistless lightning.

Arm'd thus, to make their bosoms bleed,
  Many will throng to sigh like me, love!
More constant they may prove, indeed;
  Fonder, alas! they ne'er can be, love!

LINES ADDRESSED TO A YOUNG LADY.

[As the author was discharging his pistols in a garden, two ladies passing near the spot were alarmed by the sound of a bullet hissing near them; to one of whom the following stanzas were addressed the next morning.]

DOUBTLESS, sweet girl! the hissing lead,
  Wafting destruction o'er thy charms,
And hurtling* o'er thy lovely head,
  Has fill'd that breast with fond alarms.

Surely some envious demon's force,
  Vex'd to behold such beauty here,
Impell'd the bullet's viewless course,
  Diverted from its first career.

Yes! in that nearly fatal hour
  The ball obey'd some hell-born guide;
But Heaven, with interposing power,
  In pity turn'd the death aside.

* This word is used by Gray, in his poem to the Fatal Sisters: —
    "Iron sleet of arrowy shower
      Hurtles through the darken'd air."

Yet, as perchance one trembling tear
  Upon that thrilling bosom fell;
Which I, th' unconscious cause of fear,
  Extracted from its glistening cell:

Say, what dire penance can atone
  For such an outrage done to thee?
Arraign'd before thy beauty's throne,
  What punishment wilt thou decree?

Might I perform the judge's part,
  The sentence I should scarce deplore;
It only would restore a heart
  Which but belong'd to thee before.

The least atonement I can make
  Is to become no longer free;
Henceforth I breathe but for thy sake,
  Thou shalt be all in all to me.

But thou, perhaps, may'st now reject
  Such expiation of my guilt:
Come then, some other mode elect;
  Let it be death, or what thou wilt.

Choose then, relentless! and I swear
  Nought shall thy dread decree prevent;
Yet hold — one little word forbear!
  Let it be aught but banishment.

LOVE'S LAST ADIEU.

Δει, δ' αει με φευγει. — ANACREON.

THE roses of love glad the garden of life,
  Though nurtured 'mid weeds dropping pestilent dew,
Till time crops the leaves with unmerciful knife,
  Or prunes them for ever, in love's last adieu!

In vain with endearments we soothe the sad heart,
  In vain do we vow for an age to be true;
The chance of an hour may command us to part,
  Or death disunite us in love's last adieu!

Still Hope, breathing peace through the grief-swollen breast,
  Will whisper, "Our meeting we yet may renew:"
With this dream of deceit half our sorrow's represt,
  Nor taste we the poison of love's last adieu!

Oh! mark you yon pair: in the sunshine of youth
  Love twined round their childhood his flow'rs as they grew;
They flourish awhile in the season of truth,
  Till chill'd by the winter of love's last adieu!

Sweet lady! why thus doth a tear steal its way
  Down a cheek which outrivals thy bosom in hue?
Yet why do I ask? — to distraction a prey
  Thy reason has perish'd with love's last adieu!

Oh! who is yon misanthrope, shunning mankind?
  From cities to caves of the forest he flew:
There, raving, he howls his complaint to the wind;
  The mountains reverberate love's last adieu!

Now hate rules a heart which in love's easy chains
  Once passion's tumultuous blandishments knew;
Despair now inflames the dark tide of his veins;
  He ponders in frenzy on love's last adieu!

How he envies the wretch with a soul wrapt in steel!
  His pleasures are scarce, yet his troubles are few,
Who laughs at the pang that he never can feel,
  And dreads not the anguish of love's last adieu!

Youth flies, life decays, even hope is o'ercast;
  No more with love's former devotion we sue:
He spreads his young wing, he retires with the blast;
  The shroud of affection is love's last adieu!

In this life of probation for rapture divine,
　　Astrea declares that some penance is due;
From him who has worshipp'd at love's gentle shrine,
　　The atonement is ample in love's last adieu!

Who kneels to the god, on his altar of light
　　Must myrtle and cypress alternately strew:
His myrtle, an emblem of purest delight;
　　His cypress the garland of love's last adieu!

DAMÆTAS.

In law an infant,* and in years a boy,
In mind a slave to every vicious joy;
From every sense of shame and virtue wean'd;
In lies an adept, in deceit a fiend;
Versed in hypocrisy, while yet a child;
Fickle as wind, of inclination wild;
Woman his dupe, his heedless friend a tool;
Old in the world, though scarcely broke from school;
Damætas ran through all the maze of sin,
And found the goal when others just begin:
Even still conflicting passions shake his soul,
And bid him drain the dregs of pleasure's bowl;
But, pall'd with vice, he breaks his former chain,
And what was once his bliss appears his bane.

TO MARION.

Marion! why that pensive brow?
What disgust to life hast thou?
Change that discontented air;
Frowns become not one so fair.
'Tis not love disturbs thy rest,
Love's a stranger to thy breast;

---

* In law every person is an infant who has not attained the age of twenty-one.

He in dimpling smiles appears
Or mourns in sweetly timid tears,
Or bends the languid eyelid down,
But shuns the cold forbidding frown.
Then resume thy former fire,
Some will love, and all admire;
While that icy aspect chills us,
Nought but cool indifference thrills us.
Wouldst thou wandering hearts beguile,
Smile at least, or seem to smile.
Eyes like thine were never meant
To hide their orbs in dark restraint;
Spite of all thou fain wouldst say,
Still in truant beams they play.
Thy lips — but here my modest Muse
Her impulse chaste must needs refuse:
She blushes, curt'sies, frowns — in short she
Dreads lest the subject should transport me;
And flying off in search of reason,
Brings prudence back in proper season.
All I shall therefore say (whate'er
I think, is neither here nor there)
Is, that such lips, of looks endearing,
Were form'd for better things than sneering:
Of soothing compliments divested,
Advice at least's disinterested;
Such is my artless song to thee,
From all the flow of flattery free;
Counsel like mine is as a brother's,
My heart is given to some others;
That is to say, unskill'd to cozen,
It shares itself among a dozen.
Marion, adieu! oh, pr'ythee slight not
This warning, though it may delight not;
And, lest my precepts be displeasing
To those who think remonstrance teasing.

At once I'll tell thee our opinion
Concerning woman's soft dominion:
Howe'er we gaze with admiration
On eyes of blue or lips carnation,
Howe'er the flowing locks attract us,
Howe'er those beauties may distract us,
Still fickle, we are prone to rove,
These cannot fix our souls to love:
It is not too severe a stricture
To say they form a pretty picture;
But wouldst thou see the secret chain
Which binds us in your humble train,
To hail you queens of all creation,
Know, in a word, 'tis ANIMATION.

TO A LADY

WHO PRESENTED TO THE AUTHOR A LOCK OF HAIR BRAIDED
WITH HIS OWN, AND APPOINTED A NIGHT IN DECEMBER TO
MEET HIM IN THE GARDEN.

THESE locks, which fondly thus entwine,
In firmer chains our hearts confine,
Than all th' unmeaning protestations
Which swell with nonsense love orations.
Our love is fix'd, I think we've proved it,
Nor time, nor place, nor art have moved it;
Then wherefore should we sigh and whine,
With groundless jealousy repine,
With silly whims and fancies frantic,
Merely to make our love romantic?
Why should you weep like Lydia Languish,
And fret with self-created anguish?
Or doom the lover you have chosen,
On winter nights to sigh half frozen;
In leafless shades to sue for pardon,
Only because the scene's a garden?

For gardens seem, by one consent,
Since Shakspeare set the precedent,
Since Juliet first declared her passion
To form the place of assignation.*
Oh! would some modern muse inspire,
And seat her by a sea-coal fire;
Or had the bard at Christmas written,
And laid the scene of love in Britain,
He surely, in commiseration,
Had changed the place of declaration.
In Italy I've no objection;
Warm nights are proper for reflection;
But here our climate is so rigid,
That love itself is rather frigid:
Think on our chilly situation,
And curb this rage for imitation;
Then let us meet, as oft we've done,
Beneath the influence of the sun;
Or, if at midnight I must meet you,
Within your mansion let me greet you:
There we can love for hours together,
Much better, in such snowy weather,
Than placed in all th' Arcadian groves
That ever witness'd rural loves;
Then, if my passion fail to please,
Next night I'll be content to freeze;
No more I'll give a loose to laughter,
But curse my fate for ever after.**

* In the above little piece the author has been accused by some *candid readers* of introducing the name of a lady from whom he was some hundred miles distant at the time this was written; and poor Juliet, who has slept so long in "the tomb of all the Capulets," has been converted, with a trifling alteration of her name, into an English damsel, walking in a garden of their own creation, during the month of *December,* in a village where the author never passed a winter. Such has been the candour of some ingenious critics. We would advise these *liberal* commentators on taste and arbiters of decorum to read *Shakspeare.*

** Having heard that a very severe and indelicate censure has been passed on the above poem, I beg leave to reply in a quotation from an ad-

9*

OSCAR OF ALVA.*

A TALE.

How sweetly shines through azure skies,
  The lamp of heaven on Lora's shore;
Where Alva's hoary turrets rise,   .
  And hear the din of arms no more.

But often has yon rolling moon
  On Alva's casques of silver play'd;
And view'd, at midnight's silent noon,
  Her chiefs in gleaming mail array'd:

And on the crimson'd rocks beneath,
  Which scowl o'er ocean's sullen flow,
Pale in the scatter'd ranks of death,
  She saw the gasping warrior low;

While many an eye which ne'er again
  Could mark the rising orb of day,
Turn'd feebly from the gory plain,
  Beheld in death her fading ray.

Once to those eyes the lamp of Love,
  They blest her dear propitious light;
But now she glimmer'd from above,
  A sad, funereal torch of night.

mired work, "Carr's Stranger in France."—"As we were contemplating
a painting on a large scale, in which, among other figures, is the uncovered
whole length of a warrior, a prudish-looking lady, who seemed to have
touched the age of desperation, after having attentively surveyed it through
her glass, observed to her party, that there was a great deal of indecorum
in that picture. Madame S. shrewdly whispered in my ear, 'that the indecorum was in the remark.'"
    * The catastrophe of this tale was suggested by the story of "Jeronyme
and Lorenzo," in the first volume of Schiller's "Armenian, or the Ghost-
Seer." It also bears some resemblance to a scene in the third act of
"Macbeth."

Faded is Alva's noble race,
    And gray her towers are seen afar;
No more her heroes urge the chase,
    Or roll the crimson tide of war.

But, who was last of Alva's clan?
    Why grows the moss on Alva's stone?
Her towers resound no steps of man,
    They echo to the gale alone.

And when that gale is fierce and high,
    A sound is heard in yonder hall;
It rises hoarsely through the sky,
    And vibrates o'er the mouldering wall.

Yes, when the eddying tempest sighs,
    It shakes the shield of Oscar brave;
But there no more his banners rise,
    No more his plumes of sable wave.

Fair shone the sun on Oscar's birth,
    When Angus hail'd his eldest born;
The vassals round their chieftain's hearth
    Crowd to applaud the happy morn.

They feast upon the mountain deer,
    The pibroch raised its piercing note;
To gladden more their highland cheer,
    The strains in martial numbers float:

And they who heard the war-notes wild
    Hoped that one day the pibroch's strain
Should play before the hero's child
    While he should lead the tartan train.

Another year is quickly past,
    And Angus hails another son;
His natal day is like the last,
    Nor soon the jocund feast was done.

Taught by their sire to bend the bow,
    On Alva's dusky hills of wind,
The boys in childhood chased the roe,
    And left their hounds in speed behind.

But ere their years of youth are o'er,
    They mingle in the ranks of war;
They lightly wheel the bright claymore,
    And send the whistling arrow far.

Dark was the flow of Oscar's hair,
    Wildly it stream'd along the gale;
But Allan's locks were bright and fair,
    And pensive seem'd his cheek, and pale.

But Oscar own'd a hero's soul,
    His dark eye shone through beams of truth;
Allan had early learn'd control,
    And smooth his words had been from youth.

Both, both were brave; the Saxon spear
    Was shiver'd oft beneath their steel;
And Oscar's bosom scorn'd to fear,
    But Oscar's bosom knew to feel;

While Allan's soul belied his form,
    Unworthy with such charms to dwell:
Keen as the lightning of the storm,
    On foes his deadly vengeance fell.

From high Southannon's distant tower
    Arrived a young and noble dame;
With Kenneth's lands to form her dower,
    Glenalvon's blue-eyed daughter came;

And Oscar claim'd the beauteous bride,
    And Angus on his Oscar smiled:
It soothed the father's feudal pride
    Thus to obtain Glenalvon's child.

Hark to the pibroch's pleasing note!
  Hark to the swelling nuptial song!
In joyous strains the voices float,
  And still the choral peal prolong.

See how the heroes' blood-red plumes
  Assembled wave in Alva's hall;
Each youth his varied plaid assumes,
  Attending on their chieftain's call.

It is not war their aid demands,
  The pibroch plays the song of peace;
To Oscar's nuptials throng the bands,
  Nor yet the sounds of pleasure cease.

But where is Oscar? sure 'tis late:
  Is this a bridegroom's ardent flame?
While thronging guests and ladies wait,
  Nor Oscar nor his brother came.

At length young Allan join'd the bride:
  "Why comes not Oscar," Angus said:
"Is he not here?" the youth replied;
  "With me he roved not o'er the glade:

"Perchance, forgetful of the day,
  'Tis his to chase the bounding roe;
Or ocean's waves prolong his stay;
  Yet Oscar's bark is seldom slow."

"Oh, no!" the anguish'd sire rejoin'd,
  "Nor chase, nor wave, my boy delay;
Would he to Mora seem unkind?
  Would aught to her impede his way?

"Oh, search, ye chiefs! oh, search around!
  Allan, with these through Alva fly;
Till Oscar, till my son is found,
  Haste, haste, nor dare attempt reply."

All is confusion — through the vale
  The name of Oscar hoarsely rings,
It rises on the murmuring gale,
  Till night expands her dusky wings;

It breaks the stillness of the night,
  But echoes through her shades in vain,
It sounds through morning's misty light,
  But Oscar comes not o'er the plain.

Three days, three sleepless nights, the Chief
  For Oscar search'd each mountain cave;
Then hope is lost; in boundless grief,
  His locks in gray-torn ringlets wave.

"Oscar! my son! — thou God of Heav'n
  Restore the prop of sinking age!
Or if that hope no more is given,
  Yield his assassin to my rage.

"Yes, on some desert rocky shore
  My Oscar's whiten'd bones must lie;
Then grant, thou God! I ask no more,
  With him his frantic sire may die!

"Yet he may live, — away, despair!
  Be calm, my soul! he yet may live;
T' arraign my fate, my voice forbear!
  O God! my impious prayer forgive.

"What, if he live for me no more,
  I sink forgotten in the dust,
The hope of Alva's age is o'er:
  Alas! can pangs like these be just?"

Thus did the hapless parent mourn,
  Till Time, who soothes severest woe,
Had bade serenity return,
  And made the tear-drop cease to flow.

For still some latent hope survived
  That Oscar might once more appear;
His hope now droop'd and now revived,
  'Till Time had told a tedious year.

Days roll'd along, the orb of light
  Again had run his destined race;
No Oscar bless'd his father's sight,
  And sorrow left a fainter trace.

For youthful Allan still remain'd,
  And now his father's only joy:
And Mora's heart was quickly gain'd,
  For beauty crown'd the fair-hair'd boy.

She thought that Oscar low was laid,
  And Allan's face was wondrous fair;
If Oscar lived, some other maid
  Had claim'd his faithless bosom's care.

And Angus said, if one year more
  In fruitless hope was pass'd away,
His fondest scruples should be o'er,
  And he would name their nuptial day.

Slow roll'd the moons, but blest at last
  Arrived the dearly destined morn;
The year of anxious trembling past,
  What smiles the lovers' cheeks adorn!

Hark to the pibroch's pleasing note!
  Hark to the swelling nuptial song!
In joyous strains the voices float,
  And still the choral peal prolong.

Again the clan, in festive crowd,
  Throng through the gate of Alva's hall;
The sounds of mirth re-echo loud,   .
  And all their former joy recall.

But who is he, whose darken'd brow
  Glooms in the midst of general mirth?
Before his eyes' far fiercer glow
  The blue flames curdle o'er the hearth.

Dark is the robe which wraps his form,
  And tall his plume of gory red;
His voice is like the rising storm,
  But light and trackless is his tread.

'Tis noon of night, the pledge goes round,
  The bridegroom's health is deeply quaff'd;
With shouts the vaulted roofs resound,
  And all combine to hail the draught.

Sudden the stranger-chief arose,
  And all the clamorous crowd are hush'd;
And Angus' cheek with wonder glows,
  And Mora's tender bosom blush'd.

"Old man!" he cried, "this pledge is done;
  Thou saw'st 'twas duly drank by me;
It hail'd the nuptials of thy son:
  Now will I claim a pledge from thee.

"While all around is mirth and joy.
  To bless thy Allan's happy lot,
Say, had'st thou ne'er another boy?
  Say, why should Oscar be forgot?"

"Alas!" the hapless sire replied,
  The big tear starting as he spoke,
"When Oscar left my hall, or died,
  This aged heart was almost broke.

"Thrice has the earth revolved her course
  Since Oscar's form has bless'd my sight;
And Allan is my last resource,
  Since martial Oscar's death or flight."

"'Tis well," replied the stranger stern,
  And fiercely flash'd his rolling eye;
"Thy Oscar's fate I fain would learn;
  Perhaps the hero did not die.

"Perchance, if those whom most he loved
  Would call, thy Oscar might return;
Perchance the chief has only roved;
  For him thy Beltane* yet may burn.

"Fill high the bowl the table round,
  We will not claim the pledge by stealth;
With wine let every cup be crown'd;
  Pledge me departed Oscar's health."

"With all my soul," old Angus said,
  And fill'd his goblet to the brim;
"Here's to my boy! alive or dead,
  I ne'er shall find a son like him."

"Bravely, old man, this health has sped;
  But why does Allan trembling stand?
Come, drink remembrance of the dead,
  And raise thy cup with firmer hand."

The crimson glow of Allan's face
  Was turn'd at once to ghastly hue;
The drops of death each other chase
  Adown in agonizing dew.

Thrice did he raise the goblet high,
  And thrice his lips refused to taste;
For thrice he caught the stranger's eye
  On his with deadly fury placed.

"And is it thus a brother hails
  A brother's fond remembrance here?
If thus affection's strength prevails,
  What might we not expect from fear?"

---

* Beltane Tree, a Highland festival on the first of May, held near fires
lighted for the occasion.

Roused by the sneer, he raised the bowl,
  "Would Oscar now could share our mirth!"
Internal fear appall'd his soul;
  He said, and dash'd the cup to earth.

"'Tis he! I hear my murderer's voice!"
  Loud shrieks a darkly gleaming form,
"A murderer's voice!" the roof replies,
  And deeply swells the bursting storm.

The tapers wink, the chieftains shrink,
  The stranger's gone, — amidst the crew
A form was seen in tartan green,
  And tall the shade terrific grew.

His waist was bound with a broad belt round,
  His plume of sable stream'd on high;
But his breast was bare, with the red wounds there,
  And fix'd was the glare of his glassy eye.

And thrice he smiled, with his eye so wild,
  On Angus bending low the knee;
And thrice he frown'd on a chief on the ground,
  Whom shivering crowds with horror see.

The bolts loud roll, from pole to pole,
  The thunders through the welkin ring,
And the gleaming form, through the mist of the storm,
  Was borne on high by the whirlwind's wing.

Cold was the feast, the revel ceased.
  Who lies upon the stony floor?
Oblivion press'd old Angus' breast,
  At length his life-pulse throbs once more.

"Away, away! let the leech essay
  To pour the light on Allan's eyes:"
His sand is done, — his race is run;
  Oh! never more shall Allan rise!

But Oscar's breast is cold as clay,
   His locks are lifted by the gale;
And Allan's barbed arrow lay
   With him in dark Glentanar's vale.

And whence the dreadful stranger came,
   Or who, no mortal wight can tell;
But no one doubts the form of flame,
   For Alva's sons knew Oscar well.

Ambition nerved young Allan's hand,
   Exulting demons wing'd his dart;
While Envy waved her burning brand,
   And pour'd her venom round his heart.

Swift is the shaft from Allan's bow;
   Whose streaming life-blood stains his side?
Dark Oscar's sable crest is low,
   The dart has drunk his vital tide.

And Mora's eye could Allan move,
   She bade his wounded pride rebel;
Alas! that eyes which beam'd with love
   Should urge the soul to deeds of hell.

Lo! seest thou not a lonely tomb
   Which rises o'er a warrior dead?
It glimmers through the twilight gloom;
   Oh! that is Allan's nuptial bed.

Far, distant far, the noble grave
   Which held his clan's great ashes stood;
And o'er his corse no banners wave,
   For they were stain'd with kindred blood.

What minstrel gray, what hoary bard,
   Shall Allan's deeds on harp-strings raise?
The song is glory's chief reward,
   But who can strike a murderer's praise?

Unstrung, untouch'd, the harp must stand,
　No minstrel dare the theme awake;
Guilt would benumb his palsied hand,
　His harp in shuddering chords would break.

No lyre of fame, no hallow'd verse,
　Shall sound his glories high in air:
A dying father's bitter curse,
　A brother's death-groan echoes there.

THE EPISODE OF NISUS AND EURYALUS,

A PARAPHRASE FROM THE ÆNEID, LIB. IX.

Nisus, the guardian of the portal stood,
Eager to gild his arms with hostile blood;
Well skill'd in fight the quivering lance to wield,
Or pour his arrows through th'embattled field:
From Ida torn, he left his sylvan cave,
And sought a foreign home, a distant grave.
To watch the movements of the Daunian host,
With him Euryalus sustains the post;
No lovelier mien adorn'd the ranks of Troy,
And beardless bloom yet graced the gallant boy;
Though few the seasons of his youthful life,
As yet a novice in the martial strife,
'Twas his, with beauty, valour's gifts to share —
A soul heroic, as his form was fair:
These burn with one pure flame of generous love;
In peace, in war, united still they move;
Friendship and glory form their joint reward;
And now combined they hold their nightly guard.

"What god," exclaim'd the first, "instils this fire?
Or, in itself a god, what great desire?
My labouring soul, with anxious thought oppress'd,
Abhors this station of inglorious rest;

The love of fame with this can ill accord,
Be't mine to seek for glory with my sword.
Seest thou yon camp, with torches twinkling dim,
Where drunken slumbers wrap each lazy limb?
Where confidence and ease the watch disdain,
And drowsy Silence holds her sable reign?
Then hear my thought: — In deep and sullen grief
Our troops and leaders mourn their absent chief:
Now could the gifts and promised prize be thine
(The deed, the danger, and the fame be mine),
Were this decreed, beneath yon rising mound,
Methinks, an easy path perchance were found;
Which past, I speed my way to Pallas' walls,
And lead Æneas from Evander's halls."

With equal ardour fired, and warlike joy,
His glowing friend address'd the Dardan boy: —
"These deeds, my Nisus, shalt thou dare alone?
Must all the fame, the peril, be thine own?
Am I by thee despised, and left afar,
As one unfit to share the toils of war?
Not thus his son the great Opheltes taught;
Not thus my sire in Argive combats fought;
Not thus, when Ilion fell by heavenly hate,
I track'd Æneas through the walks of fate:
Thou know'st my deeds, my breast devoid of fear,
And hostile life-drops dim my gory spear.
Here is a soul with hope immortal burns,
And life, ignoble life, for *glory* spurns.
Fame, fame is cheaply earn'd by fleeting breath:
The price of honour is the sleep of death."

Then Nisus, — "Calm thy bosom's fond alarms,
Thy heart beats fiercely to the din of arms.
More dear thy worth and valour than my own,
I swear by him who fills Olympus' throne!
So may I triumph, as I speak the truth,
And clasp again the comrade of my youth!

But should I fall, — and he who dares advance
Through hostile legions must abide by chance, —
If some Rutulian arm, with adverse blow,
Should lay the friend who ever loved thee low,
Live thou, such beauties I would fain preserve,
Thy budding years a lengthen'd term deserve.
When humbled in the dust, let some one be,
Whose gentle eyes will shed one tear for me;
Whose manly arm may snatch me back by force,
Or wealth redeem from foes my captive corse;
Or, if my destiny these last deny,
If in the spoiler's power my ashes lie,
Thy pious care may raise a simple tomb,
To mark thy love, and signalize my doom.
Why should thy doting wretched mother weep
Her only boy, reclined in endless sleep?
Who, for thy sake, the tempest's fury dared,
Who, for thy sake, war's deadly peril shared;
Who braved what woman never braved before,
And left her native for the Latian shore."
"In vain you damp the ardour of my soul,"
Replied Euryalus; "it scorns control!
Hence, let us haste!" — their brother guards arose,
Roused by their call, nor court again repose;
The pair, buoy'd up on Hope's exulting wing,
Their stations leave, and speed to seek the king.

Now o'er the earth a solemn stillness ran,
And lull'd alike the cares of brute and man;
Save where the Dardan leaders nightly hold
Alternate converse, and their plans unfold.
On one great point the council are agreed,
An instant message to their prince decreed;
Each lean'd upon the lance he well could wield,
And poised with easy arm his ancient shield;
When Nisus and his friend their leave request
To offer something to their high behest.

With anxious tremors, yet unawed by fear,
The faithful pair before the throne appear:
Iulus greets them; at his kind command,
The elder first address'd the hoary band.

"With patience" (thus Hyrtacides began)
"Attend, nor judge from youth our humble plan.
Where yonder beacons half expiring beam,
Our slumbering foes of future conquest dream,
Nor heed that we a secret path have traced,
Between the ocean and the portal placed,
Beneath the covert of the blackening smoke,
Whose shade securely our design will cloak!
If you, ye chiefs, and fortune will allow,
We'll bend our course to yonder mountain's brow,
Where Pallas' walls at distance meet the sight,
Seen o'er the glade, when not obscured by night:
Then shall Æneas in his pride return,
While hostile matrons raise their offspring's urn;
And Latian spoils and purpled heaps of dead
Shall mark the havoc of our hero's tread.
Such is our purpose, not unknown the way;
Where yonder torrent's devious waters stray,
Oft have we seen, when hunting by the stream,
The distant spires above the valleys gleam."

Mature in years, for sober wisdom famed,
Moved by the speech, Alethes here exclaim'd,
"Ye parent gods! who rule the fate of Troy,
Still dwells the Dardan spirit in the boy;
When minds like these in striplings thus ye raise,
Yours is the godlike act, be yours the praise;
In gallant youth, my fainting hopes revive,
And Ilion's wonted glories still survive."
Then in his warm embrace the boys he press'd,
And, quivering, strain'd them to his aged breast;

With tears the burning cheek of each bedew'd,
And, sobbing, thus his first discourse renew'd:
"What gift, my countrymen, what martial prize
Can we bestow, which you may not despise?
Our deities the first best boon have given —
Internal virtues are the gift of Heaven.
What poor rewards can bless your deeds on earth,
Doubtless await such young, exalted worth.
Æneas and Ascanius shall combine
To yield applause far, far surpassing mine."
Iulus then: — "By all the powers above!
By those Penates who my country love!
By hoary Vesta's sacred fane, I swear,
My hopes are all in you, ye generous pair!
Restore my father to my grateful sight,
And all my sorrows yield to one delight.
Nisus! two silver goblets are thine own,
Saved from Arisba's stately domes o'erthrown!
My sire secured them on that fatal day,
Nor left such bowls an Argive robber's prey:
Two massy tripods, also, shall be thine;
Two talents polish'd from the glittering mine;
An ancient cup, which Tyrian Dido gave,
While yet our vessels press'd the Punic wave:
But when the hostile chiefs at length bow down,
When great Æneas wears Hesperia's crown,
The casque, the buckler, and the fiery steed
Which Turnus guides with more than mortal speed,
Are thine; no envious lot shall then be cast,
I pledge my word, irrevocably past:
Nay more, twelve slaves, and twice six captive dames,
To soothe thy softer hours with amorous flames,
And all the realms which now the Latins sway
The labours of to-night shall well repay.
But thou, my generous youth, whose tender years
Are near my own, whose worth my heart reveres,

Henceforth affection, sweetly thus begun,
Shall join our bosoms and our souls in one;
Without thy aid, no glory shall be mine;
Without thy dear advice, no great design;
Alike through life esteem'd, thou godlike boy,
In war my bulwark, and in peace my joy."

To him Euryalus: — "No day shall shame
The rising glories which from this I claim.
Fortune may favour, or the skies may frown,
But valour, spite of fate, obtains renown.
Yet, ere from hence our eager steps depart,
One boon I beg, the nearest to my heart:
My mother, sprung from Priam's royal line,
Like thine ennobled, hardly less divine,
Nor Troy nor king Acestes' realms restrain
Her feeble age from dangers of the main;
Alone she came, all selfish fears above,
A bright example of maternal love.
Unknown the secret enterprise I brave,
Lest grief should bend my parent to the grave;
From this alone no fond adieus I seek,
No fainting mother's lips have press'd my cheek;
By gloomy night and thy right hand I vow
Her parting tears would shake my purpose now:
Do thou, my prince, her failing age sustain,
In thee her much-loved child may live again;
Her dying hours with pious conduct bless,
Assist her wants, relieve her fond distress:
So dear a hope must all my soul inflame,
To rise in glory, or to fall in fame."
Struck with a filial care so deeply felt,
In tears at once the Trojan warriors melt:
Faster than all, Iulus' eyes o'erflow;
Such love was his, and such had been his woe.
"All thou hast ask'd, receive," the prince replied;
"Nor this alone, but many a gift beside.

10*

To cheer thy mother's years shall be my aim,
Creusa's* style but wanting to the dame.
Fortune an adverse wayward course may run,
But bless'd thy mother in so dear a son.
Now, by my life! — my sire's most sacred oath —
To thee I pledge my full, my firmest troth,
All the rewards which once to thee were vow'd
If thou shouldst fall, on her shall be bestow'd."
Thus spoke the weeping prince, then forth to view
A gleaming falchion from the sheath he drew;
Lycaon's utmost skill had graced the steel,
For friends to envy and for foes to feel:
A tawny hide, the Moorish lion's spoil,
Slain 'midst the forest, in the hunter's toil,
Mnestheus to guard the elder youth bestows,
And old Alethes' casque defends his brows.
Arm'd, thence they go, while all th' assembled train,
To aid their cause, implore the gods in vain.
More than a boy, in wisdom and in grace,
Iulus holds amidst the chiefs his place:
His prayer he sends; but what can prayers avail,
Lost in the murmurs of the sighing gale!

    The trench is pass'd, and, favour'd by the night,
Through sleeping foes they wheel their wary flight.
When shall the sleep of many a foe be o'er?
Alas! some slumber who shall wake no more!
Chariots and bridles, mix'd with arms, are seen;
And flowing flasks, and scatter'd troops between:
Bacchus and Mars to rule the camp combine;
A mingled chaos this of war and wine.
"Now," cries the first, "for deeds of blood prepare,
With me the conquest and the labour share:
Here lies our path; lest any hand arise,
Watch thou, while many a dreaming chieftain dies:

* The mother of Iulus, lost on the night when Troy was taken.

I'll carve our passage through the heedless foe,
And clear thy road with many a deadly blow."
His whispering accents then the youth repress'd,
And pierced proud Rhamnes through his panting breast:
Stretch'd at his ease, th'incautious king reposed;
Debauch, and not fatigue, his eyes had closed:
To Turnus dear, a prophet and a prince,
His omens more than augur's skill evince;
But he, who thus foretold the fate of all,
Could not avert his own untimely fall.
Next Remus' armour-bearer, hapless, fell,
And three unhappy slaves the carnage swell;
The charioteer along his courser's sides
Expires, the steel his sever'd neck divides;
And, last, his lord is number'd with the dead:
Bounding convulsive, flies the gasping head;
From the swoll'n veins the blackening torrents pour;
Stain'd is the couch and earth with clotting gore.
Young Lamyrus and Lamus next expire,
And gay Serranus, fill'd with youthful fire;
Half the long night in childish games was pass'd;
Lull'd by the potent grape, he slept at last:
Ah! happier far had he the morn survey'd,
And till Aurora's dawn his skill display'd.

In slaughter'd folds, the keepers lost in sleep,
His hungry fangs a lion thus may steep;
'Mid the sad flock, at dead of night he prowls,
With murder glutted, and in carnage rolls:
Insatiate still, through teeming herds he roams;
In seas of gore the lordly tyrant foams.

Nor less the other's deadly vengeance came,
But falls on feeble crowds without a name;
His wound unconscious Fadus scarce can feel,
Yet wakeful Rhœsus sees the threatening steel;
His coward breast behind a jar he hides,
And vainly in the weak defence confides;

)

Full in his heart, the falchion search'd his veins,
The recking weapon bears alternate stains;
Through wine and blood, commingling as they flow,
One feeble spirit seeks the shades below.
Now where Messapus dwelt they bend their way,
Whose fires emit a faint and trembling ray;
There, unconfined, behold each grazing steed,
Unwatch'd, unheeded, on the herbage feed:
Brave Nisus here arrests his comrade's arm,
Too flush'd with carnage, and with conquest warm:
"Hence let us haste, the dangerous path is pass'd;
Full foes enough to-night have breath'd their last:
Soon will the day those eastern clouds adorn;
Now let us speed, nor tempt the rising morn."

What silver arms, with various art emboss'd,
What bowls and mantles in confusion toss'd.
They leave regardless! yet one glittering prize
Attracts the younger hero's wandering eyes;
The gilded harness Rhamnes' coursers felt,
The gems which stud the monarch's golden belt:
This from the pallid corse was quickly torn,
Once by a line of former chieftains worn.
Th' exulting boy the studded girdle wears,
Messapus' helm his head in triumph bears;
Then from the tents their cautious steps they bend,
To seek the vale where safer paths extend.

Just at this hour, a band of Latian horse
To Turnus' camp pursue their destined course:
While the slow foot their tardy march delay,
The knights, impatient, spur along the way:
Three hundred mail-clad men, by Volscens led,
To Turnus with their master's promise sped:
Now they approach the trench, and view the walls,
When, on the left, a light reflection falls;
The plunder'd helmet, through the waning night,
Sheds forth a silver radiance, glancing bright.

Volscens with question loud the pair alarms: —
"Stand, stragglers! stand! why early thus in arms?
From whence, to whom?" — He meets with no reply:
Trusting the covert of the night, they fly:
The thicket's depth with hurried pace they tread,
While round the wood the hostile squadron spread.

    With brakes entangled, scarce a path between,
Dreary and dark appears the sylvan scene:
Euryalus his heavy spoils impede,
The boughs and winding turns his steps mislead;
But Nisus scours along the forest's maze
To where Latinus' steeds in safety graze,
Then backward o'er the plain his eyes extend,
On every side they seek his absent friend.
"O God! my boy," he cries, "of me bereft,
In what impending perils art thou left!
Listening he runs — above the waving trees,
Tumultuous voices swell the passing breeze;
The war-cry rises, thundering hoofs around
Wake the dark echoes of the trembling ground.
Again he turns, of footsteps hears the noise;
The sound elates, the sight his hope destroys:
The hapless boy a ruffian train surround,
While lengthening shades his weary way confound;
Him with loud shouts the furious knights pursue,
Struggling in vain, a captive to the crew.
What can his friend 'gainst thronging numbers dare?
Ah! must he rush, his comrade's fate to share?
What force, what aid, what stratagem essay,
Back to redeem the Latian spoiler's prey?
His life a votive ransom nobly give,
Or die with him for whom he wished to live?
Poising with strength his lifted lance on high,
On Luna's orb he cast his frenzied eye: —

"Goddess serene, transcending every star!
Queen of the sky, whose beams are seen afar!
By night heaven owns thy sway, by day the grove,
When, as chaste Dian, here thou deign'st to rove;
If e'er myself, or sire, have sought to grace
Thine altars with the produce of the chase,
Speed, speed my dart to pierce yon vaunting crowd,
To free my friend, and scatter far the proud."
Thus having said, the hissing dart he flung;
Through parted shades the hurtling weapon sung;
The thirsty point in Sulmo's entrails lay,
Transfix'd his heart, and stretch'd him on the clay.
He sobs, he dies, — the troop in wild amaze,
Unconscious whence the death, with horror gaze.
While pale they stare, through Tagus' temples riven,
A second shaft with equal force is driven
Fierce Volscens rolls around his lowering eyes;
Veil'd by the night, secure the Trojan lies.
Burning with wrath, he view'd his soldiers fall.
"Thou youth accurst, thy life shall pay for all!"
Quick from the sheath his flaming glaive he drew,
And, raging, on the boy defenceless flew.
Nisus no more the blackening shade conceals,
Forth, forth he starts, and all his love reveals;
Aghast, confused, his fears to madness rise,
And pour these accents, shrieking as he flies:
"Me, me, — your vengeance hurl on me alone:
Here sheathe the steel, my blood is all your own.
Ye starry spheres! thou conscious Heaven! attest!
He could not — durst not — lo! the guile confest!
All, all was mine, — his early fate suspend;
He only loved too well his hapless friend:
Spare, spare, ye chiefs! from him your rage remove;
His fault was friendship, all his crime was love."
He pray'd in vain; the dark assassin's sword
Pierced the fair side, the snowy bosom gored;

Lowly to earth inclines his plume-clad crest,
And sanguine torrents mantle o'er his breast:
As some young rose, whose blossom scents the air,
Languid in death, expires beneath the share;
Or crimson poppy, sinking with the shower,
Declining gently, falls a fading flower;
Thus, sweetly drooping, bends his lovely head,
And lingering beauty hovers round the dead.

But fiery Nisus stems the battle's tide,
Revenge his leader, and despair his guide;
Volscens he seeks amidst the gathering host,
Volscens must soon appease his comrade's ghost;
Steel, flashing, pours on steel, foe crowds on foe;
Rage nerves his arm, fate gleams in every blow;
In vain beneath unnumber'd wounds he bleeds,
Nor wounds, nor death, distracted Nisus heeds;
In viewless circles wheel'd, his falchion flies,
Nor quits the hero's grasp till Volscens dies;
Deep in his throat its end the weapon found,
The tyrant's soul fled groaning through the wound.
Thus Nisus all his fond affection proved —
Dying, revenged the fate of him he loved;
Then on his bosom sought his wonted place,
And death was heavenly in his friend's embrace!

Celestial pair! if aught my verse can claim,
Wafted on Time's broad pinion, yours is fame!
Ages on ages shall your fate admire,
No future day shall see your names expire,
While stands the Capitol, immortal dome!
And vanquish'd millions hail their empress, Rome!

TRANSLATION FROM THE MEDEA OF EURIPIDES.

['Εϱωτες ὑπεϱ μεν ἀγαν, κ. τ. λ.]

WHEN fierce conflicting passions urge
  The breast where love is wont to glow,
What mind can stem the stormy surge
  Which rolls the tide of human woe?
The hope of praise, the dread of shame,
  Can rouse the tortured breast no more;
The wild desire, the guilty flame,
  Absorbs each wish it felt before.

But if affection gently thrills
  The soul by purer dreams possest,
The pleasing balm of mortal ills
  In love can soothe the aching breast:
If thus thou comest in disguise,
  Fair Venus! from thy native heaven,
What heart unfeeling would despise
  The sweetest boon the gods have given?

But never from thy golden bow
  May I beneath the shaft expire!
Whose creeping venom, sure and slow,
  Awakes an all-consuming fire:
Ye racking doubts! ye jealous fears!
  With others wage internal war;
Repentance, source of future tears,
  From me be ever distant far!

May no distracting thoughts destroy
  The holy calm of sacred love!
May all the hours be wing'd with joy,
  Which hover faithful hearts above!
Fair Venus! on thy myrtle shrine
  May I with some fond lover sigh,
Whose heart may mingle pure with mine—
  With me to live, with me to die!

My native soil! beloved before,
   Now dearer as my peaceful home,
Ne'er may I quit thy rocky shore,
   A hapless banish'd wretch to roam!
This very day, this very hour,
   May I resign this fleeting breath!
Nor quit my silent humble bower;
   A doom to me far worse than death.

Have I not heard the exile's sigh,
   And seen the exile's silent tear,
Through distant climes condemn'd to fly,
   A pensive weary wanderer here?
Ah! hapless dame!* no sire bewails,
   No friend thy wretched fate deplores,
No kindred voice with rapture hails
   Thy steps within a stranger's doors.

Perish the fiend whose iron heart,
   To fair affection's truth unknown,
Bids her he fondly loved depart,
   Unpitied, helpless, and alone;
Who ne'er unlocks with silver key **
   The milder treasures of his soul, —
May such a friend be far from me,
   And ocean's storms between us roll!

---

* Medea, who accompanied Jason to Corinth, was deserted by him for the daughter of Creon, king of that city. The chorus from which this is taken here addresses Medea; though a considerable liberty is taken with the original, by expanding the idea, as also in some other parts of the translation.

** The original is "Καθαρὰν ἀνοίξαντι κλῇδα φρενῶν;" literally "disclosing the bright key of the mind."

THOUGHTS SUGGESTED BY A COLLEGE EXAMINATION.

HIGH in the midst, surrounded by his peers,
MAGNUS* his ample front sublime uprears:
Placed on his chair of state, he seems a god,
While Sophs and Freshmen tremble at his nod.
As all around sit wrapt in speechless gloom,
His voice in thunder shakes the sounding dome;
Denouncing dire reproach to luckless fools,
Unskill'd to plod in mathematic rules.

Happy the youth in Euclid's axioms tried,
Though little versed in any art beside;
Who, scarcely skill'd an English line to pen,
Scans Attic metres with a critic's ken.
What, though he knows not how his fathers bled,
When civil discord piled the fields with dead,
When Edward bade his conquering bands advance,
Or Henry trampled on the crest of France:
Though marvelling at the name of Magna Charta,
Yet well he recollects the laws of Sparta;
Can tell what edicts sage Lycurgus made,
While Blackstone's on the shelf neglected laid;
Of Grecian dramas vaunts the deathless fame,
Of Avon's bard remembering scarce the name.

Such is the youth whose scientific pate
Class-honours, medals, fellowships, await;
Or even, perhaps, the declamation prize,
If to such glorious height he lifts his eyes.
But lo! no common orator can hope
The envied silver cup within his scope.

* No reflection is here intended against the person mentioned under the name of Magnus. He is merely represented as performing an unavoidable function of his office. Indeed, such an attempt could only recoil upon myself; as that gentleman is now as much distinguished by his eloquence, and the dignified propriety with which he fills his situation, as he was in his younger days for wit and conviviality.

Not that our heads much eloquence require,
Th' ATHENIAN's * glowing style, or Tully's fire.
A manner clear or warm is useless, since
We do not try by speaking to convince.
Be other orators of pleasing proud:
We speak to please ourselves, not move the crowd:
Our gravity prefers the muttering tone,
A proper mixture of the squeak and groan:
No borrow'd grace of action must be seen
The slightest motion would displease the Dean;
Whilst every staring graduate would prate
Against what he could never imitate.

The man who hopes t' obtain the promised cup
Must in one posture stand, and ne'er look up;
Nor stop, but rattle over every word —
No matter what, so it can *not* be heard.
Thus let him hurry on, nor think to rest:
Who speaks the fastest's sure to speak the best;
Who utters most within the shortest space
May safely hope to win the wordy race.

The sons of science these, who, thus repaid,
Linger in ease in Granta's sluggish shade;
Where on Cam's sedgy banks supine they lie
Unknown, unhonour'd live, unwept for die:
Dull as the pictures which adorn their halls,
They think all learning fix'd within their walls:
In manners rude, in foolish forms precise,
All modern arts affecting to despise;
Yet prizing Bentley's, Brunck's, or Porson's ** note,
More than the verse on which the critic wrote:
Vain as their honours, heavy as their ale,
Sad as their wit, and tedious as their tale;

* Demosthenes.
** The present Greek professor at Trinity College, Cambridge; a man
whose powers of mind and writings may, perhaps, justify their preference.

To friendship dead, though not untaught to feel
When Self and Church demand a bigot zeal.
With eager haste they court the lord of power,
Whether 'tis Pitt or Petty rules the hour;*
To him, with suppliant smiles, they bend the head,
While distant mitres to their eyes are spread.
But should a storm o'erwhelm him with disgrace,
They'd fly to seek the next who fill'd his place.
Such are the men who learning's treasures guard!
Such is their practice, such is their reward!
This much, at least, we may presume to say —
The premium can't exceed the price they pay.

1806.

TO A BEAUTIFUL QUAKER.

Sweet girl! though only once we met,
That meeting I shall ne'er forget;
And though we ne'er may meet again,
Remembrance will thy form retain.
I would not say, "I love," but still
My senses struggle with my will:
In vain, to drive thee from my breast,
My thoughts are more and more represt;
In vain I check the rising sighs,
Another to the last replies:
Perhaps this is not love, but yet
Our meeting I can ne'er forget.

What though we never silence broke,
Our eyes a sweeter language spoke;
The tongue in flattering falsehood deals,
And tells a tale it never feels:
Deceit the guilty lips impart;
And hush the mandates of the heart;

---

* Since this was written, Lord Henry Petty has lost his place, and
subsequently (I had almost said consequently) the honour of representing
the University. A fact so glaring requires no comment.

But soul's interpreters, the eyes,
Spurn such restraint, and scorn disguise.
As thus our glances oft conversed,
And all our bosoms felt rehearsed,
No spirit, from within, reproved us,
Say rather, "'twas the spirit moved us."
Though what they utter'd I repress,
Yet I conceive thou'lt partly guess;
For as on thee my memory ponders,
Perchance to me thine also wanders.
This for myself, at least, I'll say,
Thy form appears through night, through day:
Awake, with it my fancy teems;
In sleep, it smiles in fleeting dreams;
The vision charms the hours away,
And bids me curse Aurora's ray
For breaking slumbers of delight
Which make me wish for endless night.
Since, oh! whate'er my future fate,
Shall joy or woe my steps await,
Tempted by love, by storms beset,
Thine image I can ne'er forget.

Alas! again no more we meet,
No more our former looks repeat;
Then let me breathe this parting prayer,
The dictate of my bosom's care:
"May Heaven so guard my lovely quaker,
That anguish never can o'ertake her;
That peace and virtue ne'er forsake her,
But bliss be aye her heart's partaker!
Oh! may the happy mortal, fated
To be, by dearest ties, related,
For her each hour new joys discover,
And lose the husband in the lover!
May that fair bosom never know
What 'tis to feel the restless woe

Which stings the soul, with vain regret,
　　Of him who never can forget!"

————————

THE CORNELIAN.

No specious splendour of this stone
　　Endears it to my memory ever;
With lustre only once it shone,
　　And blushes modest as the giver.

Some, who can sneer at friendship's ties,
　　Have, for my weakness, oft reproved me;
Yet still the simple gift I prize, —
　　For I am sure the giver loved me.

He offer'd it with downcast look,
　　As fearful that I might refuse it;
I told him when the gift I took,
　　My only fear should be to lose it.

This pledge attentively I view'd,
　　And sparkling as I held it near,
Methought one drop the stone bedew'd,
　　And ever since I 've loved a tear.

Still, to adorn his humble youth,
　　Nor wealth nor birth their treasures yield;
But he who seeks the flowers of truth,
　　Must quit the garden for the field.

'Tis not the plant uprear'd in sloth,
　　Which beauty shows, and sheds perfume;
The flowers which yield the most of both
　　In Nature's wild luxuriance bloom.

Had Fortune aided Nature's care,
　　For once forgetting to be blind,
His would have been an ample share,
　　If well proportion'd to his mind.

But had the goddess clearly seen,
　　His form had fix'd her fickle breast;
Her countless hoards would his have been,
　　And none remain'd to give the rest.

AN OCCASIONAL PROLOGUE,

DELIVERED PREVIOUS TO THE PERFORMANCE OF "THE WHEEL OF
FORTUNE" AT A PRIVATE THEATRE.

SINCE the refinement of this polish'd age
Has swept immoral raillery from the stage;
Since taste has now expunged licentious wit,
Which stamp'd disgrace on all an author writ;
Since now to please with purer scenes we seek,
Nor dare to call the blush from Beauty's cheek;
Oh! let the modest Muse some pity claim,
And meet indulgence, though she find not fame.
Still, not for her alone we wish respect,
Others appear more conscious of defect:
To-night no veteran Roscii you behold,
In all the arts of scenic action old;
No Cooke, no Kemble, can salute you here,
No Siddons draw the sympathetic tear;
To-night you throng to witness the *début*
Of embryo actors, to the Drama new:
Here, then, our almost unfledged wings we try;
Clip not our pinions ere the birds can fly:
Failing in this our first attempt to soar,
Drooping, alas! we fall to rise no more.
Not one poor trembler only fear betrays,
Who hopes, yet almost dreads, to meet your praise;
But all our dramatis personæ wait
In fond suspense this crisis of their fate.
No venal views our progress can retard,
Your generous plaudits are our sole reward:
For these, each Hero all his power displays,
Each timid Heroine shrinks before your gaze.

Surely the last will some protection find;
None to the softer sex can prove unkind:
While Youth and Beauty form the female shield,
The sternest censor to the fair must yield.
Yet, should our feeble efforts nought avail,
Should, after all, our best endeavours fail,
Still let some mercy in your bosoms live,
And, if you can't applaud, at least forgive.

ON THE DEATH OF MR. FOX,

THE FOLLOWING ILLIBERAL IMPROMPTU APPEARED IN A MORNING PAPER.

"Our nation's foes lament on Fox's death,
But bless the hour when Pitt resign'd his breath:
These feelings wide, let sense and truth unclue,
We give the palm where Justice points its due."

TO WHICH THE AUTHOR OF THESE PIECES SENT THE FOLLOWING REPLY.

Oh factious viper! whose envenom'd tooth
Would mangle still the dead, perverting truth;
What though our "nation's foes" lament the fate,
With generous feeling, of the good and great,
Shall dastard tongues essay to blast the name
Of him whose meed exists in endless fame?
When Pitt expired in plenitude of power,
Though ill success obscured his dying hour,
Pity her dewy wings before him spread,
For noble spirits "war not with the dead:"
His friends, in tears, a last sad requiem gave,
As all his errors slumber'd in the grave;
He sunk, an Atlas bending 'neath the weight
Of cares o'erwhelming our conflicting state:
When, lo! a Hercules in Fox appear'd,
Who for a time the ruin'd fabric rear'd:

He, too, is fall'n, who Britain's loss supplied,
With him our fast-reviving hopes have died;
Not one great people only raise his urn,
All Europe's far-extended regions mourn.
"These feelings wide, let sense and truth unclue,
To give the palm where Justice points its due;"
Yet let not canker'd Calumny assail,
Or round our statesman wind her gloomy veil.
Fox! o'er whose corse a mourning world must weep,
Whose dear remains in honour'd marble sleep;
For whom at last, e'en hostile nations groan,
While friends and foes alike his talents own;
Fox shall in Britain's future annals shine,
Nor e'en to PITT the patriot's palm resign;
Which Envy, wearing Candour's sacred mask,
For PITT, and PITT alone, has dared to ask.

THE TEAR.

"O lachrymarum fons, tenero sacros
Ducentium ortus ex animo; quater
Felix! in imo qui scatentem
Pectore te, pia Nympha, sensit." — *Gray.*

WHEN Friendship or Love our sympathies move,
  When Truth in a glance should appear,
The lips may beguile with a dimple or smile,
  But the test of affection's a Tear.

Too oft is a smile but the hypocrite's wile,
  To mask detestation or fear;
Give me the soft sigh, whilst the soul-telling eye
  Is dimm'd for a time with a Tear.

Mild Charity's glow, to us mortals below,
  Shows the soul from barbarity clear;
Compassion will melt where this virtue is felt,
  And its dew is diffused in a Tear.

11*

The man doom'd to sail with the blast of the gale,
    Through billows Atlantic to steer,
As he bends o'er the wave which may soon be his grave,
    The green sparkles bright with a Tear.

The soldier braves death for a fanciful wreath
    In Glory's romantic career;
But he raises the foe when in battle laid low,
    And bathes every wound with a Tear.

If with high-bounding pride he return to his bride,
    Renouncing the gore-crimson'd spear,
All his toils are repaid when, embracing the maid,
    From her eyelid he kisses the Tear.

Sweet scene of my youth!* seat of Friendship and Truth,
    Where love chased each fast-fleeting year,
Loth to leave thee, I mourn'd, for a last look I turn'd,
    But thy spire was scarce seen through a Tear.

Though my vows I can pour to my Mary no more,
    My Mary to Love once so dear,
In the shade of her bower I remember the hour
    She rewarded those vows with a Tear.

By another possest, may she live ever blest!
    Her name still my heart must revere:
With a sigh I resign what I once thought was mine,
    And forgive her deceit with a Tear.

Ye friends of my heart, ere from you I depart,
    This hope to my breast is most near:
If again we shall meet in this rural retreat,
    May we meet, as we part, with a Tear.

When my soul wings her flight to the regions of night,
    And my corse shall recline on its bier,
As ye pass by the tomb where my ashes consume,
    Oh! moisten their dust with a Tear.

                 * Harrow.

May no marble bestow the splendour of woe
  Which the children of vanity rear;
No fiction of fame shall blazon my name,
  All I ask — all I wish — is a Tear.

October 26th, 1806.

REPLY TO SOME VERSES OF J. M. B. PIGOT, ESQ., ON THE CRUELTY OF HIS MISTRESS.

Why, Pigot, complain of this damsel's disdain,
  Why thus in despair do you fret?
For months you may try, yet, believe me, a sigh
  Will never obtain a coquette.

Would you teach her to love? for a time seem to rove;
  At first she may frown in a pet;
But leave her awhile, she shortly will smile,
  And then you may kiss your coquette.

For such are the airs of these fanciful fairs,
  They think all our homage a debt:
Yet a partial neglect soon takes an effect,
  And humbles the proudest coquette.

Dissemble your pain, and lengthen your chain,
  And seem her hauteur to regret;
If again you shall sigh, she no more will deny
  That yours is the rosy coquette.

If still, from false pride, your pangs she deride,
  This whimsical virgin forget;
Some other admire, who will melt with your fire,
  And laugh at the little coquette.

For me, I adore some twenty or more,
  And love them most dearly; but yet,
Though my heart they enthral, I'd abandon them all,
  Did they act like your blooming coquette.

No longer repine, adopt this design,
  And break through her slight-woven net;
Away with despair, no longer forbear
  To fly from the captious coquette.

Then quit her, my friend! your bosom defend,
  Ere quite with her snares you're beset:
Lest your deep-wounded heart, when incensed by the smart,
  Should lead you to curse the coquette.

October 27th, 1806.

TO THE SIGHING STREPHON.

Your pardon, my friend, if my rhymes did offend,
  Your pardon, a thousand times o'er;
From friendship I strove your pangs to remove,
  But I swear I will do so no more.

Since your beautiful maid your flame has repaid,
  No more I your folly regret;
She's now most divine, and I bow at the shrine
  Of this quickly reformed coquette.

Yet still, I must own, I should never have known
  From your verses, what else she deserved;
Your pain seem'd so great, I pitied your fate
  As your fair was so devilish reserved.

Since the balm-breathing kiss of this magical miss
  Can such wonderful transports produce;
Since the "world you forget, when your lips once have met,"
  My counsel will get but abuse.

You say, when "I rove, I know nothing of love;"
  'Tis true, I am given to range:
If I rightly remember, I've loved a good number,
  Yet there's pleasure, at least, in a change.

I will not advance, by the rules of romance,
    To humour a whimsical fair;
Though a smile may delight, yet a frown won't affright,
    Or drive me to dreadful despair.

While my blood is thus warm I ne'er shall reform,
    To mix in the Platonists' school;
Of this I am sure, was my passion so pure,
    Thy mistress would think me a fool.

And if I should shun every woman for one,
    Whose image must fill my whole breast —
Whom I must prefer, and sigh but for her —
    What an insult 'twould be to the rest!

Now, Strephon, good bye; I cannot deny
    Your passion appears most absurd;
Such love as you plead is pure love indeed,
    For it only consists in the word.

TO ELIZA.

ELIZA, what fools are the Mussulman sect,
    Who to woman deny the soul's future existence;
Could they see thee, Eliza, they'd own their defect,
    And this doctrine would meet with a general resistance.

Had their prophet possess'd half an atom of sense,
    He ne'er would have women from paradise driven;
Instead of his houris, a flimsy pretence,
    With women alone he had peopled his heaven.

Yet still, to increase your calamities more,
    Not content with depriving your bodies of spirit,
He allots one poor husband to share amongst four! —
    With souls you'd dispense; but this last, who could bear it?

His religion to please neither party is made;
  On husbands 'tis hard, to the wives most uncivil;
Still I can't contradict, what so oft has been said,
  "Though women are angels, yet wedlock 's the devil."

———

LACHIN Y GAIR. *

AWAY, ye gay landscapes, ye gardens of roses!
  In you let the minions of luxury rove:
Restore me the rocks, where the snow-flake reposes,
  Though still they are sacred to freedom and love:
Yet, Caledonia, beloved are thy mountains,
  Round their white summits though elements war;
Though cataracts foam 'stead of smooth-flowing fountains,
  I sigh for the valley of dark Loch na Garr.

Ah! there my young footsteps in infancy wander'd;
  My cap was the bonnet, my cloak was the plaid; **
On chieftains long perish'd my memory ponder'd,
  As daily I strode through the pine-cover'd glade:
I sought not my home till the day's dying glory
  Gave place to the rays of the bright polar star;
For fancy was cheer'd by traditional story,
  Disclosed by the natives of dark Loch na Garr.

"Shades of the dead! have I not heard your voices
  Rise on the night-rolling breath of the gale?"
Surely the soul of the hero rejoices,
  And rides on the wind, o'er his own Highland vale.

* *Lachin y Gair*, or, as it is pronounced in the Erse, *Loch na Garr*, towers proudly pre-eminent in the Northern Highlands, near Invercauld. One of our modern tourists mentions it as the highest mountain, perhaps, in Great Britain. Be this as it may, it is certainly one of the most sublime and picturesque amongst our "Caledonian Alps." Its appearance is of a dusky hue, but the summit is the seat of eternal snows. Near Lachin y Gair I spent some of the early part of my life, the recollection of which has given birth to these stanzas.

** This word is erroneously pronounced *plad*: the proper pronunciation (according to the Scotch) is shown by the orthography.

Round Loch na Garr while the stormy mist gathers,
    Winter presides in his cold icy car:
Clouds there encircle the forms of my fathers;
    They dwell in the tempests of dark Loch na Garr.

"Ill starr'd,* though brave, did no visions foreboding
    Tell you that fate had forsaken your cause?"
Ah! were you destined to die at Culloden,**
    Victory crown'd not your fall with applause:
Still were you happy in death's earthy slumber,
    You rest with your clan in the caves of Braemar;†
The pibroch resounds, to the piper's loud number,
    Your deeds on the echoes of dark Loch na Garr.

Years have roll'd on, Loch na Garr, since I left you
    Years must elapse ere I tread you again:
Nature of verdure and flow'rs has bereft you,
    Yet still are you dearer than Albion's plain.
England! thy beauties are tame and domestic
    To one who has roved on the mountains afar:
Oh for the crags that are wild and majestic!
    The steep frowning glories of dark Loch na Garr!

TO ROMANCE.

Parent of golden dreams, Romance!
    Auspicious queen of childish joys,
Who lead'st along, in airy dance,
    Thy votive train of girls and boys;

* I allude here to my maternal ancestors, "the *Gordons*," many of whom fought for the unfortunate Prince Charles, better known by the name of the Pretender. This branch was nearly allied by blood, as well as attachment, to the Stuarts. George, the second Earl of Huntley, married the Princess Annabella Stuart, daughter of James the First of Scotland. By her he left four sons: the third, Sir William Gordon, I have the honour to claim as one of my progenitors.

** Whether any perished in the battle of Culloden, I am not certain; but, as many fell in the insurrection, I have used the name of the principal action, "pars pro toto."

† A tract of the Highlands so called. There is also a Castle of Braemar.

At length, in spells no longer bound,
   I break the fetters of my youth;
No more I tread thy mystic round,
   But leave thy realms for those of Truth.

And yet 'tis hard to quit the dreams
   Which haunt the unsuspicious soul,
Where every nymph a goddess seems,
   Whose eyes through rays immortal roll;
While Fancy holds her boundless reign,
   And all assume a varied hue;
When virgins seem no longer vain,
   And even woman's smiles are true.

And must we own thee but a name,
   And from thy hall of clouds descend?
Nor find a sylph in every dame,
   A Pylades* in every friend?
But leave at once thy realms of air
   To mingling bands of fairy elves;
Confess that woman's false as fair,
   And friends have feeling for — themselves?

With shame I own I've felt thy sway
   Repentant, now thy reign is o'er:
No more thy precepts I obey,
   No more on fancied pinions soar.
Fond fool! to love a sparkling eye,
   And think that eye to truth was dear;
To trust a passing wanton's sigh,
   And melt beneath a wanton's tear!

---

* It is hardly necessary to add, that Pylades was the companion of Orestes, and a partner in one of those friendships which, with those of Achilles and Patroclus, Nisus and Euryalus, Damon and Pythias, have been handed down to posterity as remarkable instances of attachments, which in all probability never existed beyond the imagination of the poet, or the page of an historian, or modern novelist.

Romance! disgusted with deceit,
  Far from thy motley court I fly,
Where Affectation holds her seat,
  And sickly Sensibility;
Whose silly tears can never flow
  For any pangs excepting thine;
Who turns aside from real woe,
  To steep in dew thy gaudy shrine.

Now join with sable Sympathy,
  With cypress crown'd, array'd in weeds,
Who heaves with thee her simple sigh,
  Whose breast for every bosom bleeds;
And call thy sylvan female choir,
  To mourn a swain for ever gone,
Who once could glow with equal fire,
  But bends not now before thy throne.

Ye genial nymphs, whose ready tears
  On all occasions swiftly flow;
Whose bosoms heave with fancied fears,
  With fancied flames and phrensy glow;
Say, will you mourn my absent name,
  Apostate from your gentle train?
An infant bard at least may claim
  From you a sympathetic strain.

Adieu, fond race! a long adieu!
  The hour of fate is hovering nigh;
E'en now the gulf appears in view,
  Where unlamented you must lie:
Oblivion's blackening lake is seen,
  Convulsed by gales you cannot weather;
Where you, and eke your gentle queen,
  Alas! must perish altogether.

ANSWER TO SOME ELEGANT VERSES SENT BY A FRIEND
TO THE AUTHOR, COMPLAINING THAT ONE OF HIS DE-
SCRIPTIONS WAS RATHER TOO WARMLY DRAWN.

> "But if any old lady, knight, priest, or physician,
> Should condemn me for printing a second edition;
> If good Madam Squintum my work should abuse,
> May I venture to give her a smack of my muse?"
>
> *New Bath Guide.*

CANDOUR compels me, BECHER! to commend
The verse which blends the censor with the friend.
Your strong yet just reproof extorts applause
From me, the heedless and imprudent cause.
For this wild error which pervades my strain,
I sue for pardon, — must I sue in vain?
The wise sometimes from Wisdom's ways depart:
Can youth then hush the dictates of the heart?
Precepts of prudence curb, but can't control,
The fierce emotions of the flowing soul.
When Love's delirium haunts the glowing mind,
Limping Decorum lingers far behind:
Vainly the dotard mends her prudish pace,
Outstript and vanquish'd in the mental chase.
The young, the old, have worn the chains of love:
Let those they ne'er confined my lay reprove:
Let those whose souls contemn the pleasing power
Their censures on the hapless victim shower.
Oh! how I hate the nerveless, frigid song,
The ceaseless echo of the rhyming throng.
Whose labour'd lines in chilling numbers flow,
To paint a pang the author ne'er can know!
The artless Helicon I boast is youth; —
My lyre, the heart; my muse, the simple truth.
Far be't from me the "virgin's mind" to "taint:"
Seduction's dread is here no slight restraint.
The maid whose virgin breast is void of guile,
Whose wishes dimple in a modest smile,

Whose downcast eye disdains the wanton leer,
Firm in her virtue's strength, yet not severe —
She whom a conscious grace shall thus refine
Will ne'er be "tainted" by a strain of mine.
But for the nymph whose premature desires
Torment her bosom with unholy fires,
No net to snare her willing heart is spread;
She would have fallen, though she ne'er had read.
For me, I fain would please the chosen few,
Whose souls, to feeling and to nature true,
Will spare the childish verse, and not destroy
The light effusions of a heedless boy.
I seek not glory from the senseless crowd;
Of fancied laurels I shall ne'er be proud:
Their warmest plaudits I would scarcely prize,
Their sneers or censures I alike despise.

November 26. 1806.

ELEGY ON NEWSTEAD ABBEY. *

"It is the voice of years that are gone! they roll before me with all their deeds." — *Ossian.*

NEWSTEAD! fast-falling, once-resplendent dome!
　Religion's shrine! repentant HENRY's ** pride!
Of warriors, monks, and dames the cloister'd tomb,
　Whose pensive shades around thy ruins glide,

Hail to thy pile! more honour'd in thy fall
　Than modern mansions in their pillar'd state;
Proudly majestic frowns thy vaulted hall,
　Scowling defiance on the blasts of fate.

* As one poem on this subject is already printed, the author had, originally, no intention of inserting the following. It is now added at the particular request of some friends.

** Henry II. founded Newstead soon after the murder of Thomas à Becket.

No mail-clad serfs,* obedient to their lord,
   In grim array the crimson cross** demand;
Or gay assemble round the festive board
   Their chief's retainers, an immortal band:

Else might inspiring Fancy's magic eye
   Retrace their progress through the lapse of time,
Marking each ardent youth, ordain'd to die,
   A votive pilgrim in Judea's clime.

But not from thee, dark pile! departs the chief;
   His feudal realm in other regions lay:
In thee the wounded conscience courts relief,
   Retiring from the garish blaze of day.

Yes! in thy gloomy cells and shades profound
   The monk abjured a world he ne'er could view;
Or blood-stain'd guilt repenting solace found,
   Or innocence from stern oppression flew.

A monarch bade thee from that wild arise,
   Where Sherwood's outlaws once were wont to prowl;
And Superstition's crimes, of various dyes,
   Sought shelter in the priest's protecting cowl.

Where now the grass exhales a murky dew,
   The humid pall of life-extinguish'd clay,
In sainted fame the sacred fathers grew,
   Nor raised their pious voices but to pray.

Where now the bats their wavering wings extend
   Soon as the gloaming † spreads her waning shade,
The choir did oft their mingling vespers blend,
   Or matin orisons to Mary †† paid.

  * This word is used by Walter Scott, in his poem, "The Wild Hunts-
man;" synonymous with vassal.
  ** The red cross was the badge of the crusaders.
  † As "gloaming," the Scottish word for twilight, is far more poetical,
and has been recommended by many eminent literary men, particularly by
Dr. Moore in his Letters to Burns, I have ventured to use it on account of
its harmony.
  †† The priory was dedicated to the Virgin.

Years roll on years; to ages, ages yield;
    Abbots to abbots, in a line, succeed:
Religion's charter their protecting shield
    Till royal sacrilege their doom decreed.

One holy HENRY rear'd the gothic walls,
    And bade the pious inmates rest in peace;
Another HENRY* the kind gift recalls,
    And bids devotion's hallow'd echoes cease.

Vain is each threat or supplicating prayer;
    He drives them exiles from their blest abode,
To roam a dreary world in deep despair —
    No friend, no home, no refuge, but their God.

Hark how the hall, resounding to the strain,
    Shakes with the martial music's novel din!
The heralds of a warrior's haughty reign,
    High crested banners wave thy walls within.

Of changing sentinels the distant hum,
    The mirth of feasts, the clang of burnish'd arms,
The braying trumpet and the hoarser drum,
    Unite in concert with increased alarms.

An abbey once, a regal fortress** now,
    Encircled by insulting rebel powers,
War's dread machines o'erhang thy threatening brow,
    And dart destruction in sulphureous showers.

Ah vain defence! the hostile traitor's siege,
    Though oft repulsed, by guile o'ercomes the brave;
His thronging foes oppress the faithful liege,
    Rebellion's reeking standards o'er him wave.

---

* At the dissolution of the monasteries, Henry VIII. bestowed New-stead Abbey on Sir John Byron.
** Newstead sustained a considerable siege in the war between Charles I. and his parliament.

Not unavenged the raging baron yields;
 The blood of traitors smears the purple plain;
Unconquer'd still, his falchion there he wields,
 And days of glory yet for him remain.

Still in that hour the warrior wished to strew
 Self-gather'd laurels on a self-sought grave;
But Charles' protecting genius hither flew,
 The monarch's friend, the monarch's hope, to save.

Trembling, she snatched him * from th' unequal strife,
 In other fields the torrent to repel;
For nobler combats, here, reserved his life,
 To lead the band where godlike FALKLAND ** fell.

From thee, poor pile! to lawless plunder given,
 While dying groans their painful requiem sound,
Far different incense now ascends to heaven,
 Such victims wallow on the gory ground.

There many a pale and ruthless robber's corse,
 Noisome and ghast, defiles thy sacred sod;
O'er mingling man, and horse commix'd with horse,
 Corruption's heap, the savage spoilers trod.

Graves, long with rank and sighing weeds o'erspread,
 Ransack'd, resign perforce their mortal mould:
From ruffian fangs escape not e'en the dead,
 Raked from repose in search for buried gold.

Hush'd is the harp, unstrung the warlike lyre,
 The minstrel's palsied hand reclines in death;
No more he strikes the quivering chords with fire,
 Or sings the glories of the martial wreath.

 * Lord Byron, and his brother Sir William, held high commands in the
royal army. The former was general in chief in Ireland, lieutenant of the
Tower, and governor to James, Duke of York, afterwards the unhappy
James II.; the latter had a principal share in many actions.
 ** Lucius Cary, Lord Viscount Falkland, the most accomplished man
of his age, was killed at the battle of Newbury, charging in the ranks of
Lord Byron's regiment of cavalry.

At length the sated murderers, gorged with prey,
    Retire; the clamour of the fight is o'er;
Silence again resumes her awful sway,
    And sable Horror guards the massy door.

Here Desolation holds her dreary court:
    What satellites declare her dismal reign!
Shrieking their dirge, ill-omened birds resort,
    To flit their vigils in the hoary fane.

Soon a new morn's restoring beams dispel
    The clouds of anarchy from Britain's skies;
The fierce usurper seeks his native hell,
    And Nature triumphs as the tyrant dies.

With storms she welcomes his expiring groans;
    Whirlwinds, responsive, greet his labouring breath;
Earth shudders as her caves receive his bones,
    Loathing* the offering of so dark a death.

The legal ruler** now resumes the helm,
    He guides through gentle seas the prow of state;
Hope cheers, with wonted smiles, the peaceful realm,
    And heals the bleeding wounds of wearied hate.

The gloomy tenants, Newstead! of thy cells,
    Howling, resign their violated nest;
Again the master on his tenure dwells,
    Enjoy'd, from absence, with enraptured zest.

Vassals, within thy hospitable pale,
    Loudly carousing, bless their lord's return;
Culture again adorns the gladdening vale,
    And matrons, once lamenting, cease to mourn.

* This is an historical fact. A violent tempest occurred immediately subsequent to the death or interment of Cromwell, which occasioned many disputes between his partisans and the cavaliers: both interpreted the circumstance into divine interposition; but whether as approbation or condemnation, we leave to the casuists of that age to decide. I have made such use of the occurrence as suited the subject of my poem.

** Charles II.

A thousand songs on tuneful echo float,
  Unwonted foliage mantles o'er the trees;
And hark! the horns proclaim a mellow note,
  The hunters' cry hangs lengthening on the breeze.

Beneath their coursers' hoofs the valleys shake:
  What fears, what anxious hopes, attend the chase!
The dying stag seeks refuge in the Lake;
  Exulting shouts announce the finished race.

Ah happy days! too happy to endure!
  Such simple sports our plain forefathers knew:
No splendid vices glitter'd to allure;
  Their joys were many, as their cares were few.

From these descending, sons to sires succeed;
  Time steals along, and Death uprears his dart;
Another chief impels the foaming steed,
  Another crowd pursue the panting hart.

Newstead! what saddening change of scene is thine!
  Thy yawning arch betokens slow decay;
The last and youngest of a noble line
  Now holds thy mouldering turrets in his sway.

Deserted now, he scans thy gray worn towers;
  Thy vaults, where dead of feudal ages sleep;
Thy cloisters, pervious to the wintry showers;
  These, these he views, and views them but to weep.

Yet are his tears no emblem of regret:
  Cherish'd affection only bids them flow.
Pride, hope, and love, forbid him to forget,
  But warm his bosom with impassion'd glow.

Yet he prefers thee to the gilded domes
  Or gewgaw grottos of the vainly great;
Yet lingers 'mid thy damp and mossy tombs,
  Nor breathes a murmur 'gainst the will of fate.

Haply thy sun, emerging, yet may shine,
  Thee to irradiate which meridian ray;
Hours splendid as the past may still be thine,
  And bless thy future as thy former day.

CHILDISH RECOLLECTIONS.

" I cannot but remember such things were,
And were most dear to me."

WHEN slow Disease, with all her host of pains,
Chills the warm tide which flows along the veins;
When Health, affrighted, spreads her rosy wing,
And flies with every changing gale of spring;
Not to the aching frame alone confined,
Unyielding pangs assail the drooping mind:
What grisly forms, the spectre-train of woe,
Bid shuddering Nature shrink beneath the blow,
With Resignation wage relentless strife,
While Hope retires appall'd, and clings to life.
Yet less the pang when, through the tedious hour,
Remembrance sheds around her genial power,
Calls back the vanish'd days to rapture given,
When love was bliss, and Beauty form'd our heaven;
Or, dear to youth, portrays each childish scene,
Those fairy bowers, where all in turn have been.
As when through clouds that pour the summer storm
The orb of day unveils his distant form,
Gilds with faint beams the crystal dews of rain,
And dimly twinkles o'er the watery plain;
Thus, while the future dark and cheerless gleams,
The sun of memory, glowing through my dreams,
Though sunk the radiance of his former blaze,
To scenes far distant points his paler rays;
Still rules my senses with unbounded sway,
The past confounding with the present day.

12*

Oft does my heart indulge the rising thought,
Which still recurs, unlook'd for and unsought;
My soul to Fancy's fond suggestion yields,
And roams romantic o'er her airy fields:
Scenes of my youth, developed, crowd to view,
To which I long have bade a last adieu!
Seats of delight, inspiring youthful themes;
Friends lost to me for aye, except in dreams;
Some who in marble prematurely sleep,
Whose forms I now remember but to weep;
Some who yet urge the same scholastic course
Of early science, future fame the source;
Who, still contending in the studious race,
In quick rotation fill the senior place.
These with a thousand visions now unite,
To dazzle, though they please, my aching sight.
IDA! blest spot, where Science holds her reign,
How joyous once I join'd thy youthful train!
Bright in idea gleams thy lofty spire,
Again I mingle with thy playful quire;
Our tricks of mischief, every childish game,
Unchanged by time or distance, seem the same;
Through winding paths along the glade, I trace
The social smile of every welcome face;
My wonted haunts, my scenes of joy and woe,
Each early boyish friend, or youthful foe,
Our feuds dissolved, but not my friendship past: —
I bless the former, and forgive the last.
Hours of my youth! when, nurtured in my breast,
To love a stranger, friendship made me blest; —
Friendship, the dear peculiar bond of youth,
When every artless bosom throbs with truth;
Untaught by worldly wisdom how to feign,
And check each impulse with prudential rein;
When all we feel, our honest souls disclose —
In love to friends, in open hate to foes;

No varnish'd tales the lips of youth repeat,
No dear-bought knowledge purchased by deceit.
Hypocrisy, 'the gift of lengthen'd years,
Matured by age, the garb of prudence wears.
When now the boy is ripen'd into man,
His careful sire chalks forth some wary plan;
Instructs his son from candour's path to shrink,
Smoothly to speak, and cautiously to think;
Still to assent, and never to deny —
A patron's praise can well reward the lie:
And who, when Fortune's warning voice is heard,
Would lose his opening prospects for a word?
Although against that word his heart rebel,
And truth indignant all his bosom swell.

Away with themes like this! not mine the task
From flattering fiends to tear the hateful mask;
Let keener bards delight in satire's sting;
My fancy soars not on Detraction's wing:
Once, and but once, she aim'd a deadly blow,
To hurl defiance on a secret foe;
But when that foe, from feeling or from shame,
The cause unknown, yet still to me the same,
Warn'd by some friendly hint, perchance, retired,
With this submission all her rage expired.
From dreaded pangs that feeble foe to save,
She hush'd her young resentment, and forgave;
Or, if my muse a pedant's portrait drew,
Pomposus' virtues are but known to few:
I never fear'd the young usurper's nod,
And he who wields must sometimes feel the rod.
If since on Granta's failings, known to all
Who share the converse of a college hall.
She sometimes trifled in a lighter strain,
'Tis past, and thus she will not sin again,
Soon must her early song for ever cease,
And all may rail when I shall rest in peace.

Here first remember'd be the joyous band,
Who hail'd me chief, obedient to command;
Who join'd with me in every boyish sport —
Their first adviser, and their last resort;
Nor shrunk beneath the upstart pedant's frown,
Or all the sable glories of his gown;
Who, thus transplanted from his father's school —
Unfit to govern, ignorant of rule —
Succeeded him, whom all unite to praise,
The dear preceptor of my early days;
Probus, * the pride of science, and the boast,
To Ida now, alas! for ever lost.
With him, for years, we search'd the classic page,
And fear'd the master, though we loved the sage:
Retired at last, his small yet peaceful seat,
From learning's labour is the blest retreat.
Pomrosus fills his magisterial chair;
Pomposus governs, — but, my muse, forbear:
Contempt, in silence, be the pedant's lot;
His name and precepts be alike forgot;
No more his mention shall my verse degrade, —
To him my tribute is already paid.

High, through those elms, with hoary branches crown'd,
Fair Ida's bower adorns the landscape round;
There Science, from her favour'd seat, surveys
The vale where rural Nature claims her praise;
To her awhile resigns her youthful train,
Who move in joy, and dance along the plain;

* Dr. Drury. This most able and excellent man retired from his
situation in March, 1805, after having resided thirty-five years at Harrow;
the last twenty as head-master; an office he held with equal honour to himself and advantage to the very extensive school over which he presided.
Panegyric would here be superfluous: it would be useless to enumerate
qualifications which were never doubted. A considerable contest took
place between three rival candidates for his vacant chair: of this I can
only say,
            Si mea cum vestris valuissent vota, Pelasgi!
            Non foret ambiguus tanti certaminis hæres.

In scatter'd groups each favour'd haunt pursue;
Repeat old pastimes, and discover new;
Flush'd with his rays, beneath the noontide sun,
In rival bands, between the wickets run,
Drive o'er the sward the ball with active force,
Or chase with nimble feet its rapid course.
But these with slower steps direct their way,
Where Brent's cool waves in limpid currents stray;
While yonder few search out some green retreat,
And arbours shade them from the summer heat:
Others, again, a pert and lively crew,
Some rough and thoughtless stranger placed in view,
With frolic quaint their antic jests expose,
And tease the grumbling rustic as he goes;
Nor rest with this, but many a passing fray
Tradition treasures for a future day:
"'Twas here the gather'd swains for vengeance fought,
And here we earn'd the conquest dearly bought;
Here have we fled before superior might,
And here renew'd the wild tumultuous fight."
While thus our souls with early passions swell,
In lingering tones resounds the distant bell;
Th' allotted hour of daily sport is o'er,
And Learning beckons from her temple's door.
No splendid tablets grace her simple hall,
But ruder records fill the dusky wall;
There, deeply carved, behold! each tyro's name
Secures its owner's academic fame;
Here mingling view the names of sire and son —
The one long graved, the other just begun:
These shall survive alike when son and sire
Beneath one common stroke of fate expire:
Perhaps their last memorial these alone,
Denied in death a monumental stone,
Whilst to the gale in mournful cadence wave
The sighing weeds that hide their nameless grave.

And here my name, and many an early friend's,
Along the wall in lengthen'd line extends.
Though still our deeds amuse the youthful race,
Who tread our steps, and fill our former place,
Who young obey'd their lords in silent awe,
Whose nod commanded, and whose voice was law;
And now, in turn, possess the reins of power,
To rule the little tyrants of an hour; —
Though sometimes, with the tales of ancient day,
They pass the dreary winter's eve away —
"And thus our former rulers stemm'd the tide,
And thus they dealt the combat side by side;
Just in this place the mouldering walls they scaled,
Nor bolts nor bars against their strength avail'd;
Here Probus came, the rising fray to quell,
And here he falter'd forth his last farewell;
And here one night abroad they dared to roam,
While bold Pomposus bravely staid at home;" —
While thus they speak, the hour must soon arrive,
When names of these, like ours, alone survive:
Yet a few years, one general wreck will whelm
The faint remembrance of our fairy realm.

Dear honest race! though now we meet no more,
One last long look on what we were before —
Our first kind greetings, and our last adieu —
Drew tears from eyes unused to weep with you.
Through splendid circles, fashion's gaudy world,
Where folly's glaring standard waves unfurl'd,
I plunged to drown in noise my fond regret,
And all I sought or hoped was to forget.
Vain wish! if chance some well-remember'd face,
Some old companion of my early race,
Advanced to claim his friend with honest joy,
My eyes, my heart, proclaim'd me still a boy;
The glittering scene, the fluttering groups around,
Were quite forgotten when my friend was found;

The smiles of beauty — (for, alas! I've known
What 'tis to bend before Love's mighty throne) —
The smiles of beauty, though those smiles were dear,
Could hardly charm me, when that friend was near:
My thoughts bewilder'd in the fond surprise,
The woods of IDA danced before my eyes;
I saw the sprightly wand'rers pour along,
I saw and join'd again the joyous throng;
Panting, again I traced her lofty grove,
And friendship's feelings triumph'd over love.

Yet, why should I alone with such delight,
Retrace the circuit of my former flight?
Is there no cause beyond the common claim
Endear'd to all in childhood's very name?
Ah! sure some stronger impulse vibrates here,
Which whispers friendship will be doubly dear,
To one who thus for kindred hearts must roam,
And seek abroad the love denied at home.
Those hearts, dear IDA, have I found in thee —
A home, a world, a paradise to me.
Stern Death forbade my orphan youth to share
The tender guidance of a father's care.
Can rank, or e'en a guardian's name, supply
The love which glistens in a father's eye?
For this can wealth or title's sound atone,
Made, by a parent's early loss, my own?
What brother springs a brother's love to seek?
What sister's gentle kiss has prest my cheek?
For me how dull the vacant moments rise,
To no fond bosom link'd by kindred ties!
Oft in the progress of some fleeting dream
Fraternal smiles collected round me seem;
While still the visions to my heart are prest,
The voice of love will murmur in my rest:
I hear — I wake — and in the sound rejoice;
I hear again, — but, ah! no brother's voice.

A hermit, 'midst of crowds, I fain must stray
Alone, though thousand pilgrims fill the way;
While these a thousand kindred wreaths entwine,
I cannot call one single blossom mine:
What then remains? in solitude to groan,
To mix in friendship, or to sigh alone.
Thus must I cling to some endearing hand,
And none more dear than IDA's social band.

Alonzo! best and dearest of my friends,
Thy name ennobles him who thus commends:
From this fond tribute thou canst gain no praise;
The praise is his who now that tribute pays.
Oh! in the promise of thy early youth,
If hope anticipate the words of truth,
Some loftier bard shall sing thy glorious name,
To build his own upon thy deathless fame.
Friend of my heart, and foremost of the list
Of those with whom I lived supremely blest,
Oft have we drain'd the font of ancient lore;
Though drinking deeply, thirsting still the more.
Yet, when confinement's lingering hour was done,
Our sports, our studies, and our souls were one:
Together we impell'd the flying ball;
Together waited in our tutor's hall;
Together join'd in cricket's manly toil,
Or shared the produce of the river's spoil;
Or, plunging from the green declining shore,
Our pliant limbs the buoyant billows bore;
In every clement, unchanged, the same,
All, all that brothers should be, but the name.

Nor yet are you forgot, my jocund boy!
DAVUS, the harbinger of childish joy;
For ever foremost in the ranks of fun,
The laughing herald of the harmless pun;
Yet with a breast of such materials made —
Anxious to please, of pleasing half afraid;

Candid and liberal, with a heart of steel
In danger's path, though not untaught to feel.
Still I remember, in the factious strife,
The rustic's musket aim'd against my life:
High poised in air the massy weapon hung,
A cry of horror burst from every tongue;
Whilst I, in combat with another foe,
Fought on, unconscious of th' impending blow;
Your arm, brave boy, arrested his career —
Forward you sprung, insensible to fear;
Disarm'd and baffled by your conquering hand,
The grovelling savage roll'd upon the sand:
An act like this, can simple thanks repay?
Or all the labours of a grateful lay?
Oh no! whene'er my breast forgets the deed,
That instant, DAVUS, it deserves to bleed.

Lycus! on me thy claims are justly great:
Thy milder virtues could my muse relate,
To thee alone, unrivall'd, would belong
The feeble efforts of my lengthen'd song.
Well canst thou boast, to lead in senates fit,
A Spartan firmness with Athenian wit:
Though yet in embryo these perfections shine,
Lycus! thy father's fame will soon be thine.
Where learning nurtures the superior mind,
What may we hope from genius thus refined!
When time at length matures thy growing years,
How wilt thou tower above thy fellow peers!
Prudence and sense, a spirit bold and free,
With honour's soul, united beam in thee.

Shall fair EURYALUS pass by unsung?
From ancient lineage, not unworthy sprung:
What though one sad dissension bade us part,
That name is yet embalm'd within my heart;
Yet at the mention does that heart rebound,
And palpitate, responsive to the sound.

Envy dissolved our ties, and not our will:
We once were friends, — I'll think we are so still.
A form unmatch'd in nature's partial mould,
A heart untainted, we in thee behold:
Yet not the senate's thunder thou shalt wield,
Nor seek for glory in the tented field;
To minds of ruder texture these be given —
Thy soul shall nearer soar its native heaven.
Haply, in polish'd courts might be thy seat,
But that thy tongue could never forge deceit:
The courtier's supple bow and sneering smile,
The flow of compliment, the slippery wile,
Would make that breast with indignation burn,
And all the glittering snares to tempt thee spurn.
Domestic happiness will stamp thy fate;
Sacred to love, unclouded e'er by hate;
The world admire thee, and thy friends adore; —
Ambition's slave alone would toil for more.

 Now last, but nearest, of the social band,
See honest, open, generous CLEON stand;
With scarce one speck to cloud the pleasing scene,
No vice degrades that purest soul serene.
On the same day our studious race begun,
On the same day our studious race was run;
Thus side by side we pass'd our first career,
Thus side by side we strove for many a year;
At last concluded our scholastic life,
We neither conquer'd in the classic strife:
As speakers* each supports an equal name,
And crowds allow to both a partial fame:
To soothe a youthful rival's early pride,
Though Cleon's candour would the palm divide,
Yet candour's self compels me now to own,
Justice awards it to my friend alone.

 * This alludes to the public speeches delivered at the school where
the author was educated.

Oh! friends regretted, scenes for ever dear,
Remembrance hails you with her warmest tear!
Drooping, she bends o'er pensive Fancy's urn,
To trace the hours which never can return;
Yet with the retrospection loves to dwell,
And soothe the sorrows of her last farewell!
Yet greets the triumph of my boyish mind,
As infant laurels round my head were twined,
When Probus' praise repaid my lyric song,
Or placed me higher in the studious throng;
Or when my first harangue received applause,
His sage instruction the primeval cause,
What gratitude to him my soul possest,
While hope of dawning honours fill'd my breast!
For all my humble fame, to him alone
The praise is due, who made that fame my own.
Oh! could I soar above these feeble lays,
These young effusions of my early days,
To him my muse her noblest strain would give:
The song might perish, but the theme might live.
Yet why for him the needless verse essay?
His honour'd name requires no vain display:
By every son of grateful Ida blest,
It finds an echo in each youthful breast;
A fame beyond the glories of the proud,
Or all the plaudits of the venal crowd.

Ida! not yet exhausted is the theme,
Nor closed the progress of my youthful dream.
How many a friend deserves the grateful strain!
What scenes of childhood still unsung remain!
Yet let me hush this echo of the past,
This parting song, the dearest and the last;
And brood in secret o'er those hours of joy,
To me a silent and a sweet employ,
While future hope and fear alike unknown,
I think with pleasure on the past alone;

Yes, to the past alone my heart confine,
And chase the phantom of what once was mine.

Ida! still o'er thy hills in joy preside,
And proudly steer through time's eventful tide;
Still may thy blooming sons thy name revere,
Smile in thy bower, but quit thee with a tear; —
That tear, perhaps, the fondest which will flow,
O'er their last scene of happiness below.
Tell me, ye hoary few, who glide along,
The feeble veterans of some former throng,
Whose friends, like autumn leaves by tempests whirl'd,
Are swept for ever from this busy world;
Revolve the fleeting moments of your youth,
While Care as yet withheld her venom'd tooth;
Say if remembrance days like these endears
Beyond the rapture of succeeding years?
Say, can ambition's fever'd dream bestow
So sweet a balm to soothe your hours of woe?
Can treasures, hoarded for some thankless son,
Can royal smiles, or wreaths by slaughter won,
Can stars or ermine, man's maturer toys,
(For glittering baubles are not left to boys)
Recall one scene so much beloved to view,
As those where Youth her garland twined for you?
Ah, no! amidst the gloomy calm of age
You turn with faltering hand life's varied page;
Peruse the record of your days on earth,
Unsullied only where it marks your birth;
Still lingering pause above each chequer'd leaf,
And blot with tears the sable lines of grief;
Where Passion o'er the theme her mantle threw,
Or weeping Virtue sigh'd a faint adieu;
But bless the scroll which fairer words adorn,
Traced by the rosy finger of the morn;
When Friendship bow'd before the shrine of truth,
And Love, without his pinion,* smiled on youth.

* "L'Amitié est l'Amour sans ailes," is a French proverb.

ANSWER TO A BEAUTIFUL POEM, ENTITLED
"THE COMMON LOT."*

MONTGOMERY! true, the common lot
  Of mortals lies in Lethe's wave;
Yet some shall never be forgot —
  Some shall exist beyond the grave.

"Unknown the region of his birth,"
  The hero ** rolls the tide of war;
Yet not unknown his martial worth,
  Which glares a meteor from afar.

His joy or grief, his weal or woe,
  Perchance may 'scape the page of fame;
Yet nations now unborn will know
  The record of his deathless name.

The patriot's and the poet's frame
  Must share the common tomb of all:
Their glory will not sleep the same;
  That will arise, though empires fall.

The lustre of a beauty's eye
  Assumes the ghastly stare of death;
The fair, the brave, the good must die,
  And sink the yawning grave beneath.

Once more the speaking eye revives,
  Still beaming through the lover's strain;
For Petrarch's Laura still survives:
  She died, but ne'er will die again.

  * Written by James Montgomery, author of "The Wanderer in
Switzerland," &c.
  ** No particular hero is here alluded to. The exploits of Bayard, Ne-
mours, Edward the Black Prince, and, in more modern times the fame of
Marlborough, Frederick the Great, Count Saxe, Charles of Sweden, &c.
are familiar to every historical reader, but the exact places of their birth
are known to a very small proportion of their admirers.

The rolling seasons pass away,
    And Time, untiring, waves his wing;
Whilst honour's laurels ne'er decay,
    But bloom in fresh, unfading spring.

All, all must sleep in grim repose,
    Collected in the silent tomb;
·The old and young, with friends and foes,
    Festering alike in shrouds, consume.

The mouldering marble lasts its day,
    Yet falls at length an useless fane;
To ruin's ruthless fangs a prey,
    The wrecks of pillar'd pride remain.

What, though the sculpture be destroy'd,
    From dark oblivion meant to guard;
A bright renown shall be enjoy'd
    By those whose virtues claim reward.

Then do not say the common lot
    Of all lies deep in Lethe's wave;
Some few who ne'er will be forgot
    Shall burst the bondage of the grave.

1806.

TO A LADY WHO PRESENTED THE AUTHOR WITH THE VELVET BAND WHICH BOUND HER TRESSES.

THIS Band, which bound thy yellow hair,
    Is mine, sweet girl! thy pledge of love;
It claims my warmest, dearest care,
    Like relics left of saints above.

Oh! I will wear it next my heart;
    'Twill bind my soul in bonds to thee:
From me again 'twill ne'er depart,
    But mingle in the grave with me.

The dew I gather from thy lip
  Is not so dear to me as this;
That I but for a moment sip,
  And banquet on a transient bliss:

This will recall each youthful scene,
  E'en when our lives are on the wane;
The leaves of Love will still be green
  When Memory bids them bud again.

Oh! little lock of golden hue,
  In gently waving ringlet curl'd,
By the dear head on which you grew,
  I would not lose you for a world.

Not though a thousand more adorn
  The polish'd brow where once you shone,
Like rays which gild a cloudless morn,
  Beneath Columbia's fervid zone.

1806.

REMEMBRANCE.

'Tis done! — I saw it in my dreams:
No more with Hope the future beams;
  My days of happiness are few:
Chill'd by misfortune's wintry blast,
My dawn of life is overcast,
  Love, Hope, and Joy, alike adieu! —
  Would I could add Remembrance too!

1806.

LINES ADDRESSED TO THE REV. J. T. BECHER ON HIS ADVISING THE AUTHOR TO MIX MORE WITH SOCIETY.

DEAR Becher, you tell me to mix with mankind; —
  I cannot deny such a precept is wise;
But retirement accords with the tone of my mind:
  I will not descend to a world I despise.

Did the senate or camp my exertions require,
  Ambition might prompt me, at once, to go forth;
When infancy's years of probation expire,
  Perchance I may strive to distinguish my birth.

The fire in the cavern of Etna conceal'd,
  Still mantles unseen in its secret recess;—
At length, in a volume terrific reveal'd,
  No torrent can quench it, no bounds can repress.

Oh! thus, the desire in my bosom for fame
  Bids me live but to hope for posterity's praise.
Could I soar with the phœnix on pinions of flame,
  With him I would wish to expire in the blaze.

For the life of a Fox, of a Chatham the death,
  What censure, what danger, what woe would I brave!
Their lives did not end when they yielded their breath;
  Their glory illumines the gloom of their grave.

Yet why should I mingle in Fashion's full herd?
  Why crouch to her leaders, or cringe to her rules?
Why bend to the proud, or applaud the absurd?
  Why search for delight in the friendship of fools?

I have tasted the sweets and the bitters of love;
  In friendship I early was taught to believe;
My passion the matrons of prudence reprove;
  I have found that a friend may profess, yet deceive.

To me what is wealth? it may pass in an hour,
  If tyrants prevail, or if Fortune should frown;
To me what is title? — the phantom of power;
  To me what is fashion? — I seek but renown.

Deceit is a stranger as yet to my soul;
  I still am unpractised to varnish the truth:
Then why should I live in a hateful control?
  Why waste upon folly the days of my youth?   1806.

———

THE DEATH OF CALMAR AND ORLA.
AN IMITATION OF MACPHERSON'S OSSIAN. *

Dear are the days of youth! Age dwells on their remembrance through the mist of time. In the twilight he recalls the sunny hours of morn. He lifts his spear with trembling hand. "Not thus feebly did I raise the steel before my fathers!" Past is the race of heroes! But their fame rises on the harp; their souls ride on the wings of the wind; they hear the sound through the sighs of the storm, and rejoice in their hall of clouds! Such is Calmar. The gray stone marks his narrow house. He looks down from eddying tempests: he rolls his form in the whirlwind, and hovers on the blast of the mountain.

In Morven dwelt the chief; a beam of war to Fingal. His steps in the field were marked in blood. Lochlin's sons had fled before his angry spear; but mild was the eye of Calmar; soft was the flow of his yellow locks: they streamed like the meteor of the night. No maid was the sigh of his soul: his thoughts were given to friendship, — to dark-haired Orla, destroyer of heroes! Equal were their swords in battle; but fierce was the pride of Orla: — gentle alone to Calmar. Together they dwelt in the cave of Oithona.

From Lochlin, Swaran bounded o'er the blue waves. Erin's sons fell beneath his might. Fingal roused his chiefs to combat. Their ships cover the ocean. Their hosts throng on the green hills. They come to the aid of Erin.

Night rose in clouds. Darkness veils the armies: but the blazing oaks gleam through the valley. The sons of Lochlin slept: their dreams were of blood. They lift the spear in thought, and Fingal flies. Not so the host of Morven. To watch was the post of Orla. Calmar stood by his side. Their spears were in their hands. Fingal called his chiefs: they stood around. The king was in the midst. Gray were his locks, but strong was the arm of the king. Age withered not

* It may be necessary to observe, that the story, though considerably varied in the catastrophe, is taken from "Nisus and Euryalus," of which episode a translation is already given in the present volume.

13*

his powers. "Sons of Morven," said the hero, "to-morrow we meet the foe. But where is Cuthullin, the shield of Erin? He rests in the halls of Tura; he knows not of our coming. Who will speed through Lochlin to the hero, and call the chief to arms? The path is by the swords of foes; but many are my heroes. They are thunderbolts of war. Speak, ye chiefs! Who will arise?"

"Son of Trenmor! mine be the deed," said dark-haired Orla, "and mine alone. What is death to me? I love the sleep of the mighty, but little is the danger. The sons of Lochlin dream. I will seek car-borne Cuthullin. If I fall, raise the song of bards; and lay me by the stream of Lubar." — "And shalt thou fall alone?" said fair-haired Calmar. "Wilt thou leave thy friend afar? Chief of Oithona! not feeble is my arm in fight. Could I see thee die, and not lift the spear? No, Orla! ours has been the chase of the roebuck, and the feast of shells; ours be the path of danger: ours has been the cave of Oithona; ours be the narrow dwelling on the banks of Lubar." "Calmar," said the chief of Oithona, "why should thy yellow locks be darkened in the dust of Erin? Let me fall alone. My father dwells in his hall of air: he will rejoice in his boy; but the blue-eyed Mora spreads the feast for her son in Morven. She listens to the steps of the hunter on the heath, and thinks it is the tread of Calmar. Let him not say, "Calmar has fallen by the steel of Lochlin: he died with gloomy Orla, the chief of the dark brow." Why should tears dim the azure eye of Mora? Why should her voice curse Orla, the destroyer of Calmar? Live, Calmar! Live to raise my stone of moss; live to revenge me in the blood of Lochlin. Join the song of bards above my grave. Sweet will be the song of death to Orla, from the voice of Calmar. My ghost shall smile on the notes of praise." "Orla," said the son of Mora, "could I raise the song of death to my friend? Could I give his fame to the winds? No, my heart would speak in sighs: faint and broken are the sounds of sorrow. Orla! our souls shall hear the song together. One cloud shall be ours on high: the bards will mingle the names of Orla and Calmar."

They quit the circle of the chiefs. Their steps are to the host of Lochlin. The dying blaze of oak dim twinkles through the night. The northern star points the path to Tura. Swaran, the king, rests on his lonely hill. Here the troops are mixed: they frown in sleep; their shields beneath their heads. Their swords gleam at distance in heaps. The fires are faint; their embers fail in smoke. All is hushed; but the gale sighs on the rocks above. Lightly wheel the heroes through the slumbering band. Half the journey is past, when Mathon, resting on his shield, meets the eye of Orla. It rolls in flame, and glistens through the shade. His spear is raised on high. "Why dost thou bend thy brow, chief of Oithona?" said fair-haired Calmar: "we are in the midst of foes. Is this a time for delay?" "It is a time for vengeance," said Orla of the gloomy brow. "Mathon of Lochlin sleeps: seest thou his spear? Its point is dim with the gore of my father. The blood of Mathon shall reek on mine; but shall I slay him sleeping, son of Mora? No! he shall feel his wound: my fame shall not soar on the blood of slumber. Rise, Mathon, rise! The son of Conna calls; thy life is his; rise to combat." Mathon starts from sleep; but did he rise alone? No: the gathering chiefs bound on the plain. "Fly! Calmar, fly!" said dark-haired Orla. "Mathon is mine. I shall die in joy: but Lochlin crowds around. Fly through the shade of night." Orla turns. The helm of Mathon is cleft; his shield falls from his arm: he shudders in his blood. He rolls by the side of the blazing oak. Strumon sees him fall: his wrath rises: his weapon glitters on the head of Orla: but a spear pierced his eye. His brain gushes through the wound, and foams on the spear of Calmar. As roll the waves of the Ocean on two mighty barks of the north, so pour the men of Lochlin on the chiefs. As, breaking the surge in foam, proudly steer the barks of the north, so rise the chiefs of Morven on the scattered crests of Lochlin. The din of arms came to the ear of Fingal. He strikes his shield; his sons throng around; the people pour along the heath. Ryno bounds in joy. Ossian stalks in his arms. Oscar shakes the spear. The eagle wing of Fillan floats on the wind.

Dreadful is the clang of death! many are the widows of Lochlin! Morven prevails in its strength.

Morn glimmers on the hills: no living foe is seen; but the
sleepers are many; grim they lie on Erin. The breeze of
ocean lifts their locks; yet they do not awake. The hawks
scream above their prey.

Whose yellow locks wave o'er the breast of a chief? Bright
as the gold of the stranger, they mingle with the dark hair of
his friend. 'Tis Calmar: he lies on the bosom of Orla. Theirs
is one stream of blood. Fierce is the look of the gloomy Orla.
He breathes not; but his eye is still a flame. It glares in death
unclosed. His hand is grasped in Calmar's; but Calmar lives!
he lives, though low. "Rise," said the king, "rise, son of
Mora: 'tis mine to heal the wounds of heroes. Calmar may
yet bound on the hills of Morven."

"Never more shall Calmar chase the deer of Morven with
Orla," said the hero. "What were the chase to me alone?
Who would share the spoils of battle with Calmar? Orla is at
rest! Rough was thy soul, Orla! yet soft to me as the dew of
morn. It glared on others in lightning: to me a silver beam
of night. Bear my sword to blue-eyed Mora; let it hang in my
empty hall. It is not pure from blood: but it could not save
Orla. Lay me with my friend. Raise the song when I am
dark!"

They are laid by the stream of Lubar. Four gray stones
mark the dwelling of Orla and Calmar. When Swaran was
bound, our sails rose on the blue waves. The wings gave our
barks to Morven: — the bards raised the song.

"What form rises on the roar of clouds? Whose dark
ghost gleams on the red streams of tempests? His voice rolls
on the thunder. 'Tis Orla, the brown chief of Oithona. He
was unmatched in war. Peace to thy soul, Orla! thy fame
will not perish. Nor thine, Calmar! Lovely wast thou, son of
blue-eyed Mora; but not harmless was thy sword. It hangs
in thy cave. The ghosts of Lochlin shriek around its steel.
Hear thy praise, Calmar! It dwells on the voice of the mighty.
Thy name shakes on the echoes of Morven. Then raise thy

fair locks, son of Mora. Spread them on the arch of the rainbow; and smile through the tears of the storm."*

L'AMITIÉ EST L'AMOUR SANS AILES.

[WRITTEN DECEMBER, 1806.]

Why should my anxious breast repine,
   Because my youth is fled?
Days of delight may still be mine;
   Affection is not dead.
In tracing back the years of youth,
One firm record, one lasting truth
   Celestial consolation brings;
Bear it, ye breezes, to the seat,
Where first my heart responsive beat, —
   "Friendship is Love without his wings!"

Through few, but deeply chequer'd years,
   What moments have been mine!
Now half obscured by clouds of tears,
   Now bright in rays divine;
Howe'er my future doom be cast,
My soul, enraptured with the past,
   To one idea fondly clings;
Friendship! that thought is all thine own,
Worth worlds of bliss, that thought alone —
   "Friendship is Love without his wings!"

Where yonder yew-trees lightly wave
   Their branches on the gale,
Unheeded heaves a simple grave,
   Which tells the common tale;

* I fear Laing's late edition has completely overthrown every hope that Macpherson's Ossian might prove the translation of a series of poems complete in themselves; but, while the imposture is discovered, the merit of the work remains undisputed, though not without faults — particularly, in some parts, turgid and bombastic diction. — The present humble imitation will be pardoned by the admirers of the original as an attempt, however inferior, which evinces an attachment to their favourite author.

Round this unconscious schoolboys stray,
Till the dull knell of childish play
    From yonder studious mansion rings;
But here whene'er my footsteps move,
My silent tears too plainly prove,
    "Friendship is Love without his wings!"

Oh Love! before thy glowing shrine
    My early vows were paid;
My hopes, my dreams, my heart was thine,
    But these are now decay'd;
For thine are pinions like the wind,
No trace of thee remains behind,
    Except, alas! thy jealous stings.
Away, away! delusive power,
Thou shalt not haunt my coming hour;
    Unless, indeed, without thy wings.

Seat of my youth!* thy distant spire
    Recalls each scene of joy;
My bosom glows with former fire, —
    In mind again a boy.
Thy grove of elms, thy verdant hill,
Thy every path delights me still,
    Each flower a double fragrance flings;
Again, as once, in converse gay,
Each dear associate seems to say
    "Friendship is Love without his wings!"

My Lycus! wherefore dost thou weep?
    Thy falling tears restrain;
Affection for a time may sleep,
    But, oh, 'twill wake again.
Think, think, my friend, when next we meet,
Our long-wish'd interview, how sweet!

* Harrow.

From this my hope of rapture springs;
While youthful hearts thus fondly swell,
Absence, my friend, can only tell,
   "Friendship is Love without his wings!"

In one, and one alone deceived,
   Did I my error mourn?
No — from oppressive bonds relieved,
   I left the wretch to scorn.
I turn'd to those my childhood knew,
With feelings warm, with bosoms true,
   Twined with my heart's according strings;
And till those vital chords shall break,
For none but these my breast shall wake
   Friendship, the power deprived of wings!

Ye few! my soul, my life is yours,
   My memory and my hope;
Your worth a lasting love ensures,
   Unfetter'd in its scope;
From smooth deceit and terror sprung,
With aspect fair and honey'd tongue,
   Let Adulation wait on kings;
With joy elate, by snares beset,
We, we, my friends, can ne'er forget,
   "Friendship is Love without his wings!"

Fictions and dreams inspire the bard
   Who rolls the epic song;
Friendship and Truth be my reward —
   To me no bays belong;
If laurell'd Fame but dwells with lies,
Me the enchantress ever flies,
   Whose heart and not whose fancy sings;
Simple and young, I dare not feign;
Mine be the rude yet heartfelt strain,
   "Friendship is Love without his wings!"

THE PRAYER OF NATURE.
[WRITTEN DECEMBER 29. 1806.]

FATHER of Light! great God of Heaven!
  Hear'st thou the accents of despair?
Can guilt like man's be e'er forgiven?
  Can vice atone for crimes by prayer?

Father of Light, on thee I call!
  Thou see'st my soul is dark within;
Thou who canst mark the sparrow's fall,
  Avert from me the death of sin.

No shrine I seek, to sects unknown;
  Oh point to me the path of truth!
Thy dread omnipotence I own;
  Spare, yet amend, the faults of youth.

Let bigots rear a gloomy fane,
  Let superstition hail the pile,
Let priests, to spread their sable reign,
  With tales of mystic rights beguile. -

Shall man confine his Maker's sway
  To Gothic domes of mouldering stone?
Thy temple is the face of day;
  Earth, ocean, heaven thy boundless throne.

Shall man condemn his race to hell,
  Unless they bend in pompous form?
Tell us that all, for one who fell,
  Must perish in the mingling storm?

Shall each pretend to reach the skies,
  Yet doom his brother to expire,
Whose soul a different hope supplies,
  Or doctrines less severe inspire?

Shall these, by creeds they can't expound,
  Prepare a fancied bliss or woe?
Shall reptiles, groveling on the ground,
  Their great Creator's purpose know?

Shall those, who live for self alone,
    Whose years float on in daily crime —
Shall they by Faith for guilt atone,
    And live beyond the bounds of Time?

Father! no prophet's laws I seek, —
    Thy laws in Nature's works appear;
I own myself corrupt and weak,
    Yet will I pray, for thou wilt hear!

Thou, who canst guide the wandering star
    Through trackless realms of æther's space;
Who calm'st the elemental war,
    Whose hand from pole to pole I trace: —

Thou, who in wisdom placed me here,
    Who, when thou wilt, canst take me hence,
Ah! whilst I tread this earthly sphere,
    Extend to me thy wide defence.

To Thee, my God, to thee I call!
    Whatever weal or woe betide,
By thy command I rise or fall,
    In thy protection I confide.

If, when this dust to dust's restored,
    My soul shall float on airy wing,
How shall thy glorious name adored
    Inspire her feeble voice to sing!

But, if this fleeting spirit share
    With clay the grave's eternal bed,
While life yet throbs I raise my prayer,
    Though doom'd no more to quit the dead.

To Thee I breathe my humble strain,
    Grateful for all thy mercies past,
And hope, my God, to thee again
    This erring life may fly at last.

TO EDWARD NOEL LONG, ESQ.

"Nil ego contulerim jucundo sanus amico." — Hor.

Dear Long, in this sequester'd scene,
    While all around in slumber lie,
The joyous days which ours have been
    Come rolling fresh on Fancy's eye;
Thus if amidst the gathering storm,
While clouds the darken'd noon deform,
Yon heaven assumes a varied glow,
I hail the sky's celestial bow,
Which spreads the sign of future peace,
And bids the war of tempests cease.
Ah! though the present brings but pain,
I think those days may come again;
Or if, in melancholy mood,
Some lurking envious fear intrude,
To check my bosom's fondest thought,
    And interrupt the golden dream,
I crush the fiend with malice fraught,
    And still indulge my wonted theme.
Although we ne'er again can trace,
    In Granta's vale, the pedant's lore;
Nor through the groves of Ida chase
    Our ruptured visions as before,
Though Youth has flown on rosy pinion,
And Manhood claims his stern dominion —
Age will not every hope destroy,
But yield some hours of sober joy.

Yes, I will hope that Time's broad wing
Will shed around some dews of spring:
But if his scythe must sweep the flowers
Which bloom among the fairy bowers,
Where smiling Youth delights to dwell,
And hearts with early rapture swell;
If frowning Age, with cold control,
Confines the current of the soul,

Congeals the tear of Pity's eye,
Or checks the sympathetic sigh,
Or hears unmoved misfortune's groan,
And bids me feel for self alone;
Oh! may my bosom never learn
 To soothe its wonted heedless flow;
Still, still despise the censor stern,
 But ne'er forget another's woe.
Yes, as you knew me in the days
O'er which Remembrance yet delays,
Still may I rove, untutor'd, wild,
And even in age at heart a child.

Though now on airy visions borne,
 To you my soul is still the same.
Oft has it been my fate to mourn,
 And all my former joys are tame.
But, hence! ye hours of sable hue!
 Your frowns are gone, my sorrows o'er:
By every bliss my childhood knew,
 I'll think upon your shade no more.
Thus, when the whirlwind's rage is past,
 And caves their sullen roar enclose,
We heed no more the wintry blast,
 When lull'd by zephyr to repose.

Full often has my infant Muse
 Attuned to love her languid lyre;
But now, without a theme to choose,
 The strains in stolen sighs expire.
My youthful nymphs, alas! are flown;
 E— is a wife, and C— a mother,
And Carolina sighs alone,
 And Mary's given to another;
And Cora's eye, which roll'd on me,
 Can now no more my love recall:
In truth, dear Long, 'twas time to flee;
 For Cora's eye will shine on all.

And though the sun, with genial rays,
His beams alike to all displays,
And every lady's eye's a *sun*,
These last should be confined to one.
The soul's meridian don't become her,
Whose sun displays a general *summer!*
Thus faint is every former flame,
And passion's self is now a name.
As, when the ebbing flames are low,
   The aid which once improved their light,
And bade them burn with fiercer glow,
   Now quenches all their sparks in night;
Thus has it been with passion's fires,
   As many a boy and girl remembers,
While all the force of love expires,
   Extinguish'd with the dying embers.

But now, dear LONG, 'tis midnight's noon,
And clouds obscure the watery moon,
Whose beauties I shall not rehearse,
Described in every stripling's verse;
For why should I the path go o'er,
Which every bard has trod before?
Yet ere yon silver lamp of night
   Has thrice perform'd her stated round,
Has thrice retraced her path of light,
   And chased away the gloom profound,
I trust that we, my gentle friend,
Shall see her rolling orbit wend
Above the dear-loved peaceful seat
Which once contain'd our youth's retreat;
And then with those our childhood knew,
We'll mingle in the festive crew;
While many a tale of former day
Shall wing the laughing hours away:
And all the flow of souls shall pour
The sacred intellectual shower,

Nor cease till Luna's waning horn
Scarce glimmers through the mist of morn.

TO A LADY.*

Oh! had my fate been join'd with thine,
　As once this pledge appear'd a token,
These follies had not then been mine,
　For then my peace had not been broken.

To thee these early faults I owe,
　To thee, the wise and old reproving:
They know my sins, but do not know
　'Twas thine to break the bonds of loving.

For once my soul, like thine, was pure,
　And all its rising fires could smother;
But now thy vows no more endure,
　Bestow'd by thee upon another.

Perhaps his peace I could destroy,
　And spoil the blisses that await him;
Yet let my rival smile in joy,
　For thy dear sake I cannot hate him.

Ah! since thy angel form is gone,
　My heart no more can rest with any;
But what it sought in thee alone,
　Attempts, alas! to find in many.

Then fare thee well, deceitful maid!
　'Twere vain and fruitless to regret thee;
Nor Hope, nor Memory yield their aid,
　But Pride may teach me to forget thee.

Yet all this giddy waste of years,
　This tiresome round of palling pleasures;
These varied loves, these matron's fears,
　These thoughtless strains to passion's measures —

* Mrs. Musters.

If thou wert mine, had all been hush'd : —
   This cheek, now pale from early riot,
With passion's hectic ne'er had flush'd,
   But bloom'd in calm domestic quiet.

Yes, once the rural scene was sweet,
   For Nature seem'd to smile before thee ;
And once my breast abhorr'd deceit, —
   For then it beat but to adore thee.

But now I seek for other joys :
   To think would drive my soul to madness ;
In thoughtless throngs and empty noise,
   I conquer half my bosom's sadness.

Yet, even in these a thought will steal
   In spite of every vain endeavour, —
And fiends might pity what I feel, —
   To know that thou art lost for ever.

I WOULD I WERE A CARELESS CHILD.

I WOULD I were a careless child,
   Still dwelling in my Highland cave,
Or roaming through the dusky wild,
   Or bounding o'er the dark blue wave ;
The cumbrous pomp of Saxon* pride
   Accords not with the freeborn soul,
Which loves the mountain's craggy side,
   And seeks the rocks where billows roll.

Fortune ! take back these cultured lands,
   Take back this name of splendid sound !
I hate the touch of servile hands,
   I hate the slaves that cringe around.

* Sassenach, or Saxon, a Gaelic word, signifying either Lowland or
English.

Place me along the rocks I love,
  Which sound to Ocean's wildest roar;
I ask but this — again to rove
  Through scenes my youth hath known before.

Few are my years, and yet I feel
  The world was ne'er design'd for me:
Ah! why do dark'ning shades conceal
  The hour when man must cease to be?
Once I beheld a splendid dream,
  A visionary scene of bliss:
Truth! — wherefore did thy hated beam
  Awake me to a world like this?

I loved — but those I loved are gone;
  Had friends — my early friends are fled:
How cheerless feels the heart alone
  When all its former hopes are dead!
Though gay companions o'er the bowl
  Dispel awhile the sense of ill;
'Though pleasure stirs the maddening soul,
  The heart — the heart — is lonely still.

How dull! to hear the voice of those
  Whom rank or chance, whom wealth or power,
Have made, though neither friends nor foes,
  Associates of the festive hour.
Give me again a faithful few,
  In years and feelings still the same,
And I will fly the midnight crew,
  Where boist'rous joy is but a name.

And woman, lovely woman! thou,
  My hope, my comforter, my all!
How cold must be my bosom now,
  When e'en thy smiles begin to pall!

Without a sigh would I resign
  This busy scene of splendid woe,
To make that calm contentment mine,
  Which virtue knows, or seems to know.

Fain would I fly the haunts of men —
  I seek to shun, not hate mankind;
My breast requires the sullen glen,
  Whose gloom may suit a darken'd mind.
Oh! that to me the wings were given
  Which bear the turtle to her nest!
Then would I cleave the vault of heaven,
  To flee away, and be at rest.*

WHEN I ROVED A YOUNG HIGHLANDER.

When I roved a young Highlander o'er the dark heath,
  And climb'd thy steep summit, oh Morven of snow!**
To gaze on the torrent that thunder'd beneath,
  Or the mist of the tempest that gather'd below,†

Untutor'd by science, a stranger to fear,
  And rude as the rocks where my infancy grew,
No feeling, save one, to my bosom was dear;
  Need I say, my sweet Mary, 'twas centred in you?

---

* "And I said, Oh! that I had wings like a dove; for then would I fly away, and be at rest." — *Psalm* LV. 6. This verse also constitutes a part of the most beautiful anthem in our language.

** Morven, a lofty mountain in Aberdeenshire. "Gormal of snow," is an expression frequently to be found in Ossian.

† This will not appear extraordinary to those who have been accustomed to the mountains. It is by no means uncommon, on attaining the top of Ben-e-vis, Ben-y-bourd, &c. to perceive, between the summit and the valley, clouds pouring down rain, and occasionally accompanied by lightning, while the spectator literally looks down upon the storm perfectly secure from its effects.

Yet it could not be love, for I knew not the name, —
  What passion can dwell in the heart of a child?
But still I perceive an emotion the same
  As I felt, when a boy, on the crag-cover'd wild:
One image alone on my bosom impress'd,
  I loved my bleak regions, nor panted for new;
And few were my wants, for my wishes were bless'd;
  And pure were my thoughts, for my soul was with you.

I arose with the dawn; with my dog as my guide,
  From mountain to mountain I bounded along;
I breasted the billows of Dee's* rushing tide,
  And heard at a distance the Highlander's song:
At eve, on my heath-cover'd couch of repose,
  No dreams, save of Mary, were spread to my view;
And warm to the skies my devotions arose,
  For the first of my prayers was a blessing on you.

I left my bleak home, and my visions are gone;
  The mountains are vanish'd, my youth is no more;
As the last of my race, I must wither alone,
  And delight but in days I have witness'd before:
Ah! splendour has raised, but embitter'd my lot;
  More dear were the scenes which my infancy knew:
Though my hopes may have fail'd, yet they are not forgot;
  Though cold is my heart, still it lingers with you.

When I see some dark hill point its crest to the sky,
  I think of the rocks that o'ershadow Colbleen;**
When I see the soft blue of a love-speaking eye,
  I think of those eyes that endear'd the rude scene;
When, haply, some light-waving locks I behold,
  That faintly resemble my Mary's in hue,
I think on the long flowing ringlets of gold,
  The locks that were sacred to beauty, and you.

---

  * The Dee is a beautiful river, which rises near Mar Lodge, and falls
into the sea at New Aberdeen.
  ** Colbleen is a mountain near the verge of the Highlands, not far from
the ruins of Dee Castle.

14*

Yet the day may arrive when the mountains once more
   Shall rise to my sight in their mantles of snow:
But while these soar above me, unchanged as before,
   Will Mary be there to receive me? — ah, no!
Adieu, then, ye hills, where my childhood was bred!
   Thou sweet flowing Dee, to thy waters adieu!
No home in the forest shall shelter my head, —
   Ah! Mary, what home could be mine but with you?

TO GEORGE, EARL DELAWARR.

On! yes, I will own we were dear to each other;
   The friendships of childhood, though fleeting, are true;
The love which you felt was the love of a brother,
   Nor less the affection I cherish'd for you.

But Friendship can vary her gentle dominion;
   The attachment of years in a moment expires:
Like Love, too, she moves on a swift-waving pinion,
   But glows not, like Love, with unquenchable fires.

Full oft have we wander'd through Ida together,
   And blest were the scenes of our youth, I allow:
In the spring of our life, how serene is the weather!
   But winter's rude tempests are gathering now.

No more with affection shall memory blending,
   The wonted delights of our childhood retrace:
When pride steels the bosom, the heart is unbending,
   And what would be justice appears a disgrace.

However, dear George, for I still must esteem you —
   The few whom I love I can never upbraid —
The chance which has lost may in future redeem you,
   Repentance will cancel the vow you have made.

I will not complain, and though chill'd is affection,
  With me no corroding resentment shall live:
My bosom is calm'd by the simple reflection,
  That both may be wrong, and that both should forgive.

You knew that my soul, that my heart, my existence,
  If danger demanded, were wholly your own;
You knew me unalter'd by years or by distance,
. Devoted to love and to friendship alone.

You know, — but away with the vain retrospection!
  The bond of affection no longer endures;
Too late you may droop o'er the fond recollection,
  And sigh for the friend who was formerly yours.

For the present, we part, — I will hope not for ever;
  For time and regret will restore you at last:
To forget our dissension we both should endeavour,
  I ask no atonement, but days like the past.

TO THE EARL OF CLARE.

"Tu semper amoris
Sis memor, et cari comitis ne abscedat imago."
                              VAL. FLAC.

FRIEND of my youth! when young we roved,
Like striplings, mutually beloved,
  With friendship's purest glow,
The bliss which wing'd those rosy hours
Was such as pleasure seldom showers
  On mortals here below.

The recollection seems alone
Dearer than all the joys I've known,
  When distant far from you:
Though pain, 'tis still a pleasing pain,
To trace those days and hours again,
  And sigh again, adieu!

My pensive memory lingers o'er
Those scenes to be enjoy'd no more,
   Those scenes regretted ever;
The measure of our youth is full,
Life's evening dream is dark and dull,
   And we may meet — ah! never!

As when one parent spring supplies
Two streams which from one fountain rise,
   Together join'd in vain;
How soon, diverging from their source,
Each, murmuring, seeks another course,
   Till mingled in the main!

Our vital streams of weal or woe,
Though near, alas! distinctly flow,
   Nor mingle as before:
Now swift or slow, now black or clear,
Till death's unfathom'd gulf appear,
   And both shall quit the shore.

Our souls, my friend! which once supplied
One wish, nor breathed a thought beside,
   Now flow in different channels:
Disdaining humbler rural sports,
'Tis yours to mix in polish'd courts,
   And shine in fashion's annals;

'Tis mine to waste on love my time,
Or vent my reveries in rhyme,
   Without the aid of reason;
For sense and reason (critics know it)
Have quitted every amorous poet,
   Nor left a thought to seize on.

Poor LITTLE! sweet, melodious bard!
Of late esteem'd it monstrous hard

That he, who sang before all, —
He who the lore of love expanded, —
By dire reviewers should be branded
   As void of wit and moral.*

And yet, while Beauty's praise is thine,
Harmonious favourite of the Nine!
   Repine not at thy lot.
Thy soothing lays may still be read,
When Persecution's arm is dead,
   And critics are forgot.

Still I must yield those worthies merit,
Who chasten, with unsparing spirit,
   Bad rhymes, and those who write them;
And though myself may be the next,
By critic sarcasm to be vext,
   I really will not fight them.**

Perhaps they would do quite as well
To break the rudely sounding shell
   Of such a young beginner.
He who offends at pert nineteen,
Ere thirty may become, I ween,
   A very harden'd sinner.

Now, Clare, I must return to you;
And, sure, apologies are due;
   Accept, then, my concession.
In truth, dear Clare, in fancy's flight
I soar along from left to right;
   My muse admires digression.

* These stanzas were written soon after the appearance of a severe critique, in a northern review, on a new publication of the British Anacreon.

** A bard (horresco referens) defied his reviewer to mortal combat. If this example becomes prevalent, our periodical censors must be dipped in the river Styx: for what else can secure them from the numerous host of their enraged assailants?

I think I said 'twould be your fate
To add one star to royal state; —
    May regal smiles attend you!
And should a noble monarch reign,
You will not seek his smiles in vain,
    If worth can recommend you.

Yet since in danger courts abound,
Where specious rivals glitter round,
    From snares may saints preserve you;
And grant your love or friendship ne'er
From any claim a kindred care,
    But those who best deserve you!

Not for a moment may you stray
From truth's secure, unerring way!
    May no delights decoy!
O'er roses may your footsteps move,
Your smiles be ever smiles of love,
    Your tears be tears of joy!

Oh! if you wish that happiness
Your coming days and years may bless,
    And virtues crown your brow;
Be still as you were won't to be,
Spotless as you've been known to me, —
    Be still as you are now.

And though some trifling share of praise,
To cheer my last declining days
    To me were doubly dear;
Whilst blessing your beloved name,
I'd wave at once a *poet*'s fame,
    To prove a *prophet* here.

LINES WRITTEN BENEATH AN ELM IN THE CHURCHYARD
OF HARROW.

Spot of my youth! whose hoary branches sigh,
Swept by the breeze that fans thy cloudless sky;
Where now alone I muse, who oft have trod,
With those I loved, thy soft and verdant sod;
With those who, scatter'd far, perchance deplore,
Like me, the happy scenes they knew before:
Oh! as I trace again thy winding hill,
Mine eyes admire, my heart adores thee still,
Thou drooping Elm! beneath whose boughs I lay,
And frequent mused the twilight hours away;
Where, as they once were wont, my limbs recline,
But, ah! without the thoughts which then were mine:
How do thy branches, moaning to the blast,
Invite the bosom to recall the past,
And seem to whisper, as they gently swell,
"Take, while thou canst, a lingering, last farewell!"

When fate shall chill, at length, this fever'd breast,
And calm its cares and passions into rest,
Oft have I thought, 'twould soothe my dying hour, —
If aught may soothe when life resigns her power, —
To know some humbler grave, some narrow cell,
Would hide my bosom where it loved to dwell;
With this fond dream, methinks, 'twere sweet to die —
And here it linger'd, here my heart might lie;
Here might I sleep where all my hopes arose,
Scene of my youth, and couch of my repose;
For ever stretch'd beneath this mantling shade,
Press'd by the turf where once my childhood play'd;
Wrapt by the soil that veils the spot I loved,
Mix'd with the earth o'er which my footsteps moved;

Blest by the tongues that charm'd my youthful ear,
Mourn'd by the few my soul acknowledged here;
Deplored by those in early days allied,
And unremember'd by the world beside.

September 2. 1807.

ENGLISH BARDS

AND

SCOTCH REVIEWERS,

A SATIRE.

"I had rather be a kitten, and cry mew!
  Than one of these same metre ballad-mongers."
                                              SHAKSPEARE.

"Such shameless bards we have; and yet 'tis true,
  There are as mad, abandon'd critics too."
                                              POPE.

PREFACE.*

ALL my friends, learned and unlearned, have urged me
not to publish this Satire with my name. If I were to be
"turned from the career of my humour by quibbles quick, and
paper bullets of the brain," I should have complied with their
counsel. But I am not to be terrified by abuse, or bullied by
reviewers, with or without arms. I can safely say that I have
attacked none personally, who did not commence on the
offensive. An author's works are public property: he who
purchases may judge, and publish his opinion if he pleases;
and the authors I have endeavoured to commemorate may do
by me as I have done by them. I dare say they will succeed
better in condemning my scribblings, than in mending their
own. But my object is not to prove that I can write well, but,
if possible, to make others write better.

As the poem has met with far more success than I expected,
I have endeavoured in this edition to make some additions
and alterations, to render it more worthy of public perusal.

* This preface was written for the second edition, and printed with it.
The noble author had left this country previous to the publication of that
edition, and is not yet returned. — *Note to the fourth edition*, 1811.

In the first edition of this satire, published anonymously, fourteen lines on the subject of Bowles's Pope were written by, and inserted at the request of, an ingenious friend of mine*, who has now in the press a volume of poetry. In the present edition they are erased, and some of my own substituted in their stead; my only reason for this being that which I conceive would operate with any other person in the same manner, — a determination not to publish with my name any production, which was not entirely and exclusively my own composition.

With regard to the real talents of many of the poetical persons whose performances are mentioned or alluded to in the following pages, it is presumed by the author that there can be little difference of opinion in the public at large; though, like other sectaries, each has his separate tabernacle of proselytes, by whom his abilities are over-rated, his faults overlooked, and his metrical canons received without scruple and without consideration. But the unquestionable possession of considerable genius by several of the writers here censured renders their mental prostitution more to be regretted. Imbecility may be pitied, or, at worst, laughed at and forgotten; perverted powers demand the most decided reprehension. No one can wish more than the author that some known and able writer had undertaken their exposure; but Mr. Gifford has devoted himself to Massinger, and, in the absence of the regular physician, a country practitioner may, in cases of absolute necessity, be allowed to prescribe his nostrum to prevent the extension of so deplorable an epidemic, provided there be no quackery in his treatment of the malady. A caustic is here offered; as it is to be feared nothing short of actual cautery can recover the numerous patients afflicted with the present prevalent and distressing *rabies* for rhyming.—As to the Edinburgh Reviewers, it would indeed require an Hercules to crush the Hydra; but if the author succeeds in merely "bruising one of the heads of the serpent," though his own hand should suffer in the encounter, he will be amply satisfied.

* Mr. Hobhouse.

ENGLISH BARDS AND SCOTCH REVIEWERS.

STILL must I hear?* — shall hoarse Fitzgerald bawl
His creaking couplets in a tavern hall,**
And I not sing, lest, haply, Scotch reviews
Should dub me scribbler, and denounce my muse?
Prepare for rhyme — I'll publish, right or wrong:
Fools are my theme, let satire be my song.

Oh! nature's noblest gift — my gray goose-quill!
Slave of my thoughts, obedient to my will,
Torn from thy parent bird to form a pen,
That mighty instrument of little men,
The pen! foredoom'd to aid the mental throes
Of brains that labour, big with verse or prose,
Though nymphs forsake, and critics may deride
The lover's solace, and the author's pride.
What wits! what poets dost thou daily raise!
How frequent is thy use, how small thy praise!
Condemn'd at length to be forgotten quite,
With all the pages which 'twas thine to write.
But thou, at least, mine own especial pen!
Once laid aside, but now assumed again,
Our task complete, like Hamet's† shall be free;
Though spurn'd by others, yet beloved by me:

* IMIT. — "Semper ego auditor tantum? nunquamne reponam,
        Vexatus toties rauci Theseide Codri?" — *Juv.* Sat. I.
** Mr. Fitzgerald, facetiously termed by Cobbett the "Small Beer
Poet," inflicts his annual tribute of verse on the Literary Fund: not content with writing, he spouts in person, after the company have imbibed a
reasonable quantity of bad port, to enable them to sustain the operation. —
   † Cid Hamet Benengeli promises repose to his pen, in the last chapter
of Don Quixote. Oh! that our voluminous gentry would follow the example of Cid Hamet Benengeli.

Then let us soar to-day; no common theme,
No eastern vision, no distemper'd dream
Inspires — our path, though full of thorns, is plain;
Smooth be the verse, and easy be the strain.

When Vice triumphant holds her sov'reign sway,
Obey'd by all who nought beside obey;
When Folly, frequent harbinger of crime,
Bedecks her cap with bells of every clime;
When knaves and fools combined o'er all prevail,
And weigh their justice in a golden scale;
E'en then the boldest start from public sneers,
Afraid of shame, unknown to other fears,
More darkly sin, by satire kept in awe,
And shrink from ridicule, though not from law.

Such is the force of wit! but not belong
To me the arrows of satiric song;
The royal vices of our age demand
A keener weapon, and a mightier hand.
Still there are follies, e'en for me to chase,
And yield at least amusement in the race:
Laugh when I laugh, I seek no other fame;
The cry is up, and scribblers are my game.
Speed, Pegasus! — ye strains of great and small,
Ode, epic, elegy, have at you all!
I too can scrawl, and once upon a time
I pour'd along the town a flood of rhyme,
A schoolboy freak, unworthy praise or blame;
I printed — older children do the same.
'Tis pleasant, sure, to see one's name in print;
A book's a book, although there's nothing in't.
Not that a title's sounding charm can save
Or scrawl or scribbler from an equal grave:
This Lambe must own, since his patrician name
Fail'd to preserve the spurious farce from shame.*

* This ingenuous youth is mentioned more particularly, with his production, in another place.

No matter, George continues still to write,*
Though now the name is veil'd from public sight.
Moved by the great example, I pursue
The self-same road, but make my own review:
Not seek great Jeffrey's, yet, like him, will be
Self-constituted judge of poesy.

A man must serve his time to ev'ry trade
Save censure — critics all are ready made.
Take hackney'd jokes from Miller, got by rote,
With just enough of learning to misquote;
A mind well skill'd to find or forge a fault;
A turn for punning, call it Attic salt;
To Jeffrey go, be silent and discreet,
His pay is just ten sterling pounds per sheet:
Fear not to lie, 'twill seem a sharper hit;
Shrink not from blasphemy, 'twill pass for wit;
Care not for feeling — pass your proper jest,
And stand a critic, hated yet caress'd.

And shall we own such judgment? no — as soon
Seek roses in December — ice in June;
Hope constancy in wind, or corn in chaff;
Believe a woman or an epitaph,
Or any other thing that's false, before
You trust in critics, who themselves are sore;
Or yield one single thought to be misled
By Jeffrey's heart, or Lambe's Bœotian head.**
To these young tyrants,† by themselves misplaced,
Combined usurpers on the throne of taste;
To these, when authors bend in humble awe,
And hail their voice as truth, their word as law —
While these are censors, 'twould be sin to spare;
While such are critics, why should I forbear?

* In the Edinburgh Review.
** Messr. Jeffrey and Lambe are the alpha and omega, the first and last of the Edinburgh Review; the others are mentioned hereafter.
† IMIT. "Stulta est Clementia, cum tot ubique
—— occurras periturœ parcere chartœ." — Juv. Sat. I.

But yet, so near all modern worthies run,
'Tis doubtful whom to seek, or whom to shun:
Nor know we when to spare, or where to strike,
Our bards and censors are so much alike.

Then should you ask me,* why I venture o'er
The path which Pope and Gifford trod before;
If not yet sicken'd, you can still proceed:
Go on; my rhyme will tell you as you read.
"But hold!" exclaims a friend, — "here's some neglect:
This — that — and t' other line seem incorrect."
What then? the self-same blunder Pope has got,
And careless Dryden — "Ay, but Pye has not:" —
Indeed! — 'tis granted, faith! — but what care I?
Better to err with Pope, than shine with Pye.

Time was, ere yet in these degenerate days
Ignoble themes obtain'd mistaken praise,
When sense and wit with poesy allied,
No fabled graces, flourish'd side by side;
From the same fount their inspiration drew,
And, rear'd by taste, bloom'd fairer as they grew.
Then, in this happy isle, a Pope's pure strain
Sought the rapt soul to charm, nor sought in vain;
A polish'd nation's praise aspired to claim,
And raised the people's, as the poet's fame.
Like him great Dryden pour'd the tide of song,
In streams less smooth, indeed, yet doubly strong.
Then Congreve's scenes could cheer, or Otway's melt —
For nature then an English audience felt.
But why these names, or greater still, retrace,
When all to feebler bards resign their place?
Yet to such times our lingering looks are cast,
When taste and reason with those times are past.

* IMIT. "Our tamen hoc libeat potius decurrere campo
          Per quem magnus equos Auruncæ flexit alumnus:
          Si vacat, et placidi rationem admittitis, edam." — Juv. Sat. I.

Now look around, and turn each trifling page,
Survey the precious works that please the age;
This truth at least let satire's self allow,
No dearth of bards can be complain'd of now.
The loaded press beneath her labour groans,
And printers' devils shake their weary bones;
While Southey's epics cram the creaking shelves,
And Little's lyrics shine in hot-press'd twelves.
Thus saith the preacher: "Nought beneath the sun
Is new;" yet still from change to change we run:
What varied wonders tempt us as they pass!
The cow-pox, tractors, galvanism, and gas,
In turns appear, to make the vulgar stare,
Till the swoln bubble bursts — and all is air!
Nor less new schools of Poetry arise,
Where dull pretenders grapple for the prize:
O'er taste awhile these pseudo-bards prevail;
Each country book-club bows the knee to Baal,
And, hurling lawful genius from the throne,
Erects a shrine and idol of its own;
Some leaden calf — but whom it matters not,
From soaring Southey down to grovelling Stott.*

Behold! in various throngs the scribbling crew,
For notice eager, pass in long review:
Each spurs his jaded Pegasus apace,
And rhyme and blank maintain an equal race;

---

* Stott, better known in the "Morning Post" by the name of Hafiz.
This personage is at present the most profound explorer of the bathos. I
remember, when the reigning family left Portugal, a special Ode of Master
Stott's, beginning thus : —(*Stott loquitur quoad Hibernia.*) —
       "Princely offspring of Braganza,
         Erin greets thee with a stanza," &c.
Also a Sonnet to Rats, well worthy of the subject, and a most thundering
Ode, commencing as follows: —
       "Oh! for a Lay! loud as the surge
         That lashes Lapland's sounding shore.
Lord have mercy on us! the "Lay of the Last Minstrel" was nothing to
this.

Sonnets on sonnets crowd, and ode on ode;
And tales of terror jostle on the road;
Immeasurable measures move along;
For simpering folly loves a varied song,
To strange mysterious dulness still the friend,
Admires the strain she cannot comprehend.
Thus Lays of Minstrels* — may they be the last! —
On half-strung harps whine mournful to the blast.
While mountain spirits prate to river sprites,
That dames may listen to the sound at nights;
And goblin brats, of Gilpin Horner's brood,
Decoy young border-nobles through the wood,
And skip at every step, Lord knows how high,
And frighten foolish babes, the Lord knows why;
While high-born ladies in their magic cell,
Forbidding knights to read who cannot spell,
Despatch a courier to a wizard's grave,
And fight with honest men to shield a knave.

* See the "Lay of the Last Minstrel," *passim*. Never was any plan so incongruous and absurd as the groundwork of this production. The entrance of Thunder and Lightning, prologuising to Bayes' tragedy unfortunately takes away the merit of originality from the dialogue between Messieurs the Spirits of Flood and Fell in the first canto. Then we have the amiable William of Deloraine, "a stark moss-trooper," videlicet, a happy compound of poacher, sheep-stealer, and highwayman. The propriety of his magical lady's injunction not to read can only be equalled by his candid acknowledgment of his independence of the trammels of spelling, although, to use his own elegant phrase, "'twas his neck-verse at Harribee," i. e. the gallows. — The biography of Gilpin Horner, and the marvellous pedestrian page, who travelled twice as fast as his master's horse, without the aid of seven-leagued boots, are *chefs-d'oeuvre* in the improvement of taste. For incident we have the invisible, but by no means sparing box on the ear bestowed on the page, and the entrance of a knight and charger into the castle, under the very natural disguise of a wain of hay. Marmion, the hero of the latter romance, is exactly what William of Deloraine would have been, had he been able to read and write. The poem was manufactured for Messrs. Constable, Murray, and Miller, worshipful booksellers, in consideration of the receipt of a sum of money; and truly, considering the inspiration, it is a very creditable production. If Mr. Scott will write for hire, let him do his best for his pay-masters, but not disgrace his genius, which is undoubtedly great, by a repetition of black-letter ballad imitations.

Next view in state, proud prancing on his roan,
The golden-crested haughty Marmion,
Now forging scrolls, now foremost in the fight,
Not quite a felon, yet but half a knight,
The gibbet or the field prepared to grace;
A mighty mixture of the great and base.
And think'st thou, Scott! by vain conceit perchance,
On public taste to foist thy stale romance,
Though Murray with his Miller may combine
To yield thy muse just half-a-crown per line?
No! when the sons of song descend to trade,
Their bays are sear, their former laurels fade.
Let such forego the poet's sacred name,
Who rack their brains for lucre, not for fame:
Still for stern Mammon may they toil in vain!
And sadly gaze on gold they cannot gain!
Such be their meed, such still the just reward
Of prostituted muse and hireling bard!
For this we spurn Apollo's venal son,
And bid a long "good night to Marmion."*

These are the themes that claim our plaudits now;
These are the bards to whom the muse must bow;
While Milton, Dryden, Pope, alike forgot,
Resign their hallow'd bays to Walter Scott.

The time has been, when yet the muse was young,
When Homer swept the lyre, and Maro sung,
An epic scarce ten centuries could claim,
While awe-struck nations hail'd the magic name;
The work of each immortal bard appears
The single wonder of a thousand years.**

* "Good night to Marmion" — the pathetic and also prophetic exclamation of Henry Blount, Esquire, on the death of honest Marmion.

** As the Odyssey is so closely connected with the story of the Iliad, they may almost be classed as one grand historical poem. In alluding to Milton and Tasso, we consider the "Paradise Lost," and "Gierusalemme Liberata," as their standard efforts; since neither the "Jerusalem Con-

Empires have moulder'd from the face of earth,
Tongues have expired with those who gave them birth,
Without the glory such a strain can give,
As even in ruin bids the language live.
Not so with us, though minor bards content,
On one great work a life of labour spent:
With eagle pinion soaring to the skies,
Behold the ballad-monger Southey rise!
To him let Camoens, Milton, Tasso yield,
Whose annual strains, like armies, take the field.
First in the ranks see Joan of Arc advance,
The scourge of England and the boast of France!
Though burnt by wicked Bedford for a witch,
Behold her statue placed in glory's niche;
Her fetters burst, and just released from prison,
A virgin phœnix from her ashes risen.
Next see tremendous Thalaba come on, * .
Arabia's monstrous, wild, and wond'rous son;
Domdaniel's dread destroyer, who o'erthrew
More mad magicians than the world e'er knew.
Immortal hero! all thy foes o'ercome,
For ever reign — the rival of Tom Thumb!
Since startled metre fled before thy face,
Well wert thou doom'd the last of all thy race!
Well might triumphant genii bear thee hence,
Illustrious conqueror of common sense!
Now, last and greatest, Madoc spreads his sails,
Cacique in Mexico, and prince in Wales;
Tells us strange tales, as other travellers do,
More old than Mandeville's, and not so true.

quered" of the Italian, nor the "Paradise Regained" of the English bard,
obtained a proportionate celebrity to their former poems. Query: Which
of Mr. Southey's will survive?
* "Thalaba," Mr. Southey's second poem, is written in open defiance
of precedent and poetry. Mr. S. wished to produce something novel, and
succeeded to a miracle. "Joan of Arc," was marvellous enough, but
"Thalaba," was one of those poems "which," in the words of Porson,
" will be read when Homer and Virgil are forgotten, but — *not till then.*"

Oh, Southey! Southey!* cease thy varied song!
A bard may chant too often and too long:
As thou art strong in verse, in mercy, spare!
A fourth, alas! were more than we could bear.
But if, in spite of all the world can say,
Thou still wilt verseward plod thy weary way;
If still in Berkley ballads most uncivil,
Thou wilt devote old women to the devil,**
The babe unborn thy dread intent may rue:
"God help thee," Southey,† and thy readers too.

    Next comes the dull disciple of thy school,
That mild apostate from poetic rule
The simple Wordsworth, framer of a lay
As soft as evening in his favourite May,
Who warns his friend "to shake off toil and trouble,
And quit his books, for fear of growing double;"††
Who, both by precept and example, shows
That prose is verse, and verse is merely prose;
Convincing all, by demonstration plain,
Poetic souls delight in prose insane ;
And Christmas stories tortured into rhyme
Contain the essence of the true sublime.

   * We beg Mr. Southey's pardon: "Madoc disdains the degrading title of epic." See his preface. Why is epic degraded? and by whom? Certainly the late romaunts of Masters Cottle, Laureat Pye, Ogilvy, Hole, and gentle Mistress Cowley, have not exalted the epic muse; but as Mr. Southey's poem "disdains the appellation," allow us to ask — has he substituted any thing better in its stead? or must he be content to rival Sir Richard Blackmore in the quantity as well as quality of his verse?
   ** See "The Old Woman of Berkley," a ballad, by Mr. Southey, wherein an aged gentlewoman is carried away by Beelzebub, on a "high-trotting horse."
   † The last line, "God help thee," is an evident plagiarism from the Anti-Jacobin to Mr. Southey, on his Dactylics.
   †† Lyrical Ballads, p. 4. — "The Tables Turned." Stanza 1.
      "Up, up, my friend, and clear your looks ;
        Why all this toil and trouble?
      Up, up, my friend, and quit your books,
        Or surely you'll grow double.

Thus, when he tells the tale of Betty Foy,
The idiot mother of "an idiot boy;"
A moon-struck, silly lad, who lost his way,
And, like his bard, confounded night with day;*
So close on each pathetic part he dwells,
And each adventure so sublimely tells,
That all who view the "idiot in his glory,"
Conceive the bard the hero of the story.

Shall gentle Coleridge pass unnoticed here,
To turgid ode and tumid stanza dear?
Though themes of innocence amuse him best,
Yet still obscurity's a welcome guest.
If Inspiration should her aid refuse
To him who takes a pixy for a muse,**
Yet none in lofty numbers can surpass
The bard who soars to elegise an ass.
So well the subject suits his noble mind,
He brays, the laureat of the long-ear'd kind.

Oh! wonder-working Lewis! monk, or bard,
Who fain wouldst make Parnassus a church-yard!
Lo! wreaths of yew, not laurel, bind thy brow,
Thy muse a sprite, Apollo's sexton thou!
Whether on ancient tombs thou takest thy stand,
By gibb'ring spectres hail'd, thy kindred band;
Or tracest chaste descriptions on thy page,
To please the females of our modest age;

* Mr. W. in his preface labours hard to prove, that prose and verse are much the same; and certainly his precepts and practice are strictly conformable: —

"And thus to Betty's questions he
    Made answer, like a traveller bold.
The cock did crow, to-whoo, to-whoo,
    And the sun did shine so cold," &c. &c., p. 120.

** Coleridge's Poems, p. 11., Songs of the Pixies, i.e. Devonshire fairies; p. 42. we have, "Lines to a young Lady:" and, p. 52., "Lines to a young Ass."

All hail, M. P.!* from whose infernal brain
Thin sheeted phantoms glide, a grisly train;
At whose command "grim women" throng in crowds,
And kings of fire, of water, and of clouds,
With "small gray men," "wild yagers," and what-not,
To crown with honour thee and Walter Scott;
Again all hail! if tales like thine may please,
St. Luke alone can vanquish the disease;
Even Satan's self with thee might dread to dwell,
And in thy skull discern a deeper hell.

Who in soft guise, surrounded by a choir
Of virgins melting, not to Vesta's fire,
With sparkling eyes, and cheek by passion flush'd,
Strikes his wild lyre, whilst listening dames are hush'd?
'Tis Little! young Catullus of his day,
As sweet, but as immoral, in his lay!
Grieved to condemn, the muse must still be just,
Nor spare melodious advocates of lust.
Pure is the flame which o'er her altar burns;
From grosser incense with disgust she turns;
Yet kind to youth, this expiation o'er,
She bids thee "mend thy line, and sin no more."

For thee, translator of the tinsel song,
To whom such glittering ornaments belong,
Hibernian Strangford! with thine eyes of blue,**
And boasted locks of red or auburn hue,
Whose plaintive strain each love-sick miss admires,
And o'er harmonious fustian half expires,
Learn, if thou canst, to yield thine author's sense,
Nor vend thy sonnets on a false pretence.

---

* "For every one knows little Matt's an M. P." — See a poem to Mr.
Lewis, in 'The Statesman,' supposed to be written by Mr. Jekyll.

** The reader, who may wish for an explanation of this, may refer to
"Strangford's Camoëns," p. 127. note to p. 56., or to the last page of the
Edinburgh Review of Strangford's Camoëns.

Think'st thou to gain thy verse a higher place,
By dressing Camoëns* in a suit of lace?
Mend, Strangford! mend thy morals and thy taste;
Be warm, but pure; be amorous, but be chaste;
Cease to deceive; thy pilfer'd harp restore,
Nor teach the Lusian bard to copy Moore.

Behold! — ye tarts! one moment spare the text —
Hayley's last work, and worst — until his next;
Whether he spin poor couplets into plays,
Or damn the dead with purgatorial praise,
His style in youth or age is still the same,
For ever feeble and for ever tame.
Triumphant first see "Temper's Triumphs" shine!
At least I'm sure they triumph'd over mine.
Of "Music's Triumphs," all who read may swear
That luckless music never triumph'd there.**

Moravians, rise! bestow some meet reward
On dull devotion — Lo! the Sabbath bard,
Sepulchral Grahame,† pours his notes sublime
In mangled prose, nor e'en aspires to rhyme;
Breaks into blank the Gospel of St. Luke,
And boldly pilfers from the Pentateuch;
And, undisturb'd by conscientious qualms,
Perverts the Prophets, and purloins the Psalms.

Hail, Sympathy! thy soft idea brings
A thousand visions of a thousand things,

* It is also to be remarked, that the things given to the public as poems of Camoëns are no more to be found in the original Portuguese, than in the Song of Solomon.

** Hayley's two most notorious verse productions are "Triumphs of Temper," and "The Triumph of Music." He has also written much comedy in rhyme, epistles, &c. &c. As he is rather an elegant writer of notes and biography, let us recommend Pope's advice to Wycherley to Mr. H.'s consideration, viz. "to convert his poetry into prose," which may be easily done by taking away the final syllable of each couplet.

† Mr. Grahame has poured forth two volumes of cant, under the name of "Sabbath Walks," and "Biblical Pictures."

And shows, still whimpering through threescore of years,
The maudlin prince of mournful sonneteers.
And art thou not their prince, harmonious Bowles!
Thou first, great oracle of tender souls?
Whether thou sing'st with equal ease, and grief,
The fall of empires, or a yellow leaf;
Whether thy muse most lamentably tells
What merry sounds proceed from Oxford bells,*
Or, still in bells delighting, finds a friend
In every chime that jingled from Ostend;
Ah! how much juster were thy muse's hap,
If to thy bells thou wouldst but add a cap!
Delightful Bowles! still blessing and still blest,
All love thy strain, but children like it best.
'Tis thine, with gentle Little's moral song,
To soothe the mania of the amorous throng!
With thee our nursery damsels shed their tears,
Ere miss as yet completes her infant years:
But in her teens thy whining powers are vain;
She quits poor Bowles for Little's purer strain.
Now to soft themes thou scornest to confine
The lofty numbers of a harp like thine;
"Awake a louder and a loftier strain,"**
Such as none heard before, or will again!
Where all Discoveries jumbled from the flood,
Since first the leaky ark reposed in mud,
By more or less, are sung in every book,
From Captain Noah down to Captain Cook.

---

* See Bowles's "Sonnet to Oxford," and "Stanzas on hearing the Bells of Ostend."

** "Awake a louder," &c., is the first line in Bowles's "Spirit of Discovery;" a very spirited and pretty dwarf-epic. Among other exquisite lines we have the following : —

                    "A kiss
        Stole on the list'ning silence, never yet
        Here heard; they trembled even as if the power," &c. &c.

That is, the woods of Madeira trembled to a kiss; very much astonished, as well they might be, at such a phenomenon.

Nor this alone; but, pausing on the road,
The bard sighs forth a gentle episode;*
And gravely tells — attend, each beauteous miss! —
When first Madeira trembled to a kiss.
Bowles! in thy memory let this precept dwell:
Stick to thy sonnets, man! — at least they sell.**
But if some new-born whim, or larger bribe,
Prompt thy crude brain, and claim thee for a scribe;
If chance some bard, though once by dunces fear'd,
Now, prone in dust, can only be revered;
If Pope, whose fame and genius, from the first,
Have foil'd the best of critics, needs the worst,
Do thou essay: each fault, each failing scan;
The first of poets was, alas! but man.
Rake from each ancient dunghill ev'ry pearl,
Consult Lord Fanny, and confide in Curll;†
Let all the scandals of a former age
Perch on thy pen, and flutter o'er thy page;
Affect a candour which thou canst not feel,
Clothe envy in the garb of honest zeal;
Write, as if St. John's soul could still inspire,
And do from hate what Mallet†† did for hire.

* The episode above alluded to is the story of "Robert a Machin" and "Anna d'Arfet," a pair of constant lovers, who performed the kiss above mentioned, that startled the woods of Madeira.

** "Although," says Lord Byron, in 1821, "I regret having published 'English Bards and Scotch Reviewers,' the part which I regret the least is that which regards Mr. Bowles, with reference to Pope. Whilst I was writing that publication, in 1807 and 1808, Mr. Hobhouse was desirous that I should express our mutual opinion of Pope, and of Mr. Bowles's edition of his works. As I had completed my outline, and felt lazy, I requested that he would do so. He did it. His fourteen lines on Bowles's Pope are in the first edition of 'English Bards,' and are quite as severe, and much more poetical, than my own, in the second. On reprinting the work, as I put my name to it, I omitted Mr. Hobhouse's lines, by which the work gained less than Mr. Bowles."

† Curll is one of the heroes of the Dunciad, and was a bookseller. Lord Fanny is the poetical name of Lord Hervey, author of "Lines to the Imitator of Horace."

†† Lord Bolingbroke hired Mallet to traduce Pope after his decease, because the poet had retained some copies of a work by Lord Bolingbroke —

Oh! hadst thou lived in that congenial time,
To rave with Dennis, and with Ralph to rhyme;*
Throng'd with the rest around his living head,
Not raised thy hoof against the lion dead;**
A meet reward had crown'd thy glorious gains,
And link'd thee to the Dunciad for thy pains.

Another epic! Who inflicts again
More books of blank upon the sons of men?
Bœotian Cottle, rich Bristowa's boast,
Imports old stories from the Cambrian coast,
And sends his goods to market — all alive!
Lines forty thousand, cantos twenty-five!
Fresh fish from Helicon! who'll buy? who'll buy?
The precious bargain's cheap — in faith, not I.
Your turtle-feeder's verse must needs be flat,
Though Bristol bloat him with the verdant fat;
If Commerce fills the purse, she clogs the brain,
And Amos Cottle strikes the lyre in vain.
In him an author's luckless lot behold,
Condemn'd to make the books which once he sold.
Oh, Amos Cottle! — Phœbus! what a name
To fill the speaking trump of future fame! —
Oh, Amos Cottle! for a moment think
What meagre profits spring from pen and ink!
When thus devoted to poetic dreams,
Who will peruse thy prostituted reams?
Oh pen perverted! paper misapplied!
Had Cottle† still adorn'd the counter's side,

the "Patriot King," — which that splendid, but malignant, genius had
ordered to be destroyed.
  * Dennis the critic, and Ralph the rhymester. —
      "Silence, ye wolves! while Ralph to Cynthia howls,
      Making night hideous: answer him, ye owls!" — *Dunciad.*
  ** See Bowles's late edition of Pope's works, for which he received
three hundred pounds. Thus Mr. B. has experienced how much easier it
is to profit by the reputation of another, than to elevate his own.
  † Mr. Cottle, Amos, Joseph, I don't know which, but one or both, once
sellers of books they did not write, and now writers of books they do not

Bent o'er the desk, or, born to useful toils,
Been taught to make the paper which he soils,
Plough'd, delved, or plied the oar with lusty limb,
He had not sung of Wales, nor I of him.*

As Sisyphus against the infernal steep
Rolls the huge rock whose motions ne'er may sleep,
So up thy hill, ambrosial Richmond, heaves
Dull Maurice ** all his granite weight of leaves:
Smooth, solid monuments of mental pain!
The petrifactions of a plodding brain,
That, ere they reach the top, fall lumbering back again.

With broken lyre, and cheek serenely pale,
Lo! sad Alcæus wanders down the vale;
Though fair they rose, and might have bloom'd at last,
His hopes have perish'd by the northern blast:
Nipp'd in the bud by Caledonian gales,
His blossoms wither as the blast prevails!
O'er his lost works let *classic* Sheffield weep;
May no rude hand disturb their early sleep! †

Yet say! why should the bard at once resign
His claim to favour from the sacred nine?
For ever startled by the mingled howl
Of northern wolves, that still in darkness prowl;

soil, have published a pair of epics. "Alfred," — (poor Alfred! Pye has
been at him too!) — "Alfred," and the "Fall of Cambria."

  * Here Lord B. notes in 1816: — "All right. I saw some letters of this
fellow (Joseph Cottle) to an unfortunate poetess, whose productions, which
the poor woman by no means thought vainly of, he attacked so roughly and
bitterly, that I could hardly resist assailing him, even were it unjust, which
it is not — for verily he is an ass." — B. 1816.

  ** Mr. Maurice hath manufactured the component parts of a ponderous
quarto, upon the beauties of "Richmond Hill," and the like: — it also
takes in a charming view of Turnham Green, Hammersmith, Brentford,
Old and New, and the parts adjacent.

  † Poor Montgomery, though praised by every English Review, has
been bitterly reviled by the Edinburgh. After all, the bard of Sheffield is
a man of considerable genius. His "Wanderer of Switzerland" is worth
a thousand "Lyrical Ballads," and at least fifty "degraded epics."

A coward brood, which mangle as they prey,
By hellish instinct, all that cross their way;
Aged or young, the living or the dead,
No mercy find — these harpies must be fed.
Why do the injured unresisting yield
The calm possession of their native field?
Why tamely thus before their fangs retreat,
Nor hunt the bloodhounds back to Arthur's Seat?*

Health to immortal Jeffrey! once, in name,
England could boast a judge almost the same;
In soul so like, so merciful, yet just,
Some think that Satan has resign'd his trust,
And given the spirit to the world again,
To sentence letters, as he sentenced men.
With hand less mighty, but with heart as black,
With voice as willing to decree the rack;
Bred in the courts betimes, though all that law
As yet hath taught him is to find a flaw;
Since well instructed in the patriot school
To rail at party, though a party tool,
Who knows, if chance his patrons should restore
Back to the sway they forfeited before,
His scribbling toils some recompence may meet,
And raise this Daniel to the judgment-seat?
Let Jeffries' shade indulge the pious hope,
And greeting thus, present him with a rope:
"Heir to my virtues! man of equal mind!
Skill'd to condemn as to traduce mankind,
This cord receive, for thee reserved with care,
To wield in judgment, and at length to wear."

Health to great Jeffrey! Heaven preserve his life,
To flourish on the fertile shores of Fife,
And guard it sacred in its future wars,
Since authors sometimes seek the field of Mars!

* Arthur's Seat; the hill which overhangs Edinburgh.

Can none remember that eventful day,
That ever glorious, almost fatal fray,
When Little's leadless pistol met his eye,
And Bow-street myrmidons stood laughing by?*
Oh, day disastrous! On her firm-set rock,
Dunedin's castle felt a secret shock;
Dark roll'd the sympathetic waves of Forth,
Low groan'd the startled whirlwinds of the north;
Tweed ruffled half his waves to form a tear,
The other half pursued its calm career;**
Arthur's steep summit nodded to its base,
The surly Tolbooth scarcely kept her place.
The Tolbooth felt — for marble sometimes can,
On such occasions, feel as much as man —
The Tolbooth felt defrauded of his charms,
If Jeffrey died, except within her arms:†
Nay last, not least, on that portentous morn,
The sixteenth story, where himself was born,
His patrimonial garret, fell to ground,
And pale Edina shudder'd at the sound:
Strew'd were the streets around with milk-white reams,
Flow'd all the Canongate with inky streams;
This of his candour seem'd the sable dew,
That of his valour show'd the bloodless hue;
And all with justice deem'd the two combined
The mingled emblems of his mighty mind.

* In 1806, Messrs. Jeffrey and Moore met at Chalk-Farm. The duel
was prevented by the interference of the magistracy; and, on examination,
the balls of the pistols were found to have evaporated. This incident gave
occasion to much waggery in the daily prints.

** The Tweed here behaved with proper decorum; it would have been
highly reprehensible in the English half of the river to have shown the
smallest symptom of apprehension.

† This display of sympathy on the part of the Tolbooth (the principal
prison in Edinburgh), which truly seems to have been most affected on this
occasion, is much to be commended. It was to be apprehended, that the
many unhappy criminals executed in the front might have rendered the
edifice more callous. She is said to be of the softer sex, because her deli-
cacy of feeling on this day was truly feminine, though, like most feminine
impulses, perhaps a little selfish.

But Caledonia's goddess hover'd o'er
The field, and saved him from the wrath of Moore;
From either pistol snatch'd the vengeful lead,
And straight restored it to her favourite's head;
That head, with greater than magnetic pow'r,
Caught it, as Danaë caught the golden show'r,
And, though the thickening dross will scarce refine,
Augments its ore, and is itself a mine.
"My son," she cried, "ne'er thirst for gore again,
Resign the pistol, and resume the pen;
O'er politics and poesy preside,
Boast of thy country, and Britannia's guide!
For long as Albion's heedless sons submit,
Or Scottish taste decides on English wit,
So long shall last thine unmolested reign,
Nor any dare to take thy name in vain.
Behold, a chosen band shall aid thy plan,
And own thee chieftain of the critic clan.
First in the oat-fed phalanx shall be seen
The travell'd thane, Athenian Aberdeen.*
Herbert shall wield Thor's hammer,** and sometimes,
In gratitude, thou'lt praise his rugged rhymes.
Smug Sydney † too thy bitter page shall seek,
And classic Hallam,†† much renown'd for Greek;

* His lordship has been much abroad, is a member of the Athenian Society, and reviewer of "Gell's Topography of Troy."

** Mr. Herbert is a translator of Icelandic and other poetry. One of the principal pieces is a "Song on the Recovery of Thor's Hammer:" the translation is a pleasant chant in the vulgar tongue, and endeth thus: —

"Instead of money and rings, I wot,
The hammer's bruises were her lot,
Thus Odin's son his hammer got."

† The Rev. Sydney Smith, the reputed author of Peter Plymley's Letters, and sundry criticisms.

†† Mr. Hallam reviewed Payne Knight's "Taste" and was exceedingly severe on some Greek verses therein. It was not discovered that the lines were Pindar's till the press rendered it impossible to cancel the critique, which still stands an everlasting monument of Hallam's ingenuity.

Note added to second edition. — The said Hallam is incensed because he is falsely accused, seeing that he never dineth at Holland House. If this

Scott may perchance his name and influence lend,
And paltry Pillans* shall traduce his friend;
While gay Thalia's luckless votary, Lambe,**
Damn'd like the devil, devil-like will damn.
Known be thy name, unbounded be thy sway!
Thy Holland's banquets shall each toil repay;
While grateful Britain yields the praise she owes
To Holland's hirelings and to learning's foes.
Yet mark one caution ere thy next Review
Spread its light wings of saffron and of blue,
Beware lest blundering Brougham † destroy the sale,
Turn beef to bannocks, cauliflowers to kail."
Thus having said, the kilted goddess kist
Her son, and vanish'd in a Scottish mist.††

be true, I am sorry — not for having said so, but on his account, as I
understand his lordship's feasts are preferable to his compositions. — If he
did not review Lord Holland's performance, I am glad, because it must
have been painful to read, and irksome to praise it. If Mr. Hallam will
tell me who did review it, the real name shall find a place in the text;
provided, nevertheless, the said name be of two orthodox musical syllables,
and will come into the verse: till then, Hallam must stand for want of a
better.

　* Pillans is a tutor at Eton.

　** The Hon. George Lambe reviewed "Beresford's Miseries," and is
moreover, author of a farce enacted with much applause at the Priory,
Stanmore; and damned with great expedition at the late theatre, Covent
Garden. It was entitled, "Whistle for It."

　† Mr. Brougham, in No. XXV. of the Edinburgh Review, throughout
the article concerning Don Pedro de Cevallos, has displayed more politics
than policy; many of the worthy burgesses of Edinburgh being so incensed
at the infamous principles it evinces, as to have withdrawn their subscrip-
tions.

　†† I ought to apologize to the worthy deities for introducing a new
goddess with short petticoats to their notice: but, alas! what was to be
done? I could not say Caledonia's genius, it being well known there is no
such genius to be found from Clackmanan to Caithness; yet, without
supernatural agency, how was Jeffrey to be saved? The national "kelpies"
are too unpoetical, and the "brownies" and "gude neighbours" (spirits
of a good disposition) refused to extricate him. A goddess, therefore, has
been called for the purpose; and great ought to be the gratitude of Jeffrey,
seeing it is the only communication he ever held, or is likely to hold, with
any thing heavenly.

Then prosper, Jeffrey! pertest of the train
Whom Scotland pampers with her fiery grain!
Whatever blessing waits a genuine Scot,
In double portion swells thy glorious lot;
For thee Edina culls her evening sweets,
And showers their odours on thy candid sheets,
Whose hue and fragrance to thy work adhere —
This scents its pages, and that gilds its rear. *
Lo! blushing Itch, coy nymph, enamour'd grown,
Forsakes the rest, and cleaves to thee alone;
And, too unjust to other Pictish men,
Enjoys thy person, and inspires thy pen!

Illustrious Holland! hard would be his lot,
His hirelings mention'd, and himself forgot!
Holland, with Henry Petty at his back,
The whipper-in and huntsman of the pack.
Blest be the banquets spread at Holland House,
Where Scotchmen feed, and critics may carouse!
Long, long beneath that hospitable roof
Shall Grub-street dine, while duns are kept aloof.
See honest Hallam lay aside his fork,
Resume his pen, review his Lordship's work,
And, grateful for the dainties on his plate,
Declare his landlord can at least translate! **
Dunedin! view thy children with delight,
They write for food — and feed because they write:
And lest, when heated with the unusual grape,
Some glowing thoughts should to the press escape,
And tinge with red the female reader's cheek,
My lady skims the cream of each critique;
Breathes o'er the page her purity of soul,
Reforms each error, and refines the whole. †

* See the colour of the back binding of the Edinburgh Review.
** Lord Holland has translated some specimens of Lope de Vega, inserted in his life of the author. Both are bepraised by his *disinterested* guests.
† Certain it is, her ladyship is suspected of having displayed her

Now to the Drama turn — Oh! motley sight!
What precious scenes the wondering eyes invite!
Puns, and a prince within a barrel pent,*
And Dibdin's nonsense yield complete content.
Though now, thank Heaven! the Rosciomania's o'er,
And full-grown actors are endured once more;
Yet what avail their vain attempts to please,
While British critics suffer scenes like these;
While Reynolds vents his "dammes!" "poohs!" and
       "zounds!"**
And common-place and common sense confounds?
While Kenney's "World" — ah! where is Kenney's wit?—
Tires the sad gallery, lulls the listless pit;
And Beaumont's pilfer'd Caratach affords
A tragedy complete in all but words?†
Who but must mourn, while these are all the rage,
The degradation of our vaunted stage!
Heavens! is all sense of shame and talent gone?
Have we no living bard of merit? — none!
Awake, George Colman! Cumberland, awake!
Ring the alarum bell! let folly quake!
Oh, Sheridan! if aught can move thy pen,
Let Comedy assume her throne again;
Abjure the mummery of the German schools;
Leave new Pizarros to translating fools;
Give, as thy last memorial to the age,
One classic drama, and reform the stage.
Gods! o'er those boards shall Folly rear her head,
Where Garrick trod, and Siddons lives to tread?

matchless wit in the Edinburgh Review. However that may be, we know,
from good authority, that the manuscripts are submitted to her perusal —
no doubt, for correction.

  * In the melo-drama of Tekeli, that heroic prince is clapt into a barrel
on the stage; a new asylum for distressed heroes.

  ** All these are favourite expressions of Mr. Reynolds, and prominent
in his comedies, living and defunct.

  † Mr. T. Sheridan, the new manager of Drury Lane theatre, stripped
the tragedy of Bonduca of the dialogue, and exhibited the scenes as the
spectacle of Caractacus. Was this worthy of his sire? or of himself?

On those shall Farce display Buffoon'ry's mask,
And Hook conceal his heroes in a cask?
Shall sapient managers new scenes produce
From Cherry, Skeffington, and Mother Goose?
While Shakspeare, Otway, Massinger, forgot,
On stalls must moulder, or in closets rot?
Lo! with what pomp the daily prints proclaim
The rival candidates for Attic fame!
In grim array though Lewis' spectres rise,
Still Skeffington and Goose divide the prize.
And sure *great* Skeffington must claim our p'raise,
For skirtless coats and skeletons of plays
Renown'd alike; whose genius ne'er confines
Her flight to garnish Greenwood's gay designs;*
Nor sleeps with "Sleeping Beauties," but anon
In five facetious acts comes thundering on, **
While poor John Bull, bewilder'd with the scene,
Stares, wondering what the devil it can mean;
But as some hands applaud, a venal few!
Rather than sleep, why John applauds it too.

Such are we now. Ah! wherefore should we turn
To what our fathers were, unless to mourn?
Degenerate Britons! are ye dead to shame,
Or, kind to dulness, do you fear to blame?
Well may the nobles of our present race
Watch each distortion of a Naldi's face;
Well may they smile on Italy's buffoons,
And worship Catalani's pantaloons,†

---

* Mr. Greenwood is, we believe, scene-painter to Drury-lane theatre
— as such, Mr. Skeffington is much indebted to him.

** Mr. [now Sir Lumley] Skeffington is the illustrious author of the
"Sleeping Beauty;" and some comedies, particularly "Maids and Ba-
chelors:" Baccalaurii baculo magis quam lauro digni.

† Naldi and Catalani require little notice; for the visage of the one
and the salary of the other, will enable us long to recollect these amusing
vagabonds. Besides, we are still black and blue from the squeeze on the
first night of the lady's appearance in trousers.

Since their own drama yields no fairer trace
Of wit than puns, of humour than grimace.

Then let Ausonia, skill'd in every art
To soften manners, but corrupt the heart,
Pour her exotic follies o'er the town,
To sanction Vice, and hunt Decorum down:
Let wedded strumpets languish o'er Deshayes,
And bless the promise which his form displays;
While Gayton bounds before th' enraptured looks
Of hoary marquises and stripling dukes:
Let high-born lechers eye the lively Prêsle
Twirl her light limbs, that spurn the needless veil;
Let Angiolini bare her breast of snow,
Wave the white arm, and point the pliant toe;
Collini trill her love-inspiring song,
Strain her fair neck, and charm the listening throng!
Whet not your scythe, suppressors of our vice!
Reforming saints! too delicately nice!
By whose decrees, our sinful souls to save,
No Sunday tankards foam, no barbers shave;
And beer undrawn, and beards unmown, display
Your holy reverence for the Sabbath-day.

Or hail at once the patron and the pile
Of vice and folly, Greville and Argyle! *

* To prevent any blunder, such as mistaking a street for a man, I beg
leave to state, that it is the institution, and not the duke of that name,
which is here alluded to. A gentleman, with whom I am slightly acquainted, lost in the Argyle Rooms several thousand pounds at back-
gammon. It is but justice to the manager in this instance to say, that some
degree of disapprobation was manifested: but why are the implements of
gaming allowed in a place devoted to the society of both sexes? A pleasant
thing for the wives and daughters of those who are blest or cursed with
such connections, to hear the billiard-tables rattling in one room, and the
dice in another! That this is the case I myself can testify, as a late unworthy member of an institution which materially affects the morals of the
higher orders, while the lower may not even move to the sound of a tabor
and fiddle, without a chance of indictment for riotous behaviour.

Where yon proud palace, Fashion's hallow'd fanc,
Spreads wide her portals for tho motley train,
Behold the new Petronius * of the day,
Our arbiter of pleasure and of play!
There the hired eunuch, the Hesperian choir,
The melting lute, the soft lascivious lyre,
The song from Italy, the step from France,
The midnight orgy, and the mazy dance,
The smile of beauty, and the flush of wine,
For fops, fools, gamesters, knaves, and lords combine:
Each to his humour — Comus all allows;
Champaign, dice, music, or your neighbour's spouse.
Talk not to us, ye starving sons of trade!
Of piteous ruin, which ourselves have made;
In Plenty's sunshine Fortune's minions bask,
Nor think of poverty, except "en masque,"
When for the night some lately titled ass
Appears the beggar which his grandsire was,
The curtain dropp'd, the gay burletta o'er,
The audience take their turn upon the floor;
Now round the room the circling dow'gers sweep,
Now in loose waltz the thin-clad daughters leap;
The first in lengthen'd line majestic swim,
The last display the free unfetter'd limb!
Those for Hibernia's lusty sons repair
With art the charms which nature could not spare;
These after husbands wing their eager flight,
Nor leave much mystery for the nuptial night.

Oh! blest retreats of infamy and ease,
Where, all forgotten but the power to please,
Each maid may give a loose to genial thought,
Each swain may teach new systems, or be taught:
There the blithe youngster, just return'd from Spain,
Cuts the light pack, or calls the rattling main;

---

* Petronius "Arbiter elegantiarum" to Nero, "and a vory pretty fellow in his day," as Mr. Congreve's "Old Bachelor" saith of Hannibal.

The jovial caster's set, and seven's the nick,
Or — done! — a thousand on the coming trick!
If, mad with loss, existence 'gins to tire,
And all your hope or wish is to expire,
Here's Powell's pistol ready for your life,
And, kinder still, two Pagets for your wife;
Fit consummation of an earthly race,
Begun in folly, ended in disgrace;
While none but menials o'er the bed of death,
Wash thy red wounds, or watch thy wavering breath;
Traduced by liars, and forgot by all,
The mangled victim of a drunken brawl,
To live like Clodius, and like Falkland fall. *

Truth! rouse some genuine bard, and guide his hand,
To drive this pestilence from out the land.
E'en I — least thinking of a thoughtless throng,
Just skill'd to know the right and choose the wrong,
Freed at that age when reason's shield is lost,
To fight my course through passion's countless host,
Whom every path of pleasure's flow'ry way
Has lured in turn, and all have led astray —
E'en I must raise my voice, e'en I must feel
Such scenes, such men, destroy the public weal;
Although some kind, censorious friend will say,
"What art thou better, meddling fool, than they?"
And every brother rake will smile to see
That miracle, a moralist in me.
No matter — when some bard in virtue strong,
Gifford perchance, shall raise the chastening song,

---

* I know the late Lord Falkland well. On Sunday night I beheld him
presiding at his own table, in all the honest pride of hospitality; on Wed-
nesday morning, at three o'clock, I saw stretched before me all that re-
mained of courage, feeling, and a host of passions. He was a gallant and
successful officer: his faults were the faults of a sailor — as such, Britons
will forgive them. He died like a brave man in a better cause; for had
he fallen in like manner on the deck of the frigate to which he was just appointed, his last moments would have been held up by his countrymen as
an example to succeeding heroes.

Then sleep my pen for ever! and my voice
Be only heard to hail him, and rejoice;
Rejoice, and yield my feeble praise, though I
May feel the lash that Virtue must apply.

As for the smaller fry, who swarm in shoals
From silly Hafiz up to simple Bowles, *
Why should we call them from their dark abode,
In broad St. Giles's or in Tottenham-road?
Or (since some men of fashion nobly dare
To scrawl in verse) from Bond-street or the Square?
If things of ton their harmless lays indite,
Most wisely doom'd to shun the public sight,
What harm? In spite of every critic elf,
Sir T. may read his stanzas to himself;
Miles Andrews still his strength in couplets try,
And live in prologues, though his dramas die.
Lords too are bards, such things at times befall,
And 'tis some praise in peers to write at all.
Yet, did or taste or reason sway the times,
Ah! who would take their titles with their rhymes?
Roscommon! Sheffield! with your spirits fled,
No future laurels deck a noble head;
No muse will cheer, with renovating smile,
The paralytic puling of Carlisle.
The puny schoolboy and his early lay
Men pardon, if his follies pass away;
But who forgives the senior's ceaseless verse,
Whose hairs grow hoary as his rhymes grow worse?
What heterogeneous honours deck the peer!
Lord, rhymester, petit-maître, pamphleteer!**

* What would be the sentiments of the Persian Anacreon, Hafiz, could
he rise from his splendid sepulchre at Sheeraz, (where he reposes with
Ferdousi and Sadi, the oriental Homer and Catullus,) and behold his name
assumed by one Stott of Dromore, the most impudent and execrable of
literary poachers for the daily prints?

** The Earl of Carlisle has lately published an eighteen-penny pamphlet
on the state of the stage, and offers his plan for building a new theatre. It

So dull in youth, so drivelling in his age,
His scenes alone had damn'd our sinking stage;
But managers for once cried, "Hold, enough!"
Nor drugg'd their audience with the tragic stuff.
Yet at their judgment let his lordship laugh,
And case his volumes in congenial calf;
Yes! doff that covering, where morocco shines,
And hang a calf-skin * on those recreant lines.

With you, ye Druids! rich in native lead,
Who daily scribble for your daily bread;
With you I war not! Gifford's heavy hand
Has crush'd, without remorse, your numerous band.
On "all the talents" vent your venal spleen;
Want is your plea, let pity be your screen.
Let monodies on Fox regale your crew,
And Melville's Mantle ** prove a blanket too!
One common Lethe waits each hapless bard,
And, peace be with you! 'tis your best reward.
Such damning fame as Dunciads only give
Could bid your lines beyond a morning live;
But now at once your fleeting labours close,
With names of greater note in blest repose.
Far be't from me unkindly to upbraid
The lovely Rosa's prose in masquerade,
Whose strains, the faithful echoes of her mind,
Leave wondering comprehension far behind.†

is to be hoped his lordship will be permitted to bring forward any thing
for the stage — except his own tragedies.
        *   "Doff that lion's hide,
            And hang a calf-skin on those recreant limbs."
                                        Shak. King John.
Lord Carlisle's works, most resplendently bound, form a conspicuous or-
nament to his book shelves: —
            "The rest is all but leather and prunella."
    ** "Melville's Mantle," a parody on "Elijah's Mantle," a poem.
    † This lovely little Jessica, the daughter of the noted Jew King, seems
to be a follower of the Della Crusca school, and has published two volumes
of very respectable absurdities in rhyme, as times go; besides sundry
novels in the style of the first edition of the Monk.

Though Crusca's bards no more our journals fill,
Some stragglers skirmish round the columns still;
Last of the howling host which once was Bell's,
Matilda snivels yet, and Hafiz yells;
And Merry's metaphors appear anew,
Chain'd to the signature of O. P. Q. *

When some brisk youth, the tenant of a stall,
Employs a pen less pointed than his awl,
Leaves his snug shop, forsakes his store of shoes,
St. Crispin quits, and cobbles for the muse,
Heavens! how the vulgar stare! how crowds applaud!
How ladies read, and literati laud!
If chance some wicked wag should pass his jest,
'Tis sheer ill-nature — don't the world know best?
Genius must guide when wits admire the rhyme,
And Capel Lofft ** declares 'tis quite sublime.
Hear, then, ye happy sons of needless trade!
Swains! quit the plough, resign the useless spade!
Lo! Burns and Bloomfield, nay, a greater far,
Gifford was born beneath an adverse star,
Forsook the labours of a servile state,
Stemm'd the rude storm, and triumph'd over fate:
Then why no more? if Phœbus smiled on you,
Bloomfield! why not on brother Nathan too? †
Him too the mania, not the muse, has seized;
Not inspiration, but a mind diseased:
And now no boor can seek his last abode,
No common be enclosed without an ode.
Oh! since increased refinement deigns to smile
On Britain's sons, and bless our genial isle,

* These are the signatures of various worthies who figure in the poetical departments of the newspapers.

** Capel Lofft, Esq., the Mæcenas of shoemakers, and preface writer-general to distressed versemen; a kind of gratis accoucheur to those who wish to be delivered of rhyme, but do not know how to bring forth.

† See Nathaniel Bloomfield's ode, elegy, or whatever he or any one else chooses to call it, on the enclosure of "Honington Green."

Let poesy go forth, pervade the whole,
Alike the rustic, and mechanic soul!
Ye tuneful cobblers! still your notes prolong,
Compose at once a slipper and a song;
So shall the fair your handywork peruse,
Your sonnets sure shall please — perhaps your shoes.
May Moorland weavers * boast Pindaric skill,
And tailors' lays be longer than their bill!
While punctual beaux reward the grateful notes,
And pay for poems — when they pay for coats.

To the famed throng now paid the tribute due,
Neglected genius! let me turn to you.
Come forth, oh Campbell! ** give thy talents scope;
Who dares aspire if thou must cease to hope?
And thou, melodious Rogers! rise at last,
Recall the pleasing memory of the past;
Arise! let blest remembrance still inspire,
And strike to wonted tones thy hallow'd lyre;
Restore Apollo to his vacant throne,
Assert thy country's honour and thine own.
What! must deserted Poesy still weep
Where her last hopes with pious Cowper sleep?
Unless, perchance, from his cold bier she turns,
To deck the turf that wraps her minstrel, Burns!
No! though contempt hath mark'd the spurious brood,
The race who rhyme from folly, or for food,
Yet still some genuine sons 'tis hers to boast,
Who, least affecting, still affect the most:

---

* Vide "Recollections of a Weaver in the Moorlands of Stafford-
shire."
* It would be superfluous to recall to the mind of the reader the
authors of "The Pleasures of Memory" and "The Pleasures of Hope," the
most beautiful didactic poems in our language, if we except Pope's "Essay
on Man;" but so many poetasters have started up, that even the names of
Campbell and Rogers are become strange.

Feel as they write, and write but as they feel —
Bear witness Gifford,* Sotheby,** Macneil.†

   "Why slumbers Gifford?" once was ask'd in vain;
Why slumbers Gifford? let us ask again.
Are there no follies for his pen to purge?††
Are there no fools whose backs demand the scourge?
Are there no sins for satire's bard to greet?
Stalks not gigantic Vice in every street?
Shall peers or princes tread pollution's path,
And 'scape alike the law's and muse's wrath?
Nor blaze with guilty glare through future time,
Eternal beacons of consummate crime?
Arouse thee, Gifford! be thy promise claim'd,
Make bad men better, or at least ashamed.

   Unhappy White!§ while life was in its spring,
And thy young muse just waved her joyous wing,
The spoiler swept that soaring lyre away,
Which else had sounded an immortal lay.
Oh! what a noble heart was here undone,
When Science' self destroy'd her favourite son!
Yes, she too much indulged thy fond pursuit,
She sow'd the seeds, but death has reap'd the fruit.

  * Gifford, author of the Baviad and Mæviad, the first satires of the day, and translator of Juvenal.

  ** Sotheby, translator of Wieland's Oberon and Virgil's Georgics, and author of "Saul," an epic poem.

  † Macneil, whose poems are deservedly popular, particularly "Scotland's Scaith," and the "Waes of War," of which ten thousand copies were sold in one month.

  †† Mr. Gifford promised publicly that the Baviad and Mæviad should not be his last original works: let him remember, "Mox in reluctantes dracones."

  § Henry Kirke White died at Cambridge, in October, 1806, in consequence of too much exertion in the pursuit of studies that would have matured a mind which disease and poverty could not impair, and which death itself destroyed rather than subdued. His poems abound in such beauties as must impress the reader with the liveliest regret that so short a period was allotted to talents which would have dignified even the sacred functions he was destined to assume.

'Twas thine own genius gave the final blow,
And help'd to plant the wound that laid thee low:
So the struck eagle, stretch'd upon the plain,
No more through rolling clouds to soar again,
View'd his own feather on the fatal dart,
And wing'd the shaft that quiver'd in his heart;
Keen were his pangs, but keener far to feel,
He nursed the pinion which impell'd the steel;
While the same plumage that had warm'd his nest
Drank the last life-drop of his bleeding breast.

There be, who say, in these enlighten'd days,
That splendid lies are all the poet's praise;
That strain'd invention, ever on the wing,
Alone impels the modern bard to sing:
'Tis true, that all who rhyme — nay, all who write,
Shrink from that fatal word to genius — trite;
Yet Truth sometimes will lend her noblest fires,
And decorate the verse himself inspires:
This fact in Virtue's name let Crabbe attest;
Though nature's sternest painter, yet the best.

And here let Shee* and Genius find a place,
Whose pen and pencil yield an equal grace;
To guide whose hand the sister arts combine,
And trace the poet's or the painter's line;
Whose magic touch can bid the canvass glow
Or pour the easy rhyme's harmonious flow;
While honours, doubly merited, attend
The poet's rival, but the painter's friend.

Blest is the man who dares approach the bower
Where dwelt the muses at their natal hour;
Whose steps have press'd, whose eye has mark'd afar,
The clime that nursed the sons of song and war,
The scenes which glory still must hover o'er,
Her place of birth, her own Achaian shore.

* Mr. Shee, author of "Rhymes on Art," and "Elements of Art."

But doubly blest is he whose heart expands
With hallow'd feelings for those classic lands;
Who rends the veil of ages long gone by,
And views their remnants with a poet's eye!
Wright! * 'twas thy happy lot at once to view
Those shores of glory, and to sing them too;
And sure no common muse inspired thy pen
To hail the land of gods and godlike men.

And you, associate bards! ** who snatch'd to light
Those gems too long withheld from modern sight;
Whose mingling taste combined to cull the wreath
Where Attic flowers Aonian odours breathe,
And all their renovated fragrance flung,
To grace the beauties of your native tongue;
Now let those minds, that nobly could transfuse
The glorious spirit of the Grecian muse,
Though soft the echo, scorn a borrow'd tone:
Resign Achaia's lyre, and strike your own.

Let these, or such as these, with just applause,
Restore the muse's violated laws;
But not in flimsy Darwin's pompous chime,
That mighty master of unmeaning rhyme,
Whose gilded cymbals, more adorn'd than clear,
The eye delighted, but fatigued the ear;
In show the simple lyre could once surpass,
But now, worn down, appear in native brass;
While all his train of hovering sylphs around
Evaporate in similes and sound:
Him let them shun, with him let tinsel die:
False glare attracts, but more offends the eye.†

* Waller Rodwell Wright, late consul-general for the Seven Islands, is author of a very beautiful poem, just published: it is entitled "Horæ Ionicæ," and is descriptive of the isles and the adjacent coast of Greece.

** The translators of the Anthology, Bland and Merivale, have since published separate poems, which evince genius that only requires opportunity to attain eminence.

† The neglect of the "Botanic Garden" is some proof of returning taste. The scenery is its sole recommendation.

Yet let them not to vulgar Wordsworth stoop,
The meanest object of the lowly group,
Whose verse, of all but childish prattle void,
Seems blessed harmony to Lamb and Lloyd:*
Let them — but hold, my muse, nor dare to teach
A strain far, far beyond thy humble reach:
The native genius with their being given
Will point the path, and peal their notes to heaven.

And thou, too, Scott!** resign to minstrels rude
The wilder slogan of a border feud:
Let others spin their meagre lines for hire;
Enough for genius if itself inspire!
Let Southey sing, although his teeming muse,
Prolific every spring, be too profuse;
Let simple Wordsworth chime his childish verse,
And brother Coleridge lull the babe at nurse;
Let spectre-mongering Lewis aim, at most,
To rouse the galleries, or to raise a ghost;
Let Moore still sigh; the Strangford steal from Moore,
And swear that Camoëns sang such notes of yore;
Let Hayley hobble on, Montgomery rave,
And godly Grahame chant a stupid stave;
Let sonneteering Bowles his strains refine,
And whine and whimper to the fourteenth line;
Let Stott, Carlisle,† Matilda, and the rest
Of Grub street, and of Grosvenor-place the best,

* Messrs. Lamb and Lloyd, the most ignoble followers of Southey and
Co.

** By the bye, I hope that in Mr. Scott's next poem, his hero or heroine
will be less addicted to "Gramarye," and more to grammar, than the Lady
of the Lay and her bravo, William of Deloraine.

† It may be asked, why I have censured the Earl of Carlisle, my
guardian and relative, to whom I dedicated a volume of puerile poems a
few years ago? — The guardianship was nominal, at least as far as I have
been able to discover; the relationship I cannot help, and am very sorry
for it; but as his lordship seemed to forget it on a very essential occasion
to me, I shall not burden my memory with the recollection. I do not think
that personal differences sanction the unjust condemnation of a brother
scribbler; but I see no reason why they should act as a preventive, when

Scrawl on, 'till death release us from the strain,
Or Common Sense assert her rights again.
But thou, with powers that mock the aid of praise,
Shouldst leave to humbler bards ignoble lays:
Thy country's voice, the voice of all the nine,
Demand a hallow'd harp — that harp is thine.
Say! will not Caledonia's annals yield
The glorious record of some nobler field,
Than the vile foray of a plundering clan,
Whose proudest deeds disgrace the name of man?
Or Marmion's acts of darkness, fitter food
For Sherwood's outlaw tales of Robin Hood?
Scotland! still proudly claim thy native bard,
And be thy praise his first, his best reward!
Yet not with thee alone his name should live,
But own the vast renown a world can give;
Be known, perchance, when Albion is no more,
And tell the tale of what she was before;
To future times her faded fame recall,
And save her glory, though his country fall.

Yet what avails the sanguine poet's hope,
To conquer ages, and with time to cope?

the author, noble or ignoble, has, for a series of years, beguiled a "discern-
ing public" (as the advertisements have it) with divers reams of most orthodox, imperial nonsense. Besides, I do not step aside to vituperate the
earl: no — his works come fairly in review with those of other patrician
literati. If, before I escaped from my teens, I said any thing in favour of
his lordship's paper books, it was in the way of dutiful dedication, and
more from the advice of others than my own judgment, and I seize the first
opportunity of pronouncing my sincere recantation. I have heard that
some persons conceive me to be under obligations to Lord Carlisle: if so,
I shall be most particularly happy to learn what they are, and when con-
ferred, that they may be duly appreciated and publicly acknowledged.
What I have humbly advanced as an opinion on his printed things, I am
prepared to support, if necessary, by quotations from elogies, eulogies,
odes, episodes, and certain facetious and dainty tragedies bearing his name
and mark: —

> "What can ennoble knaves, or fools, or cowards?
> Alas! not all the blood of all the Howards."

So says Pope. Amen!

New eras spread their wings, new nations rise,
And other victors fill the applauding skies;
A few brief generations fleet along,
Whose sons forget the poet and his song:
E'en now, what once-loved minstrels scarce may claim
The transient mention of a dubious name!
When fame's loud trump hath blown its noblest blast,
Though long the sound, the echo sleeps at last;
And glory, like the phœnix* 'midst her fires,
Exhales her odours, blazes, and expires.

Shall hoary Granta call her sable sons,
Expert in science, more expert at puns?
Shall these approach the muse? ah, no! she flies,
Even from the tempting ore of Seaton's prize;
Though printers condescend the press to soil
With rhyme by Hoare, and epic blank by Hoyle:
Not him whose page, if still upheld by whist,
Requires no sacred theme to bid us list.**
Ye! who in Granta's honours would surpass,
Must mount her Pegasus, a full-grown ass;
A foal well worthy of her ancient dam,
Whose Helicon is duller than her Cam.

There Clarke, still striving piteously "to please,"
Forgetting doggrel leads not to degrees,
A would-be satirist, a hired buffoon,
A monthly scribbler of some low lampoon,
Condemn'd to drudge, the meanest of the mean,
And furbish falsehoods for a magazine,
Devotes to scandal his congenial mind;
Himself a living libel on mankind.†

* ["The devil take that phœnix! How came it there?" — B. 1816.]
** The "Games of Hoyle," well known to the votaries of whist, chess,
&c., are not to be superseded by the vagaries of his poetical namesake,
whose poem comprised, as expressly stated in the advertisement, all the
"plagues of Egypt."
† This person, who has lately betrayed the most rabid symptoms of
confirmed authorship, is writer of a poem denominated the "Art of
Pleasing," as "lucus a non lucendo," containing little pleasantry and less

Oh! dark asylum of a Vandal race!*
At once the boast of learning, and disgrace!
So lost to Phœbus, that nor Hodgson's** verse
Can make thee better, nor poor Hewson's† worse.
But where fair Isis rolls her purer wave,
The partial muse delighted loves to lave;
On her green banks a greener wreath she wove,
To crown the bards that haunt her classic grove;
Where Richards wakes a genuine poet's fires,
And modern Britons glory in their sires.††

For me, who, thus unask'd, have dared to tell
My country, what her sons should know too well,
Zeal for her honour bade me here engage
The host of idiots that infest her age;
No just applause her honour'd name shall lose,
As first in freedom, dearest to the muse.
Oh! would thy bards but emulate thy fame,
And rise more worthy, Albion, of thy name!
What Athens was in science, Rome in power,
What Tyre appear'd in her meridian hour,
'Tis thine at once, fair Albion! to have been —
Earth's chief dictatress, ocean's lovely queen:
But Rome decay'd, and Athens strew'd the plain,
And Tyre's proud piers lie shatter'd in the main;

poetry. He also acts as monthly stipendiary and collector of calumnies
for the "Satirist." If this unfortunate young man would exchange the
magazines for the mathematics, and endeavour to take a decent degree in
his university, it might eventually prove more serviceable than his present
salary.

* "Into Cambridgeshire the Emperor Probus transported a considerable body of Vandals." — Gibbon's Decline and Fall, vol. ii. p. 83. There
is no reason to doubt the truth of this assertion; the breed is still in high
perfection.

** This gentleman's name requires no praise: the man who in translation displays unquestionable genius may be well expected to excel in
original composition, of which it is to be hoped we shall soon see a splendid specimen.

† Hewson Clarke, *esq.* as it is written.

†† The "Aboriginal Britons," an excellent poem, by Richards.

Like these, thy strength may sink, in ruin hurl'd,
And Britain fall, the bulwark of the world.
But let me cease, and dread Cassandra's fate,
With warning ever scoff'd at, till too late;
To themes less lofty still my lay confine,
And urge thy bards to gain a name like thine.

Then, hapless Britain! be thy rulers blest,
The senate's oracles, the people's jest!
Still hear thy motley orators dispense
The flowers of rhetoric, though not of sense,
While Canning's colleagues hate him for his wit,
And old dame Portland * fills the place of Pitt.

Yet once again, adieu! ere this the sail
That wafts me hence is shivering in the gale;
And Afric's coast and Calpe's adverse height,
And Stamboul's minarets must greet my sight:
Thence shall I stray through beauty's native clime, **
Where Kaff† is clad in rocks, and crown'd with snows
     sublime.
But should I back return, no tempting press ††
Shall drag my journal from the desk's recess:

* A friend of mine being asked, why his Grace of Portland was likened to an old woman? replied, "he supposed it was because he was past bearing." — His Grace is now gathered to his grandmothers, where he sleeps as sound as ever; but even his sleep was better than his colleagues' waking. 1811.

** Georgia.

† Mount Caucasus.

†† These four lines originally stood, —

    "But should I back return, no letter'd sage
      Shall drag my common-place book on the stage;
      Let vain Valentia § rival luckless Carr,
      And equal him whose work he sought to mar."

§ Lord Valentia (whose tremendous travels are forthcoming with due decorations, graphical, topographical, typographical) deposed, on Sir John Carr's unlucky suit, that Mr. Dubois's satire prevented his purchase of the "Stranger in Ireland." — Oh, fie, my lord! has your lordship no more feeling for a fellow-tourist? — but "two of a trade," they say, &c.

Let coxcombs, printing as they come from far,
Snatch his own wreath of ridicule from Carr;
Let Aberdeen and Elgin * still pursue
The shade of fame through regions of virtù:
Waste useless thousands on their Phidian freaks,
Misshapen monuments and maim'd antiques;
And make their grand saloons a general mart
For all the mutilated blocks of art.
Of Dardan tours let dilettanti tell,
I leave topography to rapid Gell; **
And, quite content, no more shall interpose
To stun the public ear — at least with prose.

Thus far I've held my undisturb'd career,
Prepared for rancour, steel'd 'gainst selfish fear:
This thing of rhyme I ne'er disdain'd to own —
Though not obtrusive, yet not quite unknown:
My voice was heard again, though not so loud,
My page, though nameless, never disavow'd;
And now at once I tear the veil away: —
Cheer on the pack! the quarry stands at bay,
Unscared by all the din of Melbourne house,
By Lambe's resentment, or by Holland's spouse,
By Jeffrey's harmless pistol, Hallam's rage,
Edina's brawny sons and brimstone page.
Our men in buckram shall have blows enough,
And feel they too are "penetrable stuff:"
And though I hope not hence unscathed to go,
Who conquers me shall find a stubborn foe.

* Lord Elgin would fain persuade us that all the figures, with and without noses, in his stoneshop are the work of Phidias! "Credat Judæus!"
** Mr. Gell's Topography of Troy and Ithaca cannot fail to ensure the approbation of every man possessed of classical taste, as well for the information Mr. Gell conveys to the mind of the reader, as for the ability and research the respective works display. — ["Since seeing the plain of Troy, my opinions are somewhat changed as to the above note. Gell's survey was hasty and superficial." — B. 1816.]

17*

The time hath been, when no harsh sound would fall
From lips that now may seem imbued with gall;
Nor fools nor follies tempt me to despise
The meanest thing that crawl'd beneath my eyes:
But now, so callous grown, so changed since youth,
I've learn'd to think, and sternly speak the truth;
Learn'd to deride the critic's starch decree,
And break him on the wheel he meant for me;
To spurn the rod a scribbler bids me kiss,
Nor care if courts and crowds applaud or hiss:
Nay more, though all my rival rhymesters frown,
I too can hunt a poetaster down;
And, arm'd in proof, the gauntlet cast at once
To Scotch marauder, and to southern dunce.
Thus much I've dared; if my incondite lay
Hath wrong'd these righteous times, let others say:
This, let the world, which knows not how to spare,
Yet rarely blames unjustly, now declare. *

* ["The greater part of this satire I most sincerely wish had never
been written — not only on account of the injustice of much of the critical,
and some of the personal part of it — but the tone and temper are such as I
cannot approve." — BYRON. July 14. 1816. *Diodati, Geneva.*]

POSTSCRIPT

TO THE SECOND EDITION.

I HAVE been informed, since the present edition went to the press, that my trusty and well-beloved cousins, the Edinburgh Reviewers, are preparing a most vehement critique on my poor, gentle, *unresisting*, Muse, whom they have already so be-deviled with their ungodly ribaldry:

"Tantæne animis cœlestibus iræ!"

I suppose I must say of Jeffrey as Sir Andrew Aguecheek saith, "an I had known he was so cunning of fence, I had seen him damned ere I had fought him." What a pity it is that I shall be beyond the Bosphorus before the next number has passed the Tweed! But I yet hope to light my pipe with it in Persia.

My northern friends have accused me, with justice, of personality towards their great literary anthropophagus, Jeffrey; but what else was to be done with him and his dirty pack, who feed by "lying and slandering," and slake their thirst by "evil speaking?" I have adduced facts already well known, and of Jeffrey's mind I have stated my free opinion, nor has he thence sustained any injury; — what scavenger was ever soiled by being pelted with mud? It may be said that I quit England because I have censured there "persons of honour and wit about town;" but I am coming back again, and their vengeance will keep hot till my return. Those who know me can testify that my motives for leaving England are very different from fears, literary or personal: those who do not, may one day be convinced. Since the publication of this thing, my name has not been concealed; I have been mostly in London, ready to answer for my transgressions, and in daily expectation of sundry cartels; but, alas! "the age of chivalry is over," or, in the vulgar tongue, there is no spirit now-a-days.

There is a youth ycleped Hewson Clarke (subaudi *esquire*), a sizer of Emanuel College, and, I believe, a denizen of Berwick-upon-Tweed, whom I have introduced in these pages to much better company than he has been accustomed to meet; he is, notwithstanding, a very sad dog, and for no reason that I can discover, except a personal quarrel with a bear, kept by me at Cambridge to sit for a fellowship, and whom the jealousy of his Trinity contemporaries prevented from success, has been abusing me, and, what is worse, the defenceless innocent above mentioned, in "The Satirist" for one year and some months. I am utterly unconscious of having given him any provocation; indeed, I am guiltless of having heard his name till

coupled with "The Satirist." He has therefore no reason to complain,
and I dare say that, like Sir Fretful Plagiary, he is rather *pleased* than
otherwise. I have now mentioned all who have done me the honour to
notice me and mine, that is, my bear and my book, except the editor of
"The Satirist," who, it seems, is a gentleman — God wot! I wish he could
impart a little of his gentility to his subordinate scribblers. I hear that Mr.
Jerningham is about to take up the cudgels for his Mæcenas, Lord Carlisle.
I hope not: he was one of the few, who, in the very short intercourse I
had with him, treated me with kindness when a boy; and whatever he may
say or do, "pour on, I will endure." I have nothing further to add, save a
general note of thanksgiving to readers, purchasers, and publishers, and,
in the words of Scott, I wish

> " To all and each a fair good night,
> And rosy dreams and slumbers light."

THE

AGE OF BRONZE;

OR,

CARMEN SECULARE ET ANNUS HAUD MIRABILIS.

———

"Impar *Congressus* Achilli."

———

THE AGE OF BRONZE.

I.

THE "good old times" — all times when old are good —
Are gone; the present might be if they would;
Great things have been, and are, and greater still
Want little of mere mortals but their will:
A wider space, a greener field, is given
To those who play their "tricks before high heaven."
I know not if the angels weep, but men
Have wept enough — for what? — to weep again!

II.

All is exploded — be it good or bad.
Reader! remember when thou wert a lad,
Then Pitt was all; or, if not all, so much,
His very rival almost deem'd him such.
We, we have seen the intellectual race
Of giants stand, like Titans, face to face —
Athos and Ida, with a dashing sea
Of eloquence between, which flow'd all free,
As the deep billows of the Ægean roar
Betwixt the Hellenic and the Phrygian shore.
But where are they — the rivals! — a few feet
Of sullen earth divide each winding sheet.
How peaceful and how powerful is the grave
Which hushes all! a calm, unstormy wave
Which oversweeps the world. The theme is old
Of "dust to dust;" but half its tale untold:
Time tempers not its terrors — still the worm
Winds its cold folds, the tomb preserves its form,
Varied above, but still alike below;
The urn may shine, the ashes will not glow,
Though Cleopatra's mummy cross the sea
O'er which from empire she lured Anthony;

Though Alexander's urn a show be grown
On shores he wept to conquer, though unknown —
How vain, how worse than vain, at length appear
The madman's wish, the Macedonian's tear!
He wept for worlds to conquer — half the earth
Knows not his name, or but his death, and birth,
And desolation; while his native Greece
Hath all of desolation, save its peace.
He "wept for worlds to conquer!" he who ne'er
Conceived the globe, he panted not to spare!
With even the busy Northern Isle unknown,
Which holds his urn, and never knew his throne.

III.

But where is he, the modern, mightier far,
Who, born no king, made monarchs draw his car;
The new Sesostris, whose unharness'd kings,
Freed from the bit, believe themselves with wings,
And spurn the dust o'er which they crawl'd of late,
Chain'd to the chariot of the chieftain's state?
Yes! where is he, the champion and the child
Of all that's great or little, wise or wild?
Whose game was empires, and whose stakes were thrones?
Whose table earth — whose dice were human bones?
Behold the grand result in yon lone isle,
And, as thy nature urges, weep or smile.
Sigh to behold the eagle's lofty rage
Reduced to nibble at his narrow cage;
Smile to survey the queller of the nations
Now daily squabbling o'er disputed rations;
Weep to perceive him mourning, as he dines,
O'er curtail'd dishes and o'er stinted wines;
O'er petty quarrels upon petty things.
Is this the man who scourged or feasted kings?
Behold the scales in which his fortune hangs,
A surgeon's statement, and an earl's harangues!
A bust delay'd, a book refused, can shake
The sleep of him who kept the world awake.

Is this indeed the tamer of the great,
Now slave of all could tease or irritate —
The paltry gaoler and the prying spy,
The staring stranger with his note-book nigh?
Plunged in a dungeon, he had still been great;
How low, how little was this middle state,
Between a prison and a palace, where
How few could feel for what he had to bear!
Vain his complaint, — my lord presents his bill,
His food and wine were doled out duly still:
Vain was his sickness, never was a clime
So free from homicide — to doubt 's a crime;
And the stiff surgeon, who maintain'd his cause,
Hath lost his place, and gain'd the world's applause.
But smile — though all the pangs of brain and heart
Disdain, defy, the tardy aid of art;
Though, save the few fond friends and imaged face
Of that fair boy his sire shall ne'er embrace,
None stand by his low bed — though even the mind
Be wavering, which long awed and awes mankind:
Smile — for the fetter'd eagle breaks his chain,
And higher worlds than this are his again.

IV.

How, if that soaring spirit still retain
A conscious twilight of his blazing reign,
How must he smile, on looking down, to see
The little that he was and sought to be!
What though his name a wider empire found
Than his ambition, though with scarce a bound;
Though first in glory, deepest in reverse,
He tasted empire's blessings and its curse;
Though kings, rejoicing in their late escape
From chains, would gladly be *their* tyrant's ape;
How must he smile, and turn to yon lone grave,
The proudest sea-mark that o'ertops the wave!
What though his gaoler, duteous to the last,
Scarce deem'd the coffin's lead could keep him fast,

Refusing one poor line along the lid,
To date the birth and death of all it hid;
That name shall hallow the ignoble shore,
A talisman to all save him who bore:
The fleets that sweep before the eastern blast
Shall hear their sea-boys hail it from the mast;
When Victory's Gallic column shall but rise,
Like Pompey's pillar, in a desert's skies,
The rocky isle that holds or held his dust
Shall crown the Atlantic like the hero's bust,
And mighty nature o'er his obsequies
Do more than niggard envy still denies.
But what are these to him? Can glory's lust
Touch the freed spirit or the fetter'd dust?
Small care hath he of what his tomb consists;
Nought if he sleeps — nor more if he exists:
Alike the better-seeing shade will smile
On the rude cavern of the rocky isle,
As if his ashes found their latest home
In Rome's Pantheon or Gaul's mimic dome.
He wants not this; but France shall feel the want
Of this last consolation, though so scant;
Her honour, fame, and faith demand his bones,
To rear above a pyramid of thrones;
Or carried onward in the battle's van,
To form, like Guesclin's dust, her talisman.
But be it as it is — the time may come
His name shall beat the alarm, like Ziska's drum.

v.

Oh heaven! of which he was in power a feature;
Oh earth! of which he was a noble creature;
Thou isle! to be remember'd long and well,
That saw'st the unfledged eaglet chip his shell!
Ye Alps, which view'd him in his dawning flights
Hover, the victor of a hundred fights!

Thou Rome, who saw'st thy Cæsar's deeds outdone!
Alas! why pass'd he too the Rubicon —
The Rubicon of man's awaken'd rights,
To herd with vulgar kings and parasites?
Egypt! from whose all dateless tombs arose
Forgotten Pharaohs from their long repose,
And shook within their pyramids to hear
A new Cambyses thundering in their ear;
While the dark shades of forty ages stood
Like startled giants by Nile's famous flood;
Or from the pyramid's tall pinnacle
Beheld the desert peopled, as from hell,
With clashing hosts, who strew'd the barren sand
To re-manure the uncultivated land!
Spain! which, a moment mindless of the Cid,
Beheld his banner flouting thy Madrid!
Austria! which saw thy twice-ta'en capital
Twice spared to be the traitress of his fall!
Ye race of Frederick! — Frederics but in name
And falsehood — heirs to all except his fame;
Who, crush'd at Jena, crouch'd at Berlin, fell
First, and but rose to follow! Ye who dwell
Where Kosciusko dwelt, remembering yet
The unpaid amount of Catherine's bloody debt!
Poland! o'er which the avenging angel past,
But left thee as he found thee, still a waste,
Forgetting all thy still enduring claim,
Thy lotted people and extinguish'd name,
Thy sigh for freedom, thy long-flowing tear,
That sound that crashes in the tyrant's ear —
Kosciusko! On — on — on — the thirst of war
Gasps for the gore of serfs and of their czar.
The half barbaric Moscow's minarets
Gleam in the sun, but 'tis a sun that sets!
Moscow! thou limit of his long career,
For which rude Charles had wept his frozen tear

To see in vain — *he* saw thee — how? with spire
And palace fuel to one common fire.
To this the soldier lent his kindling match,
To this the peasant gave his cottage thatch,
To this the merchant flung his hoarded store,
The prince his hall — and Moscow was no more!
Sublimest of volcanos! Etna's flame
Pales before thine, and quenchless Hecla's tame;
Vesuvius shows his blaze, an usual sight
For gaping tourists, from his hackney'd height:
Thou stand'st alone unrivall'd, till the fire
To come, in which all empires shall expire!

Thou other element! as strong and stern,
To teach a lesson conquerors will not learn! —
Whose icy wing flapp'd o'er the faltering foe,
'Till fell a hero with each flake of snow;
How did thy numbing beak and silent fang
Pierce, till hosts perish'd with a single pang!
In vain shall Seine look up along his banks
For the gay thousands of his dashing ranks!
In vain shall France recall beneath her vines
Her youth — their blood flows faster than her wines;
Or stagnant in their human ice remains
In frozen mummies on the Polar plains.
In vain will Italy's broad sun awaken
Her offspring chill'd; its beams are now forsaken.
Of all the trophies gather'd from the war,
What shall return? — the conqueror's broken car!
The conqueror's yet unbroken heart! Again
The horn of Roland sounds, and not in vain.
Lutzen, where fell the Swede of victory,
Beholds him conquer, but, alas! not die:
Dresden surveys three despots fly once more
Before their sovereign, — sovereign as before;
But there exhausted Fortune quits the field,
And Leipsic's treason bids the unvanquish'd yield;

The Saxon jackal leaves the lion's side
To turn the bear's, and wolf's, and fox's guide;
And backward to the den of his despair
The forest monarch shrinks, but finds no lair!

Oh ye! and each, and all! Oh France! who found
Thy long fair fields, plough'd up as hostile ground,
Disputed foot by foot, till treason, still
His only victor, from Montmartre's hill
Look'd down o'er trampled Paris! and thou Isle,
Which seest Etruria from thy ramparts smile,
Thou momentary shelter of his pride,
Till woo'd by danger, his yet weeping bride!
Oh, France! retaken by a single march,
Whose path was through one long triumphal arch!
Oh, bloody and most bootless Waterloo!
Which proves how fools may have their fortune too,
Won half by blunder, half by treachery:
Oh, dull Saint Helen! with thy gaoler nigh —
Hear! hear Prometheus* from his rock appeal
To earth, air, ocean, all that felt or feel
His power and glory, all who yet shall hear
A name eternal as the rolling year;
He teaches them the lesson taught so long,
So oft, so vainly — learn to do no wrong!
A single step into the right had made
This man the Washington of worlds betray'd:
A single step into the wrong has given
His name a doubt to all the winds of heaven;
The reed of Fortune, and of thrones the rod,
Of Fame the Moloch or the demigod;
His country's Cæsar, Europe's Hannibal,
Without their decent dignity of fall.
Yet Vanity herself had better taught
A surer path even to the fame he sought,

* I refer the reader to the first address of Prometheus in Æschylus,
when he is left alone by his attendants, and before the arrival of the Chorus
of Sea-nymphs

By pointing out on history's fruitless page
Ten thousand conquerors for a single sage.
While Franklin's quiet memory climbs to heaven,
Calming the lightning which he thence hath riven,
Or drawing from the no less kindled earth
Freedom and peace to that which boasts his birth;
While Washington's a watchword, such as ne'er
Shall sink while there's an echo left to air:
While even the Spaniard's thirst of gold and war
Forgets Pizarro to shout Bolivar!
Alas! why must the same Atlantic wave
Which wafted freedom gird a tyrant's grave —
The king of kings, and yet of slaves the slave,
Who bursts the chains of millions to renew
The very fetters which his arm broke through, .
And crush'd the rights of Europe and his own,
To flit between a dungeon and a throne?

VI.

But 'twill not be — the spark's awaken'd — lo!
The swarthy Spaniard feels his former glow;
The same high spirit which beat back the Moor
Through eight long ages of alternate gore
Revives — and where? in that avenging clime
Where Spain was once synonymous with crime,
Where Cortes' and Pizarro's banner flew,
The infant world redeems her name of "*New*."
'Tis the *old* aspiration breathed afresh,
To kindle souls within degraded flesh,
Such as repulsed the Persian from the shore
Where Greece *was* — No! she still is Greece once more
One common cause makes myriads of one breast,
Slaves of the east, or helots of the west;
On Andes' and on Athos' peaks unfurl'd
The self-same standard streams o'er either world;
The Athenian wears again Harmodius' sword;
The Chili chief abjures his foreign lord;

The Spartan knows himself once more a Greek,
Young Freedom plumes the crest of each cácique;
Debating despots, hemm'd on either shore,
Shrink vainly from the roused Atlantic's roar;
Through Calpe's strait the rolling tides advance,
Sweep slightly by the half-tamed land of France,
Dash o'er the old Spaniard's cradle, and would fain
Unite Ausonia to the mighty main:
But driven from thence awhile, yet not for aye,
Break o'er th' Ægean, mindful of the day
Of Salamis! — there, there the waves arise,
Not to be lull'd by tyrant victories.
Lone, lost, abandon'd in their utmost need
By Christians, unto whom they gave their creed,
The desolated lands, the ravaged isle,
The foster'd feud encouraged to beguile,
The aid evaded, and the cold delay,
Prolong'd but in the hope to make a prey; —
These, these shall tell the tale, and Greece can show
The false friend worse than the infuriate foe.
But this is well: Greeks only should free Greece,
Not the barbarian, with his mask of peace.
How should the autocrat of bondage be
The king of serfs, and set the nations free?
Better still serve the haughty Mussulman,
Than swell the Cossaque's prowling caravan;
Better still toil for masters, than await,
The slave of slaves, before a Russian gate, —
Number'd by hordes, a human capital,
A live estate, existing but for thrall,
Lotted by thousands, as a meet reward
For the first courtier in the Czar's regard;
While their immediate owner never tastes
His sleep, *sans* dreaming of Siberia's wastes;
Better succumb even to their own despair,
And drive the camel than purvey the bear.

VII.

But not alone within the hoariest clime
Where Freedom dates her birth with that of Time,
And not alone where, plunged in night, a crowd
Of Incas darken to a dubious cloud,
The dawn revives: renown'd, romantic Spain
Holds back the invader from her soil again.
Not now the Roman tribe nor Punic horde
Demand her fields as lists to prove the sword;
Not now the Vandal or the Visigoth
Pollute the plains, alike abhorring both;
Nor old Pelayo on his mountain rears
The warlike fathers of a thousand years.
That seed is sown and reap'd, as oft the Moor
Sighs to remember on his dusky shore.
Long in the peasant's song or poet's page
Has dwelt the memory of Abencerrage;
The Zegri, and the captive victors, flung
Back to the barbarous realm from whence they sprung.
But these are gone — their faith, their swords, their sway,
Yet left more anti-christian foes than they:
The bigot monarch and the butcher priest,
The Inquisition, with her burning feast,
The faith's red "auto," fed with human fuel,
While sate the catholic Moloch, calmly cruel,
Enjoying, with inexorable eye,
That fiery festival of agony!
The stern or feeble sovereign, one or both
By turns; the haughtiness whose pride was sloth:
The long degenerate noble; the debased
Hidalgo, and the peasant less disgraced,
But more degraded; the unpeopled realm;
The once proud navy which forgot the helm;
The once impervious phalanx disarray'd;
The idle forge that form'd Toledo's blade;
The foreign wealth that flow'd on ev'ry shore,
Save hers who earn'd it with the natives' gore;

Lord Byron. III. 18

The very language which might vie with Rome's,
And once was known to nations like their homes,
Neglected or forgotten : — such was Spain;
But such she is not, nor shall be again.
These worst, these *home* invaders, felt and feel
The new Numantine soul of old Castile.
Up! up again! undaunted Tauridor!
The bull of Phalaris renews his roar;
Mount, chivalrous Hidalgo! not in vain
Revive the cry — "Iago! and close Spain!"
Yes, close her with your armed bosoms round,
And form the barrier which Napoleon found, —
The exterminating war, the desert plain,
The streets without a tenant, save the slain;
The wild sierra, with its wilder troop
Of vulture-plumed guerrillas, on the stoop
For their incessant prey; the desperate wall
Of Saragossa, mightiest in her fall;
The man nerved to a spirit, and the maid
Waving her more than Amazonian blade;
The knife of Arragon,* Toledo's steel;
The famous lance of chivalrous Castile;
The unerring rifle of the Catalan;
The Andalusian courser in the van;
The torch to make a Moscow of Madrid;
And in each heart the spirit of the Cid : —
Such have been, such shall be, such are.   Advance,
And win — not Spain, but thine own freedom, France!

VIII.

But lo! a Congress! What! that hallow'd name
Which freed the Atlantic! May we hope the same
For outworn Europe? With the sound arise,
Like Samuel's shade to Saul's monarchic eyes,
The prophets of young Freedom, summon'd far
From climes of Washington and Bolivar;

* The Arragonians are peculiarly dexterous in the use of this weapon,
and displayed it particularly in former French wars.

Henry, the forest-born Demosthenes,
Whose thunder shook the Philip of the seas;
And stoic Franklin's energetic shade,
Robed in the lightnings which his hand allay'd
And Washington, the tyrant-tamer, wake,
To bid us blush for these old chains, or break.
But *who* compose this senate of the few
That should redeem the many? *Who* renew
This consecrated name, till now assign'd
To councils held to benefit mankind?
Who now assemble at the holy call?
The blest Alliance, which says three are all!
An earthly trinity! which wears the shape
Of heaven's, as man is mimick'd by the ape.
A pious unity! in purpose one —
To melt three fools to a Napoleon.
Why, Egypt's gods were rational to these;
Their dogs and oxen knew their own degrees,
And, quiet in their kennel or their shed,
Cared little, so that they were duly fed;
But these, more hungry, must have something more,
The power to bark and bite, to toss and gore.
Ah! how much happier were good Æsop's frogs
Than we! for ours are animated logs,
With ponderous malice swaying to and fro,
And crushing nations with a stupid blow;
All dully anxious to leave little work
Unto the revolutionary stork.

IX.

Thrice blest Verona! since the holy three
With their imperial presence shine on thee;
Honour'd by them, thy treacherous site forgets
The vaunted tomb of "all the Capulets;"
Thy Scaligers — for what was "Dog the Great,"
"Can Grande," (which I venture to translate,)
To these sublimer pugs? Thy poet too,
Catullus, whose old laurels yield to new;

18*

Thine amphitheatre, where Romans sate;
And Dante's exile shelter'd by thy gate;
Thy good old man, whose world was all within
Thy wall, nor knew the country held him in:
Would that the royal guests it girds about
Were so far like, as never to get out!
Ay, shout! inscribe! rear monuments of shame,
To tell Oppression that the world is tame!
Crowd to the theatre with loyal rage,
The comedy is not upon the stage;
The show is rich in ribandry and stars,
Then gaze upon it through thy dungeon bars;
Clap thy permitted palms, kind Italy,
For thus much still thy fetter'd hands are free!

X.

Resplendent sight! Behold the coxcomb Czar,
The autocrat of waltzes and of war!
As eager for a plaudit as a realm,
And just as fit for flirting as the helm;
A Calmuck beauty with a Cossack wit,
And generous spirit, when 'tis not frost-bit;
Now half dissolving to a liberal thaw,
But harden'd back whene'er the morning's raw;
With no objection to true liberty,
Except that it would make the nations free.
How well the imperial dandy prates of peace!
How fain, if Greeks would be his slaves, free Greece!
How nobly gave he back the Poles their Diet,
Then told pugnacious Poland to be quiet!
How kindly would he send the mild Ukraine,
With all her pleasant pulks, to lecture Spain!
How royally show off in proud Madrid
His goodly person, from the South long hid!
A blessing cheaply purchased, the world knows,
By having Muscovites for friends or foes.
Proceed, thou namesake of great Philip's son!
La Harpe, thine Aristotle, beckons on;

And that which Scythia was to him of yore
Find with thy Scythians on Iberia's shore.
Yet think upon, thou somewhat aged youth,
Thy predecessor on the banks of Pruth;
Thou hast to aid thee, should his lot be thine,
Many an old woman, but no Catherine.*
Spain, too, hath rocks, and rivers, and defiles —
The bear may rush into the lion's toils.
Fatal to Goths are Xeres' sunny fields;
Think'st thou to thee Napoleon's victor yields?
Better reclaim thy deserts, turn thy swords
To ploughshares, shave and wash thy Bashkir hordes,
Redeem thy realms from slavery and the knout,
Than follow headlong in the fatal route,
To infest the clime whose skies and laws are pure
With thy foul legions.   Spain wants no manure:
Her soil is fertile, but she feeds no foe;
Her vultures, too, were gorged not long ago;
And wouldst thou furnish them with fresher prey?
Alas! thou wilt not conquer, but purvey.
I am Diogenes, though Russ and Hun
Stand between mine and many a myriad's sun;
But were I not Diogenes, I'd wander
Rather a worm than *such* an Alexander!
Be slaves who will, the cynic shall be free;
His tub hath tougher walls than Sinopè:
Still will he hold his lantern up to scan
The face of monarchs for an "honest man."

XI.

And what doth Gaul, the all-prolific land
Of *ne plus ultra* ultras and their band
Of mercenaries? and her noisy chambers
And tribune, which each orator first clambers

* The dexterity of Catherine extricated Peter (called the Great by
courtesy), when surrounded by the Mussulmans on the banks of the river
Pruth.

Before he finds a voice, and when 'tis found,
Hears "the lie" echo for his answer round?
Our British Commons sometimes deign to "hear!"
A Gallic senate hath more tongue than ear;
Even Constant, their sole master of debate,
Must fight next day his speech to vindicate.
But this costs little to true Franks, who had rather
Combat than listen, were it to their father.
What is the simple standing of a shot,   .
To listening long, and interrupting not?
Though this was not the method of old Rome,
When Tully fulmined o'er each vocal dome,
Demosthenes has sanction'd the transaction,
In saying eloquence meant "Action, action!"

XII.

But where's the monarch? hath he dined? or yet
Groans beneath indigestion's heavy debt?
Have revolutionary patés risen,
And turn'd the royal entrails to a prison?
Have discontented movements stirr'd the troops?
Or have *no* movements follow'd traitorous soups?
Have Carbonaro cooks not carbonadoed
Each course enough? or doctors dire dissuaded
Repletion? Ah! in thy dejected looks
I read all France's treason in her cooks!
Good classic Louis! is it, canst thou say,
Desirable to be the "Desiré?"
Why wouldst thou leave calm Hartwell's green abode,
Apician table, and Horatian ode,
To rule a people who will not be ruled,
And love much rather to be scourged than school'd?
Ah! thine was not the temper or the taste
For thrones; the table sees thee better placed;
A mild Epicurean, form'd, at best,
To be a kind host and as good a guest,
To talk of letters, and to know by heart
One *half* the poet's, *all* the gourmand's art;

A scholar always, now and then a wit,
And gentle when digestion may permit; —
But not to govern lands enslaved or free;
The gout was martyrdom enough for thee.

XIII.

Shall noble Albion pass without a phrase
From a bold Briton in her wonted praise?
"Arts — arms — and George — and glory — and the isles —
And happy Britain — wealth — and Freedom's smiles —
White cliffs, that held invasion far aloof —
Contented subjects, all alike tax-proof —
Proud Wellington, with eagle beak so curl'd,
That nose, the hook where he suspends the world!*
And Waterloo — and trade — and — (hush! not yet
A syllable of imposts or of debt) —
And ne'er (enough) lamented Castlereagh,
Whose penknife slit a goose-quill t' other day —
And 'pilots who have weather'd every storm' —
(But, no, not even for rhyme's sake, name Reform)."
These are the themes thus sung so oft before,
Methinks we need not sing them any more;
Found in so many volumes far and near,
There's no occasion you should find them here.
Yet something may remain perchance to chime
With reason, and, what's stranger still, with rhyme.
Even this thy genius, Canning! may permit,
Who, bred a statesman, still wast born a wit,
And never, even in that dull House, couldst tame
To unleaven'd prose thine own poetic flame;
Our last, our best, our only orator,
Even I can praise thee — Tories do no more:
Nay, not so much; — they hate thee, man, because
Thy spirit less upholds them than it awes.

*   "Naso suspendit adunco." — *Horace.*
The Roman applies it to one who merely was imperious to his acquaintance.

The hounds will gather to their huntsman's hollo,
And where he leads the duteous pack will follow;
But not for love mistake their yelling cry;
Their yelp for game is not an eulogy;
Less faithful far than the four-footed pack,
A dubious scent would lure the bipeds back.
Thy saddle-girths are not yet quite secure,
Nor royal stallion's feet extremely sure;
The unwieldy old white horse is apt at last
To stumble, kick, and now and then stick fast
With his great self and rider in the mud:
But what of that? the animal shows blood.

XIV.

Alas, the country! how shall tongue or pen
Bewail her now *uncountry* gentlemen?
The last to bid the cry of warfare cease,
The first to make a malady of peace.
For what were all these country patriots born?
To hunt, and vote, and raise the price of corn?
But corn, like every mortal thing, must fall,
Kings, conquerors, and markets most of all.
And must ye fall with every ear of grain?
Why would you trouble Buonaparte's reign?
He was your great Triptolemus; his vices
Destroy'd but realms, and still maintain'd your prices;
He amplified to every lord's content
The grand agrarian alchymy, hight *rent.*
Why did the tyrant stumble on the Tartars,
And lower wheat to such desponding quarters?
Why did you chain him on yon isle so lone?
The man was worth much more upon his throne.
True, blood and treasure boundlessly were spilt,
But what of that? the Gaul may bear the guilt;
But bread was high, the farmer paid his way,
And acres told upon the appointed day.
But where is now the goodly audit ale?
The purse-proud tenant, never known to fail?

The farm which never yet was left on hand?
The marsh reclaim'd to most improving land?
The impatient hope of the expiring lease?
The doubling rental? What an evil's peace!
In vain the prize excites the ploughman's skill,
In vain the Commons pass their patriot bill;
The *landed interest* — (you may understand
The phrase much better leaving out the *land*) —
The land self-interest groans from shore to shore,
For fear that plenty should attain the poor.
Up, up again, ye rents! exalt your notes,
Or else the ministry will lose their votes,
And patriotism, so delicately nice,
Her loaves will lower to the market price;
For ah! "the loaves and fishes," once so high,
Are gone — their oven closed, their ocean dry,
And nought remains of all the millions spent,
Excepting to grow moderate and content.
They who are not so, *had* their turn — and turn
About still flows from Fortune's equal urn;
Now let their virtue be its own reward,
And share the blessings which themselves prepared.
See these inglorious Cincinnati swarm,
Farmers of war, dictators of the farm;
Their ploughshare was the sword in hireling hands,
Their fields manured by gore of other lands;
Safe in their barns, these Sabine tillers sent
Their brethren out to battle — why? for rent!
Year after year they voted cent. per cent.,
Blood, sweat, and tear-wrung millions — why? for rent!
They roar'd, they dined, they drank, they swore they meant
To die for England — why then live? — for rent!
The peace has made one general malcontent
Of these high-market patriots; war was rent!
Their love of country, millions all mis-spent,
How reconcile? by reconciling rent!

And will they not repay the treasures lent?
No: down with every thing, and up with rent!
Their good, ill, health, wealth, joy, or discontent,
Being, end, aim, religion — rent, rent, rent!
Thou sold'st thy birthright, Esau! for a mess;
Thou shouldst have gotten more, or eaten less;
Now thou hast swill'd thy pottage, thy demands
Are idle; Israel says the bargain stands.
Such, landlords! was your appetite for war,
And, gorged with blood, you grumble at a scar!
What! would they spread their earthquake even o'er cash?
And when land crumbles, bid firm paper crash?
So rent may rise, bid bank and nation fall,
And found on 'Change a *Fundling* Hospital?
Lo, Mother Church, while all religion writhes,
Like Niobe, weeps o'er her offspring, Tithes;
The prelates go to — where the saints have gone,
And proud pluralities subside to one;
Church, state, and faction wrestle in the dark,
Toss'd by the deluge in their common ark.
Shorn of her bishops, banks, and dividends,
Another Babel soars — but Britain ends.
And why? to pamper the self-seeking wants,
And prop the hill of these agrarian ants.
"Go to these ants, thou sluggard, and be wise;"
Admire their patience through each sacrifice,
Till taught to feel the lesson of their pride,
The price of taxes and of homicide;
Admire their justice, which would fain deny
The debt of nations: — pray *who made it high?*

XV.

Or turn to sail between those shifting rocks,
The new Symplegades — the crushing Stocks,
Where Midas might again his wish behold
In real paper or imagined gold.

That magic palace of Alcina shows
More wealth than Britain ever had to lose,
Were all her atoms of unleaven'd ore,
And all her pebbles from Pactolus' shore.
There Fortune plays, while Rumour holds the stake,
And the world trembles to bid brokers break.
How rich is Britain! not indeed in mines,
Or peace or plenty, corn or oil, or wines;
No land of Canaan, full of milk and honey,
Nor (save in paper shekels) ready money:
But let us not to own the truth refuse,
Was ever Christian land so rich in Jews?
Those parted with their teeth to good King John,
And now, ye kings! they kindly draw your own;
All states, all things, all sovereigns they control,
And waft a loan "from Indus to the pole."
The banker — broker — baron — brethren, speed
To aid these bankrupt tyrants in their need.
Nor these alone; Columbia feels no less
Fresh speculations follow each success;
And philanthropic Israel deigns to drain
Her mild per-centage from exhausted Spain.
Not without Abraham's seed can Russia march;
'Tis gold, not steel, that rears the conqueror's arch.
Two Jews, a chosen people, can command
In every realm their scripture-promised land: —
Two Jews keep down the Romans, and uphold
The accursed Hun, more brutal than of old:
Two Jews — but not Samaritans — direct
The world, with all the spirit of their sect.
What is the happiness of earth to them?
A congress forms their "New Jerusalem,"
Where baronies and orders both invite —
Oh, holy Abraham! dost thou see the sight?
Thy followers mingling with these royal swine,
Who spit not "on their Jewish gaberdine,"

But honour them as portion of the show —
(Where now, oh pope! is thy forsaken toe?
Could it not favour Judah with some kicks?
Or has it ceased to "kick against the pricks?")
On Shylock's shore behold them stand afresh,
To cut from nations' hearts their "pound of flesh."

XVI.

Strange sight this Congress! destined to unite
All that's incongruous, all that's opposite.
I speak not of the Sovereigns — they're alike,
A common coin as ever mint could strike:
But those who sway the puppets, pull the strings,
Have more of motley than their heavy kings.
Jews, authors, generals, charlatans, combine,
While Europe wonders at the vast design:
There Metternich, power's foremost parasite,
Cajoles; there Wellington forgets to fight;
There Chateaubriand forms new books of martyrs;*
And subtle Greeks intrigue for stupid Tartars;
There Montmorenci, the sworn foe to charters,
Turns a diplomatist of great eclat,
To furnish articles for the "Débats;
Of war so certain — yet not quite so sure
As his dismissal in the "Moniteur."
Alas! how could his cabinet thus err?
Can peace be worth an ultra-minister?
He falls indeed, perhaps to rise again,
"Almost as quickly as he conquer'd Spain."

XVII.

Enough of this — a sight more mournful woos
The averted eye of the reluctant muse.

* Monsieur Chateaubriand, who has not forgotten the author in the minister, received a handsome compliment at Verona from a literary sovereign: "Ah! Monsieur C., are you related to that Chateaubriand who — who — who has written *something?*" (*écrit quelque chose!*) It is said that the author of Atala reponted him for a moment of his legitimacy.

The imperial daughter, the imperial bride,
The imperial victim — sacrifice to pride;
The mother of the hero's hope, the boy,
The young Astyanax of modern Troy;
The still pale shadow of the loftiest queen
That earth has yet to see, or e'er hath seen;
She flits amidst the phantoms of the hour,
The theme of pity, and the wreck of power.
Oh, cruel mockery! Could not Austria spare
A daughter? What did France's widow there?
Her fitter place was by St. Helen's wave,
Her only throne is in Napoleon's grave.
But, no, — she still must hold a petty reign,
Flank'd by her formidable chamberlain;
The martial Argus, whose not hundred eyes
Must watch her through these paltry pageantries.
What though she share no more, and shared in vain,
A sway surpassing that of Charlemagne,
Which swept from Moscow to the southern seas!
Yet still she rules the pastoral realm of cheese,
Where Parma views the traveller resort
To note the trappings of her mimic court.
But she appears! Verona sees her shorn
Of all her beams — while nations gaze and mourn —
Ere yet her husband's ashes have had time
To chill in their inhospitable clime;
(If e'er those awful ashes can grow cold; —
But no, — their embers soon will burst the mould;)
She comes! — the Andromache (but not Racine's,
Nor Homer's,) — Lo! on Pyrrhus' arm she leans!
Yes! the right arm, yet red from Waterloo,
Which cut her lord's half-shatter'd sceptre through,
Is offer'd and accepted! Could a slave
Do more? or less? — and *he* in his new grave!
Her eye, her cheek, betray no inward strife,
And the *ex*-empress grows as *ex* a wife!

So much for human ties in royal breasts!
Why spare men's feelings, when their own are jests?

XVIII.

But, tired of foreign follies, I turn home,
And sketch the group — the picture 's yet to come.
My muse 'gan weep, but, cre a tear was spilt,
She caught Sir William Curtis in a kilt!
While throng'd the chiefs of every Highland clan
To hail their brother, Vich Ian Alderman!
Guildhall grows Gael, and echoes with Erse roar,
While all the Common Council cry "Claymore!"
To see proud Albyn's tartans as a belt
Gird the gross sirloin of a city Celt,
She burst into a laughter so extreme,
That I awoke — and lo! it was *no* dream!

Here, reader, will we pause: — if there's no harm in
This first — you'll have, perhaps, a second "Carmen."

HINTS FROM HORACE:

BEING AN ALLUSION IN ENGLISH VERSE TO THE EPISTLE "AD PISONES, DE ARTE POETICA," AND INTENDED AS A SEQUEL TO "ENGLISH BARDS AND SCOTCH REVIEWERS."

—————

— "Ergo fungar vice cotis, acutum
Reddere quæ ferrum valet, exsors ipsa secandi."
HOR. *De Arte Poet.*

"Rhymes are difficult things — they are stubborn things, sir."
FIELDING'S *Amelia.*

—————

HINTS FROM HORACE.

Athens. Capuchin Convent, March 12. 1811.

Who would not laugh, if Lawrence, hired to grace
His costly canvass with each flatter'd face,
Abused his art, till Nature, with a blush,
Saw cits grow centaurs underneath his brush?
Or, should some limner join, for show or sale,
A maid of honour to a mermaid's tail?
Or low Dubost* — as once the world has seen —
Degrade God's creatures in his graphic spleen?
Not all that forced politeness, which defends
Fools in their faults, could gag his grinning friends.
Believe me, Moschus, like that picture seems
The book which, sillier than a sick man's dreams,
Displays a crowd of figures incomplete,
Poetic nightmares, without head or feet.

Poets and painters, as all artists know,
May shoot a little with a lengthen'd bow;
We claim this mutual mercy for our task,
And grant in turn the pardon which we ask;

> Humano capiti cervicem pictor equinam
> Jungere si velit, et varias inducere plumas,
> Undique collatis membris, ut turpiter atrum
> Desinat in piscem mulier formosa superne;
> Spectatum admissi risum teneatis, amici?
> Credite, Pisones, isti tabulæ fore librum
> Persimilem, cujus, velut ægri somnia, vanæ
> Fingontur species, ut nec pes, nec caput uni
> Reddatur formæ. Pictoribus atque poetis
> Quidlibet audendi semper fuit æqua potestas,
> Scimus, et hanc veniam petimusque damusque vicissim:

* In an English newspaper, which finds its way abroad wherever there are Englishmen, I read an account of this dirty dauber's caricature of Mr. H— as a "beast," and the consequent action, &c. The circumstance is, probably, too well known to require further comment.

But make not monsters spring from gentle dams —
Birds breed not vipers, tigers nurse not lambs.

A labour'd, long exordium, sometimes tends
(Like patriot speeches) but to paltry ends;
And nonsense in a lofty note goes down
As pertness passes with a legal gown:
Thus many a bard describes in pompous strain
The clear brook babbling through the goodly plain:
The groves of Granta, and her gothic halls,
King's Coll., Cam's stream, stain'd windows, and old walls;
Or, in advent'rous numbers, neatly aims
To paint a rainbow, or — the river Thames.*

You sketch a tree, and so perhaps may shine —
But daub a shipwreck like an alehouse sign;
You plan a *vase* — it dwindles to a *pot;*
Then glide down Grub-street — fasting and forgot;
Laugh'd into Lethe by some quaint Review,
Whose wit is never troublesome till — true.

In fine, to whatsoever you aspire,
Let it at least be simple and entire.

Sed non ut placidis coëant immitia; non ut
Serpentes avibus geminentur, tigribus agni.
  Incœptis gravibus plerumque et magna professis
Purpureus, late qui splendeat, unus et alter
Assuitur pannus; cum lucus et ara Dianæ,
Et properantis aquæ per amœnos ambitus agros,
Aut flumen Rhenum, aut pluvius describitur arcus.
Sed nunc non erat his locus: et fortasse cupressum
Scis simulare: quid hoc, si fractis enatat exspes
Navibus, ære dato qui pingitur? amphora cœpit
Institui; currente rotâ cur urceus exit?
Denique sit quod vis, simplex duntaxat et unum.

* "Where pure description held the place of sense." — POPE.

The greater portion of the rhyming tribe
(Give ear, my friend, for thou hast been a scribe)
Are led astray by some peculiar lure.
I labour to be brief — become obscure;
One falls while following elegance too fast;
Another soars, inflated with bombast;
Too low a third crawls on, afraid to fly,
He spins his subject to satiety;
Absurdly varying, he at last engraves
Fish in the woods, and boars beneath the waves!

Unless your care's exact, your judgment nice,
The flight from folly leads but into vice;
None are complete, all wanting in some part,
Like certain tailors, limited in art.
For galligaskins Slowshears is your man;
But coats must claim another artisan.*
Now this to me, I own, seems much the same
As Vulcan's feet to bear Apollo's frame;
Or, with a fair complexion, to expose
Black eyes, black ringlets, but — a bottle nose!

> Maxima pars vatum, pater, et juvenes patre digni,
> Decipimur specie recti. Brevis esse laboro,
> Obscurus fio: sectantem levia, nervi
> Deficiunt animique: professus grandia, turget:
> Serpit humi, tutus nimium, timidusque procellæ:
> Qui variare cupit rem prodigialiter unam,
> Delphinum sylvis appingit fluctibus aprum.
>   In vitium ducit culpæ fuga, si caret arte.
> Æmilium circa ludum faber unus et ungues
> Exprimet, et molles imitabitur ære capillos;
> Infelix operis summa, quia ponere totum
> Nesciet. Hunc ego me, si quid componere curem,
> Non magis esse velim, quam pravo vivere naso,
> Spectandum nigris oculis nigroque capillo.

* Mere common mortals were commonly content with one tailor and with one bill, but the more particular gentlemen found it impossible to confide their lower garments to the makers of their body clothes. I speak of the beginning of 1809: what reform may have since taken place I neither know, nor desire to know.

Dear authors! suit your topics to your strength,
And ponder well your subject, and its length;
Nor lift your load, before you're quite aware
What weight your shoulders will, or will not, bear.
But lucid Order, and Wit's siren voice,
Await the poet, skilful in his choice;
With native eloquence he soars along,
Grace in his thoughts, and music in his song.

Let judgment teach him wisely to combine
With future parts the now omitted line:
This shall the author choose, or that reject,
Precise in style, and cautious to select;
Nor slight applause will candid pens afford
To him who furnishes a wanting word.
Then fear not if 'tis needful to produce
Some term unknown, or obsolete in use,
(As Pitt* has furnish'd us a word or two,
Which lexicographers declined to do;)
So you indeed, with care, — (but be content
To take this license rarely) — may invent.

Sumito materiem vestris, qui scribitis, æquam
Viribus; et versate diu quid ferre recusent
Quid valeant humeri. Cui lecta potenter erit res,
Nec facundia deseret hunc nec lucidus ordo.
  Ordinis hæc virtus erit et venus, aut ego fallor,
Ut jam nunc dicat, jam nunc debentia dici
Pleraque differat, et præsens in tempus omittat;
Hoc amet, hoc spernat promissi carminis auctor.
  In verbis etiam tenuis cautusque serendis:
Dixeris egregie, notum si callida verbum
Reddiderit junctura novum. Si forte necesse est
Indiciis monstrare recentibus abdita rerum,
Fingere cinctutis non exaudita Cethegis
Continget; dabiturque licentia sumpta pudenter;

* Mr. Pitt was liberal in his additions to our parliamentary tongue; as
may be seen in many publications, particularly the Edinburgh Review.

New words find credit in these latter days
If neatly grafted on a Gallic phrase.
What Chaucer, Spenser did, we scarce refuse
To Dryden's or to Pope's maturer muse.
If you can add a little, say why not,
As well as William Pitt, and Walter Scott?
Since they, by force of rhyme and force of lungs,
Enrich'd our island's ill-united tongues;
'Tis then — and shall be — lawful to present
Reform in writing, as in parliament.

As forests shed their foliage by degrees,
So fade expressions which in season please;
And we and ours, alas! are due to fate,
And works and words but dwindle to a date.
Though as a monarch nods, and commerce calls,
Impetuous rivers stagnate in canals;
Though swamps subdued, and marshes drain'd, sustain
The heavy ploughshare and the yellow grain,
And rising ports along the busy shore
Protect the vessel from old Ocean's roar,
All, all must perish; but, surviving last,
The love of letters half preserves the past.

Et nova fictaque nuper habebunt verba fidem, si
Græco fonte cadant, parce detorta. Quid autem
Cæcilio Plautoque dabit Romanus, ademptum
Virgilio Varioque? ego cur, acquirere pauca
Si possum, invideor, cum lingua Catonis et Enni
Sermonem patrium ditaverit, et nova rerum
Nomina protulerit? Licuit, semperque licebit,
Signatum præsente nota producere nomen.
 Ut silvæ foliis pronos mutantur in annos;
Prima cadunt: ita verborum vetus interit ætas,
Et juvenum ritu florent modo nata, vigentque.
Debemur morti nos nostraque: sive receptus
Terra Neptunus classes aquilonibus arcet,
Regis opus; sterilisve diu palus, aptaque remis
Vicinas urbes alit, et grave sentit aratrum:
Seu cursum mutavit iniquum frugibus amnis,
Doctus iter melius; mortalia facta peribunt,
Nedum sermonum stet honos, et gratia vivax.

True, some decay, yet not a few revive;*
Though those shall sink, which now appear to thrive,
As custom arbitrates, whose shifting sway
Our life and language must alike obey.

The immortal wars which gods and angels wage,
Are they not shown in Milton's sacred page?
His strain will teach what numbers best belong
To themes celestial told in epic song.

The slow, sad stanza will correctly paint
The lover's anguish, or the friend's complaint.
But which deserves the laurel — rhyme or blank?
Which holds on Helicon the higher rank?
Let squabbling critics by themselves dispute
This point, as puzzling as a Chancery suit.

Satiric rhyme first sprang from selfish spleen.
You doubt — see Dryden, Pope, St. Patrick's dean.**

Multa renascentur, quæ jam cecidere; cadentque
Quæ nunc sunt in honore vocabula, si volet usus;
Quem penes arbitrium est, et jus, et norma loquendi.
    Res gestæ regumque ducumque et tristia bella,
Quo scribi possent numero monstravit Homerus.
    Versibus impariter junctis querimonia primum;
Post etiam inclusa est voti sententia compos.
Quis tamen exiguos elegos emiserit auctor,
Grammatici certant, et adhuc sub judice lis est.
    Archilochum proprio rabies armavit iambo;
Hunc socci cepere pedem, grandesque cothurni,
Alternis aptum sermonibus, et populares
Vincentem strepitus, et natum rebus agendis.

---

* Old ballads, old plays, and old women's stories, are at present in as much request as old wine or new speeches. In fact, this is the millennium of black letter: thanks to our Hebers, Webers, and Scotts!

** "Mac Flecknoe," the "Dunciad," and all Swift's lampooning ballads. Whatever their other works may be, these originated in personal feelings, and angry retort on unworthy rivals; and though the ability of these satires elevates the poetical, their poignancy detracts from the personal character of the writers.

Blank verse is now, with one consent, allied
To Tragedy, and rarely quits her side.
Though mad Almanzor rhymed in Dryden's days,
No sing-song hero rants in modern plays;
While modest Comedy her verse foregoes
For jest and *pun* * in very middling prose.
Not that our Bens or Beaumonts show the worse,
Or lose one point, because they wrote in verse.
But so Thalia pleases to appear,
Poor virgin! damn'd some twenty times a year!

Whate'er the scene, let this advice have weight: —
Adapt your language to your hero's state.
At times Melpomene forgets to groan,
And brisk Thalia takes a serious tone;
Nor unregarded will the act pass by
Where angry Townly lifts his voice on high.
Again, our Shakspeare limits verse to kings,
When common prose will serve for common things;
And lively Hal resigns heroic ire,
To "hollowing Hotspur"** and the sceptred sire.

> Musa dedit fidibus divos, puerosque deorum,
> Et pugilem victorem, et equum certamine primum,
> Et juvenum curas, et libera vina referre.
>   Descriptas servare vices operumque colores,
> Cur ego, si nequeo ignoroque, poeta salutor?
> Cur nescire pudens prave quam discere malo?
>   Versibus exponi tragicis res comica non vult;
> Indignatur item privatis, ac prope socco
> Dignis carminibus narrari cœna Thyestæ.
> Singula quæque locum teneant sortita decenter.
> Interdum tamen et vocem comœdia tollit,
> Iratusque Cremes tumido delitigat ore:
> Et tragicus plerumque dolet sermone pedestri.
> Telephus et Peleus, cum pauper et exul, uterque
> ·Projicit ampullas et sesquipedalia verba;
> Si curat cor spectantis tetigisse querela.

* With all the vulgar applause and critical abhorrence of *puns*, they have Aristotle on their side; who permits them to orators, and gives them consequence by a grave disquisition.

** "And in his ear I'll hollow Mortimer!" — 1 *Henry IV.*

'Tis not enough, ye bards, with all your art,
To polish poems; — they must touch the heart:
Where'er the scene be laid, whate'er the song,
Still let it bear the hearer's soul along;
Command your audience or to smile or weep,
Whiche'er may please you — any thing but sleep.
The poet claims our tears; but, by his leave,
Before I shed them, let me see him grieve.

If banish'd Romeo feign'd nor sigh nor tear,
Lull'd by his languor, I should sleep or sneer.
Sad words, no doubt, become a serious face,
And men look angry in the proper place.
At double meanings folks seem wondrous sly,
And sentiment prescribes a pensive eye;
For nature form'd at first the inward man,
And actors copy nature — when they can.
She bids the beating heart with rapture bound,
Raised to the stars, or levell'd with the ground;
And for expression's aid, 'tis said, or sung,
She gave our mind's interpreter — the tongue,
Who, worn with use, of late would fain dispense
(At least in theatres) with common sense;
O'erwhelm with sound the boxes, gallery, pit,
And raise a laugh with any thing — but wit.

Non satis est pulchra esse poemata; dulcia sunto,
Et quocunque volent, animum auditoris agunto.
Ut ridentibus arrident, ita flentibus adflent
Humani vultus; si vis me flere, dolendum est
Primum ipsi tibi; tunc tua me infortunia lædent.
Telephe, vel Peleu, male si mandata loquêris,
Aut dormitabo, aut ridebo: tristia mœstum
Vultum verba decent; iratum, plena minarum;
Ludentem, lasciva; severum, seria dictu.
Format enim natura prius nos intus ad omnem
Fortunarum habitum; juvat, aut impellit ad iram;
Aut ad humum mœrore gravi deducit, et angit;
Post effert animi motus interprete lingua.
Si dicentis erunt fortunis absona dicta,
Romani tollent equites peditesque cachinnum.

To skilful writers it will much import,
Whence spring their scenes, from common life or court;
Whether they seek applause by smile or tear,
To draw a "Lying Valet," or a "Lear,"
A sage, or rakish youngster wild from school,
A wandering "Peregrine," or plain "John Bull;"
All persons please when nature's voice prevails,
Scottish or Irish, born in Wilts or Wales.

Or follow common fame, or forge a plot.
Who cares if mimic heroes lived or not?
One precept serves to regulate the scene: —
Make it appear as if it *might* have *been*.

If some Drawcansir you aspire to draw,
Present him raving, and above all law:
If female furies in your scheme are plann'd,
Macbeth's fierce dame is ready to your hand;
For tears and treachery, for good or evil,
Constance, King Richard, Hamlet, and the Devil!
But if a new design you dare essay,
And freely wander from the beaten way,
True to your characters, till all be past,
Preserve consistency from first to last.

Intererit multum, Davusne loquatur, an heros;
Maturusne senex, an adhuc florente juventa
Fervidus; an matrona potens, an sedula nutrix;
Mercatorne vagus, cultorne virontis agelli;
Colchus, an Assyrius; Thebis nutritus, an Argis.
    Aut famam sequere, aut sibi convenientia fingo,
Scriptor. Honoratum si forte reponis Achillem;
Impiger, iracundus, inexorabilis, acer,
Jura neget sibi nata, nihil non arroget armis.
Sit Medea ferox invictaque; flebilis Ino;
Perfidus Ixion; Io vaga; tristis Orestes;
Si quid inexpertum scenæ committis, et audes
Personam formare novam; servetur ad imum
Qualis ab incepto processerit, et sibi constet.

'Tis hard to venture where our betters fail,
Or lend fresh interest to a twice-told tale;
And yet, perchance, 'tis wiser to prefer
A hackney'd plot, than choose a new, and err;
Yet copy not too closely, but record,
More justly, thought for thought than word for word,
Nor trace your prototype through narrow ways,
But only follow where he merits praise.

> Difficile est proprie communia dicere;† tuque
> Rectius Iliacum carmen deducis in actus,
> Quam si proferres ignota indictaque primus.
> Publica materies privati juris erit, si
> Nec circa vilem patulumque moraberis orbem,
> Nec verbum verbo curabis reddere fidus
> Interpres, nec desilies imitator in arctum,
> Unde pedem proferre pudor vetet, aut operis lex.

† *"Difficile est proprie communia dicere."* — Mde. Dacier, Mde. de Sévigné, Boileau, and others, have left their dispute on the meaning of this passage in a tract considerably longer than the poem of Horace. It is printed at the close of the eleventh volume of Madame de Sévigné's Letters, edited by Grouvelle, Paris, 1806. Presuming that all who *can* construe may venture an opinion on such subjects, particularly as so many who can *not* have taken the same liberty, I should have held my "farthing candle" as awkwardly as another, had not my respect for the wits of Louis the Fourteenth's Augustan siècle induced me to subjoin these illustrious authorities. 1st, Boileau: "Il est difficile de traiter des sujets qui sont à la portée de tout le monde d'une manière qui vous les rende propres, ce qui s'appelle s'approprier un sujet par le tour qu'on y donne." 2dly, Batteux: "Mais il est bien difficile de donner des traits propres et individuels aux êtres purement possibles. 3dly, Dacier: "Il est difficile de traiter convenablement ces caractères que tout le monde peut inventer." Mde. de Sévigné's opinion and translation, consisting of some thirty pages, I omit, particularly as M. Grouvelle observes, "La chose est bien remarquable, aucune de ces diverses interprétations ne parait être la véritable." But, by way of comfort, it seems, fifty years afterwards, "Le lumineux Dumarsais" made his appearance, to set Horace on his legs again, "dissiper tous les nuages, et concilier tous les dissentimens;" and some fifty years hence, somebody, still more luminous, will doubtless start up and demolish Dumarsais and his system on this weighty affair, as if he were no better than Ptolemy and Tycho, or his comments of no more consequence than astronomical calculations on the present comet. I am happy to say, "la longueur de la dissertation" of M. D. prevents M. G. from saying any more on the matter. A better poet than Boileau, and at least as good a scholar as Sévigné, has said,

"A little learning is a dangerous thing."

And, by this comparison of comments, it may be perceived how a good deal may be rendered as perilous to the proprietors.

For you, young bard! whom luckless fate may lead
To tremble on the nod of all who read,
Ere your first score of cantos time unrolls,
Beware — for God's sake, don't begin like Bowles!*
"Awake a louder and a loftier strain,"
And pray, what follows from his boiling brain? —
He sinks to Southey's level in a trice,
Whose epic mountains never fail in mice!
Not so of yore awoke your mighty sire
The temper'd warblings of his master-lyre;

> Nec sic incipies, ut scriptor cyclicus olim:
> "Fortunam Priami cantabo, et nobile bellum."
> Quid dignum tanto foret hic promissor hiatu?
> Parturiunt montes: nascetur ridiculus mus.
> Quanto rectius hic, qui nil molitur inepte:
> "Dic mihi, Musa, virum, captæ post tempora Trojæ,

* About two years ago a young man, named Townsend, was announced by Mr. Cumberland (in a review since deceased) as being engaged in an epic poem to be entitled "Armageddon." The plan and specimen promise much; but I hope neither to offend Mr. Townsend, nor his friends, by recommending to his attention the lines of Horace to which these rhymes allude. If Mr. Townsend succeeds in his undertaking, as there is reason to hope, how much will the world be indebted to Mr. Cumberland for bringing him before the public! But, till that eventful day arrives, it may be doubted whether the premature display of his plan (sublime as the ideas confessedly are) has not, — by raising expectation too high, or diminishing curiosity, by developing his argument, — rather incurred the hazard of injuring Mr. Townsend's future prospects. Mr. Cumberland (whose talents I shall not depreciate by the humble tribute of my praise) and Mr. Townsend must not suppose me actuated by unworthy motives in this suggestion. I wish the author all the success he can wish himself, and shall be truly happy to see epic poetry weighed up from the bathos where it lies sunken with Southey, Cottle, Cowley (Mrs. or Abraham), Ogilvy, Wilkie, Pye, and all the "dull of past and present days." Even if he is not a *Milton*, he may be better than *Blackmore*; if not a *Homer*, an *Antimachus*. I should deem myself presumptuous, as a young man, in offering advice, were it not addressed to one still younger. Mr. Townsend has the greatest difficulties to encounter: but in conquering them he will find employment; in having conquered them, his reward. I know too well "the scribbler's scoff, the critic's contumely;" and I am afraid time will teach Mr. Townsend to know them better. Those who succeed, and those who do not, must bear this alike, and it is hard to say which have most of it. I trust that Mr. Townsend's share will be from envy; — he will soon know mankind well enough not to attribute this expression to malice.

Soft as the gentler breathing of the lute,
"Of man's first disobedience and the fruit"
He speaks, but, as his subject swells along,
Earth, heaven, and Hades echo with the song.
Still to the midst of things he hastens on,
As if we witness'd all already done;
Leaves on his path whatever seems too mean
To raise the subject, or adorn the scene;
Gives, as each page improves upon the sight,
Not smoke from brightness, but from darkness — light;
And truth and fiction with such art compounds,
We know not where to fix their several bounds.
If you would please the public, deign to hear
What soothes the many-headed monster's ear;
If your heart triumph when the hands of all
Applaud in thunder at the curtain's fall,
Deserve those plaudits — study nature's page,
And sketch the striking traits of every age;
While varying man and varying years unfold
Life's little tale, so oft, so vainly told.
Observe his simple childhood's dawning days,
His pranks, his prate, his playmates, and his plays;

Qui mores hominum multorum vidit et urbes."
Non fumum ex fulgore, sed ex fumo dare lucem
Cogitat, ut speciosa dehinc miracula promat,
Antiphaten, Scyllamque, et cum Cyclope Charybdim.
Nec reditum Diomedis ab interitu Meleagri,
Nec gemino bellum Trojanum orditur ab ovo.
Semper ad eventum festinat; et in medias res
Non secus ac notas, auditorem rapit, et quæ
Desperat tractata nitescere posse, relinquit:
Atque ita mentitur, sic veris falsa remiscet,
Primo ne medium, medio ne discrepet imum.

    Tu, quid ego et populus mecum desideret, audi.
Si plausoris eges aulæa manentis, et usque
Sessuri, donec cantor, Vos plaudite, dicat;
Ætatis cujusque notandi sunt tibi mores,
Mobilibusque decor naturis dandus et annis.
Reddere qui voces jam scit puer, et pede certo

Till time at length the mannish tyro weans,
And prurient vice outstrips his tardy teens!

Behold him Freshman! forced no more to groan
O'er Virgil's* devilish verses and — his own;
Prayers are too tedious, lectures too abstruse,
He flies from Tavell's frown to "Fordham's Mews;"
(Unlucky Tavell!** doom'd to daily cares
By pugilistic pupils, and by bears,)
Fines, tutors, tasks, conventions threat in vain,
Before hounds, hunters, and Newmarket plain.
Rough with his elders, with his equals rash,
Civil to sharpers, prodigal of cash;
Constant to nought — save hazard and a whore,
Yet cursing both — for both have made him sore;
Unread (unless, since books beguile disease,
The p—x becomes his passage to degrees);
Fool'd, pillaged, dunn'd, he wastes his term away,
And, unexpell'd perhaps, retires M. A.;
Master of arts! as *hells* and *clubs* † proclaim,
Where scarce a blackleg bears a brighter name!

> Signat humum; gestit paribus colludore, et iram
> Colligit ac ponit temere, et mutatur in horas.
>   Imberbis juvenis, tandem custode remoto,
> Gaudet equis canibusque, et aprici gramine campi;
> Cereus in vitium flecti, monitoribus asper,
> Utilium tardus provisor, prodigus æris,
> Sublimis, cupidusque, et amata relinquere pernix.

* Harvey, the *circulator* of the *circulation* of the blood, used to fling away Virgil in his ecstasy of admiration, and say, "the book had a devil." Now, such a character as I am copying would probably fling it away also, but rather wish that the devil had the book; not from dislike to the poet, but a well founded horror of hexameters. Indeed, the public school penance of "Long and Short" is enough to beget an antipathy to poetry for the residue of a man's life, and, perhaps, so far may be an advantage.

** "Infandum, regina, jubes renovare dolorem." I dare say Mr. Tavell (to whom I mean no affront) will understand me; and it is no matter whether any one else does or no. — To the above events, "quæque ipse miserrima vidi, et quorum pars magna fui," all *times* and *terms* bear testimony.

† "Hell," a gaming-house so called, where you risk little, and are

Launch'd into life, extinct his early fire,
He apes the selfish prudence of his sire;
Marries for money, chooses friends for rank,
Buys land, and shrewdly trusts not to the Bank;
Sits in the Senate; gets a son and heir;
Sends him to Harrow, for himself was there.
Mute, though he votes, unless when call'd to cheer,
His son's so sharp — he 'll see the dog a peer!

Manhood declines — age palsies every limb;
He quits the scene — or else the scene quits him;
Scrapes wealth, o'er each departing penny grieves,
And avarice seizes all ambition leaves;
Counts cent per cent, and smiles, or vainly frets,
O'er hoards diminish'd by young Hopeful's debts;
Weighs well and wisely what to sell or buy,
Complete in all life's lessons — but to die;
Peevish and spiteful, doting, hard to please,
Commending every time, save times like these;
Crazed, querulous, forsaken, half forgot,
Expires unwept — is buried — let him rot!

But from the Drama let me not digress,
Nor spare my precepts, though they please you less.

    Conversis studiis, ætas animusque virilis
Quærit opes et amicitias, inservit honori,
Commisisse cavet quod mox mutare laboret.
    Multa senem circumveniunt incommoda; vel quod
Quærit, et inventis miser abstinet, ac timet uti;
Vel quod res omnes timide gelideque ministrat,
Dilator, spe longus, iners, avidusque futuri;
Difficilis, querulus, laudator temporis acti
Se puero, castigator censorque minorum.
Multa ferunt anni venientes commoda secum,
Multa recedentes adimunt. Ne forte seniles
Mandentur juveni partes, pueroque viriles,
Semper in adjunctis, ævoque morabimur aptis.
    Aut agitur res in scenis, aut acta refertur.

cheated a good deal. "Club," a pleasant purgatory, where you lose more,
and are not supposed to be cheated at all

Though woman weep, and hardest hearts are stirr'd
When what is done is rather seen than heard,
Yet many deeds preserved in history's page,
Are better told than acted on the stage;
The ear sustains what shocks the timid eye,
And horror thus subsides to sympathy.
True Briton all beside, I here am French —
Bloodshed 'tis surely better to retrench;
The gladiatorial gore we teach to flow
In tragic scene disgusts, though but in show;
We hate the carnage while we see the trick,
And find small sympathy in being sick.
Not on the stage the regicide Macbeth
Appals an audience with a monarch's death;
To gaze when sable Hubert threats to sear
Young Arthur's eyes, can *ours* or *nature* bear?
A haltered heroine* Johnson sought to slay --
We saved Irene, but half damn'd the play,
And (Heaven be praised!) our tolerating times
Stint metamorphoses to pantomimes;
And Lewis' self, with all his sprites, would quake
To change Earl Osmond's negro to a snake!
Because, in scenes exciting joy or grief,
We loathe the action which exceeds belief:

> Segnius irritant animos demissa per aurem
> Quam quæ sunt oculis subjecta fidelibus, et quæ
> Ipse sibi tradit spectator. Non tamen intus
> Digna geri promes in scenam; multaque tolles
> Ex oculis, quæ mox narret facundia præsens.
> Ne pueros coram populo Medea trucidet,
> Aut humana palam coquat exta nefarius Atreus;
> Aut in avem Progne vertatur, Cadmus in anguem.
> Quodcunque ostendis mihi sic, incredulus odi.
> Neve minor, neu sit quinto productior actu
> Fabula, quæ posci vult, et spectata reponi:

---

* "Irene had to speak two lines with the bowstring round her neck;
but the audience cried out 'Murder!' and she was obliged to go off the stage
alive." — *Boswell's Johnson.*

And yet, God knows! what may not authors do,
Whose postscripts prate of dyeing "heroines blue?"*

 Above all things, *Dan* Poet, if you can,
Eke out your acts, I pray, with mortal man;
Nor call a ghost, unless some cursed scrape
Must open ten trap-doors for your escape.
Of all the monstrous things I'd fain forbid,
I loathe an opera worse than Dennis did;
Where good and evil persons, right or wrong,
Rage, love, and aught but moralise, in song.
Hail, last memorial of our foreign friends,
Which Gaul allows, and still Hesperia lends!
Napoleon's edicts no embargo lay
On whores, spies, singers wisely shipp'd away.
Our giant capital, whose squares are spread
Where rustics earn'd, and now may beg, their bread,
In all iniquity is grown so nice,
It scorns amusements which are not of price.
Hence the pert shopkeeper, whose throbbing ear
Aches with orchestras which he pays to hear,
Whom shame, not sympathy, forbids to snore,
His anguish doubling by his own "encore;"
Squeezed in "Fop's Alley," jostled by the beaux,
Teased with his hat, and trembling for his toes;
Scarce wrestles through the night, nor tastes of ease,
Till the dropp'd curtain gives a glad release:
Why this, and more, he suffers — can ye guess? —
Because it costs him dear, and makes him dress!

  Nec Deus intersit, nisi dignus vindice nodus
  Inciderit. * * * *

* In the postscript to the "Castle Spectre," Mr. Lewis tells us, that though blacks were unknown in England at the period of his action, yet he has made the anachronism to set off the scene: and if he could have produced the effect "by making his heroine blue," — I quote him — "blue he would have made her!"

So prosper eunuchs from Etruscan schools;
Give us but fiddlers, and they're sure of fools!
Ere scenes were play'd by many a reverend clerk *
(What harm, if David danced before the ark?)
In Christmas revels, simple country folks
Were pleased with morrice-mumm'ry and coarse jokes.
Improving years, with things no longer known,
Produced blithe Punch and merry Madame Joan,
Who still frisk on with feats so lewdly low,
'Tis strange Benvolio ** suffers such a show;
Suppressing peer! to whom each vice gives place,
Oaths, boxing, begging, — all, save rout and race.

Farce follow'd Comedy, and reach'd her prime
In ever-laughing Foote's fantastic time:
Mad wag! who pardon'd none, nor spared the best,
And turn'd some very serious things to jest.
Nor church nor state escaped his public sneers,
Arms nor the gown, priests, lawyers, volunteers:
"Alas, poor Yorick!" now for ever mute!
Whoever loves a laugh must sigh for Foote.

We smile, perforce, when histrionic scenes
Ape the swoln dialogue of kings and queens,
When "Chrononhotonthologos must die,"
And Arthur struts in mimic majesty.

Moschus! with whom once more I hope to sit
And smile at folly, if we can't at wit;
Yes, friend! for thee I'll quit my cynic cell,
And bear Swift's motto, "Vive la bagatelle!"

* "The first theatrical representations, entitled 'Mysteries and Mora-
lities,' were generally enacted at Christmas, by monks (as the only persons
who could read), and latterly by the clergy and students of the universities.
The dramatis personæ were usually Adam, Pater Cœlestis, Faith, Vice,"
&c. &c. — See *Warton's History of English Poetry.*

** Benvolio does not bet; but every man who maintains race-horses is
a promoter of all the concomitant evils of the turf. Avoiding to bet is a
little pharisaical. Is it an exculpation? I think not. I never yet heard a
bawd praised for chastity because *she herself* did not commit fornication.

Which charm'd our days in each Ægean clime,
As oft at home, with revelry and rhyme.
Then may Euphrosyne, who sped the past,
Soothe thy life's scenes, nor leave thee in the last;
But find in thine, like pagan Plato's bed,*
Some merry manuscript of mimes, when dead.

Now to the Drama let us bend our eyes,
Where fetter'd by whig Walpole low she lies;
Corruption foil'd her, for she fear'd her glance;
Decorum left her for an opera dance!
Yet Chesterfield,** whose polish'd pen inveighs
'Gainst laughter, fought for freedom to our plays;
Uncheck'd by megrims of patrician brains,
And damning dulness of lord chamberlains.
Repeal that act! again let Humour roam
Wild o'er the stage — we've time for tears at home;
Let "Archer" plant the horns on "Sullen's" brows,
And "Estifania" gull her "Copper"† spouse;
The moral's scant — but that may be excused,
Men go not to be lectured, but amused.
He whom our plays dispose to good or ill
Must wear a head in want of Willis' skill;
Ay, but Macheath's example — psha! — no more!
It form'd no thieves — the thief was form'd before;
And spite of puritans and Collier's curse,††
Plays make mankind no better, and no worse.
Then spare our stage, ye methodistic men!
Nor burn damn'd Drury if it rise again.

---

* Under Plato's pillow a volume of the *Mimes* of Sophron was found the day he died — *Vide* Barthélémi, De Pauw, or Diogenes Laërtius, if agreeable. De Pauw calls it a jest-book. Cumberland, in his Observer, terms it moral, like the sayings of Publius Syrus.

** His speech on the Licensing Act is one of his most eloquent efforts.

† Michael Perez, the "Copper Captain," in "Rule a Wife and have a Wife."

†† Jerry Collier's controversy with Congreve, &c. on the subject of the drama, is too well known to require further comment.

But why to brain-scorch'd bigots thus appeal?
Can heavenly mercy dwell with earthly zeal?
For times of fire and faggot let them hope!
Times dear alike to puritan or pope.
As pious Calvin saw Servetus blaze,
So would new sects on newer victims gaze.
E'en now the songs of Solyma begin;
Faith cants, perplex'd apologist of sin!
While the Lord's servant chastens whom he loves,
And Simeon * kicks, where Baxter only "shoves." **

Whom nature guides, so writes, that every dunce,
Enraptured, thinks to do the same at once;
But after inky thumbs and bitten nails,
And twenty scatter'd quires, the coxcomb fails.

Let Pastoral be dumb; for who can hope
To match the youthful eclogues of our Pope?
Yet his and Phillips' faults, of different kind,
For art too rude, for nature too refined,
Instruct how hard the medium 'tis to hit
'Twixt too much polish and too coarse a wit.

A vulgar scribbler, certes, stands disgraced
In this nice age, when all aspire to taste;
The dirty language, and the noisome jest,
Which pleased in Swift of yore, we now detest;

> Ex noto fictum carmen sequar, ut sibi quivis
> Speret idem: sudet multum, frustraque laboret
> Ausus idem: tantum series juncturaque pollet;
> Tantum de medio sumtis accedit honoris.
>   Silvis deducti caveant, me judice, Fauni,
> Ne velut innati triviis, ac pæne forenses,
> Aut nimium teneris juvenentur versibus unquam,
> Aut immunda crepent, ignominiosaque dicta.

* Mr. Simeon is the very bully of beliefs, and castigator of "good works." He is ably supported by John Stickles, a labourer in the same vineyard: — but I say no more, for, according to Johnny in full congregation, *"No hopes for them as laughs."*

** "Baxter's Shove to heavy-a—d Christians" — the veritable title of a book once in good repute, and likely enough to be so again.

Proscribed not only in the world polite,
But even too nasty for a city knight!

Peace to Swift's faults! his wit hath made them pass,
Unmatch'd by all, save matchless Hudibras!
Whose author is perhaps the first we meet,
Who from our couplet lopp'd two final feet;
Nor less in merit than the longer line,
This measure moves a favourite of the Nine.
Though at first view eight feet may seem in vain
Form'd, save in ode, to bear a serious strain,
Yet Scott has shown our wondering isle of late
This measure shrinks not from a theme of weight,
And, varied skilfully, surpasses far
Heroic rhyme, but most in love and war,
Whose fluctuations, tender or sublime,
Are curb'd too much by long-recurring rhyme.

But many a skilful judge abhors to see,
What few admire — irregularity.
This some vouchsafe to pardon; but 'tis hard
When such a word contents a British bard.

And must the bard his glowing thoughts confine,
Lest censure hover o'er some faulty line?

> Offenduntur enim, quibus est equus, et pater, et res:
> Nec, si quid fricti ciceris probat et nucis emtor,
> Æquis accipiunt animis, donantve corona.
> Syllaba longa brevi subjecta vocatur iambus,
> Pes citus: unde etiam trimetris accrescere jussit
> Nomen iambeis, cum senos redderet ictus,
> Primus ad extremum similis sibi: non ita pridem,
> Tardior ut paulo graviorque veniret ad aures,
> Spondeos stabiles in jura paterna recepit
> Commodus et patiens; non ut de sede secundâ
> Cederet aut quarta socialiter. Hic et in Acci
> Nobilibus trimetris apparet rarus, et Enni
> In scenam missos magno cum pondere versus,
> Aut operæ celeris nimium, curaque carentis,
> Aut ignoratæ premit artis crimine turpi.
> Non quivis videt immodulata poemata judex;
> Et data Romanis venia est indigna poetis.

Remove whate'er a critic may suspect,
To gain the paltry suffrage of "*correct?*"
Or prune the spirit of each daring phrase,
To fly from error, not to merit praise?

Ye, who seek finish'd models, never cease,
By day and night, to read the works of Greece.
But our good fathers never bent their brains
To heathen Greek, content with native strains.
The few who read a page, or used a pen,
Were satisfied with Chaucer and old Ben;
The jokes and numbers suited to their taste
Were quaint and careless, any thing but chaste;
Yet whether right or wrong the ancient rules,
It will not do to call our fathers fools!
Though you and I, who eruditely know
To separate the elegant and low,
Can also, when a hobbling line appears,
Detect with fingers, in default of ears.

In sooth I do not know, or greatly care
To learn, who our first English strollers were;
Or if, till roofs received the vagrant art,
Our Muse, like that of Thespis, kept a cart;
But this is certain, since our Shakspeare's days,
There's pomp enough, if little else, in plays;

Idcircono vager, scribamque licentor? an omnes
Visuros peccata putem mea; tutus, et intra
Spem veniæ cautus? vitavi denique culpam,
Non laudem merui. Vos exemplaria Græca
Nocturna versate manu, versate diurna.
At vestri proavi Plautinos et numeros et
Laudavere sales; nimium patienter utrumque,
Ne dicam stulte, mirati; si modo ego et vos
Scimus inurbanum lepido seponere dicto,
Legitimumque sonum digitis callemus et aure.
    Ignotum tragicæ genus invenisse Camœnæ
Dicitur, et plaustris voxisse poemata Thespis,
Quæ canerout agerontque peruncti fæcibus ora.
Post hunc personæ pallæque reportor honestæ

Nor will Melpomene ascend her throne
Without high heels, white plume, and Bristol stone.

Old comedies still meet with much applause,
Though too licentious for dramatic laws:
At least, we moderns, wisely, 'tis confest,
Curtail, or silence, the lascivious jest.

Whate'er their follies, and their faults beside,
Our enterprising bards pass nought untried;
Nor do they merit slight applause who choose
An English subject for an English muse,
And leave to minds which never dare invent
French flippancy and German sentiment.
Where is that living language which could claim
Poetic more, as philosophic, fame,
If all our bards, more patient of delay,
Would stop, like Pope, to polish by the way?

Lords of the quill, whose critical assaults
O'erthrow whole quartos with their quires of faults,
Who soon detect, and mark where'er we fail,
And prove our marble with too nice a nail!
Democritus himself was not so bad;
He only *thought*, but *you* would make, us mad!

> Æshylus, et modicis instravit pulpita tignis,
> Et docuit magnumque loqui, nitique cothurno.
>   Successit votus his comœdia, non sine multa
> Laude; sed in vitium libertas excidit, et vim
> Dignam lege regi: lex est accepta; chorusque
> Turpiter obticuit, sublato jure nocendi.
>   Nil intentatum nostri liquere poetæ;
> Nec minimum meruere decus, vestigia Græca
> Ausi deserere, et celebrare domestica facta;
> Vel qui prætextas, vel qui docuere togatas.
> Nec virtute foret clarisve potentius armis,
> Quam lingua, Latium, si non offenderet unum-
> quemque poetarum limæ labor, et mora. Vos, ô
> Pompilius sanguis, carmen reprehendite, quod non
> Multa dies et multa litura coercuit, atque
> Præsectum decies non castigavit ad unguem.
>   Ingenium misera quia fortunatius arte
> Credit, et excludit sanos Helicone poetas

But truth to say, most rhymers rarely guard
Against that ridicule they deem so hard;
In person negligent, they wear, from sloth,
Beards of a week, and nails of annual growth;
Reside in garrets, fly from those they meet,
And walk in alleys, rather than the street.

With little rhyme, less reason, if you please,
The name of poet may be got with ease,
So that not tuns of helleboric juice
Shall ever turn your head to any use;
Write but like Wordsworth, live beside a Lake,
And keep your bushy locks a year from Blake;*
Then print your book, once more return to town,
And boys shall hunt your bardship up and down.

Am I not wise, if such some poets' plight,
To purge in spring — like Bayes — before I write?
If this precaution soften'd not my bile,
I know no scribbler with a madder style;
But since (perhaps my feelings are too nice)
I cannot purchase fame at such a price,
I'll labour gratis as a grinder's wheel,
And, blunt myself, give edge to others' steel,
Nor write at all, unless to teach the art
To those rehearsing for the poet's part;

Democritus; bona pars non ungues ponere curat,
Non barbam: secreta petit loca, balnea vitat.
Nanciscetur enim pretium nomenque poetæ,
Si tribus Anticyris caput insanabile nunquam
Tonsori Licino commiserit. O ego lævus,
Qui purgor bilem sub verni temporis horam!
Non alius faceret meliora poemata: verum
Nil tanti est: ergo fungar vice cotis, acutum
Reddere quæ ferrum valet, exsors ipsa secandi:
Munus et officium, nil scribens ipse, docebo;

* As famous a tonsor as Licinus himself, and better paid, and may, like
him, be one day a senator, having a better qualification than one half of the
heads he crops, viz. — independence

From Horace show the pleasing paths of song,
And from my own example — what is wrong.

  Though modern practice sometimes differs quite,
'Tis just as well to think before you write;
Let every book that suits your theme be read,
So shall you trace it to the fountain-head.

  He who has learn'd the duty which he owes
To friends and country, and to pardon foes;
Who models his deportment as may best
Accord with brother, sire, or stranger guest;
Who takes our laws and worship as they are,
Nor roars reform for senate, church, and bar;
In practice, rather than loud precept, wise,
Bids not his tongue, but heart, philosophise;
Such is the man the poet should rehearse,
As joint exemplar of his life and verse.

  Sometimes a sprightly wit, and tale well told,
Without much grace, or weight, or art, will hold
A longer empire o'er the public mind
Than sounding trifles, empty, though refined.

> Unde parentur opes; quid alat formetque poetam;
> Quid deceat, quid non; quo virtus, quo ferat error.
>   Scribendi recte, sapere est et principium et fons.
> Rem tibi Socraticæ poterunt ostendere chartæ:
> Verbaque provisam rem non invita sequentur.
> Qui didicit patriæ quid debeat, et quid amicis;
> Quo sit amore parens, quo frater amandus, et hospos;
> Quod sit conscripti, quod judicis officium; quæ
> Partos in bellum missi ducis; ille profecto
> Reddere personæ scit convenientia cuique.
> Respicere exemplar vitæ morumque jubebo
> Doctum imitatorem, et vivas hinc ducere voces.
>   Interdum speciosa locis, morataque recte
> Fabula, nullius veneris, sine pondere et arte,
> Valdius oblectat populum, meliusque moratur,
> Quam versus inopes rerum nugæque canoræ.

Unhappy Greece! thy sons of ancient days
The muse may celebrate with perfect praise,
Whose generous children narrow'd not their hearts
With commerce, given alone to arms and arts.
Our boys (save those whom public schools compel
To "long and short" before they're taught to spell)
From frugal fathers soon imbibe by rote,
"A penny saved, my lad, 's a penny got.'"
Babe of a city birth! from sixpence take
The third, how much will the remainder make? —
"A groat." — "Ah, bravo! Dick hath done the sum!
He'll swell my fifty thousand to a plum."

They whose young souls receive this rust betimes,
'Tis clear, are fit for any thing but rhymes;
And Locke will tell you, that the father's right
Who hides all verses from his children's sight;
For poets (says this sage,* and many more,)
Make sad mechanics with their lyric lore;
And Delphi now, however rich of old,
Discovers little silver, and less gold,
Because Parnassus, though a mount divine,
Is poor as Irus,** or an Irish mine.†

    Graiis ingenium, Graiis dedit ore rotundo
    Musa loqui, præter laudem nullius avaris.
    Romani pueri longis rationibus assom
    Discunt in partes contum diducere: dicat
    Filius Albini, Si de quincunce remota est
    Uncia, quid superat? poterat dixisse — Triens. Eu!
    Rem poteris servare tuam. Redit uncia: quid fit?
    Semis. An hæc animos ærugo et cura peculi
    Cum semel imbuerit, speramus carmina fingi
    Posse linenda cedro, et levi servanda cupresso?

* I have not the original by me, but the Italian translation runs as follows: — "E una cosa a mio credere molto stravagante, che un padre
desideri, o permetta, che suo figliuolo coltivi o perfezioni questo talento."
A little further on: "Si trovano di rado nel Parnaso le miniere d' oro e d'
argento." — *Educazione dei Fanciulli del Signor Locke.*

** "Iro pauperior:" this is the same beggar who boxed with Ulysses
for a pound of kid's fry, which he lost, and half a dozen teeth besides. —
See *Odyssey.* b. 18.

† The Irish gold mine of Wicklow, which yields just ore enough to
swear by, or gild a bad guinea.

Two objects always should the poet move,
Or one or both, — to please or to improve.
Whate'er you teach, be brief, if you desigu
For our remembrance your didactic line;
Redundance places memory on the rack,
For brains may be o'erloaded, like the back.

Fiction does best when taught to look like truth,
And fairy fables bubble none but youth:
Expect no credit for too wondrous tales,
Since Jonas only springs alive from whales!

Young men with aught but elegance dispeuse;
Maturer years require a little sense.
To end at once: — that bard for all is fit
Who mingles well instruction with his wit;
For him reviews shall smile, for him o'erflow
The patronage of Paternoster-row;
His book, with Longman's liberal aid, shall pass
(Who ne'er despises books that bring him brass);
Through three long weeks the taste of London lead,
And cross St. George's Channel and the Tweed.

But every thing has faults, nor is't unknown
That harps and fiddles often lose their toue,

Aut prodesse volunt, aut delectare poetæ;
Aut simul et jucunda ot idonea dicore vitæ
Quidquid præcipies, esto brovis: ut cito dicta
Percipiant animi dociles, teneantque fideles.
Omne supervacuum pleno do pectore manat.
  Ficta voluptatis causa, sint proxima veris:
Nec, quodcunque volet, poscat sibi fabula crodi:
Neu pransæ Lamiæ vivum puerum extrahat alvo.
  Centuriæ seniorum agitant expertia frugis:
Celsi prætereunt austera poemata Rhamnes.
Omne tulit punctum, qui miscuit utile dulci,
Lectorem delectando, pariterque monendo.
Hic meret æra liber Sosiis; hic et mare transit,
Et longum noto scriptori prorogat ævum.
  Sunt delicta tamen, quibus ignovisse velimus;
Nam neque chorda sonum reddit quem vult manus et mens,

And wayward voices, at their owner's call,
With all his best endeavours, only squall;
Dogs blink their covey, flints withhold the spark,
And double-barrels (damn them!) miss their mark.*

Where frequent beauties strike the reader's view
We must not quarrel for a blot or two;
But pardon equally to books or men,
The slips of human nature, and the pen.

Yet if an author, spite of foe or friend,
Despises all advice too much to mend,
But ever twangs the same discordant string,
Give him no quarter, howsoe'er he sing.
Let Havard's ** fate o'ertake him, who, for once,
Produced a play too dashing for a dunce:
At first none deem'd it his; but when his name
Announced the fact — what then? — it lost its fame.
Though all deplore when Milton deigns to doze,
In a long work 'tis fair to steal repose.

> Poscentique gravem persæpe remittit acutum;
> Nec semper feriet quodcunque minabitur arcus.
> Verum ubi plura nitent in carmine, non ego paucis
> Offendar maculis, quas aut incuria fudit,
> Aut humana parum cavit natura.   Quid ergo?
> Ut scriptor si peccat idem librarius usque,
> Quamvis est monitus, venia caret; ut citharœdus
> Ridetur, chorda qui semper oberrat eadem:
> Sic mihi, qui multum cessat, fit Chœrilus ille,
> Quem bis terve bonum cum risu miror; et idem
> Indignor, quandoque bonus dormitat Homerus.
> Verum operi longo fas est obrepere somnum.

* As Mr. Pope took the liberty of damning Homer, to whom he was under great obligations — "*And Homer (damn him!) calls*" — it may be presumed that any body or any thing may be damned in verse by poetical license; and, in case of accident, I beg leave to plead so illustrious a pre-cedent.

** For the story of Billy Havard's tragedy, see "Davies's Life of Garrick." I believe it is "Regulus," or "Charles the First." The moment it was known to be his the theatre thinned, and the bookseller refused to give the customary sum for the copyright.

As pictures, so shall poems be; some stand
The critic eye, and please when near at hand;
But others at a distance strike the sight;
This seeks the shade, but that demands the light,
Nor dreads the connoisseur's fastidious view
But, ten times scrutinised, is ten times new.

Parnassian pilgrims! ye whom chance, or choice,
Hath led to listen to the Muse's voice,
Receive this counsel, and be timely wise;
Few reach the summit which before you lies.
Our church and state, our courts and camps, concede
Reward to very moderate heads indeed!
In these plain common sense will travel far;
All are not Erskines who mislead the bar:
But poesy between the best and worst
No medium knows; you must be last or first;
For middling poets' miserable volumes
Are damn'd alike by gods, and men, and columns.

Again, my Jeffrey! — as that sound inspires,
How wakes my bosom to its wonted fires!
Fires, such as gentle Caledonians feel
When Southrons writhe upon their critic wheel,
Or mild Eclectics*, when some, worse than Turks,
Would rob poor Faith to decorate "good works."

Ut pictura, poesis: erit quæ, si propius stes.
Te capiet magis; et quædam, si longius abstes:
Hæc amat obscurum; volet hæc sub luce videri,
Judicis argutum quæ non formidat acumen:
Hæc placuit semel; hæc decies repetita placebit.
O major juvenum, quamvis et voce paterna
Fingeris ad rectum, et per te sapis; hoc tibi dictum
Tolle memor: certis medium et tolerabile rebus
Recte concedi: consultus juris, et actor
Causarum mediocris abest virtute diserti
Messalæ, nec scit quantum Cascellius Aulus:
Set tamen in pretio est: mediocribus esse poetis
Non homines, non dî, non concessere columnæ.

* To the Eclectic or Christian Reviewers I have to return thanks for

Such are the genial feelings thou canst claim —
My falcon flies not at ignoble game.
Mightiest of all Dunedin's beasts of chase!
For thee my Pegasus would mend his pace.
Arise, my Jeffrey! or my inkless pen
Shall never blunt its edge on meaner men;
Till thee or thine mine evil eye discerns,
Alas! I cannot "strike at wretched kernes."
Inhuman Saxon! wilt thou then resign
A muse and heart by choice so wholly thine?
Dear, d—d contemner of my schoolboy songs,
Hast thou no vengeance for my manhood's wrongs?
If unprovoked thou once could bid me bleed,
Hast thou no weapon for my daring deed?
What! not a word! — and am I then so low?
Wilt thou forbear, who never spared a foe?

the fervour of that charity which, in 1809, induced them to express a hope that a thing then published by me might lead to certain consequences, which, although natural enough, surely came but rashly from reverend lips. I refer them to their own pages, where they congratulated themselves on the prospect of a tilt between Mr. Jeffrey and myself, from which some great good was to accrue, provided one or both were knocked on the head. Having survived two years and a half those "Elegies" which they were kindly preparing to review, I have no peculiar gusto to give them "so joyful a trouble," except, indeed, "upon compulsion, Hal;" but if, as David says in the "Rivals," it should come to "bloody sword and gun fighting," we "won't run, will we, Sir Lucius?" I do not know what I had done to these Eclectic gentlemen: my works are their lawful perquisite, to be hewn in pieces like Agag, if it seem meet unto them: but why they should be in such a hurry to kill off their author, I am ignorant. "The race is not always to the swift, nor the battle to the strong:" and now, as these Christians have "smote me on one cheek," I hold them up the other; and, in return for their good wishes, give them an opportunity of repeating them. Had any other set of men expressed such sentiments, I should have smiled, and left them to the "recording angel;" but from the pharisees of Christianity decency might be expected. I can assure these brethren, that, publican and sinner as I am, I would not have treated "mine enemy's dog thus." To show them the superiority of my brotherly love, if ever the Reverend Messrs. Simeon or Ramsden should be engaged in such a conflict as that in which they requested me to fall, I hope they may escape with being "winged" only, and that Heaviside may be at hand to extract the ball.

Hast thou no wrath, or wish to give it vent?
No wit for nobles, dunces by descent?
No jest on "minors," quibbles on a name,
Nor one facetious paragraph of blame?
Is it for this on Ilion I have stood,
And thought of Homer less than Holyrood?
On shore of Euxine or Ægean sea,
My hate, untravell'd, fondly turn'd to thee.
Ah! let me cease; in vain my bosom burns,
From Corydon unkind Alexis turns:*
Thy rhymes are vain; thy Jeffrey then forego,
Nor woo that anger which he will not show.
What then? — Edina starves some lanker son,
To write an article thou canst not shun;
Some less fastidious Scotchman shall be found,
As bold in Billingsgate, though less renown'd.

As if at table some discordant dish
Should shock our optics, such as frogs for fish;
As oil in lieu of butter men decry,
And poppies please not in a modern pie;
If all such mixtures then be half a crime,
We must have excellence to relish rhyme.
Mere roast and boil'd no epicure invites;
Thus poetry disgusts, or else delights.

Who shoot not flying rarely touch a gun:
Will he who swims not to the river run?
And men unpractised in exchanging knocks
Must go to Jackson ere they dare to box.

Ut gratas inter mensas symphonia discors,
Et crassum unguentum, et Sardo cum melle papaver
Offendunt, poterat duci quia cœna sine istis;
Sic animis natum inventumque poema juvandis,
Si paulum a summo decessit, vergit ad imum.
    Ludere qui nescit, campestribus abstinet armis,
Indoctusque pilæ, discive, trochive, quiescit,

* Invenies alium, si te hic fastidit Alexin.

Whate'er the weapon, cudgel, fist, or foil,
None reach expertness without years of toil;
But fifty dunces can, with perfect ease,
Tag twenty thousand couplets, when they please.
Why not? — shall I, thus qualified to sit
For rotten boroughs, never show my wit?
Shall I, whose fathers with the quorum sate,
And lived in freedom on a fair estate;
Who left me heir, with stables, kennels, packs,
To *all* their income, and to — *twice* its tax;
Whose form and pedigree have scarce a fault,
Shall I, I say, suppress my attic salt?

   Thus think "the mob of gentlemen;" but you,
Besides all this, must have some genius too.
Be this your sober judgment, and a rule,
And print not piping hot from Southey's school,
Who (ere another Thalaba appears),
I trust, will spare us for at least nine years.
And hark 'ye, Southey!* pray — but don't be vex'd —
Burn all your last three works — and half the next.

Ne spissæ risum tollant impune coronæ:
Qui nescit, versus tamen audet fingere! — Quid ni?
Liber et ingenuus præsertim census equestrem
Summam nummorum, vitioque remotus ab omni.
Tu nihil invita dicos facieave Minerva:
Id tibi judicium est, ea mens; si quid tamen olim
Scripseris, in Metii descendat judicis auros,
Et patris, et nostras, nonumque prematur in annum.

* Mr. Southey has lately tied another canistor to his tail in the "Curse
of Kchama," maugre the neglect of Madoc &c., and has in one instance had
a wonderful effect. A literary friend of mine, walking out one lovely
evening last summer, on the eleventh bridge of the Paddington canal, was
alarmed by the cry of "one in jeopardy;" he rushed along, collected a
body of Irish haymakers (supping on butter-milk in an adjacent paddock),
procured three rakes, one eel-spear, and a landing-net, and at last (horresco
referens) pulled out — his own publisher. The unfortunate man was gone
for ever, and so was a large quarto wherewith he had taken the leap, which
proved, on enquiry, to have been Mr. Southey's last work. Its "alacrity of
sinking" was so great, that it has never since been heard of; though some

> But why this vain advice? once published, books
> Can never be recall'd — from pastry-cooks!

> Membranis intus positis, delere licebit
> Quod non edideris; nescit vox missa reverti.

maintain that it is at this moment concealed at Alderman Birch's pastry premises, Cornhill. Be this as it may, the coroner's inquest brought in a verdict of "Felo de bibliopolâ" against a "quarto unknown;" and circumstantial evidence being since strong against the "Curse of Kehama" (of which the above words are an exact description), it will be tried by its peers next session, in Grub-street. — Arthur, Alfred, Davideis, Richard Cœur de Lion, Exodus, Exodia, Epigoniad, Calvary, Fall of Cambria, Siege of Acre, Don Roderick, and Tom Thumb the Great, are the names of the twelve jurors. The judges are Pye, Bowles, and the bellman of St. Sepulchre's. The same advocates, pro and con, will be employed as are now engaged in Sir F. Burdett's celebrated cause in the Scotch courts. The public anxiously await the result, and all *live* publishers will be subpœnaed as witnesses. — But Mr. Southey has published the "Curse of Kehama," — an inviting title to quibblers. By the bye, it is a good deal beneath Scott and Campbell, and not much above Southey, to allow the booby Ballantyne to entitle them, in the Edinburgh Annual Register (of which, by the bye, Southey is editor) "the grand poetical triumvirate of the day." But, on second thoughts, it can be no great degree of praise to be the one-eyed leaders of the blind, though they might as well keep to themselves "Scott's thirty thousand copies sold," which must sadly discomfit poor Southey's unsaleables. Poor Southey, it should seem, is the "Lepidus" of this poetical triumvirate. I am only surprised to see him in such good company.

> "Such things, we know, are neither rich nor rare,
> But wonder how the devil *he* came there."

The trio are well defined in the sixth proposition of Euclid: "Because, in the triangles DBC, ACB, DB is equal to AC, and BC common to both; the two sides DB, BC, are equal to the two AC, CB, each to each, and the angle DBC is equal to the angle ACB: therefore, the base DC is equal to the base AB, and the triangle DBC (Mr. Southey) is equal to the triangle ACB, the *less* to the *greater*, which is *absurd*," &c. — The editor of the Edinburgh Register will find the rest of the theorem hard by his stabling; he has only to cross the river; 'tis the first turnpike t'other side "Pons Asinorum." †

† This Latin has sorely puzzled the University of Edinburgh. Ballantyne said it meant the "Bridge of Berwick," but Southey claimed it as half English; Scott swore it was the "Brig o' Stirling;" he had just passed two King James's and a dozen Douglasses over it. At last it was decided by Joffrey, that it meant nothing more nor less than the "counter of Archy Constable's shop."

Though "Madoc," with "Pucelle,"* instead of punk,
May travel back to Quito — on a trunk!**

　　Orpheus, we learn from Ovid and Lempriere,
Led all wild beasts but women by the ear;
And had he fiddled at the present hour,
We'd seen the lions waltzing in the Tower;
And old Amphion, such were minstrels then,
Had built St. Paul's without the aid of Wren.
Verse too was justice, and the bards of Greece
Did more than constables to keep the peace;
Abolish'd cuckoldom with much applause,
Call'd county meetings, and enforced the laws,
Cut down crown influence with reforming scythes,
And served the church — without demanding tithes;
And hence, throughout all Hellas and the East,
Each poet was a prophet and a priest,
Whose old-establish'd board of joint controls
Included kingdoms in the cure of souls.

　　Next rose the martial Homer, Epic's prince,
And fighting's been in fashion ever since;

> Sylvestres homines sacer interpresque deorum
> Cædibus et victu fœdo deterruit Orpheus:
> Dictus ob hoc lenire tigres, rabidosque leones:
> Dictus et Amphion, Thebanæ conditor arcis,
> Saxa movere sono testudinis, et prece blanda
> Ducere quo vellet: fuit hæc sapientia quondam.
> Publica privatis secernere; sacra profanis;
> Concubitu prohibere vago; dare jura maritis;
> Oppida moliri; leges incidere ligno.
> Sic honor et nomen divinis vatibus atque
> Carminibus venit.　Post hos insignis Homerus

　* Voltaire's "Pucelle" is not quite so immaculate as Mr. Southey's "Joan of Arc," and yet I am afraid the Frenchman has both more truth and poetry too on his side — (they rarely go together) than our patriotic minstrel, whose first essay was in praise of a fanatical French strumpet, whose title of witch would be correct with the change of the first letter.
　** Like Sir Bland Burgess's "Richard;" the tenth book of which I read at Malta, on a trunk of Eyres, 19. Cockspur-street.　If this be doubted, I shall buy a portmanteau to quote from.

And old Tyrtæus, when the Spartans warr'd,
(A limping leader, but a lofty bard,)
Though wall'd Ithome had resisted long,
Reduced the fortress by the force of song.

When oracles prevail'd, in times of old,
In song alone Apollo's will was told.
Then if your verse is what all verse should be,
And gods were not ashamed on't, why should we?

The Muse, like mortal females, may be woo'd;
In turns she'll seem a Paphian, or a prude;
Fierce as a bride when first she feels affright,
Mild as the same upon the second night;
Wild as the wife of alderman or peer,
Now for his grace, and now a grenadier!
Her eyes beseem, her heart belies, her zone,
Ice in a crowd, and lava when alone.

If verse be studied with some show of art,
Kind Nature always will perform her part;
Though without genius, and a native vein
Of wit, we loathe an artificial strain —
Yet art and nature join'd will win the prize,
Unless they act like us and our allies.

The youth who trains to ride, or run a race,
Must bear privations with unruffled face,
Be call'd to labour when he thinks to dine,
And, harder still, leave wenching and his wine.

> Tyrtæusque mares animos in Martia bella
> Versibus exacuit; dictæ per carmina sortes:
> Et vitæ monstrata via est: et gratia regum
> Pieriis tentata modis: ludusque repertus,
> Et longorum operum finis: ne forte pudori
> Sit tibi Musa lyræ solers, et cantor Apollo.
>   Natura fieret laudabile carmen, an arte,
> Quæsitum est: ego nec studium sine divite vena,
> Nec rude quid prosit video ingenium: alterius sic
> Altera poscit opem res, et conjurat amice.
> Qui studet optatam cursu contingere metam,
> Multa tulit fecitque puer; sudavit, et alsit;
> Abstinuit Venere et vino: qui Pythia cantat

Ladies who sing, at least who sing at sight,
Have followed music through her farthest flight;
But rhymers tell you neither more nor less,
"I've got a pretty poem for the press;"
And that's enough; then write and print so fast; —
If Satan take the hindmost, who'd be last?
They storm the types, they publish, one and all,
They leap the counter, and they leave the stall.
Provincial maidens, men of high command,
Yea, baronets have ink'd the bloody hand!
Cash cannot quell them; Pollio play'd this prank,
(Then Phœbus first found credit in a bank!)
Not all the living only, but the dead,
Fool on, as fluent as an Orpheus' head;*
Damn'd all their days, they posthumously thrive —
Dug up from dust, though buried when alive!
Reviews record this epidemic crime,
Those Books of Martyrs to the rage for rhyme.
Alas! woe worth the scribbler! often seen
In Morning Post, or Monthly Magazine.
There lurk his earlier lays; but soon, hot-press'd,
Behold a quarto! — Tarts must tell the rest.
Then leave, ye wise, the lyre's precarious chords
To muse-mad baronets, or madder lords,
Or country Crispins, now grown somewhat stale,
Twin Doric minstrels, drunk with Doric ale!

Tibicen, didicit prius, extimuitque magistrum.
Nunc satis est dixisse: ego mira poemata pango:
Occupet extremum scabies; mihi turpe relinqui est,
Et, quod non didici, sane nescire fateri.

****

* "Tum quoque marmorea caput a cervice revulsum,
   Gurgite cum medio portans Œagrius Hebrus,
   Volveret Eurydicen vox ipsa, et frigida lingua;
   Ah, miseram Eurydicen! anima fugiente vocabat;
   Eurydicen toto referebant flumine ripæ." — *Georgio* IV. 523.

Hark to those notes, narcotically soft
The cobbler-laureats* sing to Capel Lofft!** ·
Till, lo! that modern Midas, as he hears,
Adds an ell growth to his egregious ears!

* I beg Nathaniel's pardon: he is not a cobbler; it is a tailor, but begged Capel Lofft to sink the profession in his preface to two pair of panta — psha! — of cantos, which he wished the public to try on; but the sieve of a patron let it out, and so far saved the expense of an advertisement to his country customers. — Merry's "Moorfields whine" was nothing to all this. The "Della Cruscans" were people of some education, and no profession; but these Arcadians ("Arcades ambo" — bumpkins both) send out their native nonsense without the smallest alloy, and leave all the shoes and smallclothes in the parish unrepaired, to patch up Elegies on Enclosures and Pæans to Gunpowder. Sitting on a shopboard, they describe fields of battle, when the only blood they ever saw was shed from the finger; and an "Essay on War" is produced by the ninth part of a "poet."

"And own that nine such poets made a Tate."

Did Nathan ever read that line of Pope? and if he did, why not take it as his motto?

** This well meaning gentleman has spoiled some excellent shoemakers, and been accessary to the poetical undoing of many of the industrious poor.' Nathaniel Bloomfield and his brother Bobby have set all Somersetshire singing; nor has the malady confined itself to one county. Pratt too (who once was wiser) has caught the contagion of patronage, and decoyed a poor fellow named Blackett into poetry; but he died during the operation, leaving one child and two volumes of "Remains" utterly destitute. The girl, if she don't take a poetical twist, and come forth as a shoemaking Sappho, may do well; but the "tragedies" are as rickety as if they had been the offspring of an Earl or a Seatonian prize poet. The patrons of this poor lad are certainly answerable for his end; and it ought to be an indictable offence. But this is the least they have done; for, by a refinement of barbarity, they have made the (late) man posthumously ridiculous, by printing what he would have had sense enough never to print himself. Cortes these rakers of "Remains" come under the statute against "resurrection men." What does it signify whether a poor dear dead dunce is to be stuck up in Surgeons' or in Stationers' Hall? Is it so bad to unearth his bones as his blunders? Is it not better to gibbet his body on a heath, than his soul in an octavo? "We know what we are, but we know not what we may be;" and it is to be hoped we never shall know, if a man who has passed through life with a sort of éclat, is to find himself a mountebank on the other side of Styx, and made, like poor Joe Blackett, the laughing-stock of purgatory. The plea of publication is to provide for the child; now, might not some of this "Sutor ultra Crepidam's" friends and seducers have done a decent action without inveigling Pratt into biography? And then his inscription split into so many modicums! — "To the Duchess of

There lives one druid, who prepares in time
'Gainst future feuds his poor revenge of rhyme;
Racks his dull memory, and his duller muse,
To publish faults which friendship should excuse.
If friendship's nothing, self-regard might teach
More polish'd usage of his parts of speech.
But what is shame, or what is aught to him?
He vents his spleen, or gratifies his whim.
Some fancied slight has roused his lurking hate,
Some folly cross'd, some jest, or some debate;
Up to his den Sir Scribbler hies, and soon
The gather'd gall is voided in lampoon.
Perhaps at some pert speech you've dared to frown,
Perhaps your poem may have pleased the town:
If so, alas! 'tis nature in the man —
May Heaven forgive you, for he never can!
Then be it so; and may his withering bays
Bloom fresh in satire, though they fade in praise!
While his lost songs no more shall steep and stink,
The dullest, fattest weeds on Lethe's brink,
But springing upwards from the sluggish mould,
Be (what they never were before) be — sold!
Should some rich bard (but such a monster now,
In modern physics, we can scarce allow),
Should some pretending scribbler of the court,
Some rhyming peer — there's plenty of the sort* —

Somuch, the Right Hon. So-and-So, and Mrs. and Miss Somebody, these
volumes are &c. &c." — why, this is doling out the "soft milk of dedication" in gills, — there is but a quart, and he divides it among a dozen.
Why, Pratt, hadst thou not a puff left? Dost thou think six families of
distinction can share this in quiet? There is a child, a book, and a dedication: send the girl to her grace, the volumes to the grocer, and the dedication to the devil.

    * Here will Mr. Gifford allow me to introduce once more to his notice
the sole survivor, the "ultimus Romanorum," the last of the Cruscanti! —
"Edwin" the "profound," by our Lady of Punishment! here he is, as lively
as in the days of "well said Bavind the Correct." I thought Fitzgerald had
been the tail of poesy; but, alas! he is only the penultimate.

All but one poor dependent priest withdrawn
(Ah! too regardless of his chaplain's yawn!)
Condemn the unlucky curate to recite
Their last dramatic work by candle-light,
How would the preacher turn each rueful leaf,
Dull as his sermons, but not half so brief!
Yet, since 'tis promised at the rector's death,
He'll risk no living for a little breath.
Then spouts and foams, and cries at every line,
(The Lord forgive him!) "Bravo! grand! divine!"
Hoarse with those praises (which, by flatt'ry fed,
Dependence barters for her bitter bread,)
He strides and stamps along with creaking boot,
Till the floor echoes his emphatic foot;
Then sits again, then rolls his pious eye,
As when the dying vicar will not die!
Nor feels, forsooth, emotion at his heart; —
But all dissemblers overact their part.

A FAMILIAR EPISTLE TO THE EDITOR OF THE MORNING CHRONICLE.

"What reams of paper, floods of ink,"
  Do some men spoil, who never think!
And so perhaps you 'll say of me,
  In which your readers may agree.
Still I write on, and tell you why;
  Nothing 's so bad, you can't deny,
But may instruct or entertain
  Without the risk of giving pain, &c. &c.

ON SOME MODERN QUACKS AND REFORMISTS.

In tracing of the human mind
    Through all its various courses,
Though strange, 'tis true, we often find
    It knows not its recources:

And men through life assume a part
    For which no talents they possess,
Yet wonder that, with all their art,
    They meet no better with success, &c. &c.

Ye, who aspire to "build the lofty rhyme,"
Believe not all who laud your false "sublime;"
But if some friend shall hear your work, and say,
"Expunge that stanza, lop that line away,"
And, after fruitless efforts, you return
Without amendment, and he answers, "Burn!"
That instant throw your paper in the fire,
Ask not his thoughts, or follow his desire;
But (if true bard!) you scorn to condescend,
And will not alter what you can't defend,
If you will breed this bastard of your brains,* —
We'll have no words —.I've only lost my pains.

Yet, if you only prize your favourite thought,
As critics kindly do, and authors ought;
If your cool friend annoy you now and then,
And cross whole pages with his plaguy pen;
No matter, throw your ornaments aside, —
Better let him than all the world deride.
Give light to passages too much in shade,
Nor let a doubt obscure one verse you've made;
Your friend's "a Johnson," not to leave one word,
However trifling, which may seem absurd;

                    — Si carmina condes,
Nunquam te fallant anima sub vulpe latentos.
Quintilio si quid recitares, Corrige, sodes,
Hoc (aiebat) et hoc: melius te posse negaros,
Bis terque expertum frustra, delere jubebat,
Et male tornatos incudi reddere versus.
Si defendere delictum quam vertere malles,
Nullum ultra verbum, aut operam insumebat inanem,
Quin sine rivali teque et tua solus amares.
    Vir bonus et prudens versus reprehendet inortes:
Culpabit duros; incomptis allinet atrum
Transverso calamo signum; ambitiosa recidet
Ornamenta; parum claris lucem dare coget;
Arguet ambigue dictum; mutanda notabit;
Flet Aristarchus: nec dicet, Cur ego amicum

* "Bastard of your brains." — Minerva being the first by Jupiter's
headpiece, and a variety of equally unaccountable parturitions upon earth,
such as Madoc, &c. &c. &c.

Such erring trifles lead to serious ills,
And furnish food for critics,* or their quills.

As the Scotch fiddle, with its touching tune,
Or the sad influence of the angry moon,
All men avoid bad writers' ready tongues,
As yawning waiters fly** Fitzscribble's lungs;
Yet on he mouths — ten minutes — tedious each
As prelate's homily, or placeman's speech;
Long as the last years of a lingering lease,
When riot pauses until rents increase.
While such a minstrel, muttering fustian, strays
O'er hedge and ditch, through unfrequented ways,
If by some chance he walks into a well,
And shouts for succour with stentorian yell,
"A rope! help, Christians, as ye hope for grace!"
Nor woman, man, nor child will stir a pace;
For there his carcass he might freely fling,
From frenzy, or the humour of the thing.
Though this has happen'd to more bards than one;
I'll tell you Budgell's story, — and have done.

»Budgell, a rogue and rhymester, for no good,
(Unless his case be much misunderstood)

> Offendam in nugis? hæ nugæ seria ducent
> In mala derisum semel exceptumque sinistre.
>   Ut mala quem scabies aut morbus regius urget,
> Aut fanaticus error et iracunda Diana,
> Vesanum tetigisse timent fugiuntque poetam,
> Qui sapiunt; agitant pueri, incautique sequuntur.
> Hic dum sublimes versus ructatur, et errat
> Si veluti merulis intentus decidit auceps
> In puteum, foveamve; licet, Succurrite, longum
> Clamet, Io cives! non sit qui tollere curet.
> Si quis curet opem ferre, et demittere funem,
> Qui scis an prudens huc se dejecerit, atque
> Servari nolit? Dicam: Siculique poetæ

---

* "A crust for the critics." — *Bayes, in the "Rehearsal."*
** And the "waiters" are the only fortunate people who can "fly" from them; all the rest, viz. the sad subscribers to the "Literary Fund," being compelled, by courtesy, to sit out the recitation without a hope of exclaiming, "Sic" (that is, by choking Fitz with bad wine, or worse poetry) "me servavit Apollo!"

When teased with creditors' continual claims,
"To die like Cato,"* leapt into the Thames!
And therefore be it lawful through the town
For any bard to poison, hang, or drown.
Who saves the intended suicide receives
Small thanks from him who loathes the life he leaves;
And, sooth to say, mad poets must not lose
The glory of that death they freely choose.

   Nor is it certain that some sorts of verse
Prick not the poet's conscience as a curse;
Dosed** with vile drams on Sunday he was found,
Or got a child on consecrated ground!
And hence is haunted with a rhyming rage —
Fear'd like a bear just bursting from his cage.
If free, all fly his versifying fit,
Fatal at once to simpleton or wit.
But *him*, unhappy! whom he seizes, — *him*
He flays with recitation limb by limb;
Probes to the quick where'er he makes his breach,
And gorges like a lawyer — or a leech.

        Narrabo interitum. Deus immortalis haberi
        Dum cupit Empedocles, ardentem frigidus Ætnam
        Insiluit: sit jus liceatque perire poetis:
        Invitum qui servat, idem facit occidenti.
        Nec semel hoc fecit; nec, si retractus erit, jam
        Fiet homo, et ponet famosæ mortis amorem.
        Nec satis apparet cur versus factitet: utrum
        Minxerit in patrios cineres, an triste bidental
        Moverit incestus: certe furit, ac velut ursus,
        Objectos caveæ valuit si frangere clathros,
        Indoctum doctumque fugat recitator acerbus.
        Quem vero arripuit, tenet, occiditque legendo,
        Non missura cutem, nisi plenat cruoris, hirudo.

   * On his table were found these words: "*What Cato did, and Addison
approved, cannot be wrong.*" But Addison did not "approve;" and if he
had, it would not have mended the matter. He had invited his daughter
on the same water-party; but Miss Budgell, by some accident, escaped this
last paternal attention. Thus fell the sycophant of "Atticus," and the
enemy of Pope!
   ** If "dosed with," &c. be censured as low, I beg leave to refer to the
original for something still lower; and if any reader will translate "Minxerit
in patrios cineres," &c. into a decent couplet, I will insert said couplet in
lieu of the present.

THE
CURSE OF MINERVA.

—— "Pallas te hoc vulnere, Pallas
Immolat, et pœnam scelerato ex sanguine sumit."

Æneid. lib. xii.

THE CURSE OF MINERVA.

———

Athens, Capuchin Convent, March 17. 1811.

Slow sinks, more lovely ere his race be run,
Along Morea's hills the setting sun;
Not, as in northern climes, obscurely bright,
But one unclouded blaze of living light;
O'er the hush'd deep the yellow beam he throws,
Gilds the green wave that trembles as it glows;
On old Ægina's rock and Hydra's isle
The god of gladness sheds his parting smile;
O'er his own regions lingering loves to shine,
Though there his altars are no more divine.
Descending fast, the mountain-shadows kiss
Thy glorious gulf, unconquer'd Salamis!
Their azure arches through the long expanse,
More deeply purpled, meet his mellowing glance,
And tenderest tints, along their summits driven,
Mark his gay course, and own the hues of heaven;
Till, darkly shaded from the land and deep,
Behind his Delphian rock he sinks to sleep.

On such an eve his palest beam he cast
When, Athens! here thy wisest look'd his last.
How watch'd thy better sons his farewell ray,
That closed their murder'd sage's* latest day!

* Socrates drank the hemlock a short time before sunset (the hour of execution), notwithstanding the entreaties of his disciples to wait till the sun went down.

Not yet — not yet — Sol pauses on the hill,
The precious hour of parting lingers still;
But sad his light to agonising eyes,
And dark the mountain's once delightful dyes;
Gloom o'er the lovely land he seem'd to pour,
The land where Phœbus never frown'd before;
But ere he sunk below Citheron's head,
The cup of woe was quaff'd — the spirit fled;
The soul of him that scorn'd to fear or fly,
Who lived and died as none can live or die.

But, lo! from high Hymettus to the plain
The queen of night asserts her silent reign;*
No murky vapour, herald of the storm,
Hides her fair face, or girds her glowing form.
With cornice glimmering as the moonbeams play,
There the white column greets her grateful ray,
And bright around, with quivering beams beset,
Her emblem sparkles o'er the minaret:
The groves of olive scatter'd dark and wide,
Where meek Cephisus sheds his scanty tide,
The cypress saddening by the sacred mosque,
The gleaming turret of the gay kiosk,**
And sad and sombre mid the holy calm,
Near Theseus' fane, yon solitary palm;
All, tinged with varied hues, arrest the eye;
And dull were his that pass'd them heedless by.

Again the Ægean, heard no more afar,
Lulls his chafed breast from elemental war;

* The twilight in Greece is much shorter than in our own country;
the days in winter are longer, but in summer of less duration.
** The kiosk is a Turkish summer-house; the palm is without the present walls of Athens, not far from the temple of Theseus, between which
and the tree the wall intervenes. Cephisus' stream is indeed scanty, and
Ilissus has no stream at all.

Again his waves in milder tints unfold
Their long expanse of sapphire and of gold,
Mix'd with the shades of many a distant isle,
That frown, where gentler ocean deigns to smile.

As thus, within the walls of Pallas' fane,
I mark'd the beauties of the land and main,
Alone, and friendless, on the magic shore,
Whose arts and arms but live in poets' lore;
Oft as the matchless dome I turn'd to scan,
Sacred to gods, but not secure from man,
The past return'd, the present seem'd to cease,
And Glory knew no clime beyond her Greece!

Hours roll'd along, and Dian's orb on high
Had gain'd the centre of her softest sky;
And yet unwearied still my footsteps trod
O'er the vain shrine of many a vanish'd god:
But chiefly, Pallas! thine; when Hecate's glare,
Check'd by thy columns, fell more sadly fair
O'er the chill marble, where the startling tread
Thrills the lone heart like echoes from the dead.
Long had I mused, and treasured every trace
The wreck of Greece recorded of her race,
When, lo! a giant form before me strode,
And Pallas hail'd me in her own abode!

Yes, 'twas Minerva's self; but ah! how changed
Since o'er the Dardan field in arms she ranged!
Not such as erst, by her divine command,
Her form appear'd from Phidias' plastic hand:
Gone were the terrors of her awful brow,
Her idle ægis bore no Gorgon now;
Her helm was dinted, and the broken lance
Seem'd weak and shaftless e'en to mortal glance;

The olive branch, which still she deign'd to clasp,
Shrunk from her touch, and wither'd in her grasp;
And, ah! though still the brightest of the sky,
Celestial tears bedimm'd her large blue eye;
Round the rent casque her owlet circled slow,
And mourn'd his mistress with a shriek of woe!

"Mortal!"—'twas thus she spake—"that blush of shame
Proclaims thee Briton, once a noble name;
First of the mighty, foremost of the free,
Now honour'd *less* by all, and *least* by me:
Chief of thy foes shall Pallas still be found.
Seek'st thou the cause of loathing? — look around.
Lo! here, despite of war and wasting fire,
I saw successive tyrannies expire.
'Scaped from the ravage of the Turk and Goth,
Thy country sends a spoiler worse than both.
Survey this vacant, violated fane;
Recount the relics torn that yet remain:
These Cecrops placed, *this* Pericles adorn'd,*
That Adrian rear'd when drooping Science mourn'd.
What more I owe let gratitude attest —
Know, Alaric and Elgin did the rest.
That all may learn from whence the plunderer came,
The insulted wall sustains his hated name:
For Elgin's fame thus grateful Pallas pleads,
Below, his name — above, behold his deeds!
Be ever hail'd with equal honour here
The Gothic monarch and the Pictish peer:
Arms gave the first his right, the last had none,
But basely stole what less barbarians won.

* This is spoken of the city in general, and not of the Acropolis in
particular. The temple of Jupiter Olympius, by some supposed the Pantheon, was finished by Hadrian; sixteen columns are standing, of the most
beautiful marble and architecture.

So when the lion quits his fell repast,
Next prowls the wolf, the filthy jackal last:
Flesh, limbs, and blood the former make their own,
The last poor brute securely gnaws the bone.
Yet still the gods are just, and crimes are cross'd:
See here what Elgin won, and what he lost!
Another name with *his* pollutes my shrine:
Behold where Dian's beams disdain to shine!
Some retribution still might Pallas claim,
When Venus half avenged Minerva's shame." *

She ceased awhile, and thus I dared reply,
To soothe the vengeance kindling in her eye:
"Daughter of Jove! in Britain's injured name,
A true-born Briton may the deed disclaim.
Frown not on England; England owns him not:
Athena, no! thy plunderer was a Scot.
Ask'st thou the difference? From fair Phyle's towers
Survey Bœotia; — Caledonia's ours.
And well I know within that bastard land **
Hath Wisdom's goddess never held command;
A barren soil, where Nature's germs, confined
To stern sterility, can stint the mind;
Whose thistle well betrays the niggard earth,
Emblem of all to whom the land gives birth;
Each genial influence nurtured to resist;
A land of meanness, sophistry, and mist.
Each breeze from foggy mount and marshy plain
Dilutes with drivel every drizzly brain,
Till, burst at length, each wat'ry head o'erflows,
Foul as their soil, and frigid as their snows.

* His lordship's name, and that of one who no longer bears it, are
carved conspicuously on the Partheon; above, in a part not far distant, are
the torn remnants of the basso relievos, destroyed in a vain attempt to remove them.
** "Irish bastards," according to Sir Callaghan O'Brallaghan.

Then thousand schemes of petulance and pride
Despatch her scheming children far and wide :
Some east, some west, some every where but north,
In quest of lawless gain, they issue forth.
And thus — accursed be the day and year! —
She sent a Pict to play the felon here.
Yet Caledonia claims some native worth,
As dull Bœotia gave a Pindar birth;
So may her few, the letter'd and the brave,
Bound to no clime, and victors of the grave,
Shake off the sordid dust of such a land,
And shine like children of a happier strand;
As once, of yore, in some obnoxious place,
Ten names (if found) had saved a wretched race."

    "Mortal!" the blue-eyed maid resumed, "once more
Bear back my mandate to thy native shore.
Though fallen, alas! this vengeance yet is mine,
To turn my counsels far from lands like thine.
Hear then in silence Pallas' stern behest;
Hear and believe, for Time will tell the rest.

    "First on the head of him who did this deed
My curse shall light, — on him and all his seed
Without one spark of intellectual fire,
Be all the sons as senseless as the sire :
If one with wit the parent brood disgrace,
Believe him bastard of a brighter race :
Still with his hireling artists let him prate,
And folly's praise repay for Wisdom's hate;
Long of their patron's gusto let them tell,
Whose noblest, *native* gusto is — to sell :
To sell, and make — may Shame record the day! —
The state receiver of his pilfer'd prey.
Meantime, the flattering, feeble dotard, West,
Europe's worst dauber, and poor Britain's best,

With palsied hand shall turn each model o'er,
And own himself an infant of fourscore.*
Be all the bruisers cull'd from all St. Giles'
That art and nature may compare their styles;
While brawny brutes in stupid wonder stare,
And marvel at his lordship's 'stone shop'** there.
Round the throng'd gate shall sauntering coxcombs creep,
To lounge and lucubrate, to prate and peep;
While many a languid maid, with longing sigh,
On giant statues casts the curious eye;
The room with transient glance appears to skim,
Yet marks the mighty back and length of limb;
Mourns o'er the difference of *now* and *then*;
Exclaims, 'These Greeks indeed were proper men!'
Draws sly comparisons of *these* with *those*,
And envies Laïs all her Attic beaux.
When shall a modern maid have swains like these!
Alas! Sir Harry is no Hercules!
And last of all, amidst the gaping crew,
Some calm spectator, as he takes his view,
In silent indignation mix'd with grief,
Admires the plunder, but abhors the thief.
Oh, loathed in life, nor pardon'd in the dust,
May hate pursue his sacrilegious lust!
Link'd with the fool that fired the Ephesian dome,
Shall vengeance follow far beyond the tomb,
And Eratostratus and Elgin shine
In many a branding page and burning line;
Alike reserved for aye to stand accurs'd,
Perchance the second blacker than the first.

---

* Mr. West, on seeing the "Elgin Collection" (I suppose we shall hear of the "Abershaw" and "Jack Shephard" collection), declared himself "a mere tyro" in art.

** Poor Crib was sadly puzzled when the marbles were first exhibited at Elgin House: he asked if it was not "a stone shop?" — He was right; it is a shop.

"So let him stand, through ages yet unborn,
Fix'd statue on the pedestal of Scorn;
Though not for him alone revenge shall wait,
But fits thy country for her coming fate:
Hers were the deeds that taught her lawless son
To do what oft Britannia's self had done.
Look to the Baltic — blazing from afar,
Your old ally yet mourns perfidious war.
Not to such deeds did Pallas lend her aid,
Or break the compact which herself had made;
Far from such councils, from the faithless field
She fled — but left behind her Gorgon shield;
A fatal gift that turn'd your friends to stone,
And left lost Albion hated and alone.

"Look to the East, where Ganges' swarthy race
Shall shake your tyrant empire to its base;
Lo! there Rebellion rears her ghastly head,
And glares the Nemesis of native dead;
Till Indus rolls a deep purpureal flood,
And claims his long arrear of northern blood.
So may ye perish! — Pallas, when she gave
Your free-born rights, forbade ye to enslave.

"Look on your Spain! — she clasps the hand she hates,
But boldly clasps, and thrusts you from her gates.
Bear witness, bright Barossa! thou canst tell
Whose were the sons that bravely fought and fell.
But Lusitania, kind and dear ally,
Can spare a few to fight, and sometimes fly.
Oh glorious field! by Famine fiercely won,
The Gaul retires for once, and all is done!
But when did Pallas teach, that one retreat
Retrieved three long olympiads of defeat?

"Look last at home — ye love not to look there;
On the grim smile of comfortless despair:

Your city saddens: loud though Revel howls,
Here Famine faints, and yonder Rapine prowls.
See all alike of more or less bereft;
No misers tremble when there's nothing left.
'Blest paper credit'*; who shall dare to sing?
It clogs like lead Corruption's weary wing.
Yet Pallas pluck'd each premier by the ear,
Who gods and men alike disdain'd to hear;
But one, repentant o'er a bankrupt state,
On Pallas calls, — but calls, alas! too late:
Then raves for * *; to that Mentor bends,
Though he and Pallas never yet were friends.
Him senates hear, whom never yet they heard,
Contemptuous once, and now no less absurd.
So, once of yore, each reasonable frog
Swore faith and fealty to his sovereign 'log.'
Thus hail'd your rulers their patrician clod,
As Egypt chose an onion for a god.

"Now fare ye well! enjoy your little hour;
Go, grasp the shadow of your vanish'd power;
Gloss o'er the failure of each fondest scheme;
Your strength a name, your bloated wealth a dream.
Gone is that gold, the marvel of mankind,
And pirates barter all that's left behind.†
No more the hirelings, purchased near and far,
Crowd to the ranks of mercenary war.
The idle merchant on the useless quay
Droops o'er the bales no bark may bear away;
Or, back returning, sees rejected stores
Rot piecemeal on his own encumber'd shores:
The starved mechanic breaks his rusting loom,
And desperate mans him 'gainst the coming doom.

---

*   "Blest paper credit! last and best supply,
           That lends Corruption lighter wings to fly!" — Pope.
† The Deal and Dover traffickers in specie.

Then in the senate of your sinking state
Show me the man whose counsels may have weight.
Vain is each voice where tones could once command;
E'en factions cease to charm a factious land:
Yet jarring sects convulse a sister isle,
And light with maddening hands the mutual pile.

" 'Tis done, 'tis past, since Pallas warns in vain;
The Furies seize her abdicated reign:
Wide o'er the realm they wave their kindling brands,
And wring her vitals with their fiery hands.
But one convulsive struggle still remains,
And Gaul shall weep ere Albion wear her chains.
The banner'd pomp of war, the glittering files,
O'er whose gay trappings stern Bellona smiles;
The brazen trump, the spirit-stirring drum,
That bid the foe defiance ere they come;
The hero bounding at his country's call,
The glorious death that consecrates his fall,
Swell the young heart with visionary charms,
And bid it antedate the joys of arms.
But know, a lesson you may yet be taught,
With death alone are laurels cheaply bought:
Not in the conflict Havoc seeks delight,
His day of mercy is the day of fight.
But when the field is fought, the battle won,
Though drench'd with gore, his woes are but begun:
His deeper deeds as yet ye know by name;
The slaughter'd peasant and the ravish'd dame,
The rifled mansion and the foe-reap'd field,
Ill suit with souls at home, untaught to yield.
Say with what eye along the distant down
Would flying burghers mark the blazing town?
How view the column of ascending flames
Shake his red shadow o'er the startled Thames?

22*

Nay, frown not, Albion! for the torch was thine
That lit such pyres from Tagus to the Rhine:
Now should they burst on thy devoted coast,
Go, ask thy bosom who deserves them most.
The law of heaven and earth is life for life,
And she who raised, in vain regrets, the strife."

THE WALTZ;

AN APOSTROPHIC HYMN.

———

"Qualis in Eurotæ ripis, aut per juga Cynthi,
Exercet Diana choros." VIRGIL.

"Such on Eurotas' banks, or Cynthia's height,
Diana seems: and so she charms the sight,
When in the dance the graceful goddess leads
The quire of nymphs, and overtops their heads."
DRYDEN'S VIRGIL.

———

TO THE PUBLISHER.

Sir,

I am a country gentleman of a midland county. I might have been a parliament-man for a certain borough; having had the offer of as many votes as General T. at the general election in 1812.* But I was all for domestic happiness; as, fifteen years ago, on a visit to London, I married a middle-aged maid of honour. We lived happily at Hornem Hall till last season, when my wife and I were invited by the Countess of Waltzaway (a distant relation of my spouse) to pass the winter in town. Thinking no harm, and our girls being come to a marriageable (or, as they call it, *marketable*) age, and having besides a Chancery suit inveterately entailed upon the family estate, we came up in our old chariot, — of which, by the bye, my wife grew so much ashamed in less than a week, that I was obliged to buy a second-hand barouche, of which I might mount the box, Mrs. H. says, if I could drive, but never see the inside — that place being reserved for the Honourable Augustus Tiptoe, her partner-general and opera-knight. Hearing great praises of Mrs. H.'s dancing (she was famous for birthnight minuets in the latter end of the last century), I unbooted, and went to a ball at the Countess's, expecting to see a country dance, or, at most, cotillions, reels, and all the old paces to the newest tunes. But, judge of my surprise, on arriving, to see poor dear Mrs. Hornem with her arms half round the loins of a huge hussar-looking gentleman I never set eyes on before; and his, to say truth, rather more than half round her waist, turning round, and round, and round, to a d—d see-saw up-and-down sort of tune, that reminded me of

* State of the poll (last day), 5.

the "Black joke," only more "*affettuoso*," till it made me quite
giddy with wondering they were not so. By-and-by they
stopped a bit, and I thought they would sit or fall down: —
but no; with Mrs. H.'s hand on his shoulder, "*quam fami-
liariter*"* (as Terence said, when I was at school), they walked
about a minute, and then at it again, like two cockchafers
spitted on the same bodkin. I asked what all this meant,
when, with a loud laugh, a child no older than our Wilhelmina
(a name I never heard but in the Vicar of Wakefield, though
her mother would call her after the Princess of Swappenbach,)
said, "Lord! Mr. Hornem, can't you see they are valtzing?"
or waltzing (I forget which); and then up she got, and her
mother and sister, and away they went, and round-abouted it
till supper-time. Now, that I know what it is, I like it of all
things, and so does Mrs. H. (though I have broken my shins,
and four times overturned Mrs. Hornem's maid, in practising
the preliminary steps in a morning). Indeed, so much do I
like it, that having a turn for rhyme, tastily displayed in some
election ballads, and songs in honour of all the victories (but
till lately I have had little practice in that way), I sat down,
and with the aid of William Fitzgerald, Esq., and a few hints
from Dr. Busby, (whose recitations I attend, and am monstrous
fond of Master Busby's manner of delivering his father's late
successful "Drury Lane Address,") I composed the following
hymn, wherewithal to make my sentiments known to the
public; whom, nevertheless, I heartily despise, as well as the
critics.

I am, Sir, yours, &c. &c.

HORACE HORNEM.

* My Latin is all forgotten, if a man can be said to have forgotten what
he never remembered; but I bought my title-page motto of a Catholic priest
for a three-shilling bank token, after much haggling for the *even* sixpence.
I grudged the money to a papist, being all for the memory of Perceval and
"No popery," and quite regretting the downfal of the pope, because we
can't burn him any more.

THE WALTZ.

Muse of the many-twinkling feet!* whose charms
Are now extended up from legs to arms;
Terpsichore! — too long misdeem'd a maid —
Reproachful term — bestow'd but to upbraid —
Henceforth in all the bronze of brightness shine,
The least a vestal of the virgin Nine.
Far be from thee and thine the name of prude;
Mock'd, yet triumphant; sneer'd at, unsubdued;
Thy legs must move to conquer as they fly,
If but thy coats are reasonably high;
Thy breast — if bare enough — requires no shield;
Dance forth — *sans armour* thou shalt take the field,
And own — impregnable to *most* assaults,
Thy not too lawfully begotten "Waltz."

Hail, nimble nymph! to whom the young Hussar,
The whisker'd votary of waltz and war,
His night devotes, despite of spur and boots;
A sight unmatch'd since Orpheus and his brutes:
Hail, spirit-stirring Waltz! — beneath whose banners
A modern hero fought for modish manners;
On Hounslow's heath to rival Wellesley's** fame,
Cock'd — fired — and miss'd his man — but gain'd his aim;

---

* "Glance their many-twinkling feet." — GRAY.

** To rival Lord Wellesley's, or his nephew's, as the reader pleases: — the one gained a pretty woman, whom he deserved, by fighting for; and the other has been fighting in the Peninsula many a long day, "by Shrewsbury clock," without gaining any thing in *that* country but the title of "the Great Lord," and "the Lord;" which savours of profanation, having been hitherto applied only to that Being on whom " *Te Deums* " for carnage are

Hail, moving Muse! to whom the fair one's breast
Gives all it can, and bids us take the rest.
Oh! for the flow of Busby, or of Fitz,
The latter's loyalty, the former's wits,
To "energise the object I pursue,"
And give both Belial and his dance their due!

Imperial Waltz! imported from the Rhine
(Famed for the growth of pedigrees and wine),
Long be thine import from all duty free,
And hock itself be less esteem'd than thee;
In some few qualities alike — for hock
Improves our cellar — *thou* our living stock.
The head to hock belongs — thy subtler art
Intoxicates alone the heedless heart:
Through the full veins thy gentler poison swims,
And wakes to wantonness the willing limbs.

the rankest blasphemy. — It is to be presumed the general will one day return to his Sabine farm; there

"To tame the genius of the stubborn plain,
Almost as quickly as he conquor'd Spain!"

The Lord Peterborough conquered continents in a summer; we do
more — we contrive both to conquer and lose them in a shorter season. If
the "great Lord's" *Cincinnatian* progress in agriculture be no speedier than
the proportional average of time in Pope's couplet, it will, according to the
farmers' proverb, be "ploughing with dogs."

By the bye — one of this illustrious person's new titles is forgotten —
it is, however, worth remembering — "*Salvador del mundo!*" *credite,
posteri!* If this be the appellation annexed by the inhabitants of the
Peninsula to the name of a *man* who has not yet saved them — query — are
they worth saving, even in this world? for, according to the mildest modi-
fications of any Christian creed, those three words make the odds much
against them in the next. — "Saviour of the world," quotha! — it were to
be wished that he, or any one else, could save a corner of it — his country.
Yet this stupid misnomer, although it shows the near connection between
superstition and impiety, so far has its use, that it proves there can be little
to dread from those Catholics (inquisitorial Catholics too) who can confer
such an appellation on a *Protestant*. I suppose next year he will be entitled
the "Virgin Mary:" if so, Lord George Gordon himself would have nothing
to object to such liberal bastards of our Lady of Babylon.

Oh, Germany! how much to thee we owe,
As heaven-born Pitt can testify below,
Ere cursed confederation made thee France's,
And only left us thy d—d debts and dances!
Of subsidies and Hanover bereft,
We bless thee still — for George the Third is left!
Of kings the best — and last, not least in worth,
For graciously begetting George the Fourth.
To Germany, and highnesses serene,
Who owe us millions — don't we owe the queen?
To Germany, what owe we not besides?
So oft bestowing Brunswickers and brides;
Who paid for vulgar, with her royal blood,
Drawn from the stem of each Teutonic stud:
Who sent us — so be pardon'd all her faults —
A dozen dukes, some kings, a queen — and Waltz.

But peace to her — her emperor and diet,
Though now transferr'd to Buonaparte's "fiat!"
Back to my theme — O Muse of motion! say,
How first to Albion found thy Waltz her way?

Borne on the breath of hyperborean gales,
From Hamburg's port (while Hamburg yet had *mails*),
Ere yet unlucky Fame — compell'd to creep
To snowy Gottenburg — was chill'd to sleep;
Or, starting from her slumbers, deign'd arise,
Heligoland! to stock thy mart with lies;
While unburnt Moscow* yet had news to send,
Nor owed her fiery exit to a friend,

* The patriotic arson of our amiable allies cannot be sufficiently commended — nor subscribed for. Amongst other details omitted in the various
despatches of our eloquent ambassador, he did not state (being too much
occupied with the exploits of Colonel C—, in swimming rivers frozen, and
galloping over roads impassable,) that one entire province perished by
famine in the most melancholy manner, as follows: — In General Rostop-

She came — Waltz came — and with her certain sets
Of true despatches, and as true gazettes;
Then flamed of Austerlitz the blest despatch,
Which Moniteur nor Morning Post can match;
And — almost crush'd beneath the glorious news —
Ten plays, and forty tales of Kotzebue's;
One envoy's letters, six composers' airs,
And loads from Frankfort and from Leipsic fairs;
Meiner's four volumes upon womankind,
Like Lapland witches to ensure a wind;
Brunck's heaviest tome for ballast, and, to back it,
Of Heyné, such as should not sink the packet.

Fraught with this cargo — and her fairest freight,
Delightful Waltz, on tiptoe for a mate,
The welcome vessel reach'd the genial strand,
And round her flock'd the daughters of the land.
Not decent David, when, before the ark,
His grand pas-seul excited some remark;
Not love-lorn Quixote, when his Sancho thought
The knight's fandango friskier than it ought;
Not soft Herodias, when, with winning tread,
Her nimble feet danced off another's head;
Not Cleopatra on her galley's deck,
Display'd so much of *leg*, or more of *neck*,
Than thou, ambrosial Waltz, when first the moon
Beheld thee twirling to a Saxon tune!

chin's consummate conflagration, the consumption of tallow and train oil
was so great, that the market was inadequate to the demand: and thus one
hundred and thirty-three thousand persons were starved to death, by being
reduced to wholesome diet! The lamplighters of London have since subscribed a pint (of oil) a piece, and the tallow-chandlers have unanimously
voted a quantity of best moulds (four to the pound), to the relief of the
surviving Scythians; — the scarcity will soon, by such exertions, and a
proper attention to the *quality* rather than the quantity of provision, be
totally alleviated. It is said, in return, that the untouched Ukraine has
subscribed sixty thousand beeves for a day's meal to our suffering manu-
facturers.

To you, ye husbands of ten years! whose brows
Ache with the annual tributes of a spouse;
To you of nine years less, who only bear
The budding sprouts of those that you *shall* wear,
With added ornaments around them roll'd
Of native brass, or law-awarded gold;
To you, ye matrons, ever on the watch
To mar a son's, or make a daughter's, match;
To you, ye children of — whom chance accords —
Always the ladies, and *sometimes* their lords;
To you, ye single gentlemen, who seek
Torments for life, or pleasures for a week;
As Love or Hymen your endeavours guide,
To gain your own, or snatch another's bride;
To one and all the lovely stranger came,
And every ball-room echoes with her name.

Endearing Waltz! — to thy more melting tune
Bow Irish jig, and ancient rigadoon.
Scotch reels, avaunt! and country-dance, forego
Your future claims to each fantastic toe!
Waltz — Waltz alone — both legs and arms demands,
Liberal of feet, and lavish of her hands;
Hands which may freely range in public sight
Where ne'er before — but — pray "put out the light."
Methinks the glare of yonder chandelier
Shines much too far — or I am much too near;
And true, though strange — Waltz whispers this remark,
"My slippery steps are safest in the dark!"
But here the Muse with due decorum halts,
And lends her longest petticoat to Waltz.

Observant travellers of every time!
Ye quartos publish'd upon every clime!
O say, shall dull Romaika's heavy round,
Fandango's wriggle, or Bolero's bound;

Can Egypt's Almas* — tantalising group —
Columbia's caperers to the warlike whoop —
Can aught from cold Kamschatka to Cape Horn
With Waltz compare, or after Waltz be borne?
Ah, no! from Morier's pages down to Galt's,
Each tourist pens a paragraph for "Waltz."

Shades of those belles whose reign began of yore,
With George the Third's — and ended long before! —
Though in your daughters' daughters yet you thrive,
Burst from your lead, and be yourselves alive!
Back to the ball-room speed your spectred host:
Fool's Paradise is dull to that you lost.
No treacherous powder bids conjecture quake;
No stiff-starch'd stays make meddling fingers ache;
(Transferr'd to those ambiguous things that ape
Goats in their visage,** women in their shape;)

---

* Dancing girls — who do for hire what Waltz doth gratis.

** It cannot be complained now, as in the Lady Baussière's time, of the "Sieur de la Croix," that there be "no whiskers;" but how far those are indications of valour in the field, or elsewhere, may *still* be questionable. Much may be, and hath been, avouched on both sides. In the olden time philosophers had whiskers, and soldiers none — Scipio himself was shaven — Hannibal thought his one eye handsome enough without a beard; but Adrian, the emperor, wore a beard (having warts on his chin, which neither the Empress Sabina nor even the courtiers could abide) — Turenne had whiskers, Marlborough none — Buonaparte is unwhiskered, the Regent whiskered; "*argal*" greatness of mind and whiskers may or may not go together: but certainly the different occurrences, since the growth of the last mentioned, go further in behalf of whiskers than the anathema of Anselm did *against* long hair in the reign of Henry I. — Formerly, *red* was a favourite colour. See Lodowick Barrey's comedy of Ram Alley, 1661.; Act I. Scene I.

"*Taffeta.* Now for a wager — What coloured beard comes next by the window?

"*Adriana.* A black man's, I think.

"*Taffeta.* I think not so: I think a *red*, for that is most in fashion."

There is "nothing new under the sun;" but *red*, then a *favourite*, has now subsided into a *favourite's* colour.

No damsel faints when rather closely press'd,
But more caressing seems when most caress'd;
Superfluous hartshorn, and reviving salts,
Both banish'd by the sovereign cordial "Waltz."

Seductive Waltz! — though on thy native shore
Even Werter's self proclaim'd thee half a whore;
Werter — to decent vice though much inclined,
Yet warm, not wanton; dazzled, but not blind —
Though gentle Genlis, in her strife with Stael,
Would even proscribe thee from a Paris ball;
The fashion hails — from countesses to queens,
And maids and valets waltz behind the scenes;
Wide and more wide thy witching circle spreads,
And turns — if nothing else — at least our *heads;*
With thee even clumsy cits attempt to bounce,
And cockneys practise what they can't pronounce.
Gods! how the glorious theme my strain exalts,
And rhyme finds partner rhyme in praise of "Waltz!"

Blest was the time Waltz chose for her *début;*
The court, the Regent, like herself were new;*
New face for friends, for foes some new rewards;
New ornaments for black and royal guards;
New laws to hang the rogues that roar'd for bread;
New coins (most new)** to follow those that fled;
New victories — nor can we prize them less,
Though Jenky wonders at his own success;

---

* An anachronism — Waltz and the battle of Austerlitz are before said
to have opened the ball together: the bard means (if he means any thing),
Waltz was not so much in vogue till the Regent attained the acmé of his
popularity. Waltz, the comet, whiskers, and the new government, illuminated heaven and earth, in all their glory, much about the same time: of
those the comet only has disappeared; the other three continue to astonish
us still. — *Printer's Devil.*

** Amongst others a new ninepence — a creditable coin now forthcoming, worth a pound, in paper, at the fairest calculation.

New wars, because the old succeed so well,
That most survivors envy those who fell;
New mistresses — no, old — and yet 'tis true,
Though they be *old*, the *thing* is something new;
Each new, quite new — (except some ancient tricks), *
New white-sticks, gold-sticks, broom-sticks, all new sticks!
With vests or ribands — deck'd alike in hue,
New troopers strut, new turncoats blush in blue:
So saith the muse: my ——,** what say you?
Such was the time when Waltz might best maintain
Her new preferments in this novel reign;
Such was the time, nor ever yet was such;
Hoops are *no more*, and petticoats *not much;*
Morals and minuets, virtue and her stays,
And tell-tale powder — all have had their days.
The ball begins — the honours of the house
First duly done by daughter or by spouse,
Some potentate — or royal or serene —
With Kent's gay grace, or sapient Gloster's mien,
Leads forth the ready dame, whose rising flush
Might once have been mistaken for a blush.
From where the garb just leaves the bosom free,
That spot where hearts † were once supposed to be;

* "On that *right* should thus overcome *might!*" Who does not remember the "delicate investigation" in the "Merry Wives of Windsor?" —

"*Ford.* Pray you, come near: if I suspect without cause, why then make sport at me; then let me be your jest; I deserve it. How now? whither bear you this?

"*Mrs. Ford.* What have you to do whither they bear it? — you were best meddle with buck-washing."

** The gentle, or ferocious, reader may fill up the blank as he pleases — there are several dissyllabic names at *his* service (being already in the Regent's): it would not be fair to back any peculiar initial against the alphabet, as every month will add to the list now entered for the sweepstakes:—a distinguished consonant is said to be the favourite, much against the wishes of the *knowing ones.*

† "We have changed all that," says the Mock Doctor — 'tis all gone —

Round all the confines of the yielded waist,
The strangest hand may wander undisplaced;
The lady's in return may grasp as much
As princely paunches offer to her touch.
Pleased round the chalky floor how well they trip,
One hand reposing on the royal hip;
The other to the shoulder no less royal
Ascending with affection truly loyal!
Thus front to front the partners move or stand,
The foot may rest, but none withdraw the hand;
And all in turn may follow in their rank,
The Earl of — Asterisk — and Lady — Blank;
Sir — Such-a-one — with those of fashion's host,
For whose blest surnames — vide "Morning Post"
(Or if for that impartial print too late,
Search Doctors' Commons six months from my date) —
Thus all and each, in movement swift or slow,
The genial contact gently undergo;
Till some might marvel, with the modest Turk,
If "nothing follows all this palming work?"*
True, honest Mirza! — you may trust my rhyme —
Something does follow at a fitter time;
The breast thus publicly resign'd to man,
In private may resist him — if it can.

O ye who loved our grandmothers of yore,
Fitzpatrick, Sheridan, and many more!

Asmodeus knows where. After all, it is of no great importance how women's hearts are disposed of; they have nature's privilege to distribute them as absurdly as possible. But there are also some men with hearts so thoroughly bad, as to remind us of those phenomena often mentioned in natural history; viz. a mass of solid stone — only to be opened by force — and when divided, you discover a *toad* in the centre, lively, and with the reputation of being venomous.

* In Turkey a pertinent, here an impertinent and superfluous, question — literally put, as in the text, by a Persian to Morier, on seeing a waltz in Pera.— *Vide Morier's Travels.*

And thou, my prince! whose sovereign taste and will
It is to love the lovely beldames still!
Thou ghost of Queensbury! whose judging sprite
Satan may spare to peep a single night,
Pronounce — if ever in your days of bliss
Asmodeus struck so bright a stroke as this;
To teach the young ideas how to rise,
Flush in the cheek, and languish in the eyes;
Rush to the heart, and lighten through the frame,
With half-told wish and ill-dissembled flame:
For prurient nature still will storm the breast —
Who, tempted thus, can answer for the rest?

But ye — who never felt a single thought
For what our morals are to be, or ought;
Who wisely wish the charms you view to reap,
Say — would you make those beauties quite so cheap?
Hot from the hands promiscuously applied,
Round the slight waist, or down the glowing side,
Where were the rapture then to clasp the form
From this lewd grasp and lawless contact warm?
At once love's most endearing thought resign,
To press the hand so press'd by none but thine;
To gaze upon that eye which never met
Another's ardent look without regret;
Approach the lip which all, without restraint,
Come near enough — if not to touch — to taint;
If such thou lovest — love her then no more,
Or give — like her — caresses to a score;
Her mind with these is gone, and with it go
The little left behind it to bestow.

Voluptuous Waltz! and dare I thus blaspheme?
Thy bard forgot thy praises were his theme.
Terpsichore, forgive! — at every ball
My wife *now* waltzes — and my daughters *shall*;

My son — (or stop — 'tis needless to enquire —
These little accidents should ne'er transpire;
Some ages hence our genealogic tree
Will wear as green a bough for him as me) —
Waltzing shall rear, to make our name amends,
Grandsons for me — in heirs to all his friends.

———

LAMENT OF TASSO.

ADVERTISEMENT.

At Ferrara, in the Library, are preserved the original MSS. of Tasso's Gierusalemme and of Guarini's Pastor Fido, with letters of Tasso, one from Titian to Ariosto; and the inkstand and chair, the tomb and the house of the latter. But, as misfortune has a greater interest for posterity, and little or none for the contemporary, the cell where Tasso was confined in the hospital of St. Anna attracts a more fixed attention, than the residence or the monument of Ariosto — at least it had this effect on me. There are two inscriptions, one on the outer gate, the second over the cell itself, inviting, unnecessarily, the wonder and the indignation of the spectator. Ferrara is much decayed, and depopulated: the castle still exists entire; and I saw the court where Parisina and Hugo were beheaded, according to the annal of Gibbon. —

THE LAMENT OF TASSO.

I.

Long years! — It tries the thrilling frame to bear
And eagle-spirit of a Child of Song —
Long years of outrage, calumny, and wrong;
Imputed madness, prison'd solitude,
And the mind's canker in its savage mood,
When the impatient thirst of light and air
Parches the heart; and the abhorred grate,
Marring the sunbeams with its hideous shade,
Works through the throbbing eyeball to the brain,
With a hot sense of heaviness and pain;
And bare, at once, Captivity display'd
Stands scoffing through the never-open'd gate,
Which nothing through its bars admits, save day,
And tasteless food, which I have eat alone
Till its unsocial bitterness is gone;
And I can banquet like a beast of prey,
Sullen and lonely, couching in the cave
Which is my lair, and — it may be — my grave.
All this hath somewhat worn me, and may wear,
But must be borne.   I stoop not to despair;
For I have battled with mine agony,
And made me wings wherewith to overfly
The narrow circus of my dungeon wall,
And freed the Holy Sepulchre from thrall;
And revell'd among men and things divine,
And pour'd my spirit over Palestine,
In honour of the sacred war for Him,
The God who was on earth and is in heaven,
For he hath strengthen'd me in heart and limb.
That through this sufferance I might be forgiven,
I have employ'd my penance to record
How Salem's shrine was won, and how adored.

II.

But this is o'er — my pleasant task is done; —
My long-sustaining friend of many years!
If I do blot thy final page with tears,
Know, that my sorrows have wrung from me none.
But thou, my young creation! my soul's child!
Which ever playing round me came and smiled,
And woo'd me from myself with thy sweet sight,
Thou too art gone — and so is my delight:
And therefore do I weep and inly bleed
With this last bruise upon a broken reed.
Thou too art ended — what is left me now?
For I have anguish yet to bear — and how?
I know not that — but in the innate force
Of my own spirit shall be found resource.
I have not sunk, for I had no remorse,
Nor cause for such: they call'd me mad — and why?
Oh Leonora! wilt not *thou* reply?
I was indeed delirious in my heart
To lift my love so lofty as thou art;
But still my frenzy was not of the mind;
I knew my fault, and feel my punishment
Not less because I suffer it unbent.
That thou wert beautiful, and I not blind,
Hath been the sin which shuts me from mankind;
But let them go, or torture as they will,
My heart can multiply thine image still;
Successful love may sate itself away,
The wretched are the faithful; 'tis their fate
To have all feeling save the one decay,
And every passion into one dilate,
As rapid rivers into ocean pour;
But ours is fathomless, and hath no shore.

III.

Above me, hark! the long and maniac cry
Of minds and bodies in captivity.

And hark! the lash and the increasing howl,
And the half-inarticulate blasphemy!
There be some here with worse than frenzy foul,
Some who do still goad on the o'er-labour'd mind,
And dim the little light that's left behind
With needless torture, as their tyrant will
Is wound up to the lust of doing ill:
With these and with their victims am I class'd,
'Mid sounds and sights like these long years have pass'd;
'Mid sights and sounds like these my life may close:
So let it be — for then I shall repose.

IV.

I have been patient, let me be so yet,
I had forgotten half I would forget,
But it revives — Oh! would it were my lot
To be forgetful as I am forgot! —
Feel I not wroth with those who bade me dwell
In this vast lazar-house of many woes?
Where laughter is not mirth, nor thought the mind,
Nor words a language, nor ev'n men mankind;
Where cries reply to curses, shrieks to blows,
And each is tortured in his separate hell —
For we are crowded in our solitudes —
Many, but each divided by the wall,
Which echoes Madness in her babbling moods; —
While all can hear, none heed his neighbour's call —
None! save that One, the veriest wretch of all,
Who was not made to be the mate of these,
Nor bound between Distraction and Disease.
Feel I not wroth with those who placed me here?
Who have debased me in the minds of men,
Debarring me the usage of my own,
Blighting my life in best of its career,
Branding my thoughts as things to shun and fear?
Would I not pay them back these pangs again,
And teach them inward Sorrow's stifled groan?

The struggle to be calm, and cold distress,
Which undermines our Stoical success?
No! — still too proud to be vindictive — I
Have pardon'd princes' insults, and would die.
Yes, Sister of my Sovereign! for thy sake
I weed all bitterness from out my breast,
It hath no business where *thou* art a guest;
Thy brother hates — but I can not detest;
Thou pitiest not — but I can not forsake.

v.

Look on a love which knows not to despair,
But all unquench'd is still my better part,
Dwelling deep in my shut and silent heart
As dwells the gather'd lightning in its cloud,
Encompass'd with its dark and rolling shroud,
Till struck, — forth flies the all-ethereal dart!
And thus at the collision of thy name
The vivid thought still flashes through my frame,
And for a moment all things as they were
Flit by me; — they are gone — I am the same.
And yet my love without ambition grew;
I knew thy state, my station, and I knew
A Princess was no love-mate for a bard;
I told it not, I breathed it not, it was
Sufficient to itself, its own reward;
And if my eyes reveal'd it, they, alas!
Were punish'd by the silentness of thine,
And yet I did not venture to repine.
Thou wert to me a crystal-girded shrine,
Worshipp'd at holy distance, and around
Hallow'd and meekly kiss'd the saintly ground;
Not for thou wert a princess, but that Love
Had robed thee with a glory, and array'd
Thy lineaments in beauty that dismay'd - -
Oh! not dismay'd — but awed, like One above;
And in that sweet severity there was
A something which all softness did surpass —

I know not how — thy genius master'd mine —
My star stood still before thee: — if it were
Presumptuous thus to love without design,
That sad fatality hath cost me dear;
But thou art dearest still, and I should be
Fit for this cell, which wrongs me — but for *thee*.
The very love which lock'd me to my chain
Hath lighten'd half its weight; and for the rest,
Though heavy, lent me vigour to sustain,
And look to thee with undivided breast,
And foil the ingenuity of Pain.

VI.

It is no marvel — from my very birth
My soul was drunk with love, — which did pervade
And mingle with whate'er I saw on earth;
Of objects all inanimate I made
Idols, and out of wild and lonely flowers,
And rocks, whereby they grew, a paradise,
Where I did lay me down within the shade
Of waving trees, and dream'd uncounted hours,
Though I was chid for wandering; and the Wise
Shook their white aged heads o'er me, and said
Of such materials wretched men were made,
And such a truant boy would end in woe,
And that the only lesson was a blow; —
And then they smote me, and I did not weep,
But cursed them in my heart, and to my haunt
Return'd and wept alone, and dream'd again
The visions which arise without a sleep.
And with my years my soul began to pant
With feelings of strange tumult and soft pain;
And the whole heart exhaled into One Want,
But undefined and wandering, till the day
I found the thing I sought — and that was thee;
And then I lost my being all to be
Absorb'd in thine — the world was past away —
Thou didst annihilate the earth to me!

VII.

I loved all Solitude — but little thought
To spend I know not what of life, remote
From all communion with existence, save,
The maniac and his tyrant; — had I been
Their fellow, many years ere this had seen
My mind like theirs corrupted to its grave,
But who hath seen me writhe, or heard me rave?
Perchance in such a cell we suffer more
Than the wreck'd sailor on his desert shore;
The world is all before him — *mine is here*,
Scarce twice the space they must accord my bier.
What though *he* perish, he may lift his eye
And with a dying glance upbraid the sky —
I will not raise my own in such reproof,
Although 'tis clouded by my dungeon roof.

VIII.

Yet do I feel at times my mind decline,
But with a sense of its decay: — I see
Unwonted lights along my prison shine,
And a strange demon, who is vexing me
With pilfering pranks and petty pains, below
The feeling of the healthful and the free;
But much to One, who long hath suffer'd so,
Sickness of heart, and narrowness of place,
And all that may be borne, or can debase.
I thought mine enemies had been but Man,
But Spirits may be leagued with them — all Earth
Abandons — Heaven forgets me; — in the dearth
Of such defence the Powers of Evil can,
It may be, tempt me further, — and prevail
Against the outworn creature they assail.
Why in this furnace is my spirit proved
Like steel in tempering fire? because I loved?
Because I loved what not to love, and see,
Was more or less than mortal, and than me.

IX.

I once was quick in feeling — that is o'er; —
My scars are callous, or I should have dash'd
My brain against these bars, as the sun flash'd
In mockery through them; — if I bear and bore
The much I have recounted, and the more
Which hath no words, — 'tis that I would not die
And sanction with self-slaughter the dull lie
Which snared me here, and with the brand of shame
Stamp Madness deep into my memory,
And woo Compassion to a blighted name,
Sealing the sentence which my foes proclaim.
No — it shall be immortal! — and I make
A future temple of my present cell,
Which nations yet shall visit for my sake.
While thou, Ferrara! when no longer dwell
The ducal chiefs within thee, shalt fall down,
And crumbling piecemeal view thy heartless halls,
A poet's wreath shall be thine only crown, —
A poet's dungeon thy most far renown,
While strangers wonder o'er thy unpeopled walls!
And thou, Leonora! — thou — who wert ashamed
That such as I could love — who blush'd to hear
To less than monarchs that thou couldst be dear,
Go! tell thy brother, that my heart, untamed
By grief, years, weariness — and it may be
A taint of that he would impute to me —
From long infection of a den like this,
Where the mind rots congenial with the abyss,
Adores thee still; — and add — that when the towers
And battlements which guard his joyous hours
Of banquet, dance, and revel, are forgot,
Or left untended in a dull repose
This — this — shall be a consecrated spot!
But Thou — when all that Birth and Beauty throws
Of magic round thee is extinct — shalt have
One half the laurel which o'ershades my grave.
No power in death can tear our names apart,
As none in life could rend thee from my heart.
Yes, Leonora! it shall be our fate
To be entwined for ever — but too late!

ODE ON VENICE.

ODE ON VENICE.

I.

OH Venice! Venice! when thy marble walls
   Are level with the waters, there shall be
A cry of nations o'er thy sunken halls,
   A loud lament along the sweeping sea!
If I, a northern wanderer, weep for thee,
What should thy sons do? — any thing but weep:
And yet they only murmur in their sleep.
In contrast with their fathers — as the slime,
The dull green ooze of the receding deep,
Is with the dashing of the spring-tide foam,
That drives the sailor shipless to his home,
Are they to those that were; and thus they creep,
Crouching and crab-like, through their sapping streets.
Oh! agony — that centuries should reap
No mellower harvest! Thirteen hundred years
Of wealth and glory turn'd to dust and tears;
And every monument the stranger meets,
Church, palace, pillar, as a mourner greets;
And even the Lion all subdued appears,
And the harsh sound of the barbarian drum,
With dull and daily dissonance, repeats
The echo of thy tyrant's voice along
The soft waves, once all musical to song,
That heaved beneath the moonlight with the throng
Of gondolas — and to the busy hum
Of cheerful creatures, whose most sinful deeds
Were but the overbeating of the heart,
And flow of too much happiness, which needs
The aid of age to turn its course apart

From the luxuriant and voluptuous flood
Of sweet sensations, battling with the blood.
But these are better than the gloomy errors,
The weeds of nations in their last decay,
When Vice walks forth with her unsoften'd terrors,
And Mirth is madness, and but smiles to slay;
And Hope is nothing but a false delay,
The sick man's lightning half an hour ere death,
When Faintness, the last mortal birth of Pain,
And apathy of limb, the dull beginning
Of the cold staggering race which Death is winning,
Steals vein by vein and pulse by pulse away;
Yet so relieving the o'er-tortured clay,
To him appears renewal of his breath,
And freedom the mere numbness of his chain; —
And then he talks of life, and how again
He feels his spirits soaring — albeit weak,
And of the fresher air, which he would seek;
And as he whispers knows not that he gasps,
That his thin finger feels not what it clasps,
And so the film comes o'er him — and the dizzy
Chamber swims round and round — and shadows busy,
At which he vainly catches, flit and gleam,
Till the last rattle chokes the strangled scream,
And all is ice and blackness, — and the earth
That which it was the moment ere our birth.

II.

There is no hope for nations! — Search the page
   Of many thousand years — the daily scene,
The flow and ebb of each recurring age,
   The everlasting *to be* which *hath been*,
   Hath taught us nought or little: still we lean
On things that rot beneath our weight, and wear
Our strength away in wrestling with the air;
For 'tis our nature strikes us down: the beasts
Slaughter'd in hourly hecatombs for feasts

Are of as high an order — they must go
Even where their driver goads them, though to slaughter.
Ye men, who pour your blood for kings as water,
What have they given your children in return?
A heritage of servitude and woes,
A blindfold bondage, where your hire is blows.
What! do not yet the red-hot ploughshares burn,
O'er which you stumble in a false ordeal,
And deem this proof of loyalty the *real;*
Kissing the hand that guides you to your scars,
And glorying as you tread the glowing bars?
All that your sires have left you, all that Time
Bequeaths of free, and History of sublime,
Spring from a different theme! — Ye see and read,
Admire and sigh, and then succumb and bleed!
Save the few spirits, who, despite of all,
And worse than all, the sudden crimes engender'd
By the down-thundering of the prison-wall,
And thirst to swallow the sweet waters tender'd,
Gushing from Freedom's fountains — when the crowd,
Madden'd with centuries of draught, are loud,
And trample on each other to obtain
The cup which brings oblivion of a chain
Heavy and sore, — in which long yoked they plough'd
The sand, — or if there sprung the yellow grain,
'Twas not for them, their necks were too much bow'd,
And their dead palates chew'd the cud of pain: —
Yes! the few spirits — who, despite of deeds
Which they abhor, confound not with the cause
Those momentary starts from Nature's laws,
Which, like the pestilence and earthquake, smite
But for a term, then pass, and leave the earth
With all her seasons to repair the blight
With a few summers, and again put forth
Cities and generations — fair, when free —
For, Tyranny, there blooms no bud for thee!

III.

Glory and Empire! once upon these towers
  With Freedom — godlike Triad! how ye sate!
The league of mightiest nations, in those hours
  When Venice was an envy, might abate,
  But did not quench, her spirit — in her fate
All were enwrapp'd: the feasted monarchs knew
  And loved their hostess, nor could learn to hate,
Although they humbled — with the kingly few
The many felt, for from all days and climes
She was the voyager's worship; — even her crimes
Were of the softer order — born of Love,
She drank no blood, nor fatten'd on the dead,
But gladden'd where her harmless conquests spread;
For these restored the Cross, that from above
Hallow'd her sheltering banners, which incessant
Flew between earth and the unholy Crescent,
Which, if it waned and dwindled, Earth may thank
The city it has clothed in chains, which clank
Now, creaking in the ears of those who owe
The name of Freedom to her glorious struggles;
Yet she but shares with them a common woe,
And call'd the "kingdom" of a conquering foe, —
But knows what all — and, most of all, we know —
With what set gilded terms a tyrant juggles!

IV.

The name of Commonwealth is past and gone
  O'er the three fractions of the groaning globe;
Venice is crush'd, and Holland deigns to own
  A sceptre, and endures the purple robe;
If the free Switzer yet bestrides alone
His chainless mountains, 'tis but for a time,
For tyranny of late is cunning grown,
And in its own good season tramples down
The sparkles of our ashes.   One great clime,

Whose vigorous offspring by dividing ocean
Are kept apart and nursed in the devotion
Of Freedom, which their fathers fought for, and
Bequeath'd — a heritage of heart and hand,
And proud distinction from each other land,
Whose sons must bow them at a monarch's motion,
As if his senseless sceptre were a wand
Full of the magic of exploded science —
Still one great clime, in full and free defiance,
Yet rears her crest, unconquer'd and sublime,
Above the far Atlantic! — She has taught
Her Esau-brethren that the haughty flag,
The floating fence of Albion's feebler crag,
May strike to those whose red right hands have bought
Rights cheaply earn'd with blood. — Still, still, for ever
Better, though each man's life-blood were a river,
That it should flow, and overflow, than creep
Through thousand lazy channels in our veins,
Damm'd like the dull canal with locks and chains,
And moving, as a sick man in his sleep,
Three paces, and then faltering: — better be
Where the extinguish'd Spartans still are free,
In their proud charnel of Thermopylæ,
Than stagnate in our marsh, — or o'er the deep
Fly, and one current to the ocean add,
One spirit to the souls our fathers had,
One freeman more, America, to thee!

PROPHECY OF DANTE.

"'Tis the sunset of life gives me mystical lore,
And coming events cast their shadows before."
                                                CAMPBELL.

DEDICATION.

LADY! if for the cold and cloudy clime
  Where I was born, but where I would not die,
  Of the great Poet-Sire of Italy
I dare to build the imitative rhyme,
Harsh Runic copy of the South's sublime,
  THOU art the cause; and howsoever I
  Fall short of his immortal harmony,
Thy gentle heart will pardon me the crime.
Thou, in the pride of Beauty and of Youth,
  Spakest; and for thee to speak and be obey'd
Are one; but only in the sunny South
  Such sounds are utter'd, and such charms display'd,
So sweet a language from so fair a mouth —
  Ah! to what effort would it not persuade?

Ravenna, June 21. 1819.

Lord Byron. III.   24

PREFACE.

In the course of a visit to the city of Ravenna in the summer of 1819, it was suggested to the author that having composed something on the subject of Tasso's confinement, he should do the same on Dante's exile, — the tomb of the poet forming one of the principal objects of interest in that city, both to the native and to the stranger.

"On this hint I spake," and the result has been the following four cantos, in terza rima, now offered to the reader. If they are understood and approved, it is my purpose to continue the poem in various other cantos to its natural conclusion in the present age. The reader is requested to suppose that Dante addresses him in the interval between the conclusion of the Divina Commedia and his death, and shortly before the latter event, foretelling the fortunes of Italy in general in the ensuing centuries. In adopting this plan I have had in my mind the Cassandra of Lycophron, and the Prophecy of Nereus by Horace, as well as the Prophecies of Holy Writ. The measure adopted is the terza rima of Dante, which I am not aware to have seen hitherto tried in our language, except it may be by Mr. Hayley, of whose translation I never saw but one extract, quoted in the notes to Caliph Vathek; so that — if I do not err — this poem may be considered as a metrical experiment. The cantos are short, and about the same length of those of the poet, whose name I have borrowed, and most probably taken in vain.

Amongst the inconveniences of authors in the present day, it is difficult for any who have a name, good or bad, to escape translation. I have had the fortune to see the fourth canto of Childe Harold translated into Italian versi sciolti, — that is, a poem written in the *Spenserean stanza* into *blank verse*, without regard to the natural divisions of the stanza or of the sense. If the present poem, being on a national topic, should chance to undergo the same fate, I would request the Italian reader to remember that when I have failed in the imitation of his great "Padre Alighier," I have failed in imitating that which all study and few understand, since to this very day it is not yet settled what was the meaning of the allegory in the first canto of the Inferno, unless Count Marchetti's ingenious and probable conjecture may be considered as having decided the question.

He may also pardon my failure the more, as I am not quite sure that he would be pleased with my success, since the Italians, with a pardonable nationality, are particularly jealous of all that is left them as a nation — their literature; and in the present bitterness of the classic and romantic war, are but ill disposed to permit a foreigner even to approve or imitate them, without finding some fault with his ultramontane presumption. I can easily enter into all this, knowing what would be thought in England of an Italian imitator of Milton, or if a translation of Monti, or Pindemonte, or Arici, should be held up to the rising generation as a model for their future poetical essays. But I perceive that I am deviating into an address to the Italian reader, when my business is with the English one; and be they few or many, I must take my leave of both.

THE PROPHECY OF DANTE.

CANTO THE FIRST.

Once more in man's frail world! which I had left
  So long that 'twas forgotten; and I feel
  The weight of clay again, — too soon bereft
Of the immortal vision which could heal
  My earthly sorrows, and to God's own skies
  Lift me from that deep gulf without repeal,
Where late my ears rung with the damned cries
  Of souls in hopeless bale; and from that place
  Of lesser torment, whence men may arise
Pure from the fire to join the angelic race;
  Midst whom my own bright Beatrice bless'd *
  My spirit with her light; and to the base
Of the eternal Triad! first, last, best,
  Mysterious, three, sole, infinite, great God!
  Soul universal! led the mortal guest,
Unblasted by the glory, though he trod
  From star to star to reach the almighty throne.
  Oh Beatrice! whose sweet limbs the sod
So long hath press'd, and the cold marble stone,
  'Thou sole pure seraph of my earliest love,
  Love so ineffable, and so alone,
That nought on earth could more my bosom move,
  And meeting thee in heaven was but to meet
  That without which my soul, like the arkless dove,
Had wander'd still in search of, nor her feet

* The reader is requested to adopt the Italian pronunciation of Beatrice, sounding all the syllables.

Relieved her wing till found; without thy light
My paradise had still been incomplete. *
Since my tenth sun gave summer to my sight
  Thou wert my life, the essence of my thought,
  Loved ere I knew the name of love, and bright
Still in these dim old eyes, now overwrought
  With the world's war, and years, and banishment,
  And tears for thee, by other woes untaught;
For mine is not a nature to be bent
  By tyrannous faction, and the brawling crowd,
  And though the long, long conflict hath been spent
In vain, and never more, save when the cloud
  Which overhangs the Apennine, my mind's eye
  Pierces to fancy Florence, once so proud
Of me, can I return, though but to die,
  Unto my native soil, they have not yet
  Quench'd the old exile's spirit, stern and high.
But the sun, though not overcast, must set,
  And the night cometh; I am old in days,
  And deeds, and contemplation, and have met
Destruction face to face in all his ways.
  The world hath left me, what it found me, pure,
  And if I have not gather'd yet its praise,
I sought it not by any baser lure;
  Man wrongs, and Time avenges, and my name
  May form a monument not all obscure,
Though such was not my ambition's end or aim,
  To add to the vain-glorious list of those
  Who dabble in the pettiness of fame,
And make men's fickle breath the wind that blows
  Their sail, and deem it glory to be class'd
  With conquerors, and virtue's other foes,

---

*   " Che sol per le belle opre
         Che fanno in Cielo il sole e l' altre stelle
         Dentro di lui' *si crede il Paradiso,*
         Così se guardi fiso
         Ponsar ben dèi ch' ogni terren' piacore."
Canzone, in which Dante describes the person of Beatrice, Strophe third.

In bloody chronicles of ages past.
 I would have had my Florence great and free:*
 Oh Florence! Florence! unto me thou wast
Like that Jerusalem which the Almighty He
 Wept over, "but thou wouldst not;" as the bird
 Gathers its young, I would have gather'd thee
Beneath a parent pinion, hadst thou heard
 My voice; but as the adder, deaf and fierce,
 Against the breast that cherish'd thee was stirr'd
Thy venom, and my state thou didst amerce,
 And doom this body forfeit to the fire.
 Alas! how bitter is his country's curse
To him who *for* that country would expire,
 But did not merit to expire *by* her,
 And loves her, loves her even in her ire.
The day may come when she will cease to err,
 The day may come she would be proud to have
 The dust she dooms to scatter, and transfer**
Of him, whom she denied a home, the grave.
 But this shall not be granted; let my dust
 Lie where it falls; nor shall the soil which gave
Me breath, but in her sudden fury thrust
 Me forth to breathe elsewhere, so reassume
 My indignant bones, because her angry gust
Forsooth is over, and repeal'd her doom;
 No, — she denied me what was mine — my roof,
 And shall not have what is not hers — my tomb.
Too long her armed wrath hath kept aloof
 The breast which would have bled for her, the heart
 That beat, the mind that was temptation proof,

---

 * "L'Esilio che m' è dato onor mi tegno.
    * * * * *
   Cader tra' buoni è pur di lodo degno." — *Sonnet of Dante,*
in which he represents Right, Generosity, and Temperance as banished
from among men, and seeking refuge from Love, who inhabits his bosom.
 ** "Ut si quis predictorum ullo tempore in fortiam dicti communis
pervenerit, *talis perveniens igne comburatur, sic quod moriatur.*" Second
sentence of Florence against Dante, and the fourteen accused with him.
The Latin is worthy of the sentence.

The man who fought, toil'd, travell'd, and each part
  Of a true citizen fulfill'd, and saw
  For his reward the Guelf's ascendant art
Pass his destruction even into a law.
  These things are not made for forgetfulness,
  Florence shall be forgotten first; too raw
The wound, too deep the wrong, and the distress
  Of such endurance too prolong'd to make
  My pardon greater, her injustice less,
Though late repented; yet — yet for her sake
  I feel some fonder yearnings, and for thine,
  My own Beatricē, I would hardly take
Vengeance upon the land which once was mine,
  And still is hallow'd by thy dust's return,
  Which would protect the murderess like a shrine,
And save ten thousand foes by thy sole urn.
  Though, like old Marius from Minturnæ's marsh
  And Carthage ruins, my lone breast may burn
At times with evil feelings hot and harsh,
  And sometimes the last pangs of a vile foe
  Writhe in a dream before me, and o'erarch
My brow with hopes of triumph, let them go!
  Such are the last infirmities of those
  Who long have suffer'd more than mortal woe,
And yet being mortal still, have no repose
  But on the pillow of Revenge — Revenge,
  Who sleeps to dream of blood, and waking glows
With the oft-baffled, slakeless thirst of change,
  When we shall mount again, and they that trod
  Be trampled on, while Death and Atè range
O'er humbled heads and sever'd necks — Great God!
  Take these thoughts from me — to thy hands I yield
  My many wrongs, and thine almighty rod
Will fall on those who smote me, — be my shield!
  As thou hast been in peril, and in pain,
  In turbulent cities, and the tented field —

In toil, and many troubles borne in vain
   For Florence. — I appeal from her to Thee!
   Thee, whom I late saw in thy loftiest reign,
Even in that glorious vision, which to see
   And live was never granted until now,
   And yet thou hast permitted this to me.
Alas! with what a weight upon my brow
   The sense of earth and earthly things come back,
   Corrosive passions, feelings dull and low,
The heart's quick throb upon the mental rack,
   Long day, and dreary night; the retrospect
   Of half a century bloody and black,
And the frail few years I may yet expect
   Hoary and hopeless, but less hard to bear,
   For I have been too long and deeply wreck'd
On the lone rock of desolate Despair,
   To lift my eyes more to the passing sail
   Which shuns that reef so horrible and bare;
Nor raise my voice — for who would heed my wail?
   I am not of this people, nor this age,
   And yet my harpings will unfold a tale
Which shall preserve these times when not a page
   Of their perturbed annals could attract
   An eye to gaze upon their civil rage,
Did not my verse embalm full many an act
   Worthless as they who wrought it: 'tis the doom
   Of spirits of my order to be rack'd
In life, to wear their hearts out, and consume
   Their days in endless strife, and die alone;
   Then future thousands crowd around their tomb,
And pilgrims come from climes where they have known
   The name of him — who now is but a name,
   And wasting homage o'er the sullen stone,
Spread his — by him unheard, unheeded — fame;
   And mine at least hath cost me dear! to die
   Is nothing; but to wither thus — to tame

My mind down from its own infinity —
To live in narrow ways with little men,
A common sight to every common eye,
A wanderer, while even wolves can find a den,
Ripp'd from all kindred, from all home, all things
That make communion sweet, and soften pain —
To feel me in the solitude of kings
Without the power that makes them bear a crown —
To envy every dove his nest and wings
Which waft him where the Apennine looks down
On Arno, till he perches, it may be,
Within my all inexorable town,
Where yet my boys are, and that fatal she,*
Their mother, the cold partner who hath brought
Destruction for a dowry — this to see
And feel, and know without repair, hath taught
A bitter lesson; but it leaves me free:
I have not vilely found, nor basely sought,
They made an Exile — not a slave of me.

---

* This lady, whose name was *Gemma*, sprung from one of the most powerful Guelf families, named Donati. Corso Donati was the principal adversary of the Ghibellines. She is described as being "*Admodum morosa, ut de Xantippe Socratis philosophi conjuge scriptum esse legimus,*" according to Giannozzo Manetti. But Lionardo Aretino is scandalised with Boccace, in his life of Dante, for saying that literary men should not marry. "Qui il Boccaccio non ha pazienza, e dice, le mogli esser contrarie agli studj; e non si ricorda che Socrate il più nobile filosofo che mai fosse, ebbe moglie e figliuoli e uffici della Repubblica nella sua Città; e Aristotele che, &c. &c. ebbe due mogli in varj tempi, ed ebbe figliuoli, o ricchezze assai. — E Marco Tullio — e Catone — e Varrone — e Seneca — ebbero moglie," &c. &c. It is odd that honest Lionardo's examples, with the exception of Seneca, and, for any thing I know, of Aristotle, are not the most felicitous. Tully's Terentia, and Socrates' Xantippe, by no means contributed to their husbands' happiness, whatever they might as to their philosophy — Cato gave away his wife — of Varro's we know nothing — and of Seneca's, only that she was disposed to die with him, but recovered, and lived several years afterwards. But, says Lionardo, "L'uomo è *animale civile*, secondo piace a tutti i filosofi." And thence concludes that the greatest proof of the *animal's civism* is "la prima congiunzione, dalla quale multiplicata nasce la Città."

CANTO THE SECOND.

The Spirit of the fervent days of Old,
   When words were things that came to pass, and thought
   Flash'd o'er the future, bidding men behold
Their children's children's doom already brought
   Forth from the abyss of time which is to be,
   The chaos of events, where lie half-wrought
Shapes that must undergo mortality;
   What the great Seers of Israel wore within,
   That spirit was on them, and is on me,
And if, Cassandra-like, amidst the din
   Of conflict none will hear, or hearing heed
   This voice from out the Wilderness, the sin
Be theirs, and my own feelings be my meed,
 - The only guerdon I have ever known.
   Hast thou not bled? and hast thou still to bleed,
Italia? Ah! to me such things, foreshown
   With dim sepulchral light, bid me forget
   In thine irreparable wrongs my own;
We can have but one country, and even yet
   Thou'rt mine — my bones shall be within thy breast,
   My soul within thy language, which once set
With our old Roman sway in the wide West;
   But I will make another tongue arise
   As lofty and more sweet, in which express'd
The hero's ardour, or the lover's sighs,
   Shall find alike such sounds for every theme
   That every word, as brilliant as thy skies,
Shall realise a poet's proudest dream,
   And make thee Europe's nightingale of song;
   So that all present speech to thine shall seem

The note of meaner birds, and every tongue
  Confess its barbarism when compared with thine.
  This shalt thou owe to him thou didst so wrong,
Thy Tuscan Bard, the banish'd Ghibelline.
  Woe! woe! the veil of coming centuries
  Is rent, — a thousand years which yet supine
Lie like the ocean waves ere winds arise,
  Heaving in dark and sullen undulation,
  Float from eternity into these eyes;
The storms yet sleep, the clouds still keep their station,
  The unborn earthquake yet is in the womb,
  The bloody chaos yet expects creation,
But all things are disposing for thy doom;
  The elements await but for the word,
  "Let there be darkness!" and thou grow'st a tomb!
Yes! thou, so beautiful, shalt feel the sword,
  Thou, Italy! so fair that Paradise,
  Revived in thee, blooms forth to man restored:
Ah! must the sons of Adam lose it twice?
  Thou, Italy! whose ever golden fields,
  Plough'd by the sunbeams solely, would suffice
For the world's granary; thou, whose sky heaven gilds
  With brighter stars, and robes with deeper blue;
  Thou, in whose pleasant places Summer builds
Her palace, in whose cradle Empire grew,
  And form'd the Eternal City's ornaments
  From spoils of kings whom freemen overthrew;
Birthplace of heroes, sanctuary of saints,
  Where earthly first, then heavenly glory made
  Her home; thou, all which fondest fancy paints,
And finds her prior vision but portray'd
  In feeble colours, when the eye — from the Alp
  Of horrid snow, and rock, and shaggy shade
Of desert-loving pine, whose emerald scalp
  Nods to the storm — dilates and dotes o'er thee,
  And wistfully implores, as 'twere, for help
To see thy sunny fields, my Italy,

Nearer and nearer yet, and dearer still
  The more approach'd, and dearest were they free.
Thou — Thou must wither to each tyrant's will:
  The Goth hath been, — the German, Frank, and Hun
  Are yet to come, — and on the imperial hill
Ruin, already proud of the deeds done
  By the old barbarians, there awaits the new,
  Throned on the Palatine, while lost and won
Rome at her feet lies bleeding; and the hue
  Of human sacrifice and Roman slaughter
  Troubles the clotted air, of late so blue,
And deepens into red the saffron water
  Of Tiber, thick with dead; the helpless priest,
  And still more helpless nor less holy daughter,
Vow'd to their God, have shrieking fled, and ceased
  Their ministry: the nations take their prey,
  Iberian, Almain, Lombard, and the beast
And bird, wolf, vulture, more humane than they
  Are; those but gorge the flesh and lap the gore
  Of the departed, and then go their way;
But those, the human savages, explore
  All paths of torture, and insatiate yet,
  With Ugolino hunger prowl for more.
Nine moons shall rise o'er scenes like this and set;*
  The chiefless army of the dead, which late
  Beneath the traitor Prince's banner met,
Hath left its leader's ashes at the gate;
  Had but the royal Rebel lived, perchance
  Thou hadst been spared, but his involved thy fate.
Oh! Rome, the spoiler or the spoil of France,
  From Brennus to the Bourbon, never, never
  Shall foreign standard to thy walls advance
But Tiber shall become a mournful river.
  Oh! when the strangers pass the Alps and Po,
  Crush them, ye rocks! floods whelm them, and for ever!

* See "Sacco di Roma," generally attributed to Guicciardini. There is
another written by a Jacopo Buonaparte. —

Why sleep the idle avalanches so,
  To topple on the lonely pilgrim's head?
  Why doth Eridanus but overflow
The peasant's harvest from his turbid bed?
  Were not each barbarous horde a nobler prey?
  Over Cambyses' host the desert spread
Her sandy ocean, and the sea waves' sway
  Roll'd over Pharaoh and his thousands, — why,
  Mountains and waters, do ye not as they?
And you, ye men! Romans, who dare not die,
  Sons of the conquerors who overthrew
  Those who overthrew proud Xerxes, where yet lie
The dead whose tomb Oblivion never knew,
  Are the Alps weaker than Thermopylæ?
  Their passes more alluring to the view
Of an invader? is it they; or ye,
  That to each host the mountain-gate unbar,
  And leave the march in peace, the passage free,
Why, Nature's self detains the victor's car,
  And makes your land impregnable, if earth
  Could be so; but alone she will not war,
Yet aids the warrior worthy of his birth
  In a soil where the mothers bring forth men:
  Not so with those whose souls are little worth;
For them no fortress can avail, — the den
  Of the poor reptile which preserves its sting
  Is more secure than walls of adamant, when
The hearts of those within are quivering.
  Are ye not brave? Yes, yet the Ausonian soil
  Hath hearts, and hands, and arms, and hosts to bring
Against Oppression; but how vain the toil,
  While still Division sows the seeds of woe
  And weakness, till the stranger reaps the spoil.
Oh! my own beauteous land! so long laid low,
  So long the grave of thy own children's hopes,
  When there is but required a single blow

To break the chain, yet — yet the Avenger stops,
  And Doubt and Discord step 'twixt thine and thee,
  And join their strength to that which with thee copes;
What is there wanting then to set thee free,
  And show thy beauty in its fullest light?
  To make the Alps impassable; and we,
Her sons, may do this with *one* deed — Unite.

CANTO THE THIRD.

FROM out the mass of never-dying ill,
  The Plague, the Prince, the Stranger, and the Sword,
  Vials of wrath but emptied to refill
And flow again, I cannot all record
  That crowds on my prophetic eye: the earth
  And ocean written o'er would not afford
Space for the annal, yet it shall go forth;
  Yes, all, though not by human pen, is graven,
  There where the farthest suns and stars have birth,
Spread like a banner at the gate of heaven,
  The bloody scroll of our millennial wrongs
  Waves, and the echo of our groans is driven
Athwart the sound of archangelic songs,
  And Italy, the martyr'd nation's gore,
  Will not in vain arise to where belongs
Omnipotence and mercy evermore:
  Like to a harpstring stricken by the wind,
  The sound of her lament shall, rising o'er
The seraph voices, touch the Almighty Mind.
  Meantime I, humblest of thy sons, and of
  Earth's dust by immortality refined
To sense and suffering, though the vain may scoff,
  And tyrants threat, and meeker victims bow
  Before the storm because its breath is rough,
To thee, my country! whom before, as now,
  I loved and love, devote the mournful lyre
  And melancholy gift high powers allow
To read the future; and if now my fire
  Is not as once it shone o'er thee, forgive!
  I but foretell thy fortunes — then expire;

Think not that I would look on them and live.
A spirit forces me to see and speak,
And for my guerdon grants *not* to survive;
My heart shall be pour'd over thee and break:
Yet for a moment, ere I must resume
Thy sable web of sorrow, let me take
Over the gleams that flash athwart thy gloom
A softer glimpse; some stars shine through thy night,
And many meteors, and above thy tomb
Leans sculptured Beauty, which Death cannot blight;
And from thine ashes boundless spirits rise
To give thee honour, and the earth delight;
Thy soil shall still be pregnant with the wise,
The gay, the learn'd, the generous, and the brave,
Native to thee as summer to thy skies,
Conquerors on foreign shores, and the far wave,*
Discoverers of new worlds, which take their name;**
For *thee* alone they have no arm to save,
And all thy recompense is in their fame,
A noble one to them, but not to thee —
Shall they be glorious, and thou still the same?
. Oh! more than these illustrious far shall be
The being — and even yet he may be born —
The mortal saviour who shall set thee free,
And see thy diadem so changed and worn
By fresh barbarians, on thy brow replaced;
And the sweet sun replenishing thy morn,
Thy moral morn, too long with clouds defaced
And noxious vapours from Avernus risen,
Such as all they must breathe who are debased
By servitude, and have the mind in prison.
Yet through this centuried eclipse of woe
Some voices shall be heard, and earth shall listen;

---

* Alexander of Parma, Spinola, Pescara, Eugene of Savoy, Montecucco.

** Columbus, Americus Vespasius, Sebastian Cabot.

Poets shall follow in the path I show,
   And make it broader; the same brilliant sky
   Which cheers the birds to song shall bid them glow,
And raise their notes as natural and high;
   Tuneful shall be their numbers; they shall sing
   Many of love, and some of liberty,
But few shall soar upon that eagle's wing,
   And look in the sun's face with eagle's gaze,
   All free and fearless as the feather'd king,
But fly more near the earth; how many a phrase
   Sublime shall lavish'd be on some small prince
   In all the prodigality of praise!
And language, eloquently false, evince
   The harlotry of genius, which, like beauty,
   Too oft forgets its own self-reverence,
And looks on prostitution as a duty.
   He who once enters in a tyrant's hall *
   As guest is slave, his thoughts become a booty,
And the first day which sees the chain enthral
   A captive, sees his half of manhood gone — **
   The soul's emasculation saddens all
His spirit; thus the Bard too near the throne
   Quails from his inspiration, bound to *please*, —
   How servile is the task to please alone!
To smooth the verse to suit his sovereign's ease
   And royal leisure, nor too much prolong
   Aught save his eulogy, and find, and seize,
Or force, or forge fit argument of song!
   Thus trammell'd, thus condemn'd to Flattery's trebles,
   He toils through all, still trembling to be wrong:
For fear some noble thoughts, like heavenly rebels,
   Should rise up in high treason to his brain,
   He sings, as the Athenian spoke, with pebbles

---

   * A verse from the Greek tragedians, with which Pompey took leave of
Cornelia on entering the boat in which he was slain.
   ** The verse and sentiment are taken from Homer.

In's mouth, lest truth should stammer through his strain.
   But out of the long file of sonneteers
   There shall be some who will not sing in vain,
And he, their prince, shall rank among my peers,*
   And love shall be his torment; but his grief
   Shall make an immortality of tears,
And Italy shall hail him as the Chief
   Of Poet-lovers, and his higher song
   Of Freedom wreathe him with as green a leaf.
But in a farther age shall rise along
   The banks of Po two greater still than he;
   The world which smiled on him shall do them wrong
Till they are ashes, and repose with me.
   The first will make an epoch with his lyre,
   And fill the earth with feats of chivalry:
His fancy like a rainbow, and his fire,
   Like that of Heaven, immortal, and his thought
   Borne onward with a wing that cannot tire:
Pleasure shall, like a butterfly new caught,
   Flutter her lovely pinions o'er his theme,
   And Art itself seem into Nature wrought
By the transparency of his bright dream. —
   The second, of a tenderer, sadder mood,
   Shall pour his soul out o'er Jerusalem;
He, too, shall sing of arms, and Christian blood
   Shed where Christ bled for man; and his high harp
   Shall, by the willow over Jordan's flood,
Revive a song of Sion, and the sharp
   Conflict, and final triumph of the brave
   And pious, and the strife of hell to warp
Their hearts from their great purpose, until wave
   The red-cross banners where the first red Cross
   Was crimson'd from his veins who died to save,
Shall be his sacred argument; the loss
   Of years, of favour, freedom, even of fame
   Contested for a time, while the smooth gloss

* Petrarch.

Of courts would slide o'er his forgotten name,
　　And call captivity a kindness, meant
　　To shield him from insanity or shame,
Such shall be his meet guerdon! who was sent
　　To be Christ's Laureate — they reward him well!
　　Florence dooms me but death or banishment,
Ferrara him a pittance and a cell,
　　Harder to bear and less deserved, for I
　　Had stung the factions which I strove to quell;
But this meek man, who with a lover's eye
　　Will look on earth and heaven, and who will deign
　　To embalm with his celestial flattery
As poor a thing as e'er was spawn'd to reign,
　　What will *he* do to merit such a doom?
　　Perhaps he'll *love*, — and is not love in vain
Torture enough without a living tomb?
　　Yet it will be so — he and his compeer,
　　The Bard of Chivalry, will both consume
In penury and pain too many a year,
　　And, dying in despondency, bequeath
　　To the kind world, which scarce will yield a tear,
A heritage enriching all who breathe
　　With the wealth of a genuine poet's soul,
　　And to their country a redoubled wreath
Unmatch'd by time; not Hellas can unroll
　　Through her olympiads two such names, though one
　　Of hers be mighty; — and is this the whole
Of such men's destiny beneath the sun?
　　Must all the finer thoughts, the thrilling sense,
　　The electric blood with which their arteries run
Their body's self turn'd soul with the intense
　　Feeling of that which is, and fancy of
　　That which should be, to such a recompense
Conduct? shall their bright plumage on the rough
　　Storm be still scatter'd? Yes, and it must be,
　　For, form'd of far too penetrable stuff,

25*

These birds of Paradise but long to flee
    Back to their native mansion, soon they find
    Earth's mist with their pure pinions not agree,
And die or are degraded, for the mind
    Succumbs to long infection, and despair,
    And vulture passions flying close behind,
Await the moment to assail and tear;
    And when at length the winged wanderers stoop,
    Then is the prey-birds' triumph, then they share
The spoil, o'erpower'd at length by one fell swoop.
    Yet some have been untouch'd who learn'd to bear,
    Some whom no power could ever force to droop,
Who could resist themselves even, hardest care!
    And task most hopeless; but some such have been,
    And if my name amongst the number were,
That destiny austere, and yet serene,
    Were prouder than more dazzling fame unbless'd;
    The Alp's snow summit nearer heaven is seen
Than the volcano's fierce eruptive crest,
    Whose splendour from the black abyss is flung,
    While the scorch'd mountain, from whose burning breast
A temporary torturing flame is wrung,
    Shines for a night of terror, then repels
    Its fire back to the hell from whence it sprung,
The hell which in its entrails ever dwells.

CANTO THE FOURTH.

MANY are poets who have never penn'd
  Their inspiration, and perchance the best:
  They felt, and loved, and died, but would not lend
Their thoughts to meaner beings; they compress'd
  The god within them, and rejoin'd the stars
  Unlaurell'd upon earth, but far more bless'd
Than those who are degraded by the jars
  Of passion, and their frailties link'd to fame,
  Conquerors of high renown, but full of scars.
Many are poets but without the name,
  For what is poesy but to create
  From overfeeling good or ill; and aim
At an external life beyond our fate,
  And be the new Prometheus of new men,
  Bestowing fire from heaven, and then, too late,
Finding the pleasure given repaid with pain,
  And vultures to the heart of the bestower,
  Who, having lavish'd his high gift in vain,
Lies chain'd to his lone rock by the sea-shore? ·
  So be it: we can bear. — But thus all they
  Whose intellect is an o'ermastering power
Which still recoils from its encumbering clay
  Or lightens it to spirit, whatsoe'er
  The form which their creations may essay,
Are bards; the kindled marble's bust may wear .
  More poesy upon its speaking brow
  Than aught less than the Homeric page may bear;
One noble stroke with a whole life may glow,
  Or deify the canvass till it shine
  With beauty so surpassing all below,

That they who kneel to idols so divine
   Break no commandment, for high heaven is there
   Transfused, transfigurated: and the line
Of poesy, which peoples but the air
   With thought and beings of our thought reflected,
   Can do no more: then let the artist share
The palm, he shares the peril, and dejected
   Faints o'er the labour unapproved — Alas!
   Despair and Genius are too oft connected.
Within the ages which before me pass
   Art shall resume and equal even the sway
   Which with Apelles and old Phidias
She held in Hellas' unforgotten day.
   Ye shall be taught by Ruin to revive
   The Grecian forms at least from their decay,
And Roman souls at last again shall live
   In Roman works wrought by Italian hands,
   And temples, loftier than the old temples, give
New wonders to the world; and while still stands
   The austere Pantheon, into heaven shall soar
   A dome,* its image, while the base expands
Into a fane surpassing all before,
   Such as all flesh shall flock to kneel in: ne'er
   Such sight hath been unfolded by a door
As this, to which all nations shall repair,
   And lay their sins at this huge gate of heaven.
   And the bold Architect unto whose care
The daring charge to raise it shall be given,
   Whom all arts shall acknowledge as their lord,
   Whether into the marble chaos driven
His chisel bid the Hebrew,** at whose word

* The cupola of St. Peter's.
** The statue of Moses on the monument of Julius II.

SONETTO

Di Giovanni Battista Zappi.

Chi è costui, che in dura pietra scolto,
  Siede gigante; e le più illustre, e conte
  Opre dell' arte avvanza, e ha vive, e pronte
Lo labbra sì, che le parole ascolto?

Israel left Egypt, stop the waves in stone,
  Or hues of Hell be by his pencil pour'd
Over the damn'd before the Judgment throne,*
  Such as I saw them, such as all shall see,
  Or fanes be built of grandeur yet unknown,
The stream of his great thoughts shall spring from me,**
  The Ghibelline, who traversed the three realms
  Which form the empire of eternity.
Amidst the clash of swords, and clang of helms,
  The age which I anticipate, no less
  Shall be the Age of Beauty, and while whelms
Calamity the nations with distress,
  The genius of my country shall arise,
  A Cedar towering o'er the Wilderness,

> Quest' è Mosè; ben me 'l diceva il folto
>   Onor del mento, e 'l doppio raggio in fronte,
>   Quest' è Mosè, quando scendea del monte,
>   E gran parto del Nume avea nel volto.
> Tal ora allor, che le sonanti, e vasto
>   Acque oi sospese a se d' intorno, e tale
>   Quando il mar chiuse, e ne fè tomba altrui.
> E voi sue turbe un rio vitello alzaste?
>   Alzata avesto imago a questa eguale!
>   Ch' ora men fallo l' adorar costui.

> "And who is he that, shaped in sculptured stone,
>   Sits giant-like? stern monument of art
>   Unparallel'd, while language seems to start
> From his prompt lips, and we his precepts own?
>   — 'Tis Moses; by his beard's thick honours known,
>   And the twin beams that from his temples dart;
>   'Tis Moses; seated on the mount apart,
> Whilst yet the Godhead o'er his features shone.
> Such once he look'd, when ocean's sounding wave
>   Suspended hung, and such amidst the storm,
>   When o'er his foes the refluent waters roar'd.
> An idol calf his followers did engrave;
>   But had they raised this awe-commanding form,
>   Then had they with less guilt their work adored." — ROGERS.

* The Last Judgment, in the Sistine Chapel.

** I have read somewhere (if I do not err, for I cannot recollect where,) that Dante was so great a favourite of Michael Angelo's, that he had designed the whole of the Divina Commedia; but that the volume containing these studies was lost by sea.

Lovely in all its branches to all eyes,
    Fragrant as fair, and recognised afar,
    Wafting its native incense through the skies.
Sovereigns shall pause amidst their sport of war,
    Wean'd for an hour from blood, to turn and gaze
    On canvass or on stone; and they who mar
All beauty upon earth, compell'd to praise,
    Shall feel the power of that which they destroy;
    And Art's mistaken gratitude shall raise
To tyrants who but take her for a toy
    Emblems and monuments, and prostitute
    Her charms to pontiffs proud,* who but employ
The man of genius as the meanest brute
    To bear a burthen, and to serve a need,
    To sell his labours, and his soul to boot.
Who toils for nations may be poor indeed,
    But free; who sweats for monarchs is no more
    Than the gilt chamberlain, who, clothed and fee'd,
Stands sleek and slavish, bowing at his door.
    Oh, Power that rulest and inspirest! how
    Is it that they on earth, whose earthly power
Is likest thine in heaven in outward show,
    Least like to thee in attributes divine,
    Tread on the universal necks that bow,
And then assure us that their rights are thine?
    And how is it that they, the sons of fame,
    Whose inspiration seems to them to shine
From high, they whom the nations oftest name,
    Must pass their days in penury or pain,
    Or step to grandeur through the paths of shame,
And wear a deeper brand and gaudier chain?
    Or if their destiny be born aloof
    From lowliness, or tempted thence in vain,
In their own souls sustain a harder proof,

---

* See the treatment of Michael Angelo by Julius II., and his neglect by
Leo X.

The inner war of passions deep and fierce?
Florence! when thy harsh sentence razed my roof,
I loved thee; but the vengeance of my verse,
　The hate of injuries which every year
　Makes greater, and accumulates my curse,
Shall live, outliving all thou holdest dear,
　Thy pride, thy wealth, thy freedom, and even *that*,
　The most infernal of all evils here,
The sway of petty tyrants in a state;
　For such sway is not limited to kings,
　And demagogues yield to them but in date,
As swept off sooner; in all deadly things
　Which make men hate themselves, and one another,
　In discord, cowardice, cruelty, all that springs
From Death the Sin-born's incest with his mother,
　In rank oppression in its rudest shape,
　The faction Chief is but the Sultan's brother,
And the worst despot's far less human ape:
　Florence! when this lone spirit, which so long
　Yearn'd, as the captive toiling at escape,
To fly back to thee in despite of wrong,
　An exile, saddest of all prisoners,
　Who has the whole world for a dungeon strong,
Seas, mountains, and the horizon's verge for bars,
　Which shut him from the sole small spot of earth
　Where — whatsoe'er his fate — he still were hers,
His country's, and might die where he had birth —
　Florence! when this lone spirit shall return
　To kindred spirits, thou wilt feel my worth,
And seek to honour with an empty urn
　The ashes thou shalt ne'er obtain — Alas!
　"What have I done to thee, my people?"* Stern
Are all thy dealings, but in this they pass
　The limits of man's common malice, for
　All that a citizen could be I was;

---

* "E scrisse più volte non solamente a particolari cittadini del reggi-

Raised by thy will, all thine in peace or war,
   And for this thou hast warr'd with me. — 'Tis done :
   I may not overleap the eternal bar
Built up between us, and will die alone,
   Beholding with the dark eye of a seer
   The evil days to gifted souls foreshown,
Foretelling them to those who will not hear.
   As in the old time, till the hour be come
   When Truth shall strike their eyes through many a tear,
And make them own the Prophet in his tomb.

mento, ma ancora al popolo, e intra l' altre una Epistola assai lunga che
comincia: — ' *Popule mi, quid feci tibi ?* "
                    Vita di Dante scritta da Lionardo Aretino.

ODE

TO

NAPOLEON BUONAPARTE.

"Expende Annibalem: — quot libras in duce summo
Invenies?" JUVENAL, *Sat.* X.

"The Emperor Nepos was acknowledged by the Senate, by the Italians, and by the Provincials of Gaul; his moral virtues, and military talents, were loudly celebrated; and those who derived any private benefit from his government announced in prophetic strains the restoration of public felicity.

   *   *   *   *   *   *   *
   *   *   *   *   *   *   *

By this shameful abdication, he protracted his life a few years, in a very ambiguous state, between an Emperor and an Exile, till —— "

GIBBON'S *Decline and Fall*, vol. vi. p. 220.

ODE

TO

NAPOLEON BUONAPARTE.

I.

'Tis done — but yesterday a King!
  And arm'd with Kings to strive —
And now thou art a nameless thing:
  So abject — yet alive!
Is this the man of thousand thrones,
Who strew'd our earth with hostile bones,
  And can he thus survive?
Since he, miscall'd the Morning Star,
Nor man nor fiend hath fallen so far.

II.

Ill-minded man! why scourge thy kind
  Who bow'd so low the knee?
By gazing on thyself grown blind,
  Thou taught'st the rest to see.
With might unquestion'd, — power to save, —
Thine only gift hath been the grave
  To those that worshipp'd thee;
Nor till thy fall could mortals guess
Ambition's less than littleness!

III.

Thanks for that lesson — it will teach
  To after-warriors more
Than high Philosophy can preach,
  And vainly preach'd before.
That spell upon the minds of men
Breaks never to unite again,
  That led them to adore

Those Pagod things of sabre sway,
With fronts of brass, and feet of clay.

IV.

The triumph, and the vanity,
  The rapture of the strife * —
The earthquake voice of Victory,
  To thee the breath of life;
The sword, the sceptre, and that sway
Which man seem'd made but to obey,
  Wherewith renown was rife —
All quell'd! — Dark Spirit! what must be
The madness of thy memory!

V.

The Desolator desolate!
  The Victor overthrown!
The Arbiter of others' fate
  A Suppliant for his own!
Is it some yet imperial hope
That with such change can calmly cope?
  Or dread of death alone?
To die a prince — or live a slave —
Thy choice is most ignobly brave!

VI.

He who of old would rend the oak,
  Dream'd not of the rebound;
Chain'd by the trunk he vainly broke —
  Alone — how look'd he round?
Thou in the sternness of thy strength
An equal deed hast done at length,
  And darker fate hast found:
He fell, the forest prowlers' prey;
But thou must eat thy heart away!

---

* "Certaminis *gaudia*"—the expression of Attila in his harangue to his
army, previous to the battle of Chalons, given in Cassiodorus.

VII.

The Roman,* when his burning heart
  Was slaked with blood of Rome,
Threw down the dagger — dared depart,
  In savage grandeur, home. —
He dared depart in utter scorn
Of men that such a yoke had borne,
  Yet left him such a doom!
His only glory was that hour
Of self-upheld abandon'd power.

VIII.

The Spaniard, when the lust of sway
  Had lost its quickening spell,
Cast crowns for rosaries away,
  An empire for a cell;
A strict accountant of his beads,
A subtle disputant on creeds,
  His dotage trifled well:
Yet better had he neither known
A bigot's shrine, nor despot's throne.

IX.

But thou — from thy reluctant hand
  The thunderbolt is wrung —
Too late thou leav'st the high command
  To which thy weakness clung;
All Evil Spirit as thou art,
It is enough to grieve the heart
  To see thine own unstrung,
To think that God's fair world hath been
The footstool of a thing so mean;

* Sylla.

x.

And Earth hath spilt her blood for him,
  Who thus can hoard his own!
And Monarchs bow'd the trembling limb,
  And thank'd him for a throne!
Fair Freedom! we may hold thee dear,
When thus thy mightiest foes their fear.
  In humblest guise have shown.
Oh! ne'er may tyrant leave behind
A brighter name to lure mankind!

xi.

Thine evil deeds are writ in gore,
  Nor written thus in vain —
Thy triumphs tell of fame no more,
  Or deepen every stain:
If thou hadst died as honour dies,
Some new Napoleon might arise,
  To shame the world again —
But who would soar the solar height,
To set in such a starless night?

xii.

Weigh'd in the balance, hero dust
  Is vile as vulgar clay;
Thy scales, Mortality! are just
  To all that pass away:
But yet methought the living great
Some higher sparks should animate,
  To dazzle and dismay:
Nor deem'd Contempt could thus make mirth
Of these, the Conquerors of the earth.

XIII.

And she, proud Austria's mournful flower,
  Thy still imperial bride;
How bears her breast the torturing hour?
  Still clings she to thy side?
Must she too bend, must she too share
Thy late repentance, long despair,
  Thou throneless Homicide?
If still she loves thee, hoard that gem,
'Tis worth thy vanish'd diadem!

XIV.

Then haste thee to thy sullen Isle,
  And gaze upon the sea;
That element may meet thy smile —
  It ne'er was ruled by thee!
Or trace with thine all idle hand
In loitering mood upon the sand
  That Earth is now as free!
That Corinth's pedagogue hath now
Transferr'd his by-word to thy brow.

XV.

Thou Timour! in his captive's cage*
  What thoughts will there be thine,
While brooding in thy prison'd rage?
  But one — "The world *was* mine!"
Unless, like he of Babylon,
All sense is with thy sceptre gone,
  Life will not long confine
That spirit pour'd so widely forth —
So long obey'd — so little worth!

* The cage of Bajazet, by order of Tamerlane.

XVI.

Or, like the thief of fire from heaven,*
   Wilt thou withstand the shock?
And share with him, the unforgiven,
   His vulture and his rock!
Foredoom'd by God — by man accurst,
And that last act, though not thy worst,
   The very Fiend's arch mock;**
He in his fall preserved his pride,
And, if a mortal, had as proudly died!

XVII.

There was a day — there was an hour,
   While earth was Gaul's — Gaul thine —
When that immeasurable power
   Unsated to resign
Had been an act of purer fame
Than gathers round Marengo's name,
   And gilded thy decline,
Through the long twilight of all time,
Despite some passing clouds of crime.

XVIII.

But thou forsooth must be a king,
   And don the purple vest, —
As if that foolish robe could wring
   Remembrance from thy breast.
Where is that faded garment? where
The gewgaws thou wert fond to wear,
   The star — the string — the crest?
Vain froward child of empire! say,
Are all thy playthings snatch'd away?

---

* Prometheus.
**   — "The very fiend's arch mock —
    To lip a wanton, and suppose her chaste." — SHAKSPEARE.

XIX.

Where may the wearied eye repose
  When gazing on the Great;
Where neither guilty glory glows,
  Nor despicable state?
Yes — one — the first — the last — the best —
The Cincinnatus of the West,
  Whom envy dared not hate,
Bequeath'd the name of Washington,
To make man blush there was but one!

MONODY

DEATH OF THE RIGHT HON. R. B. SHERIDAN,

SPOKEN AT DRURY-LANE THEATRE.

————

WHEN the last sunshine of expiring day
In summer's twilight weeps itself away,
Who hath not felt the softness of the hour
Sink on the heart, as dew along the flower?
With a pure feeling which absorbs and awes
While Nature makes that melancholy pause,
Her breathing moment on the bridge where Time
Of light and darkness forms an arch sublime,
Who hath not shared that calm so still and deep,
The voiceless thought which would not speak but weep,
A holy concord — and a bright regret,
A glorious sympathy with suns that set?
'Tis not harsh sorrow — but a tenderer woe,
Nameless, but dear to gentle hearts below,
Felt without bitterness — but full and clear,
A sweet dejection — a transparent tear,
Unmix'd with worldly grief or selfish stain,
Shed without shame — and secret without pain.

Even as the tenderness that hour instils
When Summer's day declines along the hills,
So feels the fulness of our heart and eyes
When all of Genius which can perish dies.

26*

A mighty Spirit is eclipsed — a Power
Hath pass'd from day to darkness — to whose hour
Of light no likeness is bequeath'd — no name,
Focus at once of all the rays of Fame!
The flash of Wit — the bright Intelligence,
The beam of Song — the blaze of Eloquence,
Set with their Sun — but still have left behind
The enduring produce of immortal Mind;
Fruits of a genial morn, and glorious noon,
A deathless part of him who died too soon.
But small that portion of the wondrous whole,
These sparkling segments of that circling soul,
Which all embraced — and lighten'd over all,
To cheer — to pierce — to please — or to appal.
From the charm'd council to the festive board,
Of human feelings the unbounded lord;
In whose acclaim the loftiest voices vied,
The praised—the proud — who made his praise their pride.
When the loud cry of trampled Hindostan
Arose to Heaven in her appeal from man,
His was the thunder — his the avenging rod,
The wrath — the delegated voice of God!
Which shook the nations through his lips — and blazed
Till vanquish'd senates trembled as they praised.

And here, oh! here, where yet all young and warm
The gay creations of his spirit charm,
The matchless dialogue — the deathless wit,
Which knew not what it was to intermit;
The glowing portraits, fresh from life, that bring
Home to our hearts the truth from which they spring;
These wondrous beings of his Fancy, wrought
To fulness by the fiat of his thought,
Here in their first abode you still may meet,
Bright with the hues of his Promethean heat;
A halo of the light of other days,
Which still the splendour of its orb betrays.

But should there be to whom the fatal blight
Of failing Wisdom yields a base delight,
Men who exult when minds of heavenly tone
Jar in the music which was born their own,
Still let them pause — ah! little do they know
That what to them seem'd Vice might be but Woe.
Hard is his fate on whom the public gaze
Is fix'd for ever to detract or praise;
Repose denies her requiem to his name,
And Folly loves the martyrdom of Fame.
The secret enemy whose sleepless eye
Stands sentinel — accuser — judge — and spy,
The foe — the fool — the jealous — and the vain,
The envious who but breathe in others' pain,
Behold the host! delighting to deprave,
Who track the steps of Glory to the grave,
Watch every fault that daring Genius owes
Half to the ardour which its birth bestows,
Distort the truth, accumulate the lie,
And pile the Pyramid of Calumny!
These are his portion — but if joined to these
Gaunt Poverty should league with deep Disease,
If the high Spirit must forget to soar,
And stoop to strive with Misery at the door,
To soothe Indignity — and face to face
Meet sordid Rage — and wrestle with Disgrace,
To find in Hope but the renew'd caress,
The serpent-fold of further Faithlessness: —
If such may be the Ills which men assail,
What marvel if at last the mightiest fail?
Breasts to whom all the strength of feeling given
Bear hearts electric — charged with fire from Heaven,
Black with the rude collision, inly torn,
By clouds surrounded, and on whirlwinds borne,
Driven o'er the lowering atmosphere that nurst
Thoughts which have turn'd to thunder — scorch — and
          burst.

But far from us and from our mimic scene
Such things should be — if such have ever been;
Ours be the gentler wish, the kinder task,
To give the tribute Glory need not ask,
To mourn the vanish'd beam — and add our mite
Of praise in payment of a long delight.
Ye Orators! whom yet our councils yield,
Mourn for the veteran Hero of your field!
The worthy rival of the wondrous *Three!**
Whose words were sparks of Immortality!
Ye Bards! to whom the Drama's Muse is dear,
He was your Master — emulate him *here!*
Ye men of wit and social eloquence!
He was your brother — bear his ashes hence!
While Powers of mind almost of boundless range,
Complete in kind — as various in their change,
While Eloquence — Wit — Poesy — and Mirth,
That humbler Harmonist of care on Earth,
Survive within our souls — while lives our sense
Of pride in Merit's proud pre-eminence,
Long shall we seek his likeness — long in vain,
And turn to all of him which may remain,
Sighing that Nature form'd but one such man,
And broke the die — in moulding Sheridan!

* Fox — Pitt — Burke.

THE DREAM.

I.

Our life is twofold: Sleep hath its own world,
A boundary between the things misnamed
Death and existence: Sleep hath its own world,
And a wide realm of wild reality,
And dreams in their developement have breath,
And tears, and tortures, and the touch of joy;
They leave a weight upon our waking thoughts,
They take a weight from off our waking toils,
They do divide our being; they become
A portion of ourselves as of our time,
And look like heralds of eternity;
They pass like spirits of the past, — they speak
Like sibyls of the future; they have power —
The tyranny of pleasure and of pain;
They make us what we were not — what they will,
And shake us with the vision that's gone by,
The dread of vanish'd shadows — Are they so?
Is not the past all shadow? What are they?
Creations of the mind? — The mind can make
Substance, and people planets of its own
With beings brighter than have been, and give
A breath to forms which can outlive all flesh.
I would recall a vision which I dream'd
Perchance in sleep — for in itself a thought,
A slumbering thought, is capable of years,
And curdles a long life into one hour.

II.

I saw two beings in the hues of youth
Standing upon a hill, a gentle hill,
Green and of mild declivity, the last

As 'twere the cape of a long ridge of such,
Save that there was no sea to lave its base,
But a most living landscape, and the wave
Of woods and cornfields, and the abodes of men
Scatter'd at intervals, and wreathing smoke
Arising from such rustic roofs; — the hill
Was crown'd with a peculiar diadem
Of trees, in circular array, so fix'd,
Not by the sport of nature, but of man:
These two, a maiden and a youth, were there
Gazing — the one on all that was beneath
Fair as herself — but the boy gazed on her;
And both were young, and one was beautiful:
And both were young — yet not alike in youth.
As the sweet moon on the horizon's verge,
The maid was on the eve of womanhood;
The boy had fewer summers, but his heart
Had far outgrown his years, and to his eye
There was but one beloved face on earth,
And that was shining on him; he had look'd
Upon it till it could not pass away;
He had no breath, no being, but in hers;
She was his voice; he did not speak to her,
But trembled on her words; she was his sight,
For his eye follow'd hers, and saw with hers,
Which colour'd all his objects: — he had ceased
To live within himself; she was his life,
The ocean to the river of his thoughts,
Which terminated all: upon a tone,
A touch of hers, his blood would ebb and flow,
And his cheek change tempestuously — his heart
Unknowing of its cause of agony.
But she in these fond feelings had no share:
Her sighs were not for him; to her he was
Even as a brother — but no more; 'twas much,
For brotherless she was, save in the name
Her infant friendship had bestow'd on him;

Herself the solitary scion left
Of a time-honour'd race. — It was a name
Which pleased him, and yet pleased him not — and why?
Time taught him a deep answer — when she loved
Another; even *now* she loved another,
And on the summit of that hill she stood
Looking afar if yet her lover's steed
Kept pace with her expectancy, and flew.

III.

A change came o'er the spirit of my dream.
There was an ancient mansion, and before
Its walls there was a steed caparison'd:
Within an antique Oratory stood
The Boy of whom I spake; — he was alone,
And pale, and pacing to and fro: anon
He sate him down, and seized a pen, and traced
Words which I could not guess of; then he lean'd
His bow'd head on his hands, and shook as 'twere
With a convulsion — then arose again,
And with his teeth and quivering hands did tear
What he had written, but he shed no tears.
And he did calm himself, and fix his brow
Into a kind of quiet: as he paused,
The Lady of his love re-enter'd there;
She was serene and smiling then, and yet
She knew she was by him beloved, — she knew,
For quickly comes such knowledge, that his heart
Was darken'd with her shadow, and she saw
That he was wretched, but she saw not all.
He rose, and with a cold and gentle grasp
He took her hand; a moment o'er his face
A tablet of unutterable thoughts
Was traced, and then it faded, as it came;
He dropp'd the hand he held, and with slow steps
Retired, but not as bidding her adieu,
For they did part with mutual smiles; he pass'd
From out the massy gate of that old Hall,

And mounting on his steed he went his way;
And ne'er repass'd that hoary threshold more.

IV.

A change came o'er the spirit of my dream.
The Boy was sprung to manhood: in the wilds
Of fiery climes he made himself a home,
And his soul drank their sunbeams: he was girt
With strange and dusky aspects; he was not
Himself like what he had been; on the sea
And on the shore he was a wanderer;
There was a mass of many images
Crowded like waves upon me, but he was
A part of all; and in the last he lay
Reposing from the noontide sultriness,
Couch'd among fallen columns, in the shade
Of ruin'd walls that had survived the names
Of those who rear'd them; by his sleeping side
Stood camels grazing, and some goodly steeds
Were fasten'd near a fountain; and a man
Clad in a flowing garb did watch the while,
While many of his tribe slumber'd around:
And they were canopied by the blue sky,
So cloudless, clear, and purely beautiful,
That God alone was to be seen in Heaven.

V.

A change came o'er the spirit of my dream.
The Lady of his love was wed with One
Who did not love her better: — in her home,
A thousand leagues from his, — her native home,
She dwelt, begirt with growing Infancy,
Daughters and sons of Beauty, — but behold!
Upon her face there was the tint of grief,
The settled shadow of an inward strife,
And an unquiet drooping of the eye
As if its lid were charged with unshed tears.
What could her grief be? — she had all she loved,
And he who had so loved her was not there

To trouble with bad hopes, or evil wish,
Or ill-repress'd affliction, her pure thoughts.
What could her grief be? — she had loved him not,
Nor given him cause to deem himself beloved,
Nor could he be a part of that which prey'd
Upon her mind — a spectre of the past.

VI.

A change came o'er the spirit of my dream.
The Wanderer was return'd. — I saw him stand
Before an Altar — with a gentle bride;
Her face was fair, but was not that which made
The Starlight of his Boyhood; — as he stood
Even at the altar, o'er his brow there came
The selfsame aspect, and the quivering shock
That in the antique Oratory shook
His bosom in its solitude; and then —
As in that hour — a moment o'er his face
The tablet of unutterable thoughts
Was traced, — and then it faded as it came,
And he stood calm and quiet, and he spoke
The fitting vows, but heard not his own words,
And all things reel'd around him; he could see
Not that which was, nor that which should have been --
But the old mansion, and the accustom'd hall,
And the remember'd chambers, and the place,
The day, the hour, the sunshine, and the shade,
All things pertaining to that place and hour,
And her who was his destiny, came back
And thrust themselves between him and the light:
What business had they there at such a time?

VII.

A change came o'er the spirit of my dream.
The Lady of his love; — Oh! she was changed
As by the sickness of the soul; her mind
Had wander'd from its dwelling, and her eyes
They had not their own lustre, but the look
Which is not of the earth; she was become

The queen of a fantastic realm; her thoughts
Were combinations of disjointed things;
And forms impalpable and unperceived
Of others' sight familiar were to hers.
And this the world calls frenzy; but the wise
Have a far deeper madness, and the glance
Of melancholy is a fearful gift;
What is it but the telescope of truth?
Which strips the distance of its fantasies,
And brings life near in utter nakedness,
Making the cold reality too real!

VIII.

A change came o'er the spirit of my dream.
The Wanderer was alone as heretofore,
The beings which surrounded him were gone,
Or were at war with him; he was a mark
For blight and desolation, compass'd round
With Hatred and Contention; Pain was mix'd
In all which was served up to him, until,
Like to the Pontic monarch of old days, *
He fed on poisons, and they had no power,
But were a kind of nutriment; he lived
Through that which had been death to many men,
And made him friends of mountains: with the stars
And the quick Spirit of the Universe
He held his dialogues; and they did teach
To him the magic of their mysteries;
To him the book of Night was open'd wide,
And voices from the deep abyss reveal'd
A marvel and a secret — Be it so.

IX.

My dream was past; it had no further change.
It was of a strange order, that the doom
Of these two creatures should be thus traced out
Almost like a reality — the one
To end in madness — both in misery.   July, 1816.

* Mithridates of Pontus.

THE

VISION OF JUDGMENT,

BY

QUEVEDO REDIVIVUS.

SUGGESTED BY THE COMPOSITION SO ENTITLED BY THE AUTHOR
OF "WAT TYLER."

"A Daniel come to judgment! yea, a Daniel!
I thank thee, Jew, for teaching me that word."

PREFACE.

It hath been wisely said, that "One fool makes many;" and it hath been poetically observed,

"That fools rush in where angels fear to tread." — *Pope.*

If Mr. Southey had not rushed in where he had no business, and where he never was before, and never will be again, the following poem would not have been written. It is not impossible that it may be as good as his own, seeing that it cannot, by any species of stupidity, natural or acquired, be *worse.* The gross flattery, the dull impudence, the renegado intolerance and impious cant, of the poem by the author of "Wat Tyler," are something so stupendous as to form the sublime of himself — containing the quintessence of his own attributes.

So much for his poem — a word on his preface. In this preface it has pleased the magnanimous Laureate to draw the picture of a supposed "Satanic School," the which he doth re-commend to the notice of the legislature; thereby adding to his other laurels the ambition of those of an informer. If there exists any where, excepting in his imagination, such a School, is he not sufficiently armed against it by his own intense vanity? The truth is, that there are certain writers whom Mr. S. imagines, like Scrub, to have "talked of *him;* for they laughed consumedly."

I think I know enough of most of the writers to whom he is supposed to allude, to assert, that they, in their individual capacities, have done more good, in the charities of life, to their fellow-creatures in any one year, than Mr. Southey has done harm to himself by his absurdities in his whole life; and this is saying a great deal. But I have a few questions to ask.

'1stly, Is Mr. Southey the author of "Wat Tyler?"

2dly, Was he not refused a remedy at law by the highest judge of his beloved England, because it was a blasphemous and seditious publication?

3dly, Was he not entitled by William Smith, in full parliament, "a rancorous renegado?"

4thly, Is he not poet laureate, with his own lines on Martin the regicide staring him in the face?

And, 5thly, Putting the four preceding items together, with what conscience dare *he* call the attention of the laws to the publications of others, be they what they may?

I say nothing of the cowardice of such a proceeding; its meanness speaks for itself; but I wish to touch upon the *motive*, which is neither more nor less than that Mr. S. has been laughed at a little in some recent publications, as he has of yore in the "Anti-jacobin" by his present patrons. Hence all this "skimble scamble stuff" about "Satanic," and so forth. However, it is worthy of him — "*qualis ab incepto*."

If there is any thing obnoxious to the political opinions of a portion of the public in the following poem, they may thank Mr. Southey. He might have written hexameters, as he has written every thing else, for aught that the writer cared — had they been upon another subject. But to attempt to canonise a monarch, who, whatever were his household virtues, was neither a successful nor a patriot king, — inasmuch as several years of his reign passed in war with America and Ireland, to say nothing of the aggression upon France, — like all other exaggeration, necessarily begets opposition. In whatever manner he may be spoken of in this new "Vision," his *public* career will not be more favourably transmitted by history. Of his private virtues (although a little expensive to the nation) there can be no doubt.

With regard to the supernatural personages treated of, I can only say that I know as much about them, and (as an honest man) have a better right to talk of them than Robert

Southey. I have also treated them more tolerantly. The way in which that poor insane creature, the Laureate, deals about his judgments in the next world, is like his own judgment in this. If it was not completely ludicrous, it would be something worse. I don't think that there is much more to say at present.

Quevedo Redivivus.

P.S. — It is possible that some readers may object, in these objectionable times, to the freedom with which saints, angels, and spiritual persons discourse in this "Vision." But, for precedents upon such points, I must refer him to Fielding's "Journey from this World to the next," and to the Visions of myself, the said Quevedo, in Spanish or translated. The reader is also requested to observe, that no doctrinal tenets are insisted upon or discussed; that the person of the Deity is carefully withheld from sight, which is more than can be said for the Laureate, who hath thought proper to make him talk, not "like a school divine," but like the unscholarlike Mr. Southey. The whole action passes on the outside of heaven; and Chaucer's Wife of Bath, Pulci's Morgante Maggiore, Swift's Tale of a Tub, and the other works above referred to, are cases in point of the freedom with which saints, &c. may be permitted to converse in works not intended to be serious.

Q. R.

⁎ Mr. Southey being, as he says, a good Christian and vindictive, threatens, I understand, a reply to this our answer. It is to be hoped that his visionary faculties will in the mean time have acquired a little more judgment, properly so called: otherwise he will get himself into new dilemmas. These apostate jacobins furnish rich rejoinders. Let him take a specimen. Mr. Southey laudeth grievously "one Mr. Landor," who cultivates much private renown in the shape of Latin verses; and not long ago, the poet laureate dedicated to him, it appeareth, one of his fugitive lyrics, upon the strength of a poem called *Gebir*. Who could suppose, that in this same

Gebir the aforesaid Savage Landor (for such is his grim cognomen) putteth into the infernal regions no less a person than the hero of his friend Mr. Southey's heaven, — yea, even George the Third! See also how personal Savage becometh, when he hath a mind. The following is his portrait of our late gracious sovereign: —

(Prince Gebir having descended into the infernal regions, the shades of his royal ancestors are, at his request, called up to his view; and he exclaims to his ghostly guide) —

"Aroar, what wretch that nearest us? what wretch
Is that with eyebrows white and slanting brow?
Listen! him yonder, who, bound down supine,
Shrinks yelling from that sword there, engine-hung.
He too amongst my ancestors! I hate
The despot, but the dastard I despise.
Was he our countryman?"

"Alas, O king:
Iberia bore him, but the breed accurst
Inclement winds blew blighting from north-east."
"He was a warrior then, nor fear'd the gods?"
"Gebir, he fear'd the demons, not the gods,
Though them indeed his daily face adored;
And was no warrior, yet the thousand lives
Squander'd, as stones to exercise a sling,
And the tame cruelty and cold caprice —
Oh madness of mankind! address'd, adored!" — *Gebir*, p. 28.

I omit noticing some edifying Ithyphallics of Savagius, wishing to keep the proper veil over them, if his grave but somewhat indiscreet worshipper will suffer it; but certainly these teachers of "great moral lessons" are apt to be found in strange company.

THE VISION OF JUDGMENT.

I.

Saint Peter sat by the celestial gate;
  His keys were rusty, and the lock was dull,
So little trouble had been given of late;
  Not that the place by any means was full,
But since the Gallic era "eighty-eight"
  The devils had ta'en a longer, stronger pull,
And "a pull altogether," as they say
At sea — which drew most souls another way.

II.

The angels all were singing out of tune,
  And hoarse with having little else to do,
Excepting to wind up the sun and moon,
  Or curb a runaway young star or two,
Or wild colt of a comet, which too soon
  Broke out of bounds o'er the ethereal blue,
Splitting some planet with its playful tail,
As boats are sometimes by a wanton whale.

III.

The guardian seraphs had retired on high,
  Finding their charges past all care below;
Terrestrial business fill'd nought in the sky
  Save the recording angel's black bureau;
Who found, indeed, the facts to multiply
  With such rapidity of vice and wo,
That he had stripp'd off both his wings in quills,
And yet was in arrear of human ills.

IV.

His business so augmented of late years,
　That he was forced, against his will, no doubt,
(Just like those cherubs, earthly ministers,)
　For some resource to turn himself about,
And claim the help of his celestial peers,
　To aid him ere he should be quite worn out
By the increased demand for his remarks;
Six angels and twelve saints were named his clerks.

V.

This was a handsome board — at least for heaven;
　And yet they had even then enough to do,
So many conquerors' cars were daily driven,
　So many kingdoms fitted up anew;
Each day too slew its thousands six or seven,
　Till at the crowning carnage, Waterloo,
They threw their pens down in divine disgust —
The page was so besmear'd with blood and dust.

VI.

This by the way; 'tis not mine to record
　What angels shrink from: even the very devil
On this occasion his own work abhorr'd,
　So surfeited with the infernal revel:
Though he himself had sharpen'd every sword
　It almost quench'd his innate thirst of evil.
(Here Satan's sole good work deserves insertion —
'Tis, that he has both generals in reversion.)

VII.

Let's skip a few short years of hollow peace,
　Which peopled earth no better, hell as wont,
And heaven none — they form the tyrant's lease,
　With nothing but new names subscribed upon 't;
'Twill one day finish: meantime they increase,
　"With seven heads and ten horns," and all in front,
Like Saint John's foretold beast; but ours are born
Less formidable in the head than horn.

27*

VIII.

In the first year of freedom's second dawn
  Died George the Third; although no tyrant, one
Who shielded tyrants, till each sense withdrawn
  Left him nor mental nor external sun:
A better farmer ne'er brush'd dew from lawn,
  A worse king never left a realm undone!
He died — but left his subjects still behind,
One half as mad — and t'other no less blind.

IX.

He died! — his death made no great stir on earth;
  His burial made some pomp; there was profusion
Of velvet, gilding, brass, and no great dearth
  Of aught but tears — save those shed by collusion.
For these things may be bought at their true worth;
  Of elegy there was the due infusion —
Bought also; and the torches, cloaks, and banners,
Heralds, and relics of old Gothic manners,

X.

Form'd a sepulchral melodrame.   Of all
  The fools who flock'd to swell or see the show,
Who cared about the corpse?   The funeral
  Made the attraction, and the black the wo.
There throbb'd not there a thought which pierced the pall;
  And when the gorgeous coffin was laid low,
It seem'd the mockery of hell to fold
The rottenness of eighty years in gold.

XI.

So mix his body with the dust!   It might
  Return to what it *must* far sooner, were
The natural compound left alone to fight
  Its way back into earth, and fire, and air;
But the unnatural balsams merely blight
  What nature made him at his birth, as bare
As the mere million's base unmummied clay —
Yet all his spices but prolong decay.

XII.

He's dead — and upper earth with him has done;
   He's buried; save the undertaker's bill,
Or lapidary scrawl, the world is gone
   For him, unless he left a German will;
But where's the proctor who will ask his son?
   In whom his qualities are reigning still,
Except that household virtue, most uncommon,
Of constancy to a bad, ugly woman.

XIII.

"God save the king!" It is a large economy
   In God to save the like; but if he will
Be saving, all the better; for not one am I
   Of those who think damnation better still:
I hardly know too if not quite alone am I
   In this small hope of bettering future ill
By circumscribing, with some slight restriction,
The eternity of hell's hot jurisdiction.

XIV.

I know this is unpopular; I know
   "Tis blasphemous; I know one may be damn'd
For hoping no one else may e'er be so;
   I know my catechism; I know we are cramm'd
With the best doctrines till we quite o'erflow;
   I know that all save England's church have shamm'd,
And that the other twice two hundred churches
And synagogues have made a *damn'd* bad purchase.

XV.

God help us all! God help me too! I am,
   God knows, as helpless as the devil can wish,
And not a whit more difficult to damn
   Than is to bring to land a late-hook'd fish,
Or to the butcher to purvey the lamb;
   Not that I'm fit for such a noble dish
As one day will be that immortal fry
Of almost every body born to die.

XVI.

Saint Peter sat by the celestial gate,
    And nodded o'er his keys; when, lo! there came
A wondrous noise he had not heard of late —
    A rushing sound of wind, and stream, and flame;
In short, a roar of things extremely great,
    Which would have made aught save a saint exclaim;
But he, with first a start and then a wink,
Said, "There's another star gone out, I think!"

XVII.

But ere he could return to his repose,
    A cherub flapp'd his right wing o'er his eyes —
At which Saint Peter yawn'd, and rubb'd his nose:
    "Saint porter," said the angel, "prithee rise!"
Waving a goodly wing, which glow'd, as glows
    An earthly peacock's tail, with heavenly dyes:
To which the saint replied, "Well, what's the matter?
"Is Lucifer come back with all this clatter?"

XVIII.

"No," quoth the cherub; "George the Third is dead."
    "And who is George the Third?" replied the apostle:
"What George? what Third?" "The king of England," said
    The angel. "Well! he won't find kings to jostle
Him on his way; but does he wear his head?
    Because the last we saw here had a tustle,
And ne'er would have got into heaven's good graces,
Had he not flung his head in all our faces.

XIX.

"He was, if I remember, king of France;
    That head of his, which could not keep a crown
On earth, yet ventured in my face to advance
    A claim to those of martyrs — like my own:
If I had had my sword, as I had once
    When I cut ears off, I had cut him down;
But having but my keys, and not my brand,
I only knock'd his head from out his hand.

XX.

" And then he set up such a headless howl,
    That all the saints came out and took him in ;
And there he sits by St. Paul, cheek by jowl ;
    That fellow Paul — the parvenù ! The skin
Of Saint Bartholomew, which makes his cowl
    In heaven, and upon earth redeem'd his sin,
So as to make a martyr, never sped
Better than did this weak and wooden head.

XXI.

"But had it come up here upon its shoulders,
    There would have been a different tale to tell :
The fellow-feeling in the saints beholders
    Seems to have acted on them like a spell ;
And so this very foolish head heaven solders
    Back on its trunk : it may be very well,
And seems the custom here to overthrow
Whatever has been wisely done below."

XXII.

The angel answer'd, "Peter! do not pout:
    The king who comes has head and all entire,
And never knew much what it was about —
    He did as doth the puppet — by its wire,
And will be judged like all the rest, no doubt:
    My business and your own is not to enquire
Into such matters, but to mind our cue —
Which is to act as we are bid to do."

XXIII.

While thus they spake, the angelic caravan,
    Arriving like a rush of mighty wind,
Cleaving the fields of space, as doth the swan
    Some silver stream (say Ganges, Nile, or Inde,
Or Thames, or Tweed), and 'midst them an old man
    With an old soul, and both extremely blind,
Halted before the gate, and in his shroud
Seated their fellow traveller on a cloud.

XXIV.

But bringing up the rear of this bright host
   A Spirit of a different aspect waved
His wings, like thunder-clouds above some coast
   Whose barren beach with frequent wrecks is paved;
His brow was like the deep when tempest-toss'd;
   Fierce and unfathomable thoughts engraved
Eternal wrath on his immortal face,
And *where* he gazed a gloom pervaded space.

XXV.

As he drew near, he gazed upon the gate
   Ne'er to be enter'd more by him or sin,
With such a glance of supernatural hate,
   As made Saint Peter wish himself within;
He patter'd with his keys at a great rate,
   And sweated through his apostolic skin:
Of course his perspiration was but ichor,
Or some such other spiritual liquor.

XXVI.

The very cherubs huddled all together,
   Like birds when soars the falcon; and they felt
A tingling to the tip of every feather,
   And form'd a circle like Orion's belt
Around their poor old charge; who scarce knew whither
   His guards had led him, though they gently dealt
With royal manes (for by many stories,
And true, we learn the angels all are Tories).

XXVII.

As things were in this posture, the gate flew
   Asunder, and the flashing of its hinges
Flung over space an universal hue
   Of many-colour'd flame, until its tinges
Reach'd even our speck of earth, and made a new
   Aurora borealis spread its fringes
O'er the North Pole; the same seen, when ice-bound,
By Captain Parry's crew, in "Melville's Sound."

XXVIII.

And from the gate thrown open issued beaming
　A beautiful and mighty Thing of Light,
Radiant with glory, like a banner streaming
　Victorious from some world-o'erthrowing fight:
My poor comparisons must needs be teeming
　With earthly likenesses, for here the night
Of clay obscures our best conceptions, saving
Johanna Southcote, or Bob Southey raving.

XXIX.

"Twas the archangel Michael: all men know
　The make of angels and archangels, since
There's scarce a scribbler has not one to show,
　From the fiends' leader to the angels' prince.
There also are some altar-pieces, though
　I really can't say that they much evince
One's inner notions of immortal spirits;
But let the connoisseurs explain *their* merits.

XXX.

Michael flew forth in glory and in good;
　A goodly work of him from whom all glory
And good arise; the portal past — he stood;
　Before him the young cherubs and saints hoary —
(I say *young*, begging to be understood
　By looks, not years; and should be very sorry
To state, they were not older than St. Peter,
But merely that they seem'd a little sweeter).

XXXI.

The cherubs and the saints bow'd down before
　That arch-angelic hierarch, the first
Of essences angelical, who wore
　The aspect of a god; but this ne'er nursed
Pride in his heavenly bosom, in whose core
　No thought, save for his Maker's service, durst
Intrude, however glorified and high;
He knew him but the viceroy of the sky.

XXXII.

He and the sombre silent Spirit met —
   They knew each other both for good and ill;
Such was their power, that neither could forget
   His former friend and future foe; but still
There was a high, immortal, proud regret
   In either's eye, as if 'twere less their will
Than destiny to make the eternal years
Their date of war, and their "champ clos" the spheres.

XXXIII.

But here they were in neutral space: we know
   From Job, that Satan hath the powers to pay
A heavenly visit thrice a year or so;
   And that "the sons of God," like those of clay,
Must keep him company; and we might show
   From the same book, in how polite a way
The dialogue is held between the Powers
Of Good and Evil — but 'twould take up hours.

XXXIV.

And this is not a theologic tract,
   To prove with Hebrew and with Arabic
If Job be allegory or a fact,
   But a true narrative; and thus I pick
From out the whole but such and such an act
   As sets aside the slightest thought of trick.
'Tis every tittle true, beyond suspicion,
And accurate as any other vision.

XXXV.

The spirits were in neutral space, before
   The gate of heaven; like eastern thresholds is
The place where Death's grand cause is argued o'er,
   And souls despatch'd to that world or to this;
And therefore Michael and the other wore
   A civil aspect: though they did not kiss,
Yet still between his Darkness and his Brightness
There pass'd a mutual glance of great politeness

XXXVI.

The Archangel bow'd, not like a modern beau,
  But with a graceful oriental bend,
Pressing one radiant arm just where below
  The heart in good men is supposed to tend,
He turn'd us to an equal, not too low,
  But kindly; Satan met his ancient friend
With more hauteur, as might an old Castilian
Poor noble meet a mushroom rich civilian.

XXXVII.

He merely bent his diabolic brow
  An instant; and then raising it, he stood
In act to assert his right or wrong, and show
  Cause why King George by no means could or should
Make out a case to be exempt from woe
  Eternal, more than other kings, endued
With better sense and hearts, whom history mentions,
Who long have "paved hell with their good intentions."

XXXVIII.

Michael began: "What wouldst thou with this man,
  Now dead, and brought before the Lord? What ill
Hath he wrought since his mortal race began,
  That thou canst claim him? Speak! and do thy will,
If it be just: if in this earthly span
  He hath been greatly failing to fulfil
His duties as a king and mortal, say,
And he is thine; if not, let him have way."

XXXIX.

"Michael!" replied the Prince of Air, "even here,
  Before the Gate of him thou servest, must
I claim my subject: and will make appear
  That as he was my worshipper in dust,
So shall he be in spirit, although dear
  To thee and thine, because nor wine nor lust
Were of his weaknesses; yet on the throne
He reign'd o'er millions to serve me alone.

XL.

"Look to *our* earth, or rather *mine;* it was,
  Once, more thy master's: but I triumph not
In this poor planet's conquest; nor, alas!
  Need he thou servest envy me my lot:
With all the myriads of bright worlds which pass
  In worship round him, he may have forgot
Yon weak creation of such paltry things:
I think few worth damnation save their kings, —

XLI.

"And these but as a kind of quit-rent, to
  Assert my right as lord; and even had
I such an inclination, 'twere (as you
  Well know) superfluous: they are grown so bad,
That hell has nothing better left to do
  Than leave them to themselves: so much more mad
And evil by their own internal curse,
Heaven cannot make them better, nor I worse.

XLII.

"Look to the earth, I said, and say again:
  When this old, blind, mad, helpless, weak, poor worm
Began in youth's first bloom and flush to reign,
  The world and he both wore a different form,
And much of earth and all the watery plain
  Of ocean call'd him king: through many a storm
His isles had floated on the abyss of time;
For the rough virtues chose them for their clime.

XLIII.

"He came to his sceptre young; he leaves it old:
  Look to the state in which he found his realm,
And left it; and his annals too behold,
  Now to a minion first he gave the helm;
How grew upon his heart a thirst for gold,
  The beggar's vice, which can but overwhelm
The meanest hearts; and for the rest, but glance
Thine eye along America and France.

XLIV.

" 'Tis true, he was a tool from first to last
  (I have the workmen safe); but as a tool
So let him be consumed. From out the past
  Of ages, since mankind have known the rule
Of monarchs — from the bloody rolls amass'd
  Of sin and slaughter — from the Cæsars' school,
Take the worst pupil; and produce a reign
More drench'd with gore, more cumber'd with the slain.

XLV.

"He ever warr'd with freedom and the free:
  Nations as men, home subjects, foreign foes,
So that they utter'd the word 'Liberty!'
  Found George the Third their first opponent. Whose
History was ever stain'd as his will be
  With national and individual woes?
I grant his household abstinence; I grant
His neutral virtues, which most monarchs want;

XLVI.

"I know he was a constant consort; own
  He was a decent sire, and middling lord.
All this is much, and most upon a throne;
  As temperance, if at Apicius' board,
Is more than at an anchorite's supper shown.
  I grant him all the kindest can accord;
And this was well for him, but not for those
Millions who found him what oppression chose.

XLVII.

"The New World shook him off; the Old yet groans
  Beneath what he and his prepared, if not
Completed: he leaves heirs on many thrones
  To all his vices, without what begot
Compassion for him — his tame virtues; drones
  Who sleep, or despots who have now forgot
A lesson which shall be re-taught them, wake
Upon the thrones of earth; but let them quake!

XLVIII.

"Five millions of the primitive, who hold
  The faith which makes ye great on earth, implored
A *part* of that vast *all* they held of old, —
  Freedom to worship — not alone your Lord,
Michael, but you, and you, Saint Peter! Cold
  Must be your souls, if you have not abhorr'd
The foe to catholic participation
In all the license of a Christian nation.

XLIX.

"True! he allow'd them to pray God; but as
  A consequence of prayer, refused the law
Which would have placed them upon the same base
  With those who did not hold the saints in awe."
But here Saint Peter started from his place,
  And cried, "You may the prisoner withdraw;
Ere heaven shall ope her portals to this Guelph,
While I am guard, may I be damn'd myself!

L.

"Sooner will I with Cerberus exchange
  My office (and *his* is no sinecure)
Than see this royal Bedlam bigot range
  The azure fields of heaven, of that be sure!"
"Saint!" replied Satan, "you do well to avenge
  The wrongs he made your satellites endure;
And if to this exchange you should be given,
I'll try to coax *our* Cerberus up to heaven."

LI.

Here Michael interposed: "Good saint! and devil!
  Pray, not so fast; you both outrun discretion.
Saint Peter! you were wont to be more civil:
  Satan! excuse this warmth of his expression,
And condescension to the vulgar's level:
  Even saints sometimes forget themselves in session.
Have you got more to say?" — "No." — "If you please,
I'll trouble you to call your witnesses."

LII.

Then Satan turn'd and waved his swarthy hand,
  Which stirr'd with its electric qualities
Clouds farther off than we can understand,
  Although we find him sometimes in our skies;
Infernal thunder shook both sea and land
  In all the planets, and hell's batteries
Let off the artillery, which Milton mentions
As one of Satan's most sublime inventions.

LIII.

This was a signal unto such damn'd souls
  As have the privilege of their damnation
Extended far beyond the mere controls
  Of worlds past, present, or to come; no station
Is theirs particularly in the rolls
  Of hell assign'd; but where their inclination
Or business carries them in search of game,
They may range freely — being damn'd the same.

LIV.

They are proud of this — as very well they may,
  It being a sort of knighthood, or gilt key
Stuck in their loins; or like to an "entré"
  Up the back stairs, or such free-masonry.
I borrow my comparisons from clay,
  Being clay myself. Let not those spirits be
Offended with such base low likenesses;
We know their posts are nobler far then these.

LV.

When the great signal ran from heaven to hell —
  About ten million times the distance reckon'd
From our sun to its earth, as we can tell
  How much time it takes up, even to a second,
For every ray that travels to dispel
  The fogs of London, through which, dimly beacon'd,
The weathercocks are gilt some thrice a year,
If that the *summer* is not too severe: —

LVI.

I say that I can tell — 'twas half a minute:
  I know the solar beams take up more time
Ere, pack'd up for their journey, they begin it;
  But then their telegraph is less sublime,
And if they ran a race, they would not win it
  'Gainst Satan's couriers bound for their own clime.
The sun takes up some years for every ray
To reach its goal — the devil not half a day.

LVII.

Upon the verge of space, about the size
  Of half-a-crown, a little speck appear'd
(I've seen a something like it in the skies
  In the Ægean, ere a squall); it near'd
And, growing bigger, took another guise;
  Like an aërial ship it tack'd, and steer'd,
Or *was* steer'd (I am doubtful of the grammar
Of the last phrase, which makes the stanza stammer; —

LVIII.

But take your choice); and then it grew a cloud;
  And so it was — a cloud of witnesses.
But such a cloud! No land e'er saw a crowd
  Of locusts numerous as the heavens saw these;
They shadow'd with their myriads space; their loud
  And varied cries were like those of wild geese
(If nations may be liken'd to a goose),
And realised the phrase of "hell broke loose."

LIX.

Here crash'd a sturdy oath of stout John Bull,
  Who damn'd away his eyes as heretofore:
There Paddy brogued "By Jasus!" — "What's your wull?"
  The temperate Scot exclaim'd: the French ghost swore
In certain terms I sha'n't translate in full,
  As the first coachman will; and 'midst the war,
The voice of Jonathan was heard to express,
"*Our* president is going to war, I guess."

LX.

Besides there were the Spaniard, Dutch, and Dane;
  In short, an universal shoal of shades,
From Otaheite's isle to Salisbury Plain,
  Of all climes and professions, years and trades,
Ready to swear against the good king's reign,
  Bitter as clubs in cards are against spades:
All summon'd by this grand "subpœna," to
Try if kings mayn't be damn'd like me or you.

LXI.

When Michael saw this host, he first grew pale,
  As angels can; next, like Italian twilight,
He turn'd all colours — as a peacock's tail,
  Or sunset streaming through a Gothic skylight
In some old abbey, or a trout not stale,
  Or distant lightning on the horizon *by* night,
Or a fresh rainbow, or a grand review
Of thirty regiments in red, green, and blue.

LXII.

Then he address'd himself to Satan: "Why —
  My good old friend, for such I deem you, though
Our different parties make us fight so shy,
  I ne'er mistake you for a *personal* foe;
Our difference is *political*, and I
  Trust that, whatever may occur below,
You know my great respect for you: and this
Makes me regret whate'er you do amiss —

LXIII.

"Why, my dear Lucifer, would you abuse
  My call for witnesses? I did not mean
That you should half of earth and hell produce;
  'Tis even superfluous, since two honest, clean,
True testimonies are enough: we lose
  Our time, nay, our eternity, between
The accusation and defence: if we
Hear both, 'twill stretch our immortality."

Lord Byron. III.   28

LXIV.

Satan replied, "To me the matter is
   Indifferent, in a personal point of view:
I can have fifty better souls than this
   With far less trouble than we have gone through
Already; and I merely argued his
   Late majesty of Britain's case with you
Upon a point of form: you may dispose
Of him; I've kings enough below, God knows!"

LXV.

Thus spoke the Demon (late call'd "multifaced"
   By multo-scribbling Southey). "Then we'll call
One or two persons of the myriads placed
   Around our congress, and dispense with all
The rest," quoth Michael: "Who may be so graced
   As to speak first? there's choice enough — who shall
It be?" Then Satan answer'd, "There are many;
But you may choose Jack Wilkes as well as any."

LXVI.

A merry, cock-eyed, curious-looking sprite
   Upon the instant started from the throng,
Dress'd in a fashion now forgotten quite;
   For all the fashions of the flesh stick long
By people in the next world; where unite
   All the costumes since Adam's, right or wrong,
From Eve's fig-leaf down to the petticoat,
Almost as scanty, of days less remote.

LXVII.

The spirit look'd around upon the crowds
   Assembled, and exclaim'd, "My friends of all
The spheres, we shall catch cold amongst these clouds;
   So let's to business: why this general call?
If those are freeholders I see in shrouds,
   And 'tis for an election that they bawl,
Behold a candidate with unturn'd coat!
Saint Peter, may I count upon your vote?"

LXVIII.

"Sir," replied Michael, "you mistake; these things
  Are of a former life, and what we do
Above is more august; to judge of kings
  Is the tribunal met: so now you know."
"Then I presume those gentlemen with wings,"
  Said Wilkes, "are cherubs; and that soul below
Looks much like George the Third, but to my mind
A good deal older — Bless me! is he blind?"

LXIX.

"He is what you behold him, and his doom
  Depends upon his deeds," the Angel said.
"If you have aught to arraign in him, the tomb
  Gives license to the humblest beggar's head
To lift itself against the loftiest." — "Some,"
  Said Wilkes, "don't wait to see them laid in lead,
For such a liberty — and I, for one,
Have told them what I thought beneath the sun."

LXX.

"*Above* the sun repeat, then, what thou hast
  To urge against him," said the Archangel.   "Why,"
Replied the spirit, "since old scores are past,
  Must I turn evidence? In faith, not I.
Besides, I beat him hollow at the last,
  With all his Lords and Commons: in the sky
I don't like ripping up old stories, since
His conduct was but natural in a prince.

LXXI.

"Foolish, no doubt, and wicked, to oppress
  A poor unlucky devil without a shilling;
But then I blame the man himself much less
  Than Bute and Grafton, and shall be unwilling
To see him punish'd here for their excess,
  Since they were both damn'd long ago, and still in
Their place below: for me, I have forgiven,
And vote his 'habeas corpus' into heaven."

28*

LXXII.

"Wilkes," said the Devil, "I understand all this;
    You turn'd to half a courtier ere you died,
And seem to think it would not be amiss
    To grow a whole one on the other side
Of Charon's ferry; you forget that *his*
    Reign is concluded; whatsoe'er betide,
He won't be sovereign more: you've lost your labour,
For at the best he will but be your neighbour.

LXXIII.

"However, I knew what to think of it,
    When I beheld you in your jesting way,
Flitting and whispering round about the spit
    Where Belial, upon duty for the day,
With Fox's lard was basting William Pitt,
    His pupil; I knew what to think, I say:
That fellow even in hell breeds farther ills;
I'll have him *gagg'd* — 'twas one of his own bills.

LXXIV.

"Call Junius!" From the crowd a shadow stalk'd,
    And at the name there was a general squeeze,
So that the very ghosts no longer walk'd
    In comfort, at their own aërial ease,
But were all ramm'd, and jamm'd (but to be balk'd,
    As we shall see), and jostled hands and knees,
Like wind compress'd and pent within a bladder,
Or like a human colic, which is sadder.

LXXV.

The shadow came — a tall, thin, grey-hair'd figure,
    That look'd as it had been a shade on earth;
Quick in its motions, with an air of vigour,
    But nought to mark its breeding or its birth:
Now it wax'd little, then again grew bigger,
    With now an air of gloom, or savage mirth;
But as you gazed upon its features, they
Changed every instant — to *what*, none could say.

LXXVI.

The more intently the ghosts gazed, the less
  Could they distinguish whose the features were;
The Devil himself seem'd puzzled even to guess;
  They varied like a dream — now here, now there;
And several people swore from out the press,
  They knew him perfectly; and one could swear
He was his father: upon which another
Was sure he was his mother's cousin's brother:

LXXVII.

Another, that he was a duke, or knight,
  An orator, a lawyer, or a priest,
A nabob, a man-midwife; but the wight
  Mysterious changed his countenance at least
As oft as they their minds: though in full sight
  He stood, the puzzle only was increased;
The man was a phantasmagoria in
Himself — he was so volatile and thin.

LXXVIII.

The moment that you had pronounced him *one*,
  Presto! his face changed, and he was another;
And when that change was hardly well put on,
  It varied, till I don't think his own mother
(If that he had a mother) would her son
  Have known, he shifted so from one to t'other;
Till guessing from a pleasure grew a task,
At this epistolary "Iron Mask."

LXXIX.

For sometimes he like Cerberus would seem —
  "Three gentlemen at once" (as sagely says
Good Mrs. Malaprop); then you might deem
  That he was not even *one;* now many rays
Were flashing round him; and now a thick steam
  Hid him from sight — like fogs on London days:
Now Burke, now Tooke, he grew to people's fancies,
And certes often like Sir Philip Francis.

LXXX.

I've an hypothesis — 'tis quite my own;
    I never let it out till now, for fear
Of doing people harm about the throne,
    And injuring some minister or peer,
On whom the stigma might perhaps be blown:
    It is — my gentle public, lend thine ear!
'Tis, that what Junius we are wont to call
Was *really, truly,* nobody at all.

LXXXI.

I don't see wherefore letters should not be
    Written without hands, since we daily view
Them written without heads; and books, we see,
    Are fill'd as well without the latter too:
And really till we fix on somebody
    For certain sure to claim them as his due,
Their author, like the Niger's mouth, will bother
The world to say if *there* be mouth or author.

LXXXII.

"And who and what art thou?" the Archangel said.
    "For *that* you may consult my title-page,"
Replied this mighty shadow of a shade:
    "If I have kept my secret half an age,
I scarce shall tell it now." — "Canst thou upbraid,"
    Continued Michael, "George Rex, or allege
Aught further?" Junius answer'd, "You had better
First ask him for *his* answer to my letter:

LXXXIII.

"My charges upon record will outlast
    The brass of both his epitaph and tomb."
"Repent'st thou not," said Michael, "of some past
    Exaggeration? something which may doom
Thyself if false, as him if true? Thou wast
    Too bitter — is it not so? — in thy gloom
Of passion?" — "Passion!" cried the phantom dim,
"I loved my country, and I hated him.

LXXXIV.

"What I have written, I have written: let
  The rest be on his head or mine!" So spoke
Old "Nominis Umbra;" and while speaking yet,
  Away he melted in celestial smoke.
Then Satan said to Michael, "Don't forget
  To call George Washington, and John Horne Tooke,
And Franklin;" — but at this time there was heard
A cry for room, though not a phantom stirr'd.

LXXXV.

At length with jostling, elbowing, and the aid
  Of cherubim appointed to that post,
The devil Asmodeus to the circle made
  His way, and look'd as if his journey cost
Some trouble.   When his burden down he laid,
  "What's this?" cried Michael; "why, 'tis not a ghost?"
"I know it," quoth the incubus; "but he
Shall be one, if you leave the affair to me.

LXXXVI.

"Confound the renegado! I have sprain'd
  My left wing, he's so heavy; one would think
Some of his works about his neck were chain'd.
  But to the point; while hovering o'er the brink
Of Skiddaw (where as usual it still rain'd),
  I saw a taper, far below me, wink,
And stooping, caught this fellow at a libel —
No less on history than the Holy Bible.

LXXXVII.

"The former is the devil's scripture, and
  The latter yours, good Michael; so the affair
Belongs to all of us, you understand.
  I snatch'd him up just as you see him there,
And brought him off for sentence out of hand:
  I've scarcely been ten minutes in the air —
At least a quarter it can hardly be:
I dare say that his wife is still at tea."

LXXXVIII.

Here Satan said, "I know this man of old,
  And have expected him for some time here;
A sillier fellow you will scarce behold,
  Or more conceited in his petty sphere:
But surely it was not worth while to fold
  Such trash below your wing, Asmodeus dear:
We had the poor wretch safe (without being bored
With carriage) coming of his own accord.

LXXXIX.

"But since he's here, let 's see what he has done."
  "Done!" cried Asmodeus, "he anticipates
The very business you are now upon,
  And scribbles as if head clerk to the Fates.
Who knows to what his ribaldry may run,
  When such an ass as this, like Balaam's, prates?"
"Let's hear," quoth Michael, "what he has to say;
You know we're bound to that in every way."

XC.

Now the bard, glad to get an audience, which
  By no means often was his case below,
Began to cough, and hawk, and hem, and pitch
  His voice into that awful note of woe
To all unhappy hearers within reach
  Of poets when the tide of rhyme's in flow;
But stuck fast with his first hexameter,
Not one of all whose gouty feet would stir.

XCI.

But ere the spavin'd dactyls could be spurr'd
  Into recitative, in great dismay
Both cherubim and seraphim were heard
  To murmur loudly through their long array;
And Michael rose ere he could get a word
  Of all his founder'd verses under way,
And cried, "For God's sake stop, my friend! 'twere best —
Non Di, non homines — you know the rest."

XCII.

A general bustle spread throughout the throng,
  Which seem'd to hold all verse in detestation;
The angels had of course enough of song
  When upon service; and the generation
Of ghosts had heard too much in life, not long
  Before, to profit by a new occasion;
The monarch, mute till then, exclaim'd, "What! what!
Pye come again? No more — no more of that!"

XCIII.

The tumult grew; an universal cough
  Convulsed the skies, as during a debate,
When Castlereagh has been up long enough
  (Before he was first minister of state,
I mean — the *slaves hear now*); some cried "Off, off!"
  As at a farce; till, grown quite desperate,
The bard Saint Peter pray'd to interpose
(Himself an author) only for his prose.

XCIV.

The varlet was not an ill-favour'd knave;
  A good deal like a vulture in the face,
With a hook nose and a hawk's eye, which gave
  A smart and sharper-looking sort of grace
To his whole aspect, which, though rather grave,
  Was by no means so ugly as his case;
But that indeed was hopeless as can be,
Quite a poetic felony "*de se.*"

XCV.

Then Michael blew his trump, and still'd the noise
  With one still greater, as is yet the mode
On earth besides; except some grumbling voice,
  Which now and then will make a slight inroad
Upon decorous silence, few will twice
  Lift up their lungs when fairly overcrow'd;
And now the bard could plead his own bad cause,
With all the attitudes of self-applause.

XCVI.

He said — (I only give the heads) — he said,
    He meant no harm in scribbling; 'twas his way
Upon all topics; 'twas, besides, his bread,
    Of which he butter'd both sides; 'twould delay
Too long the assembly (he was pleased to dread),
    And take up rather more time than a day,
To name his works — he would but cite a few —
"Wat Tyler" — "Rhymes on Blenheim" — "Waterloo."

XCVII.

He had written praises of a regicide;
    He had written praises of all kings whatever
He had written for republics far and wide,
    And then against them bitterer than ever:
For pantisocracy he once had cried
    Aloud, a scheme less moral than 'twas clever;
Then grew a hearty anti-jacobin —
Had turn'd his coat — and would have turn'd his skin.

XCVIII.

He had sung against all battles, and again
    In their high praise and glory; he had call'd
Reviewing* "the ungentle craft," and then
    Become as base a critic as e'er crawl'd —
Fed, paid, and pamper'd by the very men
    By whom his muse and morals had been maul'd:
He had written much blank verse, and blanker prose,
And more of both than any body knows.

XCIX.

He had written Wesley's life: — here turning round
    To Satan, "Sir, I'm ready to write yours,
In two octavo volumes, nicely bound,
    With notes and preface, all that most allures
The pious purchaser; and there's no ground
    For fear, for I can choose my own reviewers:
So let me have the proper documents,
That I may add you to my other saints."

* See "Life of Henry Kirke White."

C.

Satan bow'd, and was silent. "Well, if you,
　With amiable modesty, decline
My offer, what says Michael? There are few
　. Whose memoirs could be render'd more divine.
Mine is a pen of all work; not so new
　As it was once, but I would make you shine
Like your own trumpet. By the way, my own
Has more of brass in it, and is as well blown.

CI.

"But talking about trumpets, here's my Vision!
　Now you shall judge, all people; yes, you shall
Judge with my judgment, and by my decision
　Be guided who shall enter heaven or fall.
I settle all these things by intuition,
　Times present, past, to come, heaven, hell, and all,
Like King Alfonso.* When I thus see double,
I save the Deity some worlds of trouble."

CII.

He ceased, and drew forth an MS.; and no
　Persuasion on the part of devils, or saints,
Or angels, now could stop the torrent; so
　He read the first three lines of the contents;
But at the fourth, the whole spiritual show
　Had vanish'd, with variety of scents,
Ambrosial and sulphureous, as they sprang,
Like lightning, off from his "melodious twang."**

CIII.

Those grand heroics acted as a spell;
　The angels stopp'd their ears and plied their pinions;
The devils ran howling, deafen'd, down to hell;
　The ghosts fled, gibbering, for their own dominions —
(For 'tis not yet decided where they dwell,
　And I leave every man to his opinions);

* Alfonso, speaking of the Ptolomean system, said, that "had he been
consulted at the creation of the world, he would have spared the Maker
some absurdities."
** See Aubrey's account of the apparition which disappeared "with a

Michael took refuge in his trump — but, lo!
His teeth were set on edge, he could not blow!

CIV.

Saint Peter, who has hitherto been known
   For an impetuous saint, upraised his keys,
And at the fifth line knock'd the poet down;
   Who fell like Phaeton, but more at ease,
Into his lake, for there he did not drown;
   A different web being by the Destinies
Woven for the Laureate's final wreath, whene'er
Reform shall happen either here or there.

CV.

He first sank to the bottom — like his works,
   But soon rose to the surface — like himself;
For all corrupted things are buoy'd like corks,*
   By their own rottenness, light as an elf,
Or wisp that flits o'er a morass: he lurks,
   It may be, still, like dull books on a shelf,
In his own den, to scrawl some "Life" or "Vision,"
As Welborn says — "the devil turn'd precisian."

CVI.

As for the rest, to come to the conclusion
   Of this true dream, the telescope is gone
Which kept my optics free from all delusion,
   And show'd me what I in my turn have shown;
All I saw farther, in the last confusion,
   Was, that King George slipp'd into heaven for one;
And when the tumult dwindled to a calm,
I left him practising the hundredth psalm.

curious perfume and a *most melodious twang;*" or see the "*Antiquary,*"
vol. I. p. 225.

   * A drowned body lies at the bottom till rotten; it then floats, as most
people know.

———

THE

MORGANTE MAGGIORE

OF PULCI.

<hr>

ADVERTISEMENT.

<hr>

THE Morgante Maggiore, of the first canto of which this
translation is offered, divides with the Orlando Innamorato
the honour of having formed and suggested the style and
story of Ariosto. The great defects of Boiardo were his treat-
ing too seriously the narratives of chivalry, and his harsh style.
Ariosto, in his continuation, by a judicious mixture of the
gaiety of Pulci, has avoided the one; and Berni, in his reformation of Boiardo's poem, has corrected the other. Pulci may
be considered as the precursor and model of Berni altogether,
as he has partly been to Ariosto, however inferior to both his
copyists. He is no less the founder of a new style of poetry
very lately sprung up in England. I allude to that of the ingenious Whistlecraft. The serious poems on Roncesvalles in
the same language, and more particularly the excellent one of

Mr. Merivale, are to be traced to the same source. It has never yet been decided entirely whether Pulci's intention was or was not to deride the religion which is one of his favourite topics. It appears to me, that such an intention would have been no less hazardous to the poet than to the priest, particularly in that age and country; and the permission to publish the poem, and its reception among the classics of Italy, prove that it neither was nor is so interpreted. That he intended to ridicule the monastic life, and suffered his imagination to play with the simple dulness of his converted giant, seems evident enough; but surely it were as unjust to accuse him of irreligion on this account, as to denounce Fielding for his Parson Adams, Barnabas, Thwackum, Supple, and the Ordinary in Jonathan Wild, — or Scott, for the exquisite use of his Covenanters in the "Tales of my Landlord."

In the following translation I have used the liberty of the original with the proper names; as Pulci uses Gan, Ganellon, or Ganellone; Carlo, Carlomagno, or Carlomano; Rondel, or Rondello, &c. as it suits his convenience; so has the translator. In other respects the version is faithful to the best of the translator's ability in combining his interpretation of the one language with the not very easy task of reducing it to the same versification in the other. The reader, on comparing it with the original, is requested to remember that the antiquated language of Pulci, however pure, is not easy to the generality of Italians themselves, from its great mixture of Tuscan proverbs; and he may therefore be more indulgent to the present attempt. How far the translator has succeeded, and whether or no he shall continue the work, are questions which the public will decide. He was induced to make the experiment partly by his love for, and partial intercourse with, the Italian language, of which it is so easy to acquire a slight knowledge, and with which it is so nearly impossible for a foreigner to become accurately conversant. The Italian language is like a capricious beauty, who accords her smiles to all, her favours to few, and sometimes least to those who have courted her longest. The translator wished also to present in an English dress a part at least of a poem never yet rendered into a northern language; at the same time that it has been the original of some of the most celebrated productions on this side of the Alps, as well as of those recent experiments in poetry in England which have been already mentioned.

———

IL MORGANTE MAGGIORE.

CANTO PRIMO.

I.

In principio era il Verbo appresso a Dio;
  Ed era Iddio il Verbo, e'l Verbo lui:
  Questo era nel principio, al parer mio;
  E nulla si può far sanza costui:
  Però, giusto Signor benigno e pio,
  Mandami solo un de gli angeli tui,
  Che m'accompagni, e rechimi a memoria
  Una famosa antica e degna storia.

II.

E tu Vergine, figlia, e madre, e sposa
  Di quel Signor, che ti dette le chiave
  Del cielo e dell' abisso, e d'ogni cosa,
  Quel dì che Gabriel tuo ti disse Ave!
  Perchè tu se' de' tuo' servi pietosa,
  Con dolce rime, e stil grato e soave,
  Ajuta i versi miei benignamente,
  E'nfino al fine allumina la mente.

III.

Era nel tempo, quando Filomena
  Con la sorella si lamenta e plora,
  Che si ricorda di sua antica pena,
  E pe' boschetti le ninfe innamora,
  E Febo il carro temperato mena,
  Che 'l suo Fetonte l'ammacstra ancora;
  Ed appariva appunto all'orizzonte,
  Tal che Titon si graffiava la fronte.

THE MORGANTE MAGGIORE.

CANTO THE FIRST.

I.

In the beginning was the Word next God;
  God was the Word, the Word no less was he:
This was in the beginning, to my mode
  Of thinking, and without him nought could be:
Therefore, just Lord! from out thy high abode,
  Benign and pious, bid an angel flee,
One only, to be my companion, who
Shall help my famous, worthy, old song through.

II.

And thou, oh Virgin! daughter, mother, bride,
  Of the same Lord, who gave to you each key
Of heaven, and hell, and every thing beside,
  The day thy Gabriel said "All hail!" to thee,
Since to thy servants pity's ne'er denied,
  With flowing rhymes, a pleasant style and free,
Be to my verses then benignly kind,
And to the end illuminate my mind.

III.

'Twas in the season when sad Philomel
  Weeps with her sister, who remembers and
Deplores the ancient woes which both befel,
  And makes the nymphs enamour'd, to the hand
Of Phaeton by Phœbus loved so well
  His car (but temper'd by his sire's command)
Was given, and on the horizon's verge just now
Appear'd, so that Tithonus scratch'd his brow:

IV.

Quand'io varai la mia barchetta, prima
  Per ubbidir chi sempre ubbidir debbe
  La mente, e faticarsi in prosa e in rima,
  E del mio Carlo Imperador m'increbbe;
  Che so quanti la penna ha posto in cima,
  Che tutti la sua gloria prevarrebbe:
  E stata quella istoria, a quel ch' i' veggio,
  Di Carlo male intesa, e scritta peggio.

V.

Diceva già Lionardo Aretino,
  Che s'egli avesse avuto scrittor degno,
  Com'egli ebbe un Ormanno il suo Pipino
  Ch'avesse diligenzia avuto e ingegno;
  Sarebbe Carlo Magno un uom divino;
  Però ch'egli ebbe gran vittorie e regno,
  E fece per la chiesa e per la fede
  Certo assai più, che non si dice o crede.

VI.

Guardisi ancora a san Liberatore
  Quella badía là presso a Manoppello,
  Giù ne gli Abbruzzi fatta per suo onore,
  Dove fu la battaglia e'l gran flaggello
  D'un re pagan, che Carlo imperadore
  Uccise, e tanto del suo popol fello:
  E vedesi tante ossa, e tanto il sanno,
  Che tutte in Giusaffà poi si vedranno.

VII.

Ma il mondo cieco e ignorante non prezza
  Le sue virtù, com'io vorrei vedere:
  E tu, Fiorenza, de la sua grandezza
  Possiedi, e sempre potrai possedere
  Ogni costume ed ogni gentilezza
  Che si potesse acquistare o avere
  Col senno col tesoro o con la lancia
  Dal nobil sangue e venuto di Francia.

IV.

When I prepared my bark first to obey,
  As it should still obey, the helm, my mind,
And carry prose or rhyme, and this my lay
  Of Charles the Emperor, whom you will find
By several pens already praised; but they
  Who to diffuse his glory were inclined,
For all that I can see in prose or verse,
Have understood Charles badly, and wrote worse.

V.

Leonardo Arctino said already,
  That if, like Pepin, Charles had had a writer
Of genius quick, and diligently steady,
  No hero would in history look brighter;
He in the cabinet being always ready,
  And in the field a most victorious fighter,
Who for the church and Christian faith had wrought,
Certes, far more than yet is said or thought.

VI.

You still may see at Saint Liberatore
  The abbey, no great way from Manopell,
Erected in the Abruzzi to his glory,
  Because of the great battle in which fell
A pagan king, according to the story,
  And felon people whom Charles sent to hell:
And there are bones so many, and so many,
Near them Giusaffa's would seem few, if any.

VII.

But the world, blind and ignorant, don't prize
  His virtues as I wish to see them: thou,
Florence, by his great bounty don't arise,
  And hast, and may have, if thou wilt allow,
All proper customs and true courtesies:
  Whate'er thou hast acquired from then till now,
With knightly courage, treasure, or the lance,
Is sprung from out the noble blood of France.

VIII.

Dodici paladini aveva in corte
  Carlo; e'l più savio e famoso era Orlando:
  Gan traditor lo condusse a la morte
  In Roncisvalle un trattato ordinando;
  Là dove il corno sonò tanto forte
  Dopo la dolorosa rotta, quando
  Ne la sua commedia Dante qui dice,
  E mettelo con Carlo in ciel felice.

IX.

Era per Pasqua quella dì natale:
  Carlo la corte avea tutta in Parígi:
  Orlando, com'io dico, il principale
  Evvi, il Danese, Astolfo, e Ansuigi:
  Fannosi feste e cose trionfale,
  E molto celebravan San Dionigi;
  Angiolin di Bajona, ed Ulivieri
  V'era venuto, e'l gentil Berlinghieri.

X.

Eravi Avolio ed Avino ed Ottone,
  Di Normandía, Riccardo Paladino,
  E'l savio Namo, e'l vecchio Salamone,
  Gualtier da Monlione, e Baldovino
  Ch'era figliuol del tristo Ganellone.
  Troppo lieto era il figliuol di Pipino;
  Tanto che spesso d'allegrezza geme
  Veggendo tutti i paladini insieme.

XI.

Ma la fortuna attenta sta nascosa,
  Per guastar sempre ciascun nostro effetto;
  Mentre che Carlo così si riposa,
  Orlando governava in fatto e in detto
  La corte e Carlo Magno ed ogni cosa:
  Gan per invidia scoppia il maladetto,
  E cominciava un dì con Carlo a dire:
  Abbiam noi sempre Orlando ad ubbidire?

VIII.

Twelve paladins had Charles in court, of whom
  The wisest and most famous was Orlando;
Him traitor Gan conducted to the tomb
  In Roncesvalles, as the villain plann'd too,
While the horn rang so loud, and knell'd the doom
  Of their sad rout, though he did all knight can do;
And Dante in his comedy has given
To him a happy seat with Charles in heaven.

IX.

"Twas Christmas-day; in Paris all his court
  Charles held; the chief, I say, Orlando was,
The Dane; Astolfo there too did resort,
  Also Ansuigi, the gay time to pass
In festival and in triumphal sport,
  The much-renown'd St. Dennis being the cause;
Angiolin of Bayonne, and Oliver,
And gentle Belinghieri too came there:

X.

Avolio, and Arino, and Othone
  Of Normandy, and Richard Paladin,
Wise Hamo, and the ancient Salemone,
  Walter of Lion's Mount and Baldovin,
Who was the son of the sad Ganellone,
  Were there, exciting too much gladness in
The son of Pepin: — when his knights came hither,
He groan'd with joy to see them altogether.

XI.

But watchful Fortune, lurking, takes good heed
  Ever some bar 'gainst our intents to bring.
While Charles reposed him thus, in word and deed,
  Orlando ruled court, Charles, and every thing;
Curst Gan, with envy bursting, had such need
  To vent his spite, that thus with Charles the king
One day he openly began to say,
"Orlando must we always then obey?

XII.

Io ho creduto mille volte dirti :
　Orlando ha in se troppa presunzione :
　Noi siam qui conti, re, duchi a servirti,
　E Namo, Ottone, Uggieri e Salamone,
　Per onorarti ognun, per ubbidirti :
　Che costui abbi ogni reputazione
　Nol sofferrem ; ma siam deliberati
　Da un fanciullo non esser governati.

XIII.

Tu cominciasti insino in Aspramonte
　A dargli a intender che fusse gagliardo,
　E facesse gran cose a quella fonte ;
　Ma se non fusse stato il buon Gherardo,
　Io so che la vittoria era d'Almonte :
　Ma egli ebbe sempre l'occhio a lo stendardo :
　Che si voleva quel dì coronarlo :
　Questo è colui ch'ha meritato, Carlo.

XIV.

Se ti ricorda già sendo in Guascogna,
　Quando e' vi venne la gente di Spagna,
　Il popol de' cristiani avea vergogna,
　Se non mostrava la sua forza magna.
　Il ver convien pur dir, quando e'bisogna :
　Sappi ch'ognuno imperador si lagna :
　Quant'io per me, ripasserò que' monti
　Ch'io passai 'n qua con sessantaduo conti

XV.

La tua grandezza dispensar si vuole,
　E far che ciascun abbi la sua parte :
　La corte tutta quanta se ne duole :
　Tu credi che costui sia forse Marte?
　Orlando un giorno udì queste parole,
　Che si sedeva soletto in disparte :
　Dispiacquegli di Gan quel che diceva ;
　Ma molto più che Carlo gli credeva.

XII.

"A thousand times I've been about to say,
    Orlando too presumptuously goes on;
Here are we, counts, kings, dukes, to own thy sway,
    Hamo, and Otho, Ogier, Solomon,
Each have to honour thee and to obey;
    But he has too much credit near the throne,
Which we won't suffer, but are quite decided
By such a boy to be no longer guided.

XIII.

"And even at Aspramont thou didst begin
    To let him know he was a gallant knight,
And by the fount did much the day to win;
    But I know *who* that day had won the fight
If it had not for good Gherardo been:
    The victory was Almonte's else; his sight
He kept upon the standard, and the laurels
In fact and fairness are his earning, Charles.

XIV.

"If thou rememberest being in Gascony,
    When there advanced the nations out of Spain,
The Christian cause had suffer'd shamefully,
    Had not his valour driven them back again.
Best speak the truth when there's a reason why:
    Know then, oh emperor! that all complain:
As for myself, I shall repass the mounts
O'er which I cross'd with two and sixty counts.

XV.

"'Tis fit thy grandeur should dispense relief,
    So that each here may have his proper part,
For the whole court is more or less in grief:
    Perhaps thou deem'st this lad a Mars in heart?"
Orlando one day heard this speech in brief,
    As by himself it chanced he sate apart:
Displeased he was with Gan because he said it,
But much more still that Charles should give him credit.

XVI.

E volle con la spada uccider Gano;
 Ma Ulivieri in quel mezzo si mise,
 E Durlindana gli trasse di mano,
 E così il me' che seppe gli divise,
 Orlando si sdegnò con Carlo Mano,
 E poco men che quivi non l'uccise;
 E dipartissi di Parigi solo,
 E scoppia e'mpazza di sdegno e di duolo.

XVII.

Ad Ermellina moglie del Danese
 Tolse Cortana, e poi tolse Rondello;
 E 'n verso Brara il suo cammin poi prese.
 Alda la bella, come vide quello,
 Per abbracciarlo le braccia distese.
 Orlando, che ismarrito avea il cervello,
 Com'ella disse: ben venga il mio Orlando:
 Gli volle in su la testa dar col brando.

XVIII.

Come colui che la furia consiglia,
 Egli pareva a Gan dar veramente:
 Alda la bella si fe' maraviglia:
 Orlando si ravvide prestamente:
 E la sua sposa pigliava la briglia,
 E scese dal caval subitamente:
 Ed ogni cosa narrava a costei,
 E riposossi alcun giorno con lei.

XIX.

Poi si partì portato dal furore,
 E terminò passare in Paganía;
 E mentre che cavalca, il traditore
 Di Gan sempre ricorda per la via:
 E cavalcando d'uno in altro errore,
 In un deserto truova una badía
 In luoghi oscuri e paesi lontani,
 Ch'era a' confin' tra cristiani e pagani.

XVI.

And with the sword he would have murder'd Gan,
    But Oliver thrust in between the pair,
And from his hand extracted Durlindan,
    And thus at length they separated were.
Orlando angry too with Carloman,
    Wanted but little to have slain him there;
Then forth alone from Paris went the chief,
And burst and madden'd with disdain and grief.

XVII.

From Ermellina, consort of the Dane,
    He took Cortana, and then took Rondell,
And on towards Brara prick'd him o'er the plain;
    And when she saw him coming, Aldabelle
Stretch'd forth her arms to clasp her lord again:
    Orlando, in whose brain all was not well,
As "Welcome, my Orlando, home," she said,
Raised up his sword to smite her on the head.

XVIII.

Like him a fury counsels; his revenge
    On Gan in that rash act he seem'd to take,
Which Aldabella thought extremely strange;
    But soon Orlando found himself awake;
And his spouse took his bridle on this change,
    And he dismounted from his horse, and spake
Of every thing which pass'd without demur,
And then reposed himself some days with her.

XIX.

Then full of wrath departed from the place,
    And far as pagan countries roam'd astray,
And while he rode, yet still at every pace
    The traitor Gan remember'd by the way;
And wandering on in error a long space,
    An abbey which in a lone desert lay,
'Midst glens obscure, and distant lands, he found,
Which form'd the Christian's and the pagan's bound.

XX.

L'abate si chiamava Chiaramonte,
  Era del sangue disceso d'Anglante:
  Di sopra a la badía v'era un gran monte,
  Dove abitava alcun fiero gigante,
  De'quali uno avea nome Passamonte,
  L'altro Alabastro, e'l terzo era Morgante:
  Con certe frombe gittavan da alto,
  Ed ogni dì facevan qualche assalto.

XXI.

I monachetti non potieno uscire
  Del monistero o per legne o per acque:
  Orlando picchia, e non volieno aprire,
  Fin che a l'abate a la fine pur piacque;
  Entrato drento cominciava a dire,
  Come colui, che di Maria già nacque
  Adora, ed era cristian battezzato,
  E com' egli era a la badía arrivato.

XXII.

Disse l'abate: il ben venuto sia
  Di quel ch'io ho volentier ti daremo,
  Poi che tu credi al figliuol di Maria;
  E la cagion, cavalier, ti diremo,
  Acciò che non l'imputi a villania,
  Perchè a l'entrar resistenza facemo,
  E non ti volle aprir quel monachetto:
  Così intervien chi vive con sospetto.

XXIII.

Quando ci venni al principio abitare
  Queste montagne, benchè sieno oscure
  Come tu vedi; pur si potea stare
  Sanza sospetto, ch' ell' eran sicure:
  Sol da le fiere t'avevi a guardare;
  Feroci spesso di brutte paure;
  Or ci bisogna, se vogliamo starci,
  Da le bestie dimestiche guardarci.

XX.

The abbot was call'd Clermont, and by blood
   Descended from Angrante: under cover
Of a great mountain's brow the abbey stood,
   But certain savage giants look'd him over;
One Passamont was foremost of the brood,
   And Alabaster and Morgante hover
Second and third, with certain slings, and throw
In daily jeopardy the place below.

XXI.

The monks could pass the convent gate no more,
   Nor leave their cells for water or for wood;
Orlando knock'd, but none would ope, before
 · Unto the prior it at length seem'd good;
Enter'd, he said that he was taught to adore
   Him who was born of Mary's holiest blood,
And was baptized a Christian; and then show'd
How to the abbey he had found his road.

XXII.   ·

Said the abbot, "You are welcome; what is mine
   We give you freely, since that you believe
With us in Mary Mother's Son divine;
   And that you may not, cavalier, conceive
The cause of our delay to let you in
   To be rusticity, you shall receive
The reason why our gate was barr'd to you:
Thus those who in suspicion live must do.

XXIII.

"When hither to inhabit first we came
   These mountains, albeit that they are obscure,
As you perceive, yet without fear or blame
   They seem'd to promise an asylum sure:
From savage brutes alone, too fierce to tame,
   'Twas fit our quiet dwelling to secure;
But now, if here we'd stay, we needs must guard
Against domestic beasts with watch and ward.

XXIV.

Queste ci fan piuttosto stare a segno
  Sonci appariti tre fieri giganti,
  Non so di quel paese o di qual regno,
  Ma molto son feroci tutti quanti:
  La forza e 'l malvoler giunt'a lo'ngegno
  Sai che può 'l tutto; e noi non siam bastanti;
  Questi perturban sì l'orazion nostra,
  Che non so più che far, s'altri nol mostra.

XXV.

Gli antichi padri nostri nel deserto,
  Se le lor opre sante erano e giuste,
  Del ben servir da Dio n'avean buon merto;
  Nè creder sol vivessin di locuste:
  Piovea dal ciel la manna, questo è certo;
  Ma qui convien che spesso assaggi e guste
  Sassi che piovon di sopra quel monte,
  Che gettano Alabastro e Passamonte.

XXVI.

E 'l terzo ch'è Morgante, assai più fiero,
  Isveglie e pini e faggi e cerri e gli oppi,
  E gettagli infin qui: questo è pur vero;
  Non posso far che d'ira non iscoppi.
  Mentre che parlan così in cimitero,
  Un sasso par che Rondel quasi sgroppi;
  Che da' giganti giù venne da alto
  Tanto, ch'e' prese sotto il tetto un salto.

XXVII.

Tirati drento, cavalier, per Dio,
  Disse l'abate, che la manna casca.
  Risponde Orlando: caro abate mio,
  Costui non vuol che'l mio caval più pasca:
  Veggo che lo guarrebbe del restìo:
  Quel sasso par che di buon braccio nasca.
  Rispose il santo padre: io non t'inganno,
  Credo che'l monte un giorno gitteranno.

XXIV.

"These make us stand, in fact, upon the watch;
For late there have appear'd three giants rough;
What nation or what kingdom bore the batch
I know not, but they are all of savage stuff;
When force and malice with some genius match,
You know, they can do all — *we* are not enough:
And these so much our orisons derange,
I know not what to do, till matters change.

XXV.

"Our ancient fathers living the desert in,
For just and holy works were duly fed;
Think not they lived on locusts sole, 'tis certain
That manna was rain'd down from heaven instead;
But here 'tis fit we keep on the alert in
Our bounds, or taste the stones shower'd down for bread,
From off yon mountain daily raining faster,
And flung by Passamont and Alabaster.

XXVI.

"The third, Morgante, 's savagest by far; he
Plucks up pines, beeches, poplar-trees, and oaks,
And flings them, our community to bury;
And all that I can do but more provokes."
While thus they parley in the cemetery,
A stone from one of their gigantic strokes,
Which nearly crush'd Rondell, came tumbling over,
So that he took a long leap under cover.

XXVII.

"For God-sake, cavalier, come in with speed;
The manna's falling now," the abbot cried.
"This fellow does not wish my horse should feed,
Dear abbot," Roland unto him replied.
"Of restiveness he 'd cure him had he need;
That stone seems with good will and aim applied."
The holy father said, "I don't deceive;
They'll one day fling the mountain, I believe."

XXVIII.

Orlando governar fece Rondello,
  E ordinar per se da colazione:
  Poi disse: abate, io voglio andare a quello
  Che dette al mio caval con quel cantone.
  Disse l'abate: come car fratello
  Consiglierotti sanza passione?
  Io ti sconforto, baron, di tal gita;
  Ch'io so che tu vi lascerai la vita.

XXIX.

Quel Passamonte porta in man tre dardi:
  Chi frombe, chi baston, chi muzzafrusti;
  Sai che giganti più di noi gagliardi
  Son per ragion, che son anco più giusti;
  E pur se vuoi andar fa che ti guardi,
  Che questi son villan molto e robusti.
  Rispose Orlando: io lo vedrò per certo
  Ed avviossi a piè su pel deserto.

XXX.

Disse l'abate col segnarlo in fronte:
  Va, che da Dio e me sia benedetto.
  Orlando, poi che salito ebbe il monte.
  Si dirizzò, come l'abate detto
  Gli avea, dove sta quel Passamonte;
  Il quale Orlando veggendo soletto,
  Molto lo squadra di drieto e davante;
  Poi domandò, se star volea per fante.

XXXI.

E' prometteva di farlo godere.
  Orlando disse: pazzo saracino,
  Io vengo a te, com'è di Dio volere,
  Per darti morte, e non per ragazzino;
  A'monaci suoi fatto hai dispiacere;
  Non può più comportarti can mastino.
  Questo gigante armar si corse a furia,
  Quando sentì ch'e'gli diceva ingiuria,

XXVIII.

Orlando bade them take care of Rondello,
  And also made a breakfast of his own:
"Abbot," he said, "I want to find that fellow
  Who flung at my good horse yon corner-stone."
Said the abbot, "Let not my advice seem shallow;
  As to a brother dear I speak alone;
I would dissuade you, baron, from this strife,
As knowing sure that you will lose your life.

XXIX.

"That Passamont has in his hand three darts —
  Such slings, clubs, ballast-stones, that yield you must;
You know that giants have much stouter hearts
  Than us, with reason, in proportion just:
If go you will, guard well against their arts,
  For these are very barbarous and robust."
Orlando answer'd, "This I'll see, be sure,
And walk the wild on foot to be secure."

XXX.

The abbot sign'd the great cross on his front,
  "Then go you with God's benison and mine:"
Orlando, after he had scaled the mount,
  As the abbot had directed, kept the line
Right to the usual haunt of Passamont;
  Who, seeing him alone in this design,
Survey'd him fore and aft with eyes observant,
Then ask'd him, "If he wish'd to stay as servant?"

XXXI.

And promised him an office of great ease.
  But, said Orlando, "Saracen insane!
I come to kill you, if it shall so please
  God, not to serve as footboy in your train;
You with his monks so oft have broke the peace —
  Vile dog! 'tis past his patience to sustain."
The giant ran to fetch his arms, quite furious,
When he received an answer so injurious

XXXII.

E ritornato ove aspettava Orlando,
 Il qual non s'era partito da bomba;
Subito venne la corda girando,
 E lascia un sasso andar fuor de la fromba,
Chè in su la testa giugnea rotolando
 Al conte Orlando, e l'elmetto rimbomba;
E'cadde per la pena tramortito;
 Ma più che morto par, tanto è stordito.

XXXIII.

Passamonte pensò che fusse morto,
 E disse: io voglio andarmi a disarmare:
Questo poltron per chi m'aveva scorto?
 Ma Cristo i suoi non suole abbandonare,
Massime Orlando, ch'egli arebbe il torto.
 Mentre il gigante l'arme va a spogliare,
Orlando in questo tempo si risente,
 E rivocava e la forza e la mente.

XXXIV.

E gridò forte: gigante, ove vai?
 Ben ti pensasti d'avermi ammazzato!
Volgiti a drieto, che, s'ale non hai,
 Non puoi da me fuggir, can rinnegato:
A tradimento ingiuriato m'hai.
 Donde il gigante allor maravigliato
Si volse a drieto, e riteneva il passo;
 Poi si chinò per tor di terra un sasso.

XXXV.

Orlando avea Cortana ignuda in mano;
 Trasse a la testa: e Cortana tagliava:
Per mezzo il teschio partì del pagano,
 E Passamonte morto rovinava:
E nel cadere il superbo e villano
 Divotamente Macon bestemmiava;
Ma mentre che bestemmia il rudo e acerbo,
 Orlando ringraziava il Padre e'l Verbo.

XXXII.

And being return'd to where Orlando stood,
  Who had not moved him from the spot, and swinging
The cord, he hurl'd a stone with strength so rude,
  As show'd a sample of his skill in slinging;
It roll'd on Count Orlando's helmet good
  And head, and set both head and helmet ringing,
So that he swooned with pain as if he died,
But more than dead, he seem'd so stupified.

XXXIII.

Then Passamont, who thought him slain outright,
  Said, "I will go, and while he lies along,
Disarm me: why such craven did I fight?"
  But Christ his servants ne'er abandons long,
Especially Orlando, such a knight,
  As to desert would almost be a wrong.
While the giant goes to put off his defences,
Orlando has recall'd his force and senses:

XXXIV.

And loud he shouted, "Giant, where dost go?
  Thou thought'st me doubtless for the bier outlaid;
To the right about — without wings thou'rt too slow
  To fly my vengeance — currish renegade!
"Twas but by treachery thou laid'st me low."
  The giant his astonishment betray'd,
And turn'd about, and stopp'd his journey on,
And then he stoop'd to pick up a great stone.

XXXV.

Orlando had Cortana bare in hand;
  To split the head in twain was what he schemed: —
Cortana clave the skull like a true brand,
  And pagan Passamont died unredeem'd,
Yet harsh and haughty, as he lay he bann'd,
  And most devoutly Macon still blasphemed;
But while his crude, rude blasphemies he heard,
Orlando thank'd the Father and the Word, —

XXXVI.

Dicendo: quanta grazia oggi m'ha 'data!
  Sempre ti sono, o signor mio, tenuto;
  Per te conosco la vita salvata;
  Però che dal gigante era abbattuto:
  Ogni cosa a ragion fai misurata;
  Non val nostro poter sanza il tuo ajuto.
  Priegoti, sopra me tenga la mano,
  Tanto che ancor ritorni a Carlo Mano.

XXXVII.

Poi ch'ebbe questo detto sen' andòe,
  Tanto che trouva Alabastro più basso
  Che si sforzava, quando e'lo trovòe,
  Di sveglier d'una ripa fuori un masso.
  Orlando, com'e' giunse a quel, gridòe:
  Che pensi tu, ghiotton, gittar quel sasso?
  Quando Alabastro questo grido intende,
  Subitamente la sua fromba prende.

XXXVIII.

E'trasse d'una pietra molto grossa,
  Tanto ch'Orlando bisognò schermisse;
  Che se l'avesse giunto la percossa,
  Non bisognava il medico venisse.
  Orlando adoperò poi la sua possa;
  Nel pettignon tutta la spada misse:
  E morto cadde questo babalone,
  E non dimenticò però Macone.

XXXIX.

Morgante aveva al suo modo un palagio
  Fatto di frasche e di schegge e di terra:
  Quivi, secondo lui, si posa ad agio;
  Quivi la notte si rinchiude e serra.
  Orlando picchia, e daragli disagio,
  Perchè il gigante dal sonno si sferra;
  Vennegli aprir come una cosa matta;
  Ch'un' aspra visione aveva fatta.

XXXVI.

Saying, "What grace to me thou'st this day given!
  And I to thee, oh Lord! am ever bound.
I know my life was saved by thee from heaven,
  Since by the giant I was fairly down'd.
All things by thee are measured just and even;
  Our power without thine aid would nought be found:
I pray thee take heed of me, till I can
At least return once more to Carloman."

XXXVII.

And having said thus much, he went his way;
  And Alabaster he found out below,
Doing the very best that in him lay
  To root from out a bank a rock or two.
Orlando, when he reach'd him, loud 'gan say,
  "How think'st thou, glutton, such a stone to throw?"
When Alabaster heard his deep voice ring,
He suddenly betook him to his sling,

· XXXVIII.

And hurl'd a fragment of a size so large,
  That if it had in fact fulfill'd its mission,
And Roland not avail'd him of his targe,
  There would have been no need of a physician.
Orlando set himself in turn to charge,
  And in his bulky bosom made incision
With all his sword. The lout fell; but o'erthrown, he
However by no means forgot Macone.

XXXIX.

Morgante had a palace in his mode,
  Composed of branches, logs of wood, and earth,
And stretch'd himself at ease in this abode,
  And shut himself at night within his birth.
Orlando knock'd, and knock'd again, to goad
  The giant from his sleep; and he came forth,
The door to open, like a crazy thing,
For a rough dream had shook him slumbering.

30*

XL.

E'gli parea ch'un feroce serpente
    L'avea assalito, e chiamar Macometto
    Ma Macometto non valea niente:
    Ond'e' chiamava Gesù benedetto;
    E liberato l'avea finalmente.
    Venne alla porta, ed ebbe così detto;
    Chi buzza qua? pur sempre borbottando.
    Tu 'l saprai tosto, gli rispose Orlando.

XLI.

Vengo per farti, come a'tuo' fratelli,
    Far de'peccati tuoi la peniténzia,
    Da' monaci mandato, cattivelli,
    Come stato è divina providenzia;
    Pel mal ch'avete fatto a torto a quelli,
    E dato in ciel così questa sentenzia;
    Sappi, che freddo già più ch'un pilastro
    Lasciato ho Passamonte e'l tuo Alabastro.

XLII.

Disse Morgante: o gentil cavaliere,
    Per lo tuo Dio non mi dir villania:
    Di grazia il nome tuo vorrei sapere;
    Se se' Cristian, deh dillo in cortesia.
    Rispose Orlando: di cotal mastiere
    Contenterotti per la fede mia:
    Adoro Cristo, ch'è Signor verace;
    E puoi tu adorarlo, se ti piace.

XLIII.

Rispose il saracin con umil voce:
    Io ho fatto una strana visione,
    Che m'assaliva un serpente feroce:
    Non mi valeva per chiamar Macone;
    Onde al tuo Dio che fu confitto in croce
    Rivolsi presto la mia intenzione:
    E' mi soccorse, e fui libero e sano,
    E son disposto al tutto esser Cristiano.

XL.

He thought that a fierce serpent had attack'd him;
    And Mahomet he call'd; but Mahomet
Is nothing worth, and not an instant back'd him;
    But praying blessed Jesu, he was set
At liberty from all the fears which rack'd him;
    And to the gate he came with great regret —
"Who knocks here?" grumbling all the while, said he.
"That," said Orlando, "you will quickly see.

XLI.

"I come to preach to you, as to your brothers,
    Sent by the miserable monks — repentance;
For Providence divine, in you and others,
    Condemns the evil done my new acquaintance.
'Tis writ on high — your wrong must pay another's;
    From heaven itself is issued out this sentence.
Know then, that colder now than a pilaster
I left your Passamont and Alabaster."

XLII.

Morgante said, "Oh gentle cavalier!
    Now by thy God say me no villany;
The favour of your name I fain would hear,
    And if a Christian, speak for courtesy."
Replied Orlando, "So much to your ear
    I by my faith disclose contentedly;
Christ I adore, who is the genuine Lord,
And, if you please, by you may be adored."

XLIII.

The Saracen rejoin'd in humble tone,
    "I have had an extraordinary vision;
A savage serpent fell on me alone,
    And Macon would not pity my condition;
Hence to thy God, who for ye did atone
    Upon the cross, preferr'd I my petition;
His timely succour set me safe and free,
And I a Christian am disposed to be."

XLIV.

Rispose Orlando: baron giusto e pio,
  Se questo buon voler terrai nel core,
  L'anima tua arà quel vero Dio
  Che ci può sol gradir d'eterno onore:
  E s'tu vorrai, sarai compagno mio,
  E amerotti con perfetto amore:
  Gl'idoli vostri son bugiardi e vani:
  Il vero Dio è lo Dio de' Cristiani.

XLV.

Venne questo Signor sanza peccato
  Ne la sua madre vergine pulzella:
  Se conoscessi quel Signor beato,
  Sanza'l qual non risplende sole o stella,
  Aresti gia Macon tuo rinnegato,
  E la sua fede iniqua ingiusta e fella:
  Battezzati al mio Dio di buon talento.
  Morgante gli risposo: io son contento.

XLVI.

E corse Orlando subito abbracciare:
  Orlando gran carezze gli facea,
  E disse: a la badía ti vo' menare.
  Morgante, andianci presto, respondea:
  Co'monaci la pace ci vuol fare.
  De la qual cosa Orlando in se godea,
  Dicendo; fratel mio divoto e buono,
  Io vò che chiegga a l'abate perdono.

XLVII.

Da poi che Dio ralluminato t'ha,
  Ed acettato per la sua umiltade;
  Vuolsi che tu ancor usi umiltà.
  Disse Morgante: per la tua bontade,
  Poi che il tuo Dio mio sempre omai sarà,
  Dimmio del nome tuo la veritade,
  Poi di me dispor puoi al tuo comando;
  Ond'e' gli disse, com 'egli era Orlando.

XLIV.

Orlando answer'd, "Baron just and pious,
  If this good wish your heart can really move
To the true God, who will not then deny us
  Eternal honour, you will go above,
And, if you please, as friends we will ally us,
  And I will love you with a perfect love.
Your idols are vain liars, full of fraud:
The only true God is the Christian's God.

XLV.

"The Lord descended to the virgin breast
  Of Mary Mother, sinless and divine;
If you acknowledge the Redeemer blest,
  Without whom neither sun nor star can shine,
Abjure bad Macon's false and felon test,
  Your renegado god, and worship mine, —
Baptize yourself with zeal, since you repent."
To which Morgante answer'd, "I'm content."

XLVI.

And then Orlando to embrace him flew,
  And made much of his convert, as he cried,
"To the abbey I will gladly marshal you."
  To whom Morgante, "Let us go," replied;
"I to the friars have for peace to sue."
  Which thing Orlando heard with inward pride,
Saying, "My brother, so devout and good,
Ask the abbot pardon, as I wish you would:

XLVII.

"Since God has granted your illumination,
  Accepting you in mercy for his own,
Humility should be your first oblation."
  Morgante said, "For goodness' sake, make known —
Since that your God is to be mine — your station,
  And let your name in verity be shown;
Then will I every thing at your command do."
On which the other said, he was Orlando

XLVIII.

Disse il gigante: Gesù benedetto
  Per mille volte ringraziato sia;
  Sentito t'ho nomar, baron perfetto,
  Per tutti i tempi de la vita mia:
  E, com'io dissi, sempremai suggetto
  Esser ti vo' per la tua gagliardia.
  Insieme molte cose ragionaro,
  E 'n verso la badía poi s'inviaro.

XLIX.

E per la via da que' giganti morti
  Orlando con Morgante sì ragiona:
  De la lor morte vo' che ti conforti;
  E poi che piace a Dio, a me perdona;
  A' monaci avean fatto mille torti;
  E la nostra scrittura aperto suona.
  Il ben remunerato, e'l mal punito;
  E mai non ha questo Signor fallito,

L.

Però ch'egli ama la giustizia tanto,
  Che vuol, che sempre il suo giudicio morda
  Ognun ch'abbi peccato tanto o quanto;
  E così il ben ristorar si ricorda:
  E non saria senza giustizia santo:
  Adunque al suo voler presto t'accorda:
  Che debbe ognun voler quel che vuol questo,
  Ed accordarsi volentieri e presto.

LI.

E sonsi i nostri dottori accordati,
  Pigliando tutti una conclusione,
  Che que che son nel ciel glorificati,
  S'avessin nel pensier compassione
  De' miseri parenti che dannati
  Son ne lo inferno in gran confusione,
  La lor felicità nulla sarebbe;
  E vedi che qui ingiusto Iddio parrebbe.

XLVIII.

"Then," quoth the giant, "blessed be Jesu
  A thousand times with gratitude and praise!
Oft, perfect baron! have I heard of you
  Through all the different periods of my days:
And, as I said, to be your vassal too
  I wish, for your great gallantry always."
Thus reasoning, they continued much to say,
And onwards to the abbey went their way.

XLIX.

And by the way about the giants dead
  Orlando with Morgante reason'd: "Be,
For their decease, I pray you, comforted;
  And, since it is God's pleasure, pardon me,
A thousand wrongs unto the monks they bred,
  And our true Scripture soundeth openly,
Good is rewarded, and chastised the ill,
Which the Lord never faileth to fulfil:

L.

"Because his love of justice unto all
  Is such, he wills his judgment should devour
All who have sin, however great or small;
  But good he well remembers to restore.
Nor without justice holy could we call
  Him, whom I now require you to adore.
All men must make his will their wishes sway,
And quickly and spontaneously obey

LI.

"And here our doctors are of one accord,
  Coming on this point to the same conclusion, —
That in their thoughts who praise in heaven the Lord
  If pity e'er was guilty of intrusion
For their unfortunate relations stored
  In hell below, and damn'd in great confusion, —
Their happiness would be reduced to nought,
And thus unjust the Almighty's self be thought.

LII.

Ma egli anno posto in Gesù ferma spene;
  E tanto pare a lor, quanto a lui pare;
  Afferman ciò ch'e'fa, che facci bene,
  E che non possi in nessun modo errare:
  Se padre o madre è nell' eterne pene,
  Di questo non si posson conturbare:
  Che quel che piace a Dio, sol piace a loro:
  Questo s'osserva ne l'eterno coro.

LIII.

Al savio suol bastar poche parole,
  Disse Morgante; tu il potrai vedere,
  De' miei fratelli, Orlando, se mi duole,
  E s' io m'accorderò di Dio al volere,
  Come tu di' che in ciel servar si suole:
  Morti co' morti; or pensiam di godere;
  Io vo tagliar le mani a tutti quanti,
  E porterolle a que' monaci santi,

LIV.

Acciò ch'ognun sia più sicuro e certo,
  Com' e' son morti, e non abbin paura
  Andar soletti per questo deserto;
  E perchè veggan la mia mente pura
  A quel Signor che m'ha il suo regno aperto,
  E tratto fuor di tenebre sì oscura.
  E poi tagliò le mani a' due fratelli,
  E lasciagli a le fiere ed agli uccelli.

LV.

A la badía insieme se ne vanno,
  Ove l'abate assai dubbioso aspetta:
  I monaci che'l fatto ancor non sanno,
  Correvano a l'abate tutti in fretta,
  Dicendo paurosi e pien' d'affanno:
  Volete voi costui drento si metta?
  Quando l'abate vedeva il gigante,
  Si turbò tutto nel primo sembiante.

LII.

"But they in Christ have firmest hope, and all
　　Which seems to him, to them too must appear
Well done; nor could it otherwise befall:
　　He never can in any purpose err.
If sire or mother suffer endless thrall,
　　They don't disturb themselves for him or her;
What pleases God to them must joy inspire; —
Such is the observance of the eternal choir."

LIII.

"A word unto the wise," Morgante said,
　　"Is wont to be enough, and you shall see
How much I grieve about my brethren dead;
　　And if the will of God seem good to me,
Just, as you tell me, 'tis in heaven obey'd —
　　Ashes to ashes, — merry let us be!
I will cut off the hands from both their trunks,
And carry them unto the holy monks.

LIV.

"So that all persons may be sure and certain
　　That they are dead, and have no further fear
To wander solitary this desert in,
　　And that they may perceive my spirit clear
By the Lord's grace, who hath withdrawn the curtain
　　Of darkness, making his bright realm appear."
He cut his brethren's hands off at these words,
And left them to the savage beasts and birds.

LV.

Then to the abbey they went on together,
　　Where waited them the abbot in great doubt.
The monks who knew not yet the fact, ran thither
　　To their superior, all in breathless rout,
Saying with tremor, "Please to tell us whether
　　You wish to have this person in or out?"
The abbot, looking through upon the giant,
Too greatly fear'd, at first, to be compliant.

LVI.

Orlando che turbato così il vede,
  Gli disse presto: abate, datti pace,
  Qesto è Cristiano, e in Cristo nostro crede,
  E rinnegato ha il suo Macon fallace.
  Morgante i moncherin mostrò per fede,
  Come i giganti ciascun morto giace;
  Donde l'abate ringraziavia Iddio,
  Dicendo; or m' hai contento, Signor mio.

LVII.

E risguardava, e squadrava Morgante,
  La sua grandezza e una volta e due,
  E poi gli disse: O famoso gigante
  Sappi ch'io non mi maraviglio piùe
  Che tu sveglicssi e gittassi le piante,
  Quand'io riguardo or le fattezze tue:
  Tu sarai or perfetto e vero amico
  A Cristo, quanto tu gli eri nimico.

LVIII.

Un nostro apostol, Saul già chiamato,
  Perseguì molto la fede di Cristo:
  Un giorno poi da la spirto infiammato.
  Perchè pur mi persegui? disse Cristo:
  E' si ravvide allor del suo peccato
  Andò poi predicando sempre Cristo;
  E fatto è or de la fede una tromba,
  La qual per tutto risuona e rimbomba.

LIX.

Così farai tu ancor, Morgante mio:
  E chi s'emenda, è scritto nel Vangelo,
  Che maggior festa fa d'un solo Iddio,
  Che di novantanove altri su in cielo:
  Io ti conforto ch'ogni tuo disio
  Rivolga a quel Signor con giusto zelo,
  Che tu sarai felice in sempiterno,
  Ch'eri perduto, e dannato all'inferno.

LVI.

Orlando seeing him thus agitated,
   Said quickly, "Abbot, be thou of good cheer;
He Christ believes, as Christian must be rated,
   And hath renounced his Macon false;" which here
Morgante with the hands corroborated,
   A proof of both the giants' fate quite clear:
Thence, with due thanks, the abbot God adored,
Saying, "Thou hast contented me, oh Lord!"

LVII.

He gazed; Morgante's height he calculated,
   And more than once contemplated his size;
And then he said, "Oh giant celebrated!
   Know, that no more my wonder will arise,
How you could tear and fling the trees you late did,
   When I behold your form with my own eyes.
You now a true and perfect friend will show
Yourself to Christ, as once you were a foe.

LVIII.

"And one of our apostles, Saul once named,
   Long persecuted sore the faith of Christ,
Till, one day, by the Spirit being inflamed,
   'Why dost thou persecute me thus?' said Christ;
And then from his offence he was reclaim'd,
   And went for ever after preaching Christ,
And of the faith became a trump, whose sounding
O'er the whole earth is echoing and rebounding.

LIX.

"So, my Morgante, you may do likewise;
   He who repents — thus writes the Evangelist —
Occasions more rejoicing in the skies
   Than ninety-nine of the celestial list.
You may be sure, should each desire arise
   With just zeal for the Lord, that you'll exist
Among the happy saints for evermore;
But you were lost and damn'd to hell before!"

LX.

E grande onore a Morgante faceva
  L'abate, e molti dì si son posti:
  Un giorno, come ad Orlando piaceva,
  A spasso in quà e in là si sono andati:
  L'abate in una camera sua aveva
  Molte armadure e certi archi appiccati:
  Morgante gliene piacque un che ne vede;
  Onde e' sel cinse bench oprar nol crede.

LXI.

Avea quel luogo d'acqua carestia:
  Orlando disse come buon fratello:
  Morgante, vo' che di piacer ti sia
  Andar per l'acqua; ond' e' rispose a quello:
  Comanda ciò che vuoi che fatto sia;
  E posesi in ispalla un gran tinello,
  Ed avviossi là verso una fonte
  Dove solea ber sempre appiè del monte.

LXII.

Giunto a la fonte, sente un gran fracasso
  Di subito venir per la foresta:
  Una saetta cavò del turcasso,
  Posela a l'arco, ed alzava la testa;
  Ecco apparire un gran gregge al passo
  Di porci, e vanno con molta tempesta;
  E arrivorno alla fontana appunto
  Donde il gigante è da lor sopraggiunto.

LXIII.

Morgante a la ventura a un saetta;
  Appunto ne l'orecchio lo 'ncarnava:
  Da l'altro lato passò la verretta;
  Onde il cinghial giù morto gambettava;
  Un altro, quasi per farne vendetta,
  Addosso al gran gigante irato andava;
  E perchè e' giunse troppo tosto al varco,
  Non fu Morgante a tempo a trar con l'arco.

LX.

And thus great honour to Morgante paid
  The abbot: many days they did repose.
One day, as with Orlando they both stray'd,
  And saunter'd here and there, where'er they chose,
The abbot show'd a chamber, where array'd
  Much armour was, and hung up certain bows;
And one of these Morgante for a whim
Girt on, though useless, he believed, to him.

LXI.

There being a want of water in the place,
  Orlando, like a worthy brother, said,
"Morgante, I could wish you in this case
  To go for water." "You shall be obey'd
In all commands," was the reply, "straightways."
  Upon his shoulder a great tub he laid,
And went out on his way unto a fountain,
Where he was wont to drink below the mountain.

LXII.

Arrived there, a prodigious noise he hears,
  Which suddenly along the forest spread;
Whereat from out his quiver he prepares
  An arrow for his bow, and lifts his head;
And lo! a monstrous herd of swine appears,
  And onward rushes with tempestuous tread,
And to the fountain's brink precisely pours;
So that the giant's join'd by all the boars.

LXIII.

Morgante at a venture shot an arrow,
  Which pierced a pig precisely in the ear,
And pass'd unto the other side quite thorough;
  So that the boar, defunct, lay tripp'd up near.
Another, to revenge his fellow farrow,
  Against the giant rush'd in fierce career,
And reach'd the passage with so swift a foot,
Morgante was not now in time to shoot.

LXIV.

Vedendosi venuto il porco adosso,
  Gli dette in su la testa un gran punzone *
  Per modo che gl'infranse insino a l'osso,
  E morto allato a quell'altro lo pone:
  Gli altri porci veggendo quel percosso,
  Si misson tutti in fuga pel vallone;
  Morgante si levò il tinello in collo,
  Ch'era pien d'acqua, e non si muove un crollo.

LXV.

Da l'una spalla il tinello avea posto,
  Da l'altra i porci, e spacciava il terreno;
  E torna a la badìa, ch'è pur discosto,
  Ch' una gocciola d'acqua non va in seno.
  Orlando che'l vedea tornar sì tosto
  Co' porci morti, e con quel vaso pieno;
  Maravigliossi che sia tanto forte;
  Così l'abate; e spalancan le porte.

LXVI.

I monaci veggendo l'acqua fresca
  Si rallegrorno, ma più de' cinghiali;
  Ch'ogni animal si rallegra de l'esca;
  E posano a dormire i breviali:
  Ognun s'affanna, e non par che gl'incresca,
  Acciò che questa carne nog s'insali,
  E che poi secca sapesse di vieto:
  E la digiune si restorno a drieto.

LXVII.

E ferno a scoppia corpo per un tratto,
  E scuffian, che parien de l'acqua usciti;
  Tanto che'l cane sen doleva e 'l gatto,
  Che gli ossi rimanean troppo puliti.
  L'abate, poi che molto onoro ha fatto
  A tutti, un dì dopo questi conviti
  Dette a Morgante un destrier molto bello,
  Che lungo tempo tenuto avea quello.

* See Note pag. 492.

LXIV.

Perceiving that the pig was on him close,
  He gave him such a punch upon the head
As floor'd him so that he no more arose,
  Smashing the very bone; and he fell dead
Next to the other. Having seen such blows,
  The other pigs along the valley fled;
Morgante on his neck the bucket took,
Full from the spring, which neither swerved nor shook.

LXV.

The ton was on one shoulder, and there were
  The hogs on t'other, and he brush'd apace
On to the abbey, though by no means near,
  Nor spilt one drop of water in his race.
Orlando, seeing him so soon appear
  With the dead boars, and with that brimful vase,
Marvell'd to see his strength so very great;
So did the abbot, and set wide the gate.

LXVI.

The monks, who saw the water fresh and good,
  Rejoiced, but much more to perceive the pork; —
All animals are glad at sight of food:
  They lay their breviaries to sleep, and work
With greedy pleasure, and in such a mood,
  That the flesh needs no salt beneath their fork.
Of rankness and of rot there is no fear,
For all the fasts are now left in arrear.

LXVII.

As though they wish'd to burst at once, they ate;
  And gorged so that, as if the bones had been
In water, sorely grieved the dog and cat,
  Perceiving that they all were pick'd too clean.
The abbot, who to all did honour great,
  A few days after this convivial scene,
Gave to Morgante a fine horse, well train'd,
Which he long time had for himself maintain'd.

LXVIII.

Morgante in su 'n un prato il caval mena,
  E vuol che corra, e che facci ogni pruova,
  E pensa che di ferro abbi la schiena,
  O forse non credeva schiacciar l'uova:
  Questo caval s'accoscia per la pena,
  E scoppia, e 'n su la terra si ritruova.
  Dicea Morgante: lieva su, rozzone;
  E va pur punzecchiando co lo sprone.

LXIX.

Ma finalmente convien ch' egli smonte,
  E disse: io son pur leggier come penna,
  Ed è scoppiato; che ne di' tu, conte?
  Rispose Orlando: un arbore d'antenna
  Mi par piuttosto, e la gaggia la fronte:
  Lascialo andar, che la fortuna accenna
  Che meco appiede ne venga, Morgante.
  Ed io così verrò, disse il gigante.

LXX.

Quando serà mestier, tu mi vedrai
  Com'io mi proverò ne la battaglia.
  Orlando disse: io credo tu farai
  Come buon cavalier, se Dio mi vaglia;
  Ed anco me dormir non mirerai:
  Di questo tuo caval non te ne caglia:
  Vorrebbesi portarlo in qualche bosco;
  Ma il modo nè la via non ci conosco.

LXXI.

Disse il gigante: io il porterò ben io,
  Da poi che portar me non ha voluto,
  Per render ben per mal, come fa Dio;
  Ma vo' che a porlo addosso mi dia ajute.
  Orlando gli dicea: Morgante mio,
  S'al mio consiglio ti sarai attenuto,
  Questo caval tu non ve 'l porteresti,
  Che ti farà come tu a lui facesti.

LXVIII.

The horse Morgante to a meadow led,
  To gallop, and to put him to the proof,
Thinking that he a back of iron had,
  Or to skim eggs unbroke was light enough;
But the horse, sinking with the pain, fell dead,
  And burst, while cold on earth lay head and hoof.
Morgante said, "Get up, thou sulky cur!"
And still continued pricking with the spur.

LXIX.

But finally he thought fit to dismount,
  And said, "I am as light as any feather,
And he has burst; — to this what say you, count?"
  Orlando answer'd, "Like a ship's mast rather
You seem to me, and with the truck for front: —
  Let him go; Fortune wills that we together
Should march, but you on foot Morgante still."
To which the giant answer'd, "So I will.

LXX.

"When there shall be occasion, you will see
  How I approve my courage in the fight."
Orlando said, "I really think you'll be,
  If it should prove God's will, a goodly knight;
Nor will you napping there discover me.
  But never mind your horse, though out of sight
T'were best to carry him into some wood,
If but the means or way I understood."

LXXI.

The giant said, "Then carry him I will,
  Since that to carry me he was so slack —
To render, as the gods do, good for ill;
  But lend a hand to place him on my back."
Orlando answer'd, "If my counsel still
  May weigh, Morgante, do not undertake
To lift or carry this dead courser, who,
  As you have done to him, will do to you.

31*

LXXII.

Guarda che non facesse la vendetta,
  Come fece già Nesso così morto:
  Non so se la sua istoria hai inteso o letta
  E' ti farà scoppiar; datti conforto.
 . Disse Morgante: ajuta ch'io me 'l metta
  Addosso, e poi vedrai s'io ve lo porto:
  Io porterei, Orlando mio gentile,
  Con le campane la quel campanile.

LXXIII.

Disse l'abate: il campanil v'è bene;
  Ma le campane voi l'avete rotte.
  Dicea Morgante, e' ne porton le pene
  Color che morti son là in quelle grotte;
  E levossi il cavallo in su le schiene,
  E disse: guarda s'io sento di gotte,
  Orlando, nelle gambe, e s' io lo posso;
  E fe' duo salti col cavallo addosso.

LXXIV.

Era Morgante come una montagna:
  Se facea questo, non è maraviglia
  Ma pure Orlando con seco si lagna;
  Perchè pur era omai di sua famiglia
  Temenza avea non pigliasse magagna.
  Un' altra volta costui riconsiglia:
  Posalo ancor, nol portare al deserto.
  Disse Morgante: il porterò per certo.

LXXV.

E portollo, e gittollo in luogo strano,
  E tornò a la badìa subitamente.
  Diceva Orlando: or che più dimoriano?
  Morgante, qui non facciam noi niente;
  E prese un giorno l'abate per mano,
  E disse a quel molto discretamente,
  Che vuol partir de la sua reverenzia,
  E domandava e perdono e licenzia.

LXXII.

"Take care he don't revenge himself, though dead,
　As Nessus did of old beyond all cure.
I don't know if the fact you've heard or read;
　But he will make you burst, you may be sure."
"But help him on my back," Morgante said,
　"And you shall see what weight I can endure.
In place, my gentle Roland, of this palfrey,
With all the bells, I'd carry yonder belfry."

LXXIII.

The abbot said, "The steeple may do well,
　But, for the bells, you've broken them, I wot."
Morgante answer'd, "Let them pay in hell
　The penalty who lie dead in yon grot;
And hoisting up the horse from where he fell,
　He said, "Now look if I the gout have got,
Orlando, in the legs — or if I have force;"
And then he made two gambols with the horse.

LXXIV.

Morgante was like any mountain framed;
　So if he did this, 'tis no prodigy;
But secretly himself Orlando blamed,
　Because he was one of his family;
And fearing that he might be hurt or maim'd,
　Once more he bade him lay his burden by:
"Put down, nor bear him further the desert in."
Morgante said, "I'll carry him for certain."

LXXV.

He did; and stow'd him in some nook away,
　And to the abbey then return'd with speed.
Orlando said, "Why longer do we stay?
　"Morgante, here is nought to do indeed."
The abbot by the hand he took one day,
　And said, with great respect, he had agreed
To leave his reverence; but for this decision
He wish'd to have his pardon and permission.

LXXVI.

E de gli onor ricevuti da questi,
  Qualche volta potendo, arà buon merito;
  E dice: io intendo ristorare e presto
  I persi giorni del tempo preterito:
  E' son più dì che licenzia arei chiesto,
  Benigno padre, se non ch' io mi perito;
  Non so mostrarvi quel che drento sento;
  Tanto vi veggo del mio star-contento.

LXXVII.

Io me ne porto per sempre nel core
  L'abate, la badìa, questo deserto;
  Tanto v'ho posto in picciol tempo amore:
  Rendavi su nel ciel per me buon merto
  Quel vero Dio, quello eterno Signore,
  Che vi serba il suo regno al fine aperto:
  Noi aspettiam vostra benedizione,
  Raccomandiamci a le vostre orazione.

LXXVIII.

Quando l'abate il conte Orlando intese,
  Rintenerì nel cor per la dolcezza,
  Tanto fervor nel petto se gli accese;
  E disse: cavalier, se a tua prodezza
  Non sono stato benigno e cortese,
  Come conviensi a la gran gentillezza;
  Che so che ciò ch'i'ho fatto è stato poco,
  Incolpa la ignoranzia nostra e il loco.

LXXIX.

Noi ti potremo di messe onorare,
  Dì prediche di laude e paternostri,
  Piuttosto che da cena o desinare,
  O d'altri convenevol che da chiostri:
  Tu m'hai di te sì fatto innamorare
  Per mille alte eccellenzie che tu mostri;
  Ch'io me ne vengo ove tu andrai con teco,
  E d'altra parte tu resti quì meco.

LXXVI.

The honours they continued to receive
 Perhaps exceeded what his merits claim'd:
He said, "I mean, and quickly, to retrieve
 The lost days of time past, which may be blamed;
Some days ago I should have ask'd your leave,
 Kind father, but I really was ashamed,
And know not how to show my sentiment,
So much I see you with our stay content.

LXXVII.

"But in my heart I bear through every clime
 The abbot, abbey, and this solitude —
So much I love you in so short a time;
 For me, from heaven reward you with all good
The God so true, the eternal Lord sublime!
 Whose kingdom at the last hath open stood.
Meantime we stand expectant of your blessing,
And recommend us to your prayers with pressing."

LXXVIII.

Now when the abbot Count Orlando heard,
 His heart grew soft with inner tenderness,
Such fervour in his bosom bred each word;
 And, "Cavalier," he said, "if I have less
Courteous and kind to your great worth appear'd,
 Than fits me for such gentle blood to express,
I know I have done too little in this case;
But blame our ignorance, and this poor place.

LXXIX.

"We can indeed but honour you with masses,
 And sermons, thanksgivings, and pater-nosters,
Hot suppers, dinners (fitting other places
 In verity much rather than the cloisters);
But such a love for you my heart embraces,
 For thousand virtues which your bosom fosters,
That wheresoe'er you go I too shall be,
And, on the other part, you rest with me.

LXXX.

Tanto ch'a questo par contraddizione;
  Ma so che tu se' savio, e 'ntendi e gusti,
  E intendi il mio parlar per discrizione;
  De' beneficj tuoi pietosi e giusti
  Renda il Signore a te munerazione,
  Da cui mandato in queste selve fusti;
  Per le virtù del qual liberi siamo,
  E grazie a lui e a te noi ne rendiamo.

LXXXI.

Tu ci hai salvato l'anima e la vita:
  Tanta perturbazion già que' giganti
  Ci detton, che la strada era smarrita
  Da ritrovar Gesù con gli altri santi:
  Però troppo ci duol la tua partita,   -
  E sconsolati restiam tutti quanti;
  Nè ritener possiamti i mesi e gli anni:
  Che tu non se' da vestir questi panni,

LXXXII.

Ma da portar la lancia e l'armadura:
  E puossi meritar con essa, come
  Con questa cappa; e leggi la scrittura:
  Questo gigante al ciel drizzò le some
  Per tua virtù; va in pace a tua ventura
  Chi tu ti sia, ch'io non ricerco il nome;
  Ma dirò sempre, s'io son domandato,
  Ch' un angiol qui da Dio fussi mandato.

LXXXIII.

Se c'è armadura o cosa che tu voglia,
  Vattene in zambra e pigliane tu stessi,
  E cuopri a questo gigante le scoglia.
  Rispose Orlando: se armadura avessi
  Prima che noi uscissim de la soglia,
  Che questo mio compagno difendessi:
  Questo accetto io, e sarammi piacere.
  Disse l'abate: venite a vedere.

LXXX.

"This may involve a seeming contradiction;
　But you I know are sage, and feel, and taste,
And understand my speech with full conviction.
　For your just pious deeds may you be graced
With the Lord's great reward and benediction,
　By whom you were directed to this waste:
To his high mercy is our freedom due,
For which we render thanks to him and you.

LXXXI.

"You saved at once our life and soul: such fear
　The giants caused us, that the way was lost
By which we could pursue a fit career
　In search of Jesus and the saintly host;
And your departure breeds such sorrow here,
　That comfortless we all are to our cost;
But months and years you would not stay in sloth,
Nor are you form'd to wear our sober cloth;

LXXXII.

"But to bear arms, and wield the lance; indeed,
　With these as much is done as with this cowl;
In proof of which the Scripture you may read.
　This giant up to heaven may bear his soul
By your compassion: now in peace proceed.
　Your state and name I seek not to unroll;
But, if I'm ask'd, this answer shall be given,
That here an angel was sent down from heaven.

LXXXIII.

"If you want armour or aught else, go in,
　Look o'er the wardrobe, and take what you choose,
And cover with it o'er this giant's skin."
　Orlando answer'd, "If there should lie loose
Some armour, ere our journey we begin,
　Which might be turn'd to my companion's use,
The gift would be acceptable to me."
The abbot said to him, "Come in and see."

LXXXIV.

E in certa cameretta entrati sono,
  Che d'armadure vecchie era copiosa;
  Dice l'abate: tutte ve le dono;
  Morgante va rovistando ogni cosa;
  Ma solo un certo sbergo gli fu buono,
  Ch'avea tutta la maglia rugginosa:
  Maravigliossi che lo cuopra appunto:
  Che mai più gnun forse glien' era aggiunto.

LXXXV.

Questo fu d'un gigante smisurata,
  Ch'a la badía fu morto per antico
  Dal gran Milon d'Angrante, ch' arrivato?
  V' era, s'appunto questa istoria dico;
  Ed era ne le mura istoriato,
  Come e' fu morto questo gran nimico
  Che fece a la badía già lunga guerra:
  E Milon v'è com 'e' l'abbatte in terra.

LXXXVI.

Veggendo questa istoria il conte Orlando,
  Fra suo cor disse: o Dio, che sai sol tutto,
  Come venne Milon qui capitando,
  Che ha questo gigante qui distrutto
  E lesse certe lettere lacrimando,
  Che non potè tenir più il viso asciutto,
  Com'io dirò ne la seguente istoria:
  Di mal vi guardi il Re de l'alta gloria.

LXXXIV.

And in a certain closet, where the wall
  Was cover'd with old armour like a crust,
The abbot said to them, "I give you all."
  Morgante rummaged piecemeal from the dust
The whole, which, save one cuirass, was too small,
  And that too had the mail inlaid with rust.
They wonder'd how it fitted him exactly,
Which ne'er has suited others so compactly.

LXXXV.

'Twas an immeasurable giant's, who
  By the great Milo of Agrante fell
Before the abbey many years ago.
  The story on the wall was figured well;
In the last moment of the abbey's foe,
  Who long had waged a war implacable:
Precisely as the war occurr'd they drew him,
And there was Milo as he overthrew him.

LXXXVI.

Seeing this history, Count Orlando said
  In his own heart, "Oh God, who in the sky
Know'st all things! how was Milo hither led?
  Who caused the giant in this place to die?"
And certain letters, weeping, then he read,
  So that he could not keep his visage dry, —
As I will tell in the ensuing story.
From evil keep you the high King of glory!

NOTE.

Page 480.

* "Gli dette in su la testa un gran punzone." It is strange that Pulci should have literally anticipated the technical terms of my old friend and master, Jackson, and the art which he has carried to its highest pitch. "*A punch on the head*," or "*a punch in the head*," — "un punzone in su la testa," — is the exact and frequent phrase of our best pugilists, who little dream that they are talking the purest Tuscan.

FRANCESCA OF RIMINI.

FRANCESCA DA RIMINI.

DANTE, L'INFERNO.

CANTO V.

SIEDE la terra dove nata fui
    Su la marina, dove il Po discende,
    Per aver pace coi seguaci sui.
Amor, che al cor gentil ratto s' apprende,
    Prese costui della bella persona
    Che mi fu tolta; e il modo ancor m' offende.
Amor, che a nullo amato amar perdona,
    Mi prese del costui piacer si forte,
    Che, come vedi, ancor non m'abbandona;
Amor condusse noi ad una morte:
    Cainà attende chi in vita ci spense:
    Queste parole da lor ci fur porte.
Da ch' io intesi quell' anime offense
    Chinai il viso, e tanto il tenni basso
    Fin che il Poeta mi disse: "Che pense?"
Quando risposi incomminciai: "Ahi lasso!
    Quanti dolci pensier, quanto desio
    Menò costoro al doloroso passo!"
Poi mi rivolsi a loro, e parlai io,
    E cominciai: Francesca, i tuoi martiri
    A lagrimar mi fanno tristo e pio.
Ma dimmi: al tempo de' dolci sospiri
    A che, e come concedette Amore
    Che conosceste i dubbiosi desiri?

FRANCESCA OF RIMINI.

FROM THE INFERNO OF DANTE.

CANTO V.

———

" The land where I was born [1] sits by the seas,
    Upon that shore to which the Po descends,
    With all his followers, in search of peace.
Love, which the gentle heart soon apprehends,
    Seized him for the fair person which was ta'en [2]
    From me, and me even yet the mode offends.
Love, who to none beloved to love again
    Remits, seized me with wish to please, so strong,
    That, as thou seest, yet, yet it doth remain.
Love to one death conducted us along,
    But Cainà [3] waits for him our life who ended:"
    These were the accents utter'd by her tongue. —
Since I first listen'd to these souls offended,
    I bow'd my visage, and so kept it till —
    "What think'st thou?" said the bard; when I unbended,
And recommenced: "Alas! unto such ill
    How many sweet thoughts, what strong ecstasies
    Led these their evil fortune to fulfil!"
And then I turn'd unto their side my eyes,
    And said, "Francesca, thy sad destinies
    Have made me sorrow till the tears arise.
But tell me, in the season of sweet sighs,
    By what and how thy love to passion rose,
    So as his dim desires to recognise?"

1—3 See Notes on pag. 498.

Ed ella a me: nessun maggior dolore
   Che ricordarsi del tempo felice
   Nella miseria; e ciò sa il tuo dottore.
Ma se a conoscer la prima radice
   Del nostro amor tu hai cotanto affetto
   Farò come colui che piange e dice.
Noi leggevamo un giorno per diletto
   Di Lancillotto, come Amor lo strinse:
   Soli eravamo, e senza alcun sospetto.
Per più fiate gli occhi ci sospinse
   Quella lettura, e scolorocci il viso:
   Ma solo un punto fu quel che ci vinse.
Quando leggemmo il disiato riso
   Esser baciato da cotanto amante,
   Questi, che mai da me non fia diviso,
La bocca mi baciò tutto tremante:
   Galeotto fu il libro, e chi lo scrisse —
   Quel giorno più non vi leggemmo avante.
Mentre che l' uno spirto questo disse,
   L'altro piangeva sì che di pietade
   Io venni men così com' io morisse,
E caddi come corpo morto cade.

Then she to me: "The greatest of all woes
  Is to remind us of our happy days [1]
  In misery, and that thy teacher knows. [2]
But if to learn our passion's first root preys
  Upon thy spirit with such sympathy,
  I will do even as he who weeps and says. [3] —
We read one day for pastime, seated nigh,
  Of Lancilot, how love enchain'd him too.
  We were alone, quite unsuspiciously.
But oft our eyes met, and our cheeks in hue
  All o'er discoloured by that reading were;
  But one point only wholly us o'erthrew; [4]
When we read the long-sigh'd-for smile of her,
  To be thus kiss'd by such devoted lover, [5]
  He who from me can be divided ne'er
Kiss'd my mouth, trembling in the act all over.
  Accursed was the book and he who wrote!
  That day no further leaf we did uncover." —
While thus one spirit told us of their lot,
  The other wept, so that with pity's thralls
  I swoon'd as if by death I had been smote,
And fell down even as a dead body falls.

[1]—[5] See Notes on the next page.

NOTES.

[1] Ravenna.

[2] Among Lord Byron's unpublished letters we find the following: —
"Varied readings of the translation from Dante.

> Seized him for the fair person, which in its
> Bloom was ta'en from me, yet the mode offends.
>   *or,*
> Seized him for the fair form, of which in its
> Bloom I was reft, and yet the mode offends.
> Love, which to none beloved to love remits,

> Seized me { with mutual wish to please / with wish of pleasing him / with the desire to please } so strong,

> That, as thou see'st, not yet that passion quits, &c.

You will find these readings vary from the MS. I sent you. They are closer, but rougher: take which is liked best; or, if you like, print them as variations. They are all close to the text." — *B. Letters.*

[3] From Cain, the first fratricide. By Cainà we are to understand that part of the Inferno to which murderers are condemned.

[1] MS. — "Is to { recall to mind / remind us of } our happy days."

[2] MS. — "In misery and { this / that } thy teacher knows."

[3] MS. — I will { relate / do even } as he weeps and says."

[4] MS. — "But one point only us { overthrew / o'erthrew }."

[5] MS. — "To be thus kiss'd by such { a fervent / devoted } lover."

THE BLUES;

A LITERARY ECLOGUE.

"Nimium ne crede colori." — VIRGIL.

O trust not, ye beautiful creatures, to hue,
Though your *hair* were as *red*, as your *stockings* are *blue*.

THE BLUES,

A LITERARY ECLOGUE.

ECLOGUE FIRST.

London — Before the Door of a Lecture Room.

Enter TRACY, *meeting* INKEL.

Ink. You're too late.
Tra.   Is it over?
Ink.   Nor will be this hour.
But the benches are cramm'd, like a garden in flower,
With the pride of our belles, who have made it the fashion;
So, instead of "beaux arts," we may say "la *belle* passion"
For learning, which lately has taken the lead in
The world, and set all the fine gentlemen reading.
   Tra. I know it too well, and have worn out my patience
With studying to study your new publications.
There's Vamp, Scamp, and Mouthy, and Wordswords and Co.
With their damnable —
   Ink.   Hold, my good friend, do you know
Whom you speak to?
   Tra.   Right well, boy, and so does "the Row:"
You're an author — a poet —
   Ink.   And think you that I
Can stand tamely in silence, to hear you decry
The Muses?
   Tra.   Excuse me: I meant no offence
To the Nine; though the number who make some pretence
To their favours is such — but the subject to drop
I am just piping hot from a publisher's shop,
(Next door to the pastry-cook's; so that when I
Cannot find the new volume I wanted to buy

On the bibliopole's shelves, it is only two paces,
As one finds every author in one of those places;)
Where I just had been skimming a charming critique,
So studded with wit, and so sprinkled with Greek!
Where your friend — you know who — has just got such a
		threshing,
That it is, as the phrase goes, extremely *"refreshing."*
What a beautiful word!
 Ink.   Very true; 'tis so soft
And so cooling — they use it a little too oft;
And the papers have got it at last — but no matter.
So they've cut up our friend then?
 Tra.   Not left him a tatter—
Not a rag of his present or past reputation,
Which they call a disgrace to the age and the nation.

 Ink. I'm sorry to hear this! for friendship, you know —
Our poor friend! — but I thought it would terminate so.
Our friendship is such, I'll read nothing to shock it.
You don't happen to have the Review in your pocket?
 Tra. No; I left a round dozen of authors and others
(Very sorry, no doubt, since the cause is a brother's)
All scrambling and jostling, like so many imps,
And on fire with impatience to get the next glimpse.
 Ink. Let us join them.
 Tra.   What, won't you return to the lecture?
 Ink. Why, the place is so cramm'd, there's not room for a
		spectre.
Besides, our friend Scamp is to-day so absurd —
 Tra. How can you know that till you hear him?
 Ink.   I heard
Quite enough; and, to tell you the truth, my retreat
Was from his vile nonsense, no less than the heat.
 Tra. I have had no great loss then?
 Ink.   Loss! — such a palaver!
I'd inoculate sooner my wife with the slaver
Of a dog when gone rabid, than listen two hours
To the torrent of trash which around him he pours,

Pump'd up with such effort, disgorged with such labour,
That — come — do not make me speak ill of one's neighbour.

 Tra. I make you!

 Ink.   Yes, you! I said nothing until
You compell'd me, by speaking the truth —

 Tra.   *To speak ill?*
Is that your deduction?

 Ink.   When speaking of Scamp ill,
I certainly *follow, not set* an example.
The fellow's a fool, an impostor, a zany.

 Tra. And the crowd of to-day shows that one fool makes
   many.
But we two will be wise.

 Ink.   Pray, then, let us retire.

 Tra. I would, but —

 Ink.   There must be attraction much higher
Than Scamp, or the Jews' harp he nicknames his lyre,
To call *you* to this hotbed.

 Tra.   I own it — 'tis true —
A fair lady —

 Ink.   A spinster?

 Tra.   Miss Lilac!

 Ink.   The Blue!
The heiress?

 Tra.   The angel!

 Ink.   The devil! why, man!
Pray get out of this hobble as fast as you can.
You wed with Miss Lilac! 'twould be your perdition:
She's a poet, a chymist, a mathematician.

 Tra. I say she's an angel.

 Ink.   Say rather an *angle.*
If you and she marry, you'll certainly wrangle.
I say she's a Blue, man, as blue as the ether.

 Tra. And is that any cause for not coming together?

 Ink. Humph! I can't say I know any happy alliance
Which has lately sprung up from a wedlock with science.

She's so learned in all things, and fond of concerning
Herself in all matters connected with learning,
That —

    Tra. What?

    Ink.   I perhaps may as well hold my tongue;
But there's five hundred people can tell you you're wrong.

    Tra. You forget Lady Lilac's as rich as a Jew.

    Ink. Is it miss or the cash of mamma you pursue?

    Tra. Why, Jack, I'll be frank with you — something of
         both.

The girl's a fine girl.

    Ink.   And you feel nothing loth
To her good lady-mother's reversion; and yet
Her life is as good as your own, I will bet.

    Tra. Let her live, and as long as she likes; I demand
Nothing more than the heart of her daughter and hand.

    Ink. Why, that heart's in the inkstand — that hand on the
         pen.

    Tra. A propos — Will you write me a song now and then?

    Ink. To what purpose?

    Tra.   You know, my dear friend, that in prose
My talent is decent, as far as it goes;
But in rhyme —

    Ink.   You're a terrible stick, to be sure.

    Tra. I own it; and yet, in these times, there's no lure
For the heart of the fair like a stanza or two;
And so, as I can't, will you furnish a few?

    Ink. In your name?

    Tra.   In my name. I will copy them out,
To slip into her hand at the very next rout.

    Ink. Are you so far advanced as to hazard this?

    Tra.   Why,
Do you think me subdued by a Blue-stocking's eye,
So far as to tremble to tell her in rhyme
What I've told her in prose, at the least, as sublime?

    Ink. *As sublime!* If it be so, no need of my Muse.

    Tra. But consider, dear Inkel, she's one of the "Blues.'

Ink. As sublime! — Mr. Tracy — I've nothing to say.
Stick to prose — As sublime!! — but I wish you good day.

Tra. Nay, stay, my dear fellow — consider — I'm wrong;
I own it; but, prithee, compose me the song.

Ink. *As* sublime!!

Tra.   I but used the expression in haste.

Ink. That may be, Mr. Tracy, but shows damn'd bad taste.

Tra. I own it — I know it — acknowledge it — what
Can I say to you more?

Ink.   I see what you'd be at:
You disparage my parts with insidious abuse,
Till you think you can turn them best to your own use.

Tra. And is that not a sign I respect them?

Ink.   Why that
To be sure makes a difference.

Tra.   I know what is what:
And you, who're a man of the gay world, no less
Than a poet of t'other, may easily guess
That I never could mean, by a word, to offend
A genius like you, and moreover my friend.

Ink. No doubt; you by this time should know what is due
To a man of — but come — let us shake hands.

Tra.   You knew,
And you *know*, my dear fellow, how heartily I,
Whatever you publish, am ready to buy.

Ink. That's my bookseller's business; I care not for sale;
Indeed the best poems at first rather fail.
There were Renegade's epics, and Botherby's plays,
And my own grand romance —

Tra.   Had its full share of praise.
I myself saw it puff'd in the "Old Girl's Review."

Ink. What Review?

Tra.   'Tis the English "Journal de Trevoux;"
A clerical work of our jesuits at home.
Have you never yet seen it?

Ink.   That pleasure's to come.

Tra. Make haste then,

Ink.   **Why so?**

Tra.   I have heard people say
That it threaten'd to give up the *ghost* t'other day.

    Ink. Well, that is a sign of some *spirit.*

    Tra.   No doubt.
Shall you be at the Countess of Fiddlecome's rout?

    Ink. I've a card, and shall go: but at present, as soon
As friend Scamp shall be pleased to step down from the moon
(Where he seems to be soaring in search of his wits),
And an interval grants from his lecturing fits,
I'm engaged to the Lady Bluebottle's collation,
To partake of a luncheon and learn'd conversation:
'Tis a sort of re-union for Scamp, on the days
Of his lecture, to treat him with cold tongue and praise.
And I own, for my own part, that 'tis not unpleasant.
Will you go? There's Miss Lilac will also be present.

    Tra. That "metal's attractive."

    Ink.   No doubt — to the pocket.

    Tra. You should rather encourage my passion than
        shock it.
But let us proceed; for I think, by the hum —

    Ink. Very true; let us go, then, before they can come,
Or else we'll be kept here an hour at their levy,
On the rack of cross questions, by all the blue bevy.
Hark! Zounds, they'll be on us; I know by the drone
Of old Botherby's spouting ex-cathedrâ tone.
Ay! there he is at it. Poor Scamp! better-join
Your friends, or he'll pay you back in your own coin.

    Tra. All fair; 'tis but lecture for lecture.

    Ink.   That's clear.
But for God's sake let's go, or the Bore will be here.
Come, come: nay, I'm off.   [*Exit* INKEL.

    Tra.   You are right, and I'll follow;
'Tis high time for a "*Sic me servavit Apollo.*"
And yet we shall have the whole crew on our kibes,
Blues, dandies, and dowagers, and second-hand scribes,

All flocking to moisten their exquisite throttles
With a glass of Madeira at Lady Bluebottle's.

[*Exit* TRACY.

ECLOGUE SECOND.

An Apartment in the House of LADY BLUEBOTTLE. — *A Table prepared.*

SIR RICHARD BLUEBOTTLE *solus.*

WAS there ever a man who was married so sorry?
Like a fool, I must needs do the thing in a hurry.
My life is reversed, and my quiet destroy'd;
My days, which once pass'd in so gentle a void,
Must now, every hour of the twelve, be employ'd:
The twelve, do I say? — of the whole twenty-four,
Is there one which I dare call my own any more?
What with driving and visiting, dancing and dining,
What with learning, and teaching, and scribbling, and
        shining
In science and art, I'll be cursed if I know
Myself from my wife; for although we are two,
Yet she somehow contrives that all things shall be done
In a style which proclaims us eternally one.
But the thing of all things which distresses me more
Than the bills of the week (though they trouble me sore)
Is the numerous, humorous, backbiting crew
Of scribblers, wits, lecturers, white, black, and blue,
Who are brought to my house as an inn, to my cost
— For the bill here, it seems, is defray'd by the host —
No pleasure! no leisure! no thought for my pains,
But to hear a vile jargon which addles my brains:
A smatter and chatter, glean'd out of reviews,
By the rag, tag, and bobtail, of those they call "BLUES;"
A rabble who know not — But soft, here they come!
Would to God I were deaf! as I'm not, I'll be dumb.

Enter Lady Bluebottle, Miss Lilac, Lady Bluemount, Mr.
Botherby, Inkel, Tracy, Miss Mazarine, *and others*, *with*
Scamp *the Lecturer*, &c. &c.

> *Lady Blueb.* Ah! Sir Richard, good morning; I've brought
>   you some friends.
> *Sir Rich.* (*bows, and afterwards aside.*) If friends, they're
>   the first.
> *Lady Blueb.*   But the luncheon attends.
> I pray ye be seated, "*sans cérémonie.*"
> Mr. Scamp, you're fatigued; take your chair there, next me.
>   [*They all sit.*
> *Sir Rich.* (*aside.*) If he does, his fatigue is to come.
> *Lady Blueb.*   ·   Mr. Tracy —
> Lady Bluemount — Miss Lilac — be pleased, pray, to place ye;
> And you, Mr. Botherby —
> *Both.*   Oh, my dear Lady,
> I obey.
> *Lady Blueb.* Mr. Inkel, I ought to upbraid ye:
> You were not at the lecture.
> *Ink.*   Excuse me, I was;
> But the heat forced me out in the best part — alas!
> And when —
> *Lady Blueb.* To be sure it was broiling; but then
> You have lost such a lecture!
> *Both.*   The best of the ten.
> *Tra.* How can you know that? there are two more.
> *Both.*   Because
> I defy him to beat this day's wondrous applause.
> The very walls shook.
> *Ink.*   Oh, if that be the test,
> I allow our friend Scamp has this day done his best.
> Miss Lilac, permit me to help you; — a wing?
> *Miss Lil.* No more, sir I thank you. Who lectures next
>   spring?
> *Both.* Dick Dunder.
> *Ink.*   That is, if he lives.

Miss Lil. And why not?

Ink. No reason whatever, save that he's a sot.
Lady Bluemount! a glass of Madeira?

Lady Bluem. With pleasure.

Ink. How does your friend Wordswords, that Windermere
treasure?
Does he stick to his lakes, like the leeches he sings,
And their gatherers, as Homer sung warriors and kings?

Lady Blueb. He has just got a place.

Ink. As a footman?

Lady Bluem. For shame!
Nor profane with your sneers so poetic a name.

Ink. Nay, I meant him no evil, but pitied his master;
For the poet of pedlers 'twere, sure, no disaster
To wear a new livery; the more, as 'tis not
The first time he has turn'd both his creed and his coat.

Lady Bluem. For shame! I repeat. If Sir George could
but hear —

Lady Blueb. Never mind our friend Inkel; we all know,
my dear,
'Tis his way.

Sir Rich. But this place —

Ink. Is perhaps like friend Scamp's,
A lecturer's.

Lady Blueb. Excuse me — 'tis one in "the Stamps:"
He is made a collector.

Tra. Collector!

Sir Rich. How?

Miss Lil. What?

Ink. I shall think of him oft when I buy a new hat:
There his works will appear —

Lady Bluem. Sir, they reach to the Ganges.

Ink. I sha'n't go so far — I can have them at Grange's.*

Lady Blueb. Oh fie!

Miss Lil. And for shame!

Lady Bluem. You're too bad.

* Grange is or was a famous pastry-cook and fruiterer in Piccadilly.

Both.   Very good!

Lady Bluem. How good?

Lady Blueb. He means nought — 'tis his phrase.

Lady Bluem.   He grows rude.

Lady Blueb. He means nothing; nay, ask him.

Lady Bluem.   Pray, sir! did you mean
What you say?

Ink.   Never mind if he did; 'twill be seen
That whatever he means won't alloy what he says.

Both. Sir!

Ink. Pray be content with your portion of praise;
'Twas in your defence.

Both.   If you please, with submission,
I can make out my own.

Ink.   It would be your perdition.
While you live, my dear Botherby, never defend
Yourself or your works; but leave both to a friend.
A propos — Is your play then accepted at last?

Both. At last?

Ink. Why I thought — that's to say — there had pass'd
A few green-room whispers, which hinted — you know
That the taste of the actors at best is so so.

Both. Sir, the green-room's in rapture, and so's the com-
            mittee.

Ink. Ay — yours are the plays for exciting our "pity
And fear," as the Greek says: for "purging the mind,"
I doubt if you'll leave us an equal behind.

Both. I have written the prologue, and meant to have
            pray'd
For a spice of your wit in an epilogue's aid.

Ink. Well, time enough yet, when the play's to be play'd.
Is it cast yet?

Both.   The actors are fighting for parts,
As is usual in that most litigious of arts.

Lady Blueb. We'll all make a party, and go the *first* night.

Tra. And you promised the epilogue, Inkel.

Ink.   Not quite.

However, to save my friend Botherby trouble,
I'll do what I can, though my pains must be double.
   Tra. Why so?
   Ink.   To do justice to what goes before.
   Both. Sir, I'm happy to say, I have no fears on that score.
Your parts, Mr. Inkel, are —
   Ink.   Never mind *mine;*
Stick to those of your play, which is quite your own line.
   Lady Bluem. You're a fugitive writer, I think, sir, of
      rhymes?
   Ink. Yes, ma'am; and a fugitive reader sometimes.
On Wordswords, for instance, I seldom alight,
Or on Mouthey, his friend, without taking to flight.
   Lady Bluem. Sir, your taste is too common; but time and
      posterity
Will right these great men, and this age's severity
Become its reproach.
   Ink.   I've no sort of objection,
So I'm not of the party to take the infection.
   Lady Blueb. Perhaps you have doubts that they ever will
      take?
   Ink. Not at all; on the contrary, those of the lake
Have taken already, and still will continue
To take — what they can, from a groat to a guinea,
Of pension or place; — but the subject's a bore.
   Lady Bluem. Well, sir, the time's coming.
   Ink.   Scamp! don't you feel sore?
What say you to this?
   Scamp.   They have merit, I own;
Though their system's absurdity keeps it unknown.
   Ink. Then why not unearth it in one of your lectures?
   Scamp. It is only time past which comes under my stric-
      tures.
   Lady Blueb. Come, a truce with all tartness: — the joy of
      my heart
Is to see Nature's triumph o'er all that is art.
Wild Nature! — Grand Shakspeare!

Both.   And down Aristotle!

Lady Bluem. Sir George thinks exactly with Lady Blue-
  bottle;
And my Lord Seventy-four, who protects our dear Bard,
And who gave him his place, has the greatest regard
For the poet, who, singing of pedlers and asses,
Has found out the way to dispense with Parnassus.

Tra. And you, Scamp! —

Scamp.   I needs must confess I'm embarrass'd.

Ink. Don't call upon Scamp, who's already so harass'd
With old *schools*, and new *schools*, and no *schools*, and all
  schools.

Tra. Well, one thing is certain, that *some* must be fools.
I should like to know who.

Ink.   .   And I should not be sorry
To know who are *not:* — it would save us some worry.

Lady Blueb. A truce with remark, and let nothing control
This "feast of our reason, and flow of the soul."
Oh! my dear Mr. Botherby! sympathise! — I
Now feel such a rapture, I'm ready to fly,
I feel so elastic — "*so buoyant — so buoyant!*"*

Ink. Tracy! open the window.

Tra.   I wish her much joy on't.

Both. For God's sake, my Lady Bluebottle, check not
This gentle emotion, so seldom our lot
Upon earth. Give it way; 'tis an impulse which lifts
Our spirits from earth; the sublimest of gifts;
For which poor Prometheus was chain'd to his mountain:
'Tis the source of all sentiment — feeling's true fountain:
'Tis the Vision of Heaven upon Earth: 'tis the gas
Of the soul: 'tis the seizing of shades as they pass,
And making them substance: 'tis something divine: —

Ink. Shall I help you, my friend, to a little more wine?

Both. I thank you; not any more, sir, till I dine.

* Fact from life, with the words.

Ink. A propos — Do you dine with Sir Humphry to-day?

Tra. I should think with *Duke* Humphry was more in your
      way.

Ink. It might be of yore; but we authors now look
To the knight, as a landlord, much more than the Duke.
The truth is, each writer now quite at his ease is,
And (except with the publisher) dines where he pleases.
But 'tis now nearly five, and I must to the Park.

Tra. And I'll take a turn with you there till 'tis dark.
And you, Scamp —

Scamp.   Excuse me; I must to my notes,
For my lecture next week.

Ink.   He must mind whom he quotes
Out of "Elegant Extracts."

Lady Blueb.   Well, now we break up;
But remember Miss Diddle invites us to sup.

Ink. Then at two hours past midnight we all meet again,
For the sciences, sandwiches, hock, and champaigne!

Tra. And the sweet lobster salad!

Both.   I honour that meal;
For 'tis then that our feelings most genuinely — feel.

Ink. True; feeling is truest *then*, far beyond question:
I wish to the gods 'twas the same with digestion!

Lady Blueb. Pshaw! — never mind that; for one moment
         of feeling
Is worth — God knows what.

Ink.   'Tis at least worth concealing
For itself, or what follows — But here comes your carriage.

Sir Rich. (*aside*). I wish all these people were d—d with *my*
         marriage!   [*Exeunt.*

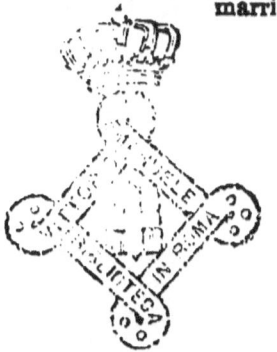

PRINTING OFFICE OF THE PUBLISHER.